STONE & SEA

Graham Edwards was born in Somerset in 1965, and grew up in Bournemouth. He attended art school in London and now works in a special effects design studio. He lives in Nottingham with his wife Helen and their two children. *Stone & Sea* is his fifth novel.

Voyager

GRAHAM EDWARDS

STONE & SEA

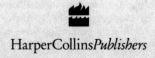

HarperCollins*Publishers*

Voyager
An Imprint of HarperCollins*Publishers*
77–85 Fulham Palace Road,
Hammersmith, London W6 8JB

The *Voyager* World Wide Web site address is
http://www.harpercollins.co.uk/voyager

A Paperback Original 2000
1 3 5 7 9 8 6 4 2

A catalogue record for this book
is available from the British Library

ISBN 0 00 651071 X

Set in Meridien by
Rowland Phototypesetting Ltd
Bury St Edmunds, Suffolk

Printed and bound in Great Britain by
Caledonian International Book Manufacturing Ltd, Glasgow

to mum
everything changes
nothing goes

'And then anon Sir Tristram took the sea, and La Beale Isoud; and when they were in their cabin, it happed so that they were thirsty, and they saw a little flasket of gold stand by them, and it seemed by the colour and the taste that it was noble wine . . . But by that their drink was in their bodies, they loved either other so well that never their love departed for weal neither for woe.'

**La Morte D'Arthur,
Sir Thomas Malory**

'and the waters were a wall unto them on their right hand . . .'

Exodus 14:22

Prologue

Aeons flew past like clouds of lead. She resisted the temptation to pause and breathe too deeply; like lead, the taste of ages past was certain poison. Besides, there was no time to pause: Red Dragon was behind her and closing all the while. She was not a voyager here; she was the hunted.

Close to her breast: the white scale that drew Archan to her. The magnet drawing the iron soul of the immortal beast. One hand to hold the scale, one to part the black veils through which she fled. Time slithered past, faster at every turn, as she plunged deep into memory, her haunted face cast forever back over her shoulder.

Faster, yes, and smaller too. Every turn an increase in the pace, and every turn a *diminution*. Already she was a billion times smaller than she had been in her Earthly life, and she would diminish a billion times more before her journey was done. That it would end she had no doubt: there would come a time when she would stop running and simply hide.

But not yet, not yet.

The aeons passed, their momentous bulk dissected by the Turnings. World after world, history after history, time after time after time . . .

Hive-world, where the memories were those of a gestalt creature with many minds and only one purpose – to eat all it surveyed. The dreadful moment of self-immolation as it returned to its own tail.

The world surrounded by a thousand suns. The light absolute. A world without shadow, its sleepless denizens ignorant of the night.

Memories of worlds of ice, worlds of deep ravines and sentient clouds, worlds where gas congealed into minds bent on conflict, wars raging high in the atmosphere unseen on the barren land below.

Strange pasts, untold histories of the world, distant memories.

Memories through which the faery queen fled with a single dragon scale, growing smaller every time she blinked her eye.

The pursuit continued, with Archan now closer, now further away, but less far each time. An underlying approach, a drawing-near that would not be stopped. The need to find a hiding-place was overwhelming.

She rested in the space between two atoms of hydrogen suspended in a vast, sun-hot sea. But even here she was vulnerable; after the briefest of pauses she hurried on, vanishingly small yet vast in the all-seeing eye of the huntress. The scale made her shine.

More worlds turned past as she sped deeper and deeper into the past. The memory rod through which she raced was hers to command now. She could not change its nature as Jonah could but she could enter and leave it at will; she could navigate but not manipulate. It would have to be enough.

There! An unexpected prize! A history of the world where time itself did not exist. Dropping out of the memory rod she found herself in a realm of frozen thunder and shadowless light. Massive, hulking creatures squatted in unmoving fog, their minds cast in single, irreconcilable thoughts, trapped forever in the moulds into which they had been pressed when this dreadful world had first been created. A place where she might hide forever, for how could the huntress track down her prey when neither one could move, nor even force a way forward along the great river of time?

2

Falling from the safety of the memory rod, the faery queen planted herself in this timeless place. Thus embedded, she became a fragment of a world that had existed many millions of Turnings before her own. As her thoughts began to slow she found time to wonder at this daunting fact, at the distance she had placed between herself and her own era.

'Come, Red Dragon,' she whispered. Each syllable took ten thousand years to enunciate. All around her, nothing changed. 'Come and join me. At last I have found us a tomb.'

The final thought, the one that remained like a cast inside her mind when she finally adjusted to the world in which she had chosen to hide, was surprise. For, just as she lost her grip on the flow of time, she was aware of a massive object hurtling past, barely an electron's width away.

Red Dragon! You were closer than I thought. Oh, so much closer!

No matter: she had been passed by. Now, perhaps, Archan would keep going back to the beginning of eternity, if such a place existed. She had made her choice: here she would stay.

Here she would never be found.

1

Annie's Journal – One

Jonah measured Stone today.

Wait, I should start somewhere else.

I can't decide how to track time. We don't count weeks – there are none, nor months. We count days but they're shorter than the days back home, and we don't bother keeping much of a record. Jonah started off making marks on a scrap of wood, but even he's lost interest in the last few days. Yes, Jonah! Who likes to count *everything*. Maybe he's starting to accept this place, you know, relax a little.

Accept Stone? No. I don't think even Jonah's gotten to do that yet.

Look at that. I can't even write his name without the pen shaking.

Today it's sunny, like it was sunny yesterday and like it will most likely be sunny tomorrow. Which is not to say the weather doesn't change sometimes. Sometimes the wind veers from pure vertical to a little on-shore, and then we get heavy breakers and great combs of cloud rolling in from the ocean. Then the rain comes. Most times we take shelter. The rain is warm and sweet, but it ain't just made of water . . .

What I'm trying to say is that it doesn't matter we don't know what day it is. Of us all, it's dear Jonah who's found this the hardest to accept. Gerent and Kythe don't know any different of course, and as for me, well, in some ways Stone isn't so different from the plains of Kansas. Big skies and a far horizon. Changeless days. I'll miss the seasons, I reckon, but I've not been here long enough yet to notice they're gone. Perhaps Stone has its own ideas about summer and winter. So I'm just going to start writing this journal and see where it takes me.

You'll be wondering where I found a book as splendid as this in such a barren place. It *is* splendid. Its cover is something like leather, but smoother and not so soft. I don't imagine it's as strong as leather but it's a good enough substitute. Such a brilliant red colour too, and the pages so beautifully bound, even if they are warped by the damp. The pen is a miraculous thing too, made of some smooth brittle stuff with a tube of ink held inside it. Gerent was fascinated when we found it, and spent a long time examining it before announcing there was actually a tiny ball of brass, or something like it, held at the very tip, around which the ink flows. Fiendishly clever, Jonah said. I guess I have to agree, but right now I'm just glad it writes. I have two more like it. What happens when the ink runs out I don't know.

But I'm getting ahead of myself again.

I've tried hard to understand my purpose in writing this journal. Do I really believe anybody will read it? – except maybe one of my companions if I wind up dead or one of them develops more curiosity than sense. (If I catch Jonah reading it before I'm dead – or Gerent for that matter, if he ever learns to read English – I'll stake him out on the beach and wait for the waves to come rolling on in.) I guess some part of me still believes there's a way off Stone, even a way home. And maybe if I don't make it, my words will.

And it's a way of keeping busy, I guess, until I start painting again. If I ever do.

If I'm honest, I guess I want to write because, well, because I *have* to write. Like once I had to paint. Jonah laughs – he thinks it's funny I should struggle so hard to record things when all around us the hidden machinery of Stone is recording every breath of every beast that ever walked the Earth. He thinks my efforts are pointless. He calls my paintings 'dead memories', because the moment the tip of my brush touches the ivory tile the world it's trying to describe has already changed. I argue with him that that's what memories are – frozen moments, not dead at all but still very much alive in the heart of the person who owns them. He says only Stone contains memories that are truly alive – and he knows, of course, because he's seen them, he's touched them. He even believes he can change them.

He scares me when he talks like that.

Oh! This is getting me nowhere! I started off meaning to describe what it's like on Stone, and how Jonah reckons he's found out something about Stone's actual shape and size. Whether his theory's true or not . . . I don't know. It sounds right enough, but who knows? Perhaps I should remember what Jonah did for me, you know, learn to trust him a little more. I know I love him. I guess trust is a little bit different.

Where to begin then?

Stone.

Well, Stone is a world beyond our world. We came to it through a kind of tunnel that was opened up by the eruption of a volcano called Krakatoa in the year 1883. Both Jonah and I were on that island when it blew; so I reckon as far as our world's concerned we're dead and gone.

Stone's no ordinary place though – I guess the easiest way to describe it is like the biggest damned wall you could ever imagine – it just goes on for ever. Up and down, side to side, it fades away into the mist. Endless, infinite, call it what you like. It's just damned *big*.

The thing is, Stone is connected to our world by memories. It's a kind of giant storehouse of memories. What's more, travelling on Stone is like travelling backwards or forwards in time in our world. We came through from 1883 and travelled downStone (which means to your right if you're standing on one of Stone's ledges and staring straight out into the sky) and ended up here, beyond a place called the Threshold. The Threshold marks a moment way back in ancient history called the 'turning of the world'.

And, according to the new history Jonah and I have been forced to learn, the turning of the world . . . well, that was the moment in time when the magic went away.

So now we're back beyond that point, sitting on Stone's topsy-turvy version of a beach, loosely connected to an era in our world when magic still ruled and the skies were filled with dragons. There's no way back upStone across the desert surrounding the Threshold. There's no way off this beach except out across the ocean, and that's easier for Kythe and Gerent than it is for me or Jonah. They've both got wings, you see. Kythe's a dragon, and as for Gerent . . . well, he used to be a man. I don't know quite what he is now. Archan would have called him a faery.

But I don't want to write about Archan. Not yet.

Back to the point.

It happened this morning, the Great Measuring of Stone.

I thought for a while Jonah's urge to explore the forest would win out, but he's been planning the Measuring for several days already and today the weather was perfect: as clear as it gets on Stone (it's almost permanently hazy) and the falling wind a steady tumble (permanently windy, too). He'd already picked his spot on the beach; now all he needed was for our winged companions to fly out to sea and do all the hard work for him.

We call it a beach, but there's no sand on it. In fact, it's nothing like a beach at all! The ocean, like the rest of Stone, is tilted almost to the vertical – Jonah reckons it's about ten degrees short of sheer. Apart from that it looks much like the Pacific. It's a dizzying sight, and even though I've woken up to it every morning for what must be nearly a month now, it still doesn't fail to take my breath away. An ocean tipped on its side. Incredible.

There's no clue as to what keeps the water from falling. Kythe, who knows a little about such things, reckons it's magic, or 'charm' as she calls it. Whatever it is – magnetism or some damned thing – it exerts just enough pull to keep the main body of the water suspended, but nothing else.

Spray, for instance. If the wind's particularly strong, the waves come careening down from up high. As soon as the wavetops reach a certain height (sorry, I suppose they're not 'high' at all but 'wide'. You even have to turn your words on end when you're on Stone) they break up into spray – and the spray suddenly gets grabbed by gravity and pulled downwards. I've even seen Stone's version of a dolphin leap clear of the sea altogether and fall in the same way. It really is like a magnet – if you get too far away it just doesn't pull you any longer.

The dolphin was all right, by the way. It just fell for a half-mile or so before meeting up with the ocean again, thanks to Stone's ten-degree tilt. Later on I saw it do the exact same thing. I reckon it just liked the sport.

So much for the ocean.

The beach is really more like an upturned dockside. It's a slab of dark grey material, hard as granite that's – you guessed it – inclined at ten degrees off vertical. It's about two miles high, by Jonah's reckoning, and a few hundred yards wide. A gigantic grey cliff. Luckily for us it's criss-crossed by wide ledges and deep cracks, so we can move across and up it without feeling too much like mountain climbers. And this is where we've set up home – for now at least – in a series of deep niches cut into this world-sized wall.

The word 'dockside' isn't so far from the truth. Along the ocean-edge of the beach are heaps of metalwork and wrecked machinery. A lot of what used to be there must have long since rusted and fallen away (falling is a constant danger on Stone); what's left is clinging on by its fingernails, so to speak. We haven't tried exploring there yet – it looks precarious.

So, halfway to the dockside there's a polished metal disc projecting slightly proud of the beach itself. A ledge runs directly underneath it so that standing on the ledge and looking at the disc is a bit like looking into a round mirror hanging on a giant's bath-house wall – except this mirror is nearly twenty feet in diameter. We pass the disc most days on our way to the waterhole (a huge scoop in the beach that collects the fresh water running constantly down the surface of Stone) but it was only after one of Kythe's exploratory flights out to sea that Jonah really took notice of it.

Kythe came back dejected, announcing she had flown for the best part of a day and seen no sign of an opposite shore. All she had seen was a silver disc much like our bath-house mirror, except it was twice the size, sticking clear of the waves. It was several miles off-shore, but if you squint hard you can just see the sun glinting off it, way off on the horizon – or the 'vertex' as Jonah insists on calling it. Stupid name, I reckon, whatever the geometry.

Right away something connected in Jonah's head. I could almost hear the spark.

He spent the rest of the day whittling down two branches until they were exactly the same length – and I do mean *exactly* the same. Then he fastened some shorter lengths of wood to the ends to make a pair of L-shaped brackets, braced across the angle to make them rigid. He worked hard to make sure the right-angles were as close as possible to ninety degrees, though he said that so long as the two pieces were identical, it didn't much matter what the angle actually was.

I was thoroughly confused, and when I asked him what the hell he was doing, he just smiled at me and said I was to wait and see. Infuriating man!

So then we waited, and Jonah continued to be infuriating and I nagged at him and he went on refusing to let us in on his secret. Gerent didn't seem at all curious, even this morning when Jonah explained to him exactly what it was he wanted him to do. Gerent is solemn, but then he has every reason to be: he saw the woman he loved murdered by her own father. Grief has turned him in on himself. There's a fire burning away inside him though; I have a feeling we'll be seeing it spill out before long.

Kythe had her instructions too. Dear Kythe! Even though she's a dragon I can't help thinking of her as a ten-year-old girl. She's so bright and full of vigour! She listened to Jonah's strange request with a big, dragon smile on her face, then took off into the sky with a yell of delight. She loves to be flying; I think she'd stay in the sky all day if she could.

So off they went, Kythe and Gerent. Gerent's wings – made from shining dragon scales, striped red and black – are almost as glorious as Kythe's. He still hates to use them. I don't really know why – perhaps flying makes him feel less human. Or perhaps it just reminds him of Malya and her treacherous father, Frey.

Gerent carried with him one of Jonah's curious instruments, a length of twine cut from our precious supply, and one of my miraculous pens, with an instruction as to what he should do with them but no clue why.

On they flew, dwindling gradually downStone until

they were just specks in the vast, blue sky. Halfway to the island-disc Kythe stopped and took up station, hovering in the falling wind. Gerent flew on and soon disappeared from sight completely.

Jonah and I went to our mirror-disc and waited.

After what seemed an age, Kythe started to perform loops in the air. We could barely see her as she circled like a tiny insect. I could hear Jonah counting them under his breath: 'One . . . two . . . three!' At the end of the third loop she folded her wings and dropped like a stone.

At once Jonah leaped up and pressed his L-shaped apparatus on to the flat surface of the mirror-disc. The sun, still only halfway to its noon zenith, cast a long, sharp shadow across the metal. Jonah unravelled a length of twine on which, using another of my pens, he recorded the length of the shadow.

On the island-disc, he explained, Gerent was doing the exact same thing.

Then it was back to waiting again, only this time Jonah was so excited he couldn't keep still. He kept scratching at his beard and asking if I thought he should shave. I said it suited him, which it does. His red hair's nearly down to his shoulders now, and his skin's almost showing signs of a tan, except in the laugh-lines around his eyes – they're still white as snow. He looks like some weather-beaten Scottish laird! I laughed at him and went to fetch him a drink of water, which I ended up throwing all over him. We laughed together like a couple of kids and, well, it was easy to make the time go by.

Kythe and Gerent got back at the same time. They were as eager as I was to learn what it was all about, but even then Jonah kept up the suspense. He buried himself away in his niche and wouldn't come out until he'd finished his calculations. It must have taken him over an hour, by which time I was ready to explode!

When he finally emerged he looked grave again.

'What's the matter?' I asked him anxiously. 'Nothing,' he answered. We all sat down together, and he explained what he had learned.

He said this:

'I had always assumed that Stone was an infinite, near-vertical plane. A wall that went on forever, if you like. However, having spent some time near this outlandish ocean, I began to wonder if that assumption had any basis in fact.' (Like all Englishmen, Jonah can get a bit wordy sometimes.) 'Consider this: on clear days, or as near as they get to clear at any rate, there is the impression of a near-vertical horizon, or *vertex* as I like to think of it, far out to sea. And, as you, Annie, know, such a phenomenon is caused, on Earth at least, by the curvature of the planet. So I began to speculate, and finally asked myself the simple question: "Is Stone curved?"

'At first I thought there was no way to investigate such a thing, until I remembered a story my father told me many years ago about a Greek scholar called Eratosthenes, who worked at the great library in Alexandria. He was the first man to measure the curvature of the Earth. One day he heard a story about Aswan, another Egyptian town over five hundred miles away.

'At the summer solstice, somewhere near Aswan, the sun was directly overhead. The proof of this was that it cast no shadow – none at all. But he noticed that back home in Alexandria, at the exact same time, the sun *did* cast a shadow. He used the difference in the angle of the sunlight, and his knowledge of the distance between the two towns, to calculate the diameter of the Earth. The figure was incredibly accurate too, considering the tools he had at his disposal.

'All one needs to re-create his experiment is a matched pair of measuring sticks, and some friends who are willing to travel. I can only estimate the distance to the disc where Gerent measured his stick's shadow, but the theory holds true regardless of the precise measurements. The fact is that the two shadows were of different lengths, therefore the sunlight was striking them from a different angle. We assume the sun's rays are parallel, so it must be Stone that is curved!'

At this point Jonah beamed at us. I was frowning, though I think I'd cottoned what he was saying. But Gerent and Kythe were clearly puzzled. As natives of Stone, neither of them had even bothered to wonder what shape their home might be, it was just . . . there.

Seeing this, Jonah asked if he could use one of the pages from my book. Reluctantly I tore one out (see the ripped edge?) and gave it to him. Then he drew a diagram that looked more or less like this:

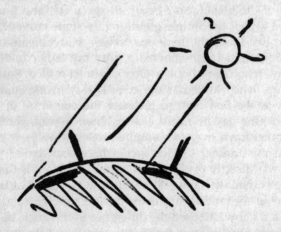

Our winged friends understood at once. That's all it took, just that one drawing, to change the way they saw their world. But then Gerent has always had a knack of seeing to the heart of things faster than the rest of us. And Kythe? Well, dragons are gifted with a good sense of space. All that flying, I guess.

'What does all this mean for Stone?' I asked Jonah.

'Are we on a planet like our own, except somebody tinkered with the gravity so we feel like we're hanging off the edge instead of sitting on the top?' I found myself thinking of when my mama told me about Australia, and how I'd laughed and laughed to think of all those convicts dropping off the bottom of the world!

But Jonah shook his head. 'I don't think so.' He fetched a deep sigh. 'I can't be absolutely sure of anything, but even on the days when I have perceived a vertex downStone, I have perceived none either above or below us. Yes, I do believe Stone has a curvature, but in one plane only.'

'So it is like this,' said Gerent, making the shape of a cylinder with his hands. I shivered – his mind was so goddamn quick! I was still trailing way behind.

'Perhaps,' Jonah said. 'But, my Neolithic friend, you are forgetting that the wall of Stone is not vertical but tipped back at approximately ten degrees. That means that if my hypothesis is correct, and Stone is straight in the vertical dimension but curved in the horizontal, then it is neither a sphere nor a cylinder. It is a cone!'

If he was expecting us to gasp in amazement he must have been sorely disappointed. His final flourish went off like a damp firecracker. 'So . . . we're clinging on to the side of a giant witch's hat,' I commented unhelpfully. 'It doesn't stop us being stuck on this damn beach!'

All the same, somewhere deep inside my head, I could feel something scratching away, like a dream that escapes you the minute you wake up. Except it felt like all I needed to do was fall asleep and I'd be in that dream, living it for real. I didn't like the way it felt. I didn't like the memories it brought back, memories of being trapped in that same, deep place myself, trapped screaming, a prisoner inside my own mind.

Memories of Archan.

Jonah was drawing again, and Gerent was poring over

his diagrams and even sketching a few of his own. Kythe had flown off, bored, and I went too. Leave the men to their maps and measures, I thought. All they needed was a couple of snifters of brandy and they'd have been comfortable for the rest of the day. The whole night, for that matter. The sun was hot and my head was thumping. I made my way along the ledge to the waterhole, stripped off my clothes and dived in.

The water in the scoop is reassuringly horizontal – whatever power keeps the sea tipped on its side doesn't extend this far up the beach. Fresh water pours into the scoop down a narrow channel. It could almost be a mountain pool fed by a waterfall, back in our world. I surfaced and swam on my back for a while, staring up into the infinite heights of Stone.

The water isn't pure, of course. It's saturated with charm, as is the ocean and the occasional rain-shower. But it's the only water we've got, and if we want to get clean we have no choice but to bathe in it, and if we feel thirsty we have no choice but to drink it. The magical air of Stone, so warm and spicy it could almost have come from some Oriental kitchen, nourishes and sustains us, so that as long as we are here we don't really need food or drink at all. But our bodies crave those things, especially water, and often the days are so warm we feel parched. And so we drink.

There's no way of knowing what the charm might be doing to our bodies. Perhaps it passes straight through – undigested, so to speak. Somehow I don't think that's the case. I reckon we absorb it, just a little. Even when we take a breath, we take a little more magic in.

I wonder what it's doing to us.

2

Forest

Three days before Jonah performed his experiment to determine the shape of Stone, he was lying on his back on one of Stone's broad ledges, looking up into the forest.

Giant coat-hooks lined on a wall, he thought dizzily. *The plasterwork needs repair though.*

The forest hung suspended some twenty yards above his head, the massive, lowermost trees – which Jonah thought of as the *anchormen* – bursting from countless great rips in the face of Stone. Rank upon rank, their trunks extended horizontally for many tens of yards before turning through an abrupt ninety degrees to soar upwards into a thundercloud of foliage.

An immense forest clinging to Stone like a beard to the face of a giant.

Jonah was curious about the forest, as he was curious about everything on Stone, but getting up to it meant undertaking a major expedition. The beach was almost smooth here, making a straight climb impossible. Kythe had flown close to the trees on several occasions, but she had seen nothing through the thickly-matted branches and had no desire to fight her way inside.

'Dragons and trees are not made for each other!' she had said decisively.

It occurred to him now that all he really needed was

17

a knotted rope and a grapnel. Once he had reached the first tree the climbing should be relatively easy. As to what he might find within . . .

'A way out,' he muttered. 'A way *on*! How is it that we are trapped here, imprisoned in one small corner of a world so vast?' Frustration welled and he turned his head to look downStone across the ocean.

Trapped indeed! There was no way back upStone – the uncrossable desert surrounding the Threshold saw to that. And the mysterious laws of Stone itself dictated that to ascend or descend too far was to risk insanity or even death. 'It's a lesson all dragons are taught,' Kythe had explained. 'It hurts to climb too high – or dive too low, for that matter. It's like someone's got inside your brains and chewed them all to pieces!'

Which left only downStone, the direction in which they had been travelling ever since Krakatoa had blown them clean across the gap between the worlds. DownStone, over the vertical sea to whatever lay on the other side. *But how to cross such an ocean?*

Several times he had urged his two winged companions to make the journey. 'I know you cannot carry either me or Annie very far,' he pleaded, 'but if only one of you were to reach the other side you might find a means by which we can all cross over.'

But young Kythe was too afraid to make the journey alone. As for Gerent – he simply refused. The look on the Neolithic's face whenever flying was mentioned was enough to convince Jonah he would not be persuaded.

A wind gusted briefly through the nearest branches, causing them to rock down in Jonah's direction; still too far away to reach though. They whistled like reeds. Gradually the wind dropped. The trees continued to move for a while, then settled. Jonah heard the gentle pad of footsteps and looked up to see Annie crouching down beside him.

'Hello,' she said. Her voice thrilled him. 'See anything?'

'Not a tremendous amount, I'm afraid to say. How I wish we could get up there.'

'What would we gain?'

'Knowledge! Information! We might learn some of the answers to the questions that plague our minds! Why, we may even . . .' She pressed her fingers against his mouth and silenced his outburst.

'Hush, Jonah. Your mind may be full of questions but . . . well . . .'

Reluctantly Jonah removed her hand from his lips and said, 'Well what, my dear?'

She laughed, the rich tinkling sound that echoed in his dreams. 'Don't be so damned impatient, Jonah Lightfoot! And think about what it means if we're stuck here for good. You could spend the rest of your life exploring this world and never see what's in front of your face!'

'And what, pray, is that?'

A ghost of a smile. Her face filled his vision. But she did not get a chance to reply; as her lips parted the trees shivered once more, except this time the shivering was accompanied by an ominous crashing sound. They both looked upwards.

The trees were moving. It seemed to Jonah that the whole forest was moving. Not the rhythmic swaying of a windblown dance but pitching and jerking as though shaken by giants. Beyond the deafening rustle of the leaves was an irregular thump-thump and a long, drawn-out groaning sound.

'Jonah, my God, what the hell is *that*?'

'I have absolutely no idea, but I think we would be well-advised to retreat.'

Annie was already hauling him to his feet. Together they scrambled backwards, trying desperately to get out of the shadow of the trees.

The shaking was more localized now, focused in the

anchormen immediately above where Jonah had been lying. The thumping came less frequently, but each impact resounded more strongly than ever. With the impacts came cracks and the explosions of shattering timbers. A shape swelled in the darkness above these bottom-most trees, a pale object falling through.

It lodged momentarily between two of the anchormen, tantalizingly close yet still almost completely obscured by the foliage. Soil was raining freely, filling the air with dense black dust. Then came a final, tearing groan and the shape was falling free, smashing against the wicked slope of the beach and turning completely over as it slid gracelessly down towards the ledge. It broke through the rain of soil and they saw it for what it was.

'I'll be damned,' breathed Annie. 'It's a boat!'

Its hull, once white, was streaked with grime and smears of yellow sap. A broken mast sprang clear of a compact superstructure. At the stern a large rudder flapped wildly behind a gleaming screw propeller. A harsh metallic screaming accompanied its descent, flakes of white paint joining the dispersing dust. It was the size of a small schooner and beneath the bow its name was clearly visible, picked out in gold paint: *Bonaventure*.

Halfway to the ledge the boat lurched and turned end over end. A huge hole opened up in the hull, revealing a skeleton of ribs and bulkheads. Jonah saw a tiny cabin, had the briefest glimpse of a bedsheet billowing like a sail and a sudden explosion of glass. Something flew from the hole, a small, dark object following its own trajectory.

The boat struck the ledge bow-first. The hull crumpled like tin and the entire vessel turned a lazy cartwheel before somersaulting outwards and falling on down into the ever-hungry abyss. Crashing sounds continued to echo up to them as it continued to impact with Stone's sloping wall. Jonah and Annie rushed to the ledge's outer perimeter and leaned over to watch its death throes. It was not long before the fragments were swallowed by the haze and the boat was gone; nevertheless they continued to watch for some time.

'A boat,' whispered Annie.

'Could it have sailed on such an ocean as this?'

He turned to find her face right in front of his. Her breath was warm against his cheek and her eyes were wide. He raised his hand and, finding it shaking, smiled nervously. He touched her cheek and watched her lips part.

'I . . .' he began, faltering, the boat thrown suddenly from his mind. 'I think I have always loved you, Annie. Ever since Krakatoa, ever since I saw you on that beach.'

'I know, Jonah. I'm only just beginning to realize that. And you never gave up on me, even when all you could see in my eyes was Archan glaring back at you. Even when she was in control you still believed I was there.'

'I was not going to rest until you were free. I wish I could have freed you myself.'

'You wanted to, Jonah. That's what counts. You wanted to.'

Her breath had become his breath. For a second her lips brushed against his, their touch like a butterfly's kiss, then her arms had enfolded his neck and the kiss was real. Her hands moved down to the small of his back and pulled him close; the soft press of her body against his was like a second pulse. The boat forgotten, the forest and the ocean forgotten, all sense of place and world put aside, they found ways to draw closer still until it seemed they would never be separated. Charm fell around them, carried silent and invisible on the falling wind.

By the time Kythe and Gerent arrived they were standing again at the edge of the ledge, holding hands and looking down into the haze.

'We heard the commotion!' exclaimed the dragon-child. 'What was it?'

'Something magical,' replied Jonah, returning Annie's smile. She squeezed his hand. Suddenly he remembered the object that had been ejected from the boat.

It had landed a short distance away, in a clump of vegetation. Litter fell constantly from the forest on to the ledge here – dead needles and scraps of bark – and a veritable carpet had been laid down. As short as a neatly cropped lawn, it consisted largely of a tiny-leafed bracken. Walking on it was a little like walking on moss, soft and springy.

Jonah reached it first. It was a trunk or travelling case of strange manufacture, dark grey and very hard; its surface was slightly pitted, its texture curiously like orange peel, and marked with a single word: *Samsonite*. It meant nothing to any of them.

'It may be the substance from which the case is made,' suggested Jonah. 'Some new and highly durable chemical element, one might surmise.'

'One might,' agreed Annie, imitating his English accent with a chuckle.

Opening it proved more challenging than they had hoped. There were three small thumbwheels set into the side of the case behind an artfully moulded handle, each of which showed a number; together they read: *1 – 4 – 5*.

'A number lock,' sighed Jonah, disappointed. Then he brightened. 'Still, there can only be nine hundred and ninety-nine possible combinations.' Thereupon he seated himself, hoisted the case up on to his knees and set the thumbwheels so that they read: *0 – 0 – 0*.

'Nought, nought, one,' he muttered under his breath as he began methodically to turn them. 'Nought, nought, two. Nought, nought, three.' Each time he set the wheels he pulled at what was clearly a pair of locking clasps, set almost flush with the corners of the case. Gerent and

Kythe looked on curiously as Jonah slowly counted.

'Where did it come from?' Annie wondered, looking up uncertainly. The forest was a distant ceiling of ebony tree trunks, casually supporting a mountain of branches and rich green foliage. The ragged wound through which the boat had fallen was clearly visible.

'From the boat, of course,' answered Jonah unhelpfully. 'As to where the boat came from, that is quite another matter indeed. Ah-ha, we are in luck!'

With the thumbwheels set at $1 - 1 - 5$ the case opened with a sharp click. They all drew close as Jonah gingerly opened the lid and peered inside.

'Clothing,' he announced, showing them.

Annie whooped with delight and without ceremony started to rummage through the contents.

'Goddamn!' she cried. 'At last I can get rid of these damned leathers.' The only clothes they possessed were the ill-fitting garments they had acquired from the castle occupied by Gerent's doomed tribe, the Denneth. This motley selection of gear had proven entirely inappropriate for the warm atmosphere of Stone; Jonah too was relieved at the prospect of exchanging his own coarse cloak for something more suitable.

From the pile Annie extricated a pair of what looked like striped stockings; without hesitation she peeled off her trousers. Jonah glanced away as she undressed, feeling foolish considering their new-found intimacy. Gerent looked on openly, much to Jonah's chagrin.

The garment Annie had chosen turned out to be a pair of tight-fitting leggings made from a highly flexible material as mysterious as that from which the case had been formed. Stripes alternating brown and black ran vertically from waist to ankle. A faded white label inside the waistband displayed a line of unidentifiable symbols, but what writing there had been on it had been worn almost completely away.

She replaced her upper garments with a thin, white, sleeveless blouse which, because it had no buttons, had to be pulled over her head. Thus garbed, she turned a pirouette in the sunlight, her bare arms spread wide, a beatific smile on her face.

'At last my body can breathe again!' she exclaimed. 'Anything in there for you boys?'

'Should we?' said Jonah belatedly, but she urged him on.

'Come on, Englishman. They're no good to anyone else!'

But to whom did they belong in the first place? wondered Jonah.

Gerent was not tempted, but watched with interest as Jonah selected a similar white blouse and a pair of pale blue denim trousers which fitted him well enough, though they were a little large in the hip and short in the leg. A leather belt cinched in the waist enough to keep them up. 'A lady's wardrobe, I suspect,' he speculated as he paced back and forth in his new outfit. 'All the same, the clothes are comfortable enough.'

They caught each other's eye at the same time, Jonah and Annie. Both wore expressions of such intense concentration that they burst out laughing.

'I don't understand it at all,' sighed Kythe, who was perched on the edge of the ledge looking bemused. 'Why do you need to cover your bodies? I know you don't have scales like me but it isn't as if you need protection from the cold, or the weather, not here on Stone.'

'An Englishman must maintain propriety at all times, young dragon,' replied Jonah with a tone so earnest that Annie exploded with laughter once more. He regarded her with a pained expression for a moment then chuckled himself. 'Well, perhaps there is no very good reason for it other than that . . . that it is what we *do*.'

'I just don't understand faeries,' grumbled Kythe,

wiping her snout with the end of one orange wingtip.

Jonah was amazed at how much better he felt in fresh clothes. Pressing aside the vague guilt he felt at requisitioning someone else's possessions he squatted down to investigate what was left in the case. There were more clothes, much like those they had just donned. Jonah picked up a small triangle of lace-trimmed black fabric of a particularly scant and flimsy nature; Annie regarded it solemnly and proclaimed it a lady's undergarment, at which Jonah dropped it quickly, his face and ears burning.

At the bottom of the case, underneath all the clothes, were two identical books and three odd-looking writing instruments, which turned out to be ingeniously contrived ink pens. The first book was filled with blank pages; the pages of the second were covered with broad, looping handwriting.

'It's a diary,' breathed Annie. She leafed through the first few pages. 'It's a woman's hand. It tells of a sea voyage. Here's the name of the boat: *Bonaventure*. It must have come . . .' here she faltered, '. . . it . . . all these things came through from our world, Jonah, didn't they?'

He nodded. 'Yes. Book and boat: they both came from our world. And that is something which puzzles me greatly.'

'Why?'

'Because they are quite out of place.' Jonah rubbed his chin, thought for a moment, then continued. 'Consider this: we emerged into this world at a point far upStone from here, a point which may usefully be considered to be a marker for the year 1883. From there we travelled downStone, passing more markers along the way which defined earlier and earlier moments in our history: a mediaeval castle, a Roman sword and so forth. By the time we reached the Threshold we had already travelled far back in time, beyond the point where human history began.

'And so we find ourselves here, beyond even the Threshold, on the shore of a mighty ocean. Whatever markers we find here must surely have come from a time long before man walked on the Earth, before even the turning of the world.'

'From the time of charm,' added Kythe.

'So this shouldn't be here at all,' said Annie, closing the book.

'The boat and its contents certainly did not come this far downStone of their own accord,' agreed Jonah. 'Which can mean only one thing: they must have been brought here.'

'But why? And by whom?'

Jonah looked up into the trees. 'I cannot answer those questions. But I believe we already know where the answers must lie.'

With those words Jonah's desperation turned to hope. As soon as the measuring experiment was completed, confirming his theory of the curvature of Stone, he turned his attention fully to the exploration of the forest. To his surprise it was Gerent, who had been so reluctant to fly out to sea for him, who was most eager to join him in this latest expedition.

'We will climb together,' the Neolithic man announced. Jonah gladly agreed.

Gerent insisted they try to assemble some equipment before attempting the ascent. The day after the measuring of Stone, he set off alone for the perilous dockside, where until now none of them had dared to venture. Exploiting the Denneth knack of unearthing and re-using what others had left behind, he rummaged through the precarious heaps of rust and twisted ironwork and returned with two lengths of rope – into which they subsequently spaced a series of knots. A second visit yielded two little swords, glossy and untarnished, and a small, three-pronged grapnel salvaged from what sounded to Jonah like a miniature crane.

'Whatever people once lived here and worked that machinery,' Gerent concluded, 'were smaller than we are. About so high.' He flattened his hand at the level of his waist.

'Pygmies?' ventured Jonah.

'Or faeries. It matters not; they are gone now.'

Annie was not keen on the expedition at all.

'It's foolhardy,' she said that evening as she lay in Jonah's arms. 'An unnecessary risk. Kythe wants no part of it . . . and neither do I.'

Jonah brushed a lock of hair from her cheek. 'Are you not curious about the things we found?' he asked. 'The clothes you wear, that book? The boat itself, for goodness' sake!'

'Of course I'm curious! I just think it's dangerous, that's all!'

Outside the cave-like niche the sky was deep blue. Dark circles rimmed her eyes.

'You do not sleep soundly, Annie. Last night I heard you cry out. What is wrong?'

'Nothing!' she brushed his hand away, then grasped it and held it against her breast. 'Oh, I mean . . . Jonah, I don't know. I guess I'm just a little scared of everything right now. It's been hard, you know?'

'Is it Archan? Do you still have memories of her?'

She nodded, her lip trembling.

'Do you want me to stay with you?'

She hesitated, then shook her head. 'I think you should go, Jonah. I think you will find something there. But I will stay. I'll be all right. Don't worry about me.'

Neither Annie nor Kythe came with them when they set out for the ledge running below the forest. After three attempts Gerent managed to secure the grapnel in the bark of one of the largest trees and the two men began their climb.

Jonah felt as though he were carrying Annie with him as he ascended the rope, so heavy did his heart feel. He could feel her pulling him down like gravity, a universal force that would not be denied. That he loved her he had no doubt.

He forced himself to concentrate on the task at hand. The friction of the knotted rope against his fingers was salutary and before long he had reached the sanctuary of the nearest of the anchormen. With a final heave he pulled himself up around the trunk and lay gasping on its curved upper surface. Then, having caught his breath, he called down to Gerent to begin his ascent.

Looking out through the weave of the branches he found the tall sweep of the sea. Perched here, he began for the first time to grasp the immensity of this sideways ocean, and for the first time he wondered – *really* wondered – what lay on the opposite shore.

Everything looked different from this altered perspective. Sitting in a tree extending horizontally out from Stone was not unlike sitting in a treetop on Earth. Above all else it expanded the view: the fabulous turquoise ocean; the blue-brown hump that broke clear of the waves about a mile off-shore – a sandbank perhaps, or Stone's equivalent; swirls of vapour drifting away from the wave-tops only to be torn apart by the wind; the endless march of crest and trough into the all-consuming distance. Sometimes great shoals of fish ascended laboriously through the shallows like salmon fighting their way up-river; their silver backs scintillated just behind the waves, marking their stately progress.

Perched here, Jonah knew he was right about the shape of Stone.

The day was remarkably clear and the vertex where the sea met the sky, though blurred, was unmistakable. Of course his calculations were rudimentary, and of course his conclusions were really only speculations: in truth Stone might have been anything from a tilted cylinder to an egg, or even the immeasurable product of some irregular geometry he was not equipped to survey. But his heart told him that its structure was regular and his instinct true. That, despite the tweeness of the rhyme it prompted, Stone was shaped like a cone.

Cone or not, he thought, *the important thing is that Stone is not the infinite wall we originally thought it to be. Somewhere, somehow, it curves completely around and meets itself. Somewhere the circle is closed.*

Does that mean that somewhere, at some unimaginable seam, the past and the future are one?

He scanned the broad ledges, looking for Annie. There she was, swimming in the warm, clear water of the scoop. Jonah was not surprised to find her there; it had become her haven. From this remote vantage she was little more than a doll, her tanned limbs the size of matchsticks.

At his feet the grapnel lurched suddenly, turning twice over and scoring a groove through the bark at least six feet long before it finally bit again. Belatedly he lunged for it, wondering at the same time what might have happened had he grabbed it before it had regained its hold.

'I would have been pulled over the edge,' he muttered. 'And we both would have been killed.' Well, perhaps not Gerent, whose reflexes would probably have opened his wings in time to break his fall.

All the same he dropped to his knees and pressed his hands on to the slick metal of the grapnel, ensuring its hold was fast. Thick yellow sap welled from the wound it had made in the tree's coarse bark; the smell it gave off was like pine, sharp and fresh. From close by, somewhere beneath the tree, he heard Gerent's heartfelt curses. A few seconds later the Neolithic man's hands appeared, gripping the knotted rope ferociously. His wings were half-open, although as Jonah watched they furled themselves against the man's back where they lay folded like a red and black cloak.

As soon as Gerent had reached the safety of the upper part of the trunk he rounded on Jonah.

'You should have been watching for me, Jonah Lightfoot! Where was your mind this time, as if I did not know?'

'There was nothing I could have done,' Jonah retorted. 'The grapnel slipped. Had I taken hold of it we should both have been dragged down!'

'So you value your own life above those of your companions!'

'You did not need the rope. You could just as well have used your wings.'

'They are not mine, as you well know!'

Jonah was about to snap back when he checked himself. Gerent stood before him like some Norse god, not heavily muscled but tall and lean, naked but for the breech-cloth that had become his only garment. He saw the hidden king of the Denneth struggling to free himself from behind Gerent's haunted features, the king whose entire people had fallen to their deaths along with the castle that had become their prison. A lonely heir to a Stone Age kingdom that no longer existed.

'Gerent . . .' he began.

'Be silent!' The Neolithic's voice was like a whip-crack. Jonah flinched, unbalanced by the sudden fire in his eyes. Then Gerent whispered, 'Do not move. Do not even breathe.'

Jonah blinked, and wondered if he was permitted to do even that. Then he became aware of a sound – a small, scraping sound, scarcely audible – and he realized that

Gerent was not glaring at him at all, but at something behind him.

'Take a step towards me,' said the Neolithic. 'Move slowly.'

At first Jonah thought his legs had locked themselves rigid. He bit down on his lip, drawing blood; the sudden pain galvanized his limbs and he jerked forward. 'Be careful,' hissed Gerent, reaching for him.

The scraping grew loud and seemed to surround Jonah. Now it was accompanied by a fearful chattering. His vision tunnelled; all he could see was Gerent bending slowly and precisely to prise the grapnel free from the bark. Tiny black splinters sprayed across his bare feet as he raised the three-pronged anchor and hefted it. At the same time he took a step to the side, allowing Jonah to rush past him, to slow his headlong flight and turn, to look upon his pursuer.

It was not one but two, a pair of eyeless worms, pale as milk, each as thick in the body as a man. At the tips of their identical heads they bore serrated beaks that chattered in unison, their blurred movements as ruthless as a threshing machine. It dawned on Jonah that it was not just their beaks that moved together – so did the worms themselves. Like grotesque dancing partners they swayed and looped their pallid, segmented bodies in perfect synchrony. The stench of their breath washed over his face.

Then Gerent swung the grapnel in a clean arc, embedding one of its prongs in the head of the worm nearer to him. It dropped instantly on to the tree, the connection with its twin broken, the dance over.

Strangely, the felled worm did not bleed. Instead, the instant the grapnel struck it, a gaping wound opened in the head of the untouched worm. This was vividly clear to Jonah, for the vile creature's beak was sawing at the air bare inches in front of his nose when its head literally

31

peeled itself apart, revealing brightly glowing flesh within. Crimson blood and what might have been electrical sparks exploded outwards; the worm writhed, spraying gore and trails of miniature lightning. It raised its blind head, uttering a single, piercing shriek and then fell with a hollow thud next to its sibling.

Gasping, the two men leaned against each other. Jonah had to clutch at Gerent's shoulder to prevent himself from collapsing; the Neolithic man held him around his waist.

'They came from there,' said Gerent. Jonah was astonished how steady his voice was.

He was pointing towards the place where the tree trunk was rooted. Here Stone's skin was buckled outwards; plates of Stone-stuff clung to the bole of the tree like pieces of blackened eggshell. At the base of the trunk, banked heavily against the sheer wall of Stone itself, was a tremendous wedge of earth and debris. It was riddled with holes. Were these worms the caretakers of the forest, tunnelling through the litter and processing the debris? Or were they predators, angry at having their territory invaded?

'I do not think we should stay here,' said Jonah, eyeing the tunnel mouths suspiciously. 'Next time we may not be so fortunate.'

'You wish to go back down? You want to give up?'

'Give up? No. We must go on and up, Gerent, on and up.'

'Stone says we cannot climb far.'

'I do not care a damn for what Stone may or may not say! We have come this far and I at least will not be turned from my path by a pair of overgrown earthworms! You may go back if you wish; I will go on!'

'You are a pompous man, Lightfoot!' cried Gerent, wrenching the grapnel free of the worm's head with a sickening, damp sound. He wiped it clean against the creature's flabby hide and grimaced. 'But in this case you happen to be right. Come – the climbing will be easier from now on.'

And so it proved. The trees were packed tight and boasted innumerable boughs thick enough to support their weight. Gerent went first, with the rope coiled and slung around his neck and the grapnel lodged between his wings. Following the Neolithic king up into the forest's maze, Jonah observed the tiny movements of those wings as they cushioned and supported the grapnel: instinctive movements of which Gerent himself was quite unaware.

The trees became more entangled the further they ascended, dulling their sense of direction. It was no longer like being in an upturned forest, more like climbing up through the branches of a single, enormous tree. They passed clots of rotting leaves and mounds of richly scented compost; as they rounded one such pile they observed another of the twin-worms. This specimen was a little smaller than the one Gerent had slain and dark green in colour. The two men crept past as quietly as they could; the beast (for they agreed that it was not two creatures but one) showed no sign of registering their presence, preferring instead to scythe at a clump of ferns with its chattering beaks.

Noticing its tendency to graze, Jonah wondered if its cousin had intended only to warn them away in response to some territorial instinct. He was reluctant to put the theory to the test, and breathed a silent sigh of relief as they passed out of earshot of the creature's idiot chattering.

Turning his attention to the trees themselves, Jonah judged them all to be of the same species. The thick, black bark was like nothing he had seen before – and their tremendous girth was certainly unearthly; their heavy needles and the sweet scent of resin reminded him of terrestrial pines. Yet he would have expected to find more than one variety of tree in such a large plantation.

'Not on Stone, it seems,' he mused.

There was something else the black trees reminded him of too. Clambering up them was unnervingly like clambering through the labyrinth of twisted memory rods they had found exposed in the Threshold. Each time he reached for the next handhold he winced, half-expecting the familiar jolt of energy as his uniquely adept fingers tapped into the memory-store concealed beneath Stone's skin. Occasionally he believed he *did* feel something – a tingle of electricity, a tiny spark of memory coursing up his arm. But, of course, it was only his imagination.

Part of him wanted the contact, wanted to experience again the miracle of delving into the past – or perhaps this time into the future . . . But mostly he was fearful of the power only he and Archan had possessed: the power not only to read the memory rods of Stone but to change them as well.

The power to alter the course of history.

Pausing, he gazed past Gerent's body into the forest. Branches swarmed, an intricate, three-dimensional web, in the recesses of which he saw strange shadows and half-formed shapes. It was like looking through the eyes of a child, seeing witches skulking in the corners of his room as night comes on, and elves dancing on the wain-scotting. Darting movements caught his attention, but when he turned to look all was still. Yet the forest creaked and whispered and made its intricate shadow-play, leaving him tense and uncertain.

In fact they saw no living things during the climb other than the twin-worms, and Jonah found this in itself unsettling. Terrestrial woodlands were home to thousands of varieties of creatures, yet in this Stone equivalent

34

there was no birdsong, nor any sign of rodent or foraging insect.

Sightlines through to the sky grew sparse; all sense of the world outside the forest had gone. Despite this it did not seem unduly dark. The forest interior was intensely sculptural, its elaborate contours modelled by rich green light and deep, deep shadows. Looking down at his hands Jonah saw the same green cast across his skin, as though his blood had turned to sap. He became aware of the subtlest noise: a shallow breathing he was almost unable to separate from the sound of the air his lungs claimed for their own: the voice of the woodland.

They had planned to follow the trail of destruction left by the *Bonaventure* as it had tumbled through the trees; in fact there was little damage to be found beyond the broken anchormen. A few of the bigger trunks bore scratches and even the odd scorch-mark, but there were almost no broken limbs and in all directions the branches bore well-established growths of needles and scores of hanging vines.

'It cannot have grown back so quickly,' cried Jonah, stopping to catch his breath. 'It has been a matter of only a few days since the *Bonaventure* fell through.'

'Charm?' suggested Gerent, grateful of the chance to rest.

'Pah! Are we to put everything down to magic now?'

Gerent looked at him and said nothing.

'Well, whatever it is that has happened, it will soon be impossible to track the boat's progress. We shall very soon be exploring blind.'

'We may have been doing that from the beginning, Lightfoot.'

Huffing melodramatically, Jonah took the lead, but they had advanced only a little further when a chill infiltrated his spine. 'Do you feel that?' he whispered, glancing around nervously. 'It seems suddenly cold. This is most unlike Stone, I must say. Oh – it's gone.'

'I felt nothing, Lightfoot.'

Jonah's apprehension increased as he studied the woodland. It seemed to be closing in on them, fat branches twisting across every available pathway, closing off escape. The deep shadows – impossible though it seemed – grew steadily deeper and darker, but more than that they appeared to acquire solidity, as if they were no longer voids but had substance. Where once they had receded now the shadows swelled, advancing through the spaces between the branches and pressing away the green light until all was black and sombre. Within these bloated shadows Jonah fancied he could see movement, jerky and uncontrolled.

He shrank against Gerent and felt the man tense against him. 'Should we retreat?' Jonah gulped, but Gerent shook his head.

'It is the same behind and below us,' he answered curtly. 'There is nowhere for us to go.'

A wind gusted down from above, disrupting the advancing shadows as though they were but flimsy shrouds and scattering the remains. The forest was restored, except now it was different: there were strange objects hulked behind the trees, giant structures that seemed at once familiar yet, because of the strange green light in which they were bathed, quite alien.

Jonah stared at these things – they were all around them, as well as above and below – turning his head as though trying to puzzle out a child's drawing. There was a profile that reminded him of a long, hooked nose; there a shape like a rabbit's ear; there a hard mechanical sil-houette. What were they? The answer floated and dipped just out of reach.

Squinting at the nearest of them he managed to resolve the outline of a long spar from which hung several thick ropes and countless vines. From the top of the spar was suspended a long, triangular pennant. A second spar intersected with the first at a sharp angle; attached to this was a greenish-white sail. The object locked itself into focus and he had it!

'It's a boat!' he gasped, and suddenly the discovery seemed inevitable. 'Another boat – or rather, a ship.' He cast his gaze around. 'And there, another. And another, and another! By God, Gerent, there are scores of the things! This is a veritable ships' graveyard!'

Heedless of any danger, Jonah scrambled along a bough towards the nearest ship; Gerent followed more cautiously. Having forced his way between several close-set branches Jonah emerged into what was almost a clearing. The ship was hanging exactly on a level with his eyes, supported and wrapped around by hundreds of limber branches and lianas. Examining it more closely he saw that many of these were not simply holding the ship but had actually grown into it – or were growing from it, he could not tell which. Moreover, some parts of the vessel were so twisted out of shape that it was hard to see where ship left off and tree began.

'A strange fruit,' commented Gerent, his voice so close behind that it made Jonah jump.

Jonah wiped his brow, yearning for Stone's eternal wind to blow away the forest's stuffy air. 'Indeed,' he replied. 'I wonder if this one has a name.'

Both men peered at the ship. It was of a type Jonah could not easily identify. It dated perhaps from the Elizabethan era, and something about its design made him think of pirates. A raised deck near the prow bore several small cannon. The hull was long and shallow, its bottom half painted dirty white and its top half coloured black and decorated with gilded swirls and flourishes. Its two enormous sails were triangular, slung from sloping yards, and looked quite intact; this surprised Jonah, who would have expected the surrounding trees to have long since torn them to shreds.

Yet that may not be so, he corrected himself. *We are the intruders here, not this vessel. Unlike us, it belongs.*

'There!' called Gerent. 'Is that its name?'

Jonah followed the direction he was pointing. There were words carved high up on the stern but he could barely read them, wreathed as they were in shadow. 'Yes, I can see part of it . . . it looks like *Reinara* . . . something. I cannot read the rest.' Not for the first time he wondered at the selectivity of Stone's magic: the airborne charm that allowed him and Gerent – and Kythe for that matter – to understand each other's speech fell short when it came to the written word. Gerent could no more read English than Jonah could the strange marks the Neolithic man sometimes made.

'Does it mean anything to you?'

'No, I am afraid not. My knowledge of history might be good when it comes to you and your prehistoric contemporaries, Gerent, but I never paid much attention to the Middle Ages. The name sounds Italian, but I can tell you little else about it.'

'So it is from your world?'

Jonah frowned at the obvious question. 'Yes, yes it is. *Our* world, Gerent, yours and mine. It is, you might say, a relic from my past and a vision of your future.' He smiled, pleased with himself.

'Here is another.'

Adjacent to the Italian pirate ship was a vessel rather older and of a type more familiar to Jonah's eyes. Like the *Reinara* it was welded to the forest by vast numbers of branches and woven vines. One particularly thick branch sprouted from its keel, looking for all the world like a massive umbilicus pumping life-giving fluids into its belly. Apart from a few wooden carvings and the dramatically upraised bow and stern, both of which were curled into stylized serpents' heads, this vessel was much more workmanlike in its construction. Its single, central mast bore a square sail, and its rudder was a heavy oar lashed with ropes beside the stern.

'A Viking longboat,' announced Jonah with relish. 'This is the sort of boat your people might have learned to build had they remained on Earth, Gerent.'

'It is from the place you call *Scandinavia*?'

'Indeed it is! Is it not splendid?'

Gerent seemed genuinely affected by the longboat, and managed to climb close enough to touch the nails holding its hull-planks in place. Heroically posed, with his long, golden hair flowing down his naked back, he looked again like a character from Nordic myth, or maybe a Viking warrior in search of lands to conquer. There was in his eyes a yearning, an emptiness that begged to be filled.

There were too many ships to catalogue. Here was a small boat with a rounded hull and a sail decorated with fantastic beasts; here an eighteenth-century brig. Here hung a real curiosity – a truly enormous metal construction whose long deck was encrusted with towers and cranes and massive guns. To Jonah's Victorian eyes it looked impossibly futuristic. Each one unique, each one sharing the same weird symbiosis with the forest.

'A ships' graveyard,' repeated Jonah as the strangeness of the place finally overwhelmed him. Walking back to the root of an enormous branch he slumped against the trunk of its parent tree, staring up at a vessel that looked more like a steel shark than a ship. Stubby square fins jutted inelegantly from its rounded bow; rising like a fat dorsal fin from its spine was a mast-topped tower bearing not a name but a number: 'S101'.

Entranced by its streamlined elegance, Jonah imagined it travelling not above the waves but beneath them, a sub-aquatic leviathan large enough to hold a hundred men.

Gerent slid down beside him, a look of profound concentration on his face, an expression that had become very familiar to Jonah over the weeks he had known the Neolithic man. Gerent was an extraordinary problem-solver, and Jonah knew that when he looked like this all he could do was wait for the gears in his mind to turn full circuit, which eventually they did.

'What we said before,' Gerent began slowly, 'about the vessels coming here from our world.'

'They can have come from nowhere else,' agreed Jonah.

'Hmm. And yet . . . Oh, these ships are wholly foreign to me, Jonah, though I sensed their purpose immediately. Such a bold idea, to mould wood in such a way that man might voyage upon the waters!'

'Bold indeed. It was the ship that opened up the world to trade, Gerent. Why, the English Navy is the pride of the Empire . . .'

'Indeed.' Gerent cut him short, waving his words aside while keeping his own eyes fixed on the distant longboat. 'But these vessels, Lightfoot. Look at them! They have not come from our world – how can they have? They are as much a part of this forest as the trees themselves. See how the trunk of this monster flows into the belly of the ship of Scandinavia! They have not been brought here: they have been *made* here!'

'Made in the forest? Gerent, it is not only the ships themselves but everything they contain. Do you include the *Bonaventure* in your hypothesis? Do you not remember the case that fell from its hull? The books and pens? These clothes I am wearing, for Heaven's sake!' He tugged at the blue denim trousers. 'Are you trying to tell me that these are not real?'

'Of course they are *real*, Lightfoot. They are simply not from where you think they are from.'

40

'So . . . so they grew on the trees? Is that what you are trying to tell me?'

Gerent shrugged. 'As I said before – strange fruit.'

Jonah laughed – he could not help himself. 'I'm sorry, Gerent. But it seems far more likely a proposition to suggest that these ships have simply been washed here, just as we were washed here. To use a metaphor, of course.'

'Are you not forgetting what you yourself said: that whatever markers we find in this place will have come not from the age of Man but the age of Charm?'

The lack of a breeze was giving Jonah a headache. Outside the forest, he suspected, night was already falling. He massaged his forehead. 'No, Gerent, I did not forget that. But is it not possible that the ships came through further upStone and were somehow transported here?'

'But why? We ourselves made such a journey but at what cost? How could so many things of such tremendous size be moved such a distance?'

Jonah buried his head. 'I do not know. Perhaps yours is the correct answer, Gerent. I simply do not know.'

The tree against which they were both leaning suddenly moved. They jerked clear of the trunk, scrambling some distance along the branch before stopping to look behind them.

Things seemed to be sliding about just beneath the ebony bark; it looked for all the world like the throat of a giant, flexing and swallowing as weird ripples distorted its skin. It bloated outwards then sank in upon itself, changing its dimensions as if it were made of rubber. Accompanying the transformation was a syrupy sound, the sound of oil moving thickly through hidden pipes.

Gradually the sinuous movement slowed, and then stopped altogether.

Where once there had been a random mosaic of knots and grooves, now there was a face.

It was hard to see, and Jonah had to look very hard indeed to convince himself it was there at all. The heavy green illumination, previously so informative, somehow failed to enlighten the scene, reducing it instead to two dimensions. Yet when he concentrated he could see it, it was there.

A human face, or approximately so, but on a gigantic scale: from crown to chin it was fully twelve feet high. Heavy brows and deep eyes. A sharp nose presiding over drooping lips and heavy jowls. A heavily bearded chin, and the suggestion of pointed ears that extended up, far up into the upper branches. The face of a strange old man carved from the bark of an alien tree.

Green liquid sparkled in the depths of those remarkable eyes. The lips moved.

'To your friend you should listen. What's your name . . . *Lightfoot*?'

Its voice was deep and dry and somehow primaeval. It sounded as if it were trying to repress a laugh. Jonah could think of absolutely nothing to say.

The tree yawned, revealing pale brown teeth and a huge chasm of a mouth.

'But right or wrong is not worth the worry,' the voice went on cheerfully. 'My boats are real enough if real you like, so explore them if you must. Make the most, in fact. I warn you – it's all coming down. Just the beginning was the *Bonaventure*. I can't keep up with the curse-woven dryads any more. Let them do their business and be done. When you've been here as long as I have and seen what I've seen – and can see what I see coming – then you stop fussing. Times come and times go, and even Stone gets old. Oh ye, mighty old.'

It chuckled with what might have been bitter humour, then fell silent.

'I beg your pardon,' ventured Jonah, 'but . . . are you really a tree?'

'Oh, no tree I, but that you can call me if you wish.' It paused, seemed to consider this. 'Ye, that will do nicely. Call me Grandfather Tree.'

3

Lesky

'The time you have chosen to find me – auspicious it is. A time of great change for me and all I am. Ye, great change.

'Grandfather Tree you may call me, but lesky is what I am. My name, my kind, all of me. A long time have I dwelt here, with few visitors. Now you have come. I feel glad. The feeling is strange but not unwelcome. Like an old friend met beneath the moon. And good fortune it may be too. Ye, for us all.

'Stone has raised the night and so the time has come for stories. Mine first. You shall forgive me if I don't invite a fire. Fire is not for the leskies. We ignite. You shall forgive me if I speak too much – alone I have been for many ages, for the dryads and I have little between us in the way of kindness. Once we might have shared a bond, but no more. Those thrown together by fate must find a way to live together. We have found such a way, the dryads and I. It is called war.

'I have a long memory. I remember a time before all this, when leskies lived in the world behind Stone, in what I used to think of as the real world. In those times the forest was called taiga. Huge it was, not like this feeble beard. The taiga was all that lay east of the Spine; between its trees beasts prowled, beasts of the old world

44

and the new, beasts of charm and beasts of nature. Young races there were among the old, their eyes empty of memory, hungry for life. Some moved on, some remained. Thronged it was, ever-changing.

'Among the old were the leskies and the beautiful leso-vikha and peris and rusalka and all the hidden folk of the taiga. Charm was losing its hold on us all and we were slipping out of the world. Strong were the leskies though, strong in our hold on the trees, and we looked set to last it out longer than most. Words came from the west, from the injured lands. They said that soon the world would turn and all magic would be wiped from its skin. It was denied by faces but believed in hearts. All knew change was coming. Leskies more than most.

'So I made ready.

'I am a tree-spirit. Only the strongest, oldest forests hold leskies. In all the taiga there were fewer than two hundred leskies. All of us old, some wiser than others, each jealous of his territory and proud of his existence. Those of us who remained true to our souls remained within our trees, nurturing the taiga through our roots and leaves. Some leskies, as they learned of the fall of charm, became rogue and wandered the taiga by night, setting traps for the unwary and consuming their dreams. They believed they could live on in a world without charm by sucking the magic from those who still possessed it. Twisted they became, and inward-looking. Many embraced evil itself and looked deep into the heart of the flame.

'All this I saw, I saw my brethren sink into the abyss of despair. But while they hurled curses upon the new force of nature I bided my time and saved my strength.

'Then there came a time, shortly before my prime tree reached its one thousandth year. I found myself thinking of the future and of the past. Places they were to me, not ages, and both connected through my roots in the present. Past and future held apart, my branches spanning the gap. So I encouraged my tree to root itself deeper. Digging down is like exploring the past. On the broken backs of our ancestors we stand, we feed on their remains. So digging down is a way to make yourself strong. In my case, strong enough to withstand the storm of a charmless world.

'I dug down further than any other.

'At first it was like ordinary soil, but soon it developed a texture like none I had known. Coarse-grained, set through with thin strands like an unbreakable web. Deeper I went, infiltrating immovable web with sinuous root, pressing through the impossible density of the hard-packed earth with filaments of pure charm. Thin was the charm by then but I sucked it down from the air, leached it out of the rain and wind. Yes, I even stole it from my neighbours. I was obsessed. Deeper and deeper I travelled with every day that passed, never stopping. Roots entered ancient bones, strange relics. Down, all the time down, with no desire to stop or even slow.

'Then, something strange. The soil grew thin again, like powder. Speed, suddenly. Tree senses accelerated as everything in the world turned over. No longer was I digging down but *out*, no longer a descent but a movement to the side. Thin soil compacted against hard plates. Against this sudden wall I pressed with all my charm. It broke, and out I broke. All turned around, top and bottom exchanged and tipped on their sides. Leaves so far distant drew close, merged and then were flung out into a new sky, a sideways sky set with falling clouds. This sky. The sky of Stone.

'I'd broken through. Through the past the roots of my tree had moved themselves, and in doing so they'd taken me across the gap between the worlds. Young was my tree again, a mere sapling, and strong I felt. A single tree, a single lesky, alone on a great wall. A brilliant sun and a sky filled with charm.

'Time was kind then, as was charm. Each root brought forth a new sapling, each sapling ten more. From that one tree grew a forest, and though one tree became many there remained only one lesky. I am in all this forest, I am the lesky in all these trees. How much greater am I than any other of my kind, and how blessed, for I can be with the young as with the old, in the sapling as in the aged giant lying crashed to the floor. Leaf and bark I am, branch and bud and hidden root. I am the forest, and I am the lesky.

'But still, if you prefer, you may call me Grandfather Tree.'

The face in the tree dropped its eyes. Jonah was glad to be free of that weird, liquid gaze. The lesky's features were still only faintly defined, but those eyes! The references meant little to him. He fancied *taiga* was an old Russian name, but the instant translation afforded by Stone's magical air made it hard to assess the origins of words.

'Stay the night you may,' the lesky was saying to them both, 'but come the dawn you should be gone from here. For one night I shall protect you against the dryads, but you should not be found here thereafter. Now, you have a story of your own?'

Jonah started in faltering fashion, wondering how much of their tale to tell, wondering how much he could even remember. To his surprise he remembered and told almost all of it, lingering especially on his own recollections of Esh.

'During our journey to the Threshold she was our guide. She was one of the Ypoth, whom you may know as the caretakers of Stone.' The face in the tree showed no sign of recognition. 'Whenever there is a breach in

47

the fabric of Stone, such as that which was caused by the eruption of Krakatoa, the Ypoth emerge and repair the damage. During that time they evolve at a remarkable rate, developing from mindless beasts of labour to intelligent creatures able to reason and communicate and . . . and to love. Esh loved us all, I think, and at the end she gave up her life for us.'

'What of the Ypoth when the breaches are repaired?' asked the lesky.

'They lose their intelligence. They regress to their former mindless state until eventually they are absorbed back into the body of Stone.'

The lesky considered this. 'A noble end.'

'A sad end.'

'Ye, indeed. I have heard rumour of the Ypoth but never have I met one. Nor have I met one of their acquaintance. Your knowledge is unique.'

Around them the forest was utterly silent; even the rustle of leaf and creak of bough had ceased. Jonah began to feel decidedly uneasy. His sense of time, already affected by Stone's shorter days and undefined moonless months, had deserted him altogether and he had no idea how long they had been here exchanging their stories. The overwhelming greenness of the tree-scape was making his eyes ache; fatigue had crept up on him like sudden age.

'Are these dryads dangerous?' he asked abruptly. 'Are they the dryads of Greek mythology? I always imagined them to be kindly spirits, though they were said to have a fearsome beauty. Is that where their peril lies?'

'Myths have truth, and dangerous the dryads are. As to their beauty, don't be deceived by their skins. Within they fester. Cruel they are and warlike, and if you leave now you will become their prey. The dryads move by night; only by day are travellers safe in the taiga. Even then caution is wise. Stay with Grandfather Tree – he will keep watch.'

Jonah sighed and turned to Gerent. 'It seems we have little choice.'

Gerent pressed his hands against his face then lowered them again. 'Tell us how you came to make the ocean vessels. You *did* make them, did you not?'

The face wavered and almost disappeared altogether. When it resolved itself again it was smiling. 'Ah ye, the ships! They are mine! Splendid they are, you shall agree?'

The lesky was interrupted by a hissing noise coming from the trees directly above them. To Jonah it sounded like the safety valve on an over-strained boiler. He even ducked, expecting to feel the scalding vapour washing across the back of his neck. Grandfather Tree hissed a single word in response: 'Dryads!'

Something was whipping the leaves into motion, something unseen within the foliage. The movements were jerky, erratic; they proceeded outwards from a central point in horribly uncoordinated waves. Jonah imagined a destructive steam engine scything through the forest, a mobile machine of war armed with spinning blades and lethal pointed rams. Leaves showered on their heads like green confetti. Then, as quickly as it had begun, the movement stopped. The hissing sound faded, only to be replaced by a dreadful growling that grew in intensity; it was as if all Africa's lions had been brought to Stone. It was a guttural, animal sound, full of malevolence and scarcely restrained power; hearing it made the hairs on Jonah's neck stand erect.

'Can you truly protect us against these things?' Gerent asked calmly.

'They feed on fear,' the lesky replied. 'That's why they make such noise.'

'Do you mean that their bark is worse than their bite?' asked Jonah. The lesky regarded him with that irresistible gaze then laughed heartily.

'Oh ye! An apt phrase, faery-man. Apt indeed, oh ye!'

'But they are still dangerous,' prompted Gerent.

'I have told as much. Dangerous they are, but most dangerous they are when feared. Stick with Grandfather Tree and safe you should be. Then, when morning comes, you go.'

Despite the growling Jonah felt at least a little reassured. Gerent on the other hand was frowning. 'Tell me something, *Grandfather*. If you can protect us as you say, why do you let the dryads destroy your work?'

The giant face in the tree narrowed its expression to one of suspicion. 'I don't know what you mean.'

'It is very simple. How can we trust in your ability to resist the dryads when we have seen the result of their sabotage? These ships you create – the dryads are destroying them one by one, knocking them out of the forest. Is that not true? If you cannot stop them from doing that, what dominion do you have over them at all?' Jonah tried to interrupt, acutely aware of the dark cloud of anger descending over the lesky's face, but Gerent would not be stopped. 'Furthermore, are we to take sides in a war we do not even understand? We have only your word that the dryads are evil. Were we to talk to them what might we learn? Might they not tell us that it is you who are the enemy?'

'Cursed may you be!' bellowed Grandfather Tree. Bright green sap sprayed from the lesky's cavernous mouth, spattering the ground by Jonah's feet. 'Where is your gratitude? You intrude and I embrace you, but with suspicion you repay me! Go then, if you think me evil! Face the dryads and see what they really are! Grandfather Tree will not come to you again! I rid myself of you! Begone!'

The tree trunk shuddered and suddenly the face was there no more. Fresh green light cascaded like water but the bark was just bark; Grandfather Tree was gone.

Now the growling was all around them, and growing

louder with every breath. 'I think we should beat a retreat,' suggested Jonah. 'For goodness' sake, Gerent, what possessed you to talk to him like that? Could you not see how angry he was becoming?'

'Anger breeds truth,' answered Gerent tersely. 'Come! We can discuss this later!'

So saying he launched himself down through the branches, crashing and sliding in a barely controlled descent. Jonah hesitated before pursuing him, remembering how the *Bonaventure* had burst from the base of the forest after just such a fall, remembering that to fall on Stone was to fall a very long way indeed, perhaps forever. Then something growled right next to his ear and he cried out. Scrambling after Gerent he began descending hand by hand, grasping at individual limbs and lowering himself quickly but safely. But as the animal presence intensified, as the growls grew louder still, he abandoned caution and flung himself headlong, heedless of the lashing branches and the irresistible pull of gravity. Leaves blurred into a green patchwork; he crashed into one trunk and rebounded into another. Robbed of breath he sucked helplessly at the thick, hot air. A third tree trunk, black as pitch, exploded into his vision. Seconds before striking it he managed to roll so that it was his hunched back that met the wood first. He hit hard, his shocked lungs screaming with pain. His neck snapped back, slamming the back of his head against the tree, and then everything was black.

He was under the sea. Not branches but fronds of seaweed; not bark but rough coral. Above him swam exotic fish, their long, languid bodies like those of mermaids. They spiralled down towards him, talking in silent voices as they cocked their beautiful heads towards him. The nearer they drew the less like fish they seemed, the more human, the more female. One of them flashed close enough to brush her tail against his thighs then disappeared in a stream of darting blue bubbles. Her touch was like the softest moleskin. Another reached sinuous arms behind her head and grasped the tip of her tail, spinning herself into a perfect circle that drew a vortex in the water. The first mermaid reappeared, floated above him momentarily then kissed him back to sleep.

He sat up with a start, instinctively holding his breath against the press of the water. But surrounding him was not an undersea realm but the familiar terrain of branch and bough; he was still in the sideways forest.

His head throbbed. All at once he remembered the twin-worms and jumped to his feet, looking warily around. He sensed it was still night, though the green light remained as flat and unedifying as before. What had he been dreaming about?

The trunk on which he stood – a horizontal cylinder of ebony wood at least twenty feet in diameter – felt none too stable beneath his feet, a fact which, given its prodigious size, gave Jonah some cause for concern. Looking along its length he saw why: a large patch of bark was rippling like water. Tiny waves were racing energetically across its width, and at first Jonah thought that the lesky was about to manifest itself again.

Then something did indeed emerge from the rippling bark, but it was not Grandfather Tree.

Human forms, very many of them, raised themselves up through the skin of the tree like breaching whales. Except the tree did not exactly break in the places where they emerged, rather it seemed to melt and merge into the slowly forming bodies. It was less a process of emergence than of metamorphosis. Watching these slender bodies solidify from the very substance of the tree on which he stood, Jonah had no doubt he was witnessing the same order of charm used by Grandfather Tree himself; these beings were as much a part of the forest as the lesky. Nor did he have any doubt as to what, or who, they were: they were the dryads.

They did not stand – they had no legs. Just like mermaids, they possessed the upper body of the human female and the lower body of the fish. However, these fish-tails were clad not with scales but needles, thousands of dark green pine needles; as the dryads moved they rustled like straw. When Jonah tried to locate the ends of their tails he found they simply merged back into the tree from which they had been spawned. These creatures were literally rooted to the spot. They swayed like seaweed.

One of the dryads – he counted fifteen – followed his gaze with bright, grey eyes and smiled. Her face was flushed deep pink, its smooth skin marked by neither care nor age. Long red hair, much darker than his own auburn locks, flowed across her shoulders; she was devastatingly pretty. Her voice, when she spoke, was deep and liquid.

'Do you think we cannot move, Jonah?'

She was almost too quick for him. With a single flick of her tail she surged forwards, throwing up a crackling bow wave of tree-bark as she sped across to where Jonah stood. Behind her the bark sealed itself instantaneously. Jonah took a step back as she rose up before him, her smile exposing blue-white teeth. Her canines were long and sharp. Behind her tongue, in the back of her throat, he fancied he saw a faint glow.

'H-how do you know my name?' he stammered. The creature (woman?) smelt of spice and citrus; the aroma was sharp, intoxicating and he had to fight to keep his thoughts level.

'We have tracked you and Gerent since first you came into the forest. We chose to wait before revealing ourselves to you.'

Another of the dryads had rustled forwards to join her

53

companion. The two looked very much alike, like sisters close in age. 'We were interested in how Lesky would react to your presence,' she said.

'We heard you talking to each other,' continued the first, finally answering Jonah's question. 'You are Jonah Lightfoot; he is simply Gerent.'

'And you?'

'I think you know that by now. We are dryads.'

'Do you have names?'

'Of course, but it is not for the likes of you to know such things.'

Jonah studied the dryads, and was unnerved to find them studying him back just as hard. His initial thrill of fear had become a kind of nervous curiosity. These were neither the ferocious creatures the lesky had described, nor were they the tree-nymphs of Greek myth. Or were they? Now he thought about it, his preconception of the classical dryads as essentially benevolent spirits was wrong. As the attendants of the huntress, Artemis, had their duty not been to deter mortals from entering the woods, and to harm them if they disobeyed? He rubbed his forehead and wished he had devoted as much study to the classics as he had to the brave new science of prehistory.

'We know what Lesky has told you of us,' said the second dryad, whose voice was even more mellifluous than her sister's – that they *were* sisters seemed a reasonable assumption given their similarity.

I could be seduced so readily, he thought, aware of the hypnotic power of their words, their beautiful faces. *They are fearsome indeed!*

'Tales are two-faced,' said the first. 'Which means they deceive. Do you wish to be deceived, Jonah, or do you wish to hear our story too, so that you may decide which is the face on which you wish to gaze? The face of the dryad, or the face of the lesky?'

'Where is Gerent?' Jonah demanded. 'He was ahead of me – did he fall too? Did you see him?'

'He is not here. If you wish, we will look for him, after we have told our story.'

'Damnation! Still, Gerent would choose to hear your side of things; I do not think he believed one iota of what the lesky said. Tell it then, but be hasty, for I would be on my way.'

The two dryads spoke in turns, and afterwards Jonah found he could not remember where one had finished and the other had started.

'Much of what Lesky had told you is true, about his own origins at least. He comes from the taiga, which is a wide forest in the cold lands east of the Spine. He was among the first in that land to believe the rumours of the fall of charm, and he was the only one to make provision. In digging down as he did, using what charm he had left to force his roots out of the world altogether and on to Stone, he opened the way for others to follow. Not many others, but enough. Us, the dryads.'

'Our homeland was warm, a small family of islands in the inland sea called Heldwater. Where the taiga was large our woodlands were small; where the taiga was cold our homes were warm with the sun. We lived our days in peace, and learned many ways to keep travellers away, to protect our trees. We loved our land and were respected by it in return.'

'Then we had to flee. New creatures were roaming the Heartland, natural faeries with cruel, blunt faces and charmless eyes. Even before the turning of the world they crossed the water to our islands on their pitiful floating craft. They took our trees and cut them and burned them and defied the curses we brought upon them, and in the end we fled into the east, into the icy clutches of the taiga where we had to battle against the cold-hearted leskies and all their minions, of which Lesky has named but a few. They gave us only the poorest saplings, and with each year that passed our domain became smaller and smaller. Travellers were few.'

'The trees were growing smaller too. As charm leaked from the world so the scale of all things changed. The trolls were long gone by then but there were still giants – giants of earth and ice, salt and clay. But without charm the world diminished, and with it diminished all things of great size, including the trees.'

'All except Lesky's tree. While ours and others failed so his flourished. His roots had spread across the entire taiga by then, sucking in every drop of charm they could find, at the same time depriving all others of its nourishment. A root system spanning almost an entire continent, all devoted to feeding a single tree. Lesky's appetite grew more voracious with every day that passed, and so the dryads plotted to pay him back for his greed.'

'The plan was simple. On a given day we would enter his tree and dislodge him from it. Why had we not thought to do it earlier, you may wonder? If it was so easy to evict a lesky why did it not happen all the time?'

'The answer is that it was simply forbidden. Oh, not merely forbidden in law, spoken or otherwise, but forbidden in spirit. To understand fully takes the mind of an aethereal, not a merely natural creature such as yourself. To evict a spirit from its dwelling is to murder and flay it, to consume its organs and bathe in its blood. It is a crime of the highest order.

'But one we were prepared to commit for the sake of our race.'

'We were the last of our kind, do you see?'

'Lesky would not have perished. He would have been taken in by his neighbours, pampered and simpered over, re-established and revered as the greatest of martyrs. We dryads would have become outcasts, shunned and despised, alive yet unloved.

'Yet alive.'

'So, on the appointed day, we entered Lesky's tree. But he was gone! We scoured every branch, every twig, every hidden bud and found nothing. Then one of our number reported back from the deepest roots, crying that she had dug deeper than any had before, that she had found a wonder benèath the world. We descended and found ourselves on Stone. Fifteen only came through before the portal closed behind us forever.'

'We had found a way to live on. And so had Lesky.'

'And since then?' asked Jonah.

'We have been at war. All we ask of Lesky is what we asked of him before: trees of our own. Yet still he is greedy. Still he must possess all that he sees. All this woodland, this soon-to-be taiga, is *him*! We exist merely as parasites beneath his skin, able only to sip at the sap through which we swim, barred from the heart of the wood by the barriers he has erected. By the time we reached Stone he had already wielded mighty charm to create a stronghold we have not yet managed to penetrate. If we could only reach him we could evict him as we once planned. He would move on, establish a new taiga and, after a space of time, we would all be able to live in peace. Is it so much to ask?'

Jonah thought he would fall into those grey eyes, so wide and pleading had they become. 'Why do *you* not move on and leave the lesky to his forest?'

'Dryads cannot survive without trees for more than one day. In the old world, once we had crossed the water the journey from Heldwater to taiga was easy, so rich was the land. We simply moved from tree to tree, crossing fields between woodlands as you might leap from one stepping-stone to the next. But here it is different. Look around: this forest is all there is. *And it is all Lesky!'*

The dryads' faces were very close to Jonah's now; he could see a thread of spittle stretched between the sharp canines of the first, could hear her hungry panting. Though their features were human there was much of the animal lurking beneath.

'Who to believe?' he said, trying to keep his voice light. 'Is it true you are destroying the ships constructed by the lesky? Did you cause the *Bonaventure* to fall?'

'What of it?' The second dryad adopted a haughty tone. 'If Lesky elects to abuse the trees then it is up to us to stop him!'

'It is delinquent,' explained her sister. 'A spirit – dryad or lesky, it does not matter – must respect her or his dwelling. To fashion such vulgar fruits is . . .'

'Forbidden?' suggested Jonah.

'Obscene!' snapped the dryad in reply. 'It offends us, so we take whatever action we must!'

'What about me? Do I offend you?'

A silk-smooth arm draped itself around his neck. 'No, Jonah. You intrigue us.' He tried to pull away as she advanced but she was stronger than he had realized. Her lips hovered over his and he thought she would kiss him; instead she licked his cheek just above the line of his beard, sighing as she did so. Her tongue was completely smooth; inhuman. Jonah cried out in sudden revulsion and pushed her away. Hard, unyielding flesh crackled under his fingers. She laughed throatily and advanced on him once more.

'Like repels like,' she intoned. 'You may not be of charm as we are, Jonah, but charm has touched you all the same, and you are ambitious. You might succeed where we have failed. Find your way through his defences, open a way in for us and you will be well rewarded. Oh yes, we can reward you in ways you could never imagine, even in your dreams.'

'And if I do not care for your rewards?'

'Then there is always punishment.'

Closing his eyes he pushed her again, pushed her hard. This time she fell backwards against her sister; they both growled like wolves and lunged at Jonah, who stumbled backwards, then changed his mind and stood his ground. 'I am getting a little tired of constantly falling down!' he shouted, as much in exasperation as anger. 'Now get away from me, you damned harridans, and let me make my own choices!'

All the dryads, both the sisters and the others crowded behind them, bared their teeth and screamed aloud. 'Do not delude yourself, *natural*!' shrieked one from the midst of the group. 'Choice is not for the likes of you!'

Something pulled at them, an unseen force. They became a tangle of spinning, writhing bodies, evergreen tails shedding needles as they lashed across each other, dark flesh resilient against the blows it received. Then the ebony bark reached up like a surging wave and sucked them down into the tree. A whirlpool opened, dragging them under; the last thing Jonah saw before they disappeared altogether was a single hand, utterly human, reaching up eloquently towards him. Then they were gone.

Though he called out for Gerent over and over again the Neolithic did not respond, nor was there any clue as to where he was. The forest was as undisturbed as it had been in the wake of the *Bonaventure*'s plunge. Jonah imagined the lesky frantically repairing any damage as soon as it occurred, then found himself wondering just what the lesky's relationship with the forest really was.

A tree spirit. Does it invest the unthinking woodland with mind, much as the human brain animates the body? If so, what are the dryads? Are they indeed parasites, swarming through the body of the lesky as fleas might crawl over human skin?

Roaming with little concern as to where he was going, traversing the forest rather than climbing either up or down, Jonah considered the dryads. They were indeed beautiful, their blushing faces delicate as china. Even their forms, so unexpected, had not disturbed him unduly (some deep part of his mind even whispered that the smooth junction between skin and needle had been sensual, enticing). Human enough to be attractive, but underneath . . . *hard, crackling skin. The audacious touch of her tongue.*

'They are whores,' he muttered under his breath. 'Every one of them. I can very well imagine how they might have diverted unwary travellers who strayed too far into their woods.'

Jonah had been walking – or rather clambering – for some time when he noticed a change in his surroundings. The branches were thickening, and he guessed he was moving in towards the face of Stone itself. Still he felt as though he were not in a forest but poised in the heights of a single unimaginably large tree. There was no ground, only an endless series of gaps through which he might at any moment fall. Progress was made by leaps and lunges, ropewalks and belly-crawls along trunks and limbs. He had never felt such an affinity with his ape ancestors. And all around him the forest seemed to be gathering itself.

As well as many more, thicker branches, thrusting in every direction from horizontal tree trunks that were truly gigantic, there was a proliferation of undergrowth. Ferns and fungi sprouted from crevices in the tough bark, creating a veritable jungle through which he was forced to beat his way. Soon he brought the blade Gerent had given him into play, hacking machete-like at the vegetation. The air was hot and stale and in no time he was sweating profusely. Everywhere wafted the scent of pine.

At one point it became so humid he could see water condensing from the air right in front of his eyes. Individual droplets sprang from nowhere then hung magically suspended, fattening quickly before bursting in sudden showers of rainbow particles. He closed his mouth around one of the larger droplets just before it exploded; the taste of charm was like electricity on his tongue.

Crossing a black trunk even more massive than any he had encountered so far, he battled through dense thickets until he could go no further. His way forward was completely blocked by a screen woven haphazardly from branches as thick as his waist. This shielded his view of what lay ahead, and effectively stopped him in his tracks.

It was little better to the sides: towers of peeled bark and splintered wood rose to dizzying heights, creating a tortured cathedral. The construction was hasty but looked immensely durable.

He turned back to find the barricade had closed in on him from all sides, even from behind. Black spears jutted towards him from the trunk itself; twisted cocoons dripping with sap dangled around his head; the flat green light limped down through a grid-work of limbs and lianas. There was barely a yard's grace in any direction. He had been neatly and effectively trapped.

Is this what the dryads told me about? Am I near to the place where Grandfather Tree actually lives?

If so, he could not understand why a merely physical obstruction such as this, while impenetrable by a human being, should cause any problem for 'aethereal' creatures such as the dryads. Were they not able to move through the substance of the forest like fish through water? Such had been his impression at least.

None of which helped his predicament.

'Grandfather Tree!' he shouted. 'I know you must be

nearby. Please let me through, or else open a passage by which I might retrace my steps.' There was no reply; the forest, and whatever lived in it, held their tongues. 'Please, I am sorry if you were offended. It was not my intention.'

He waited for what seemed an eternity, then shouted some more. Still there was no response. Jonah fell to his knees. He was hot and exhausted; it was almost certainly the middle of the night, and he had all but forgotten why he had ventured into the forest in the first place.

The ship, yes, the ship. Remembering the *Bonaventure* he was reminded, with sudden, stunning clarity, of Annie. His frustration boiled over; he wanted nothing more than to be rid of the claustrophobia of this place, to be free again with Annie on the clean slope of Stone.

Snatching up Gerent's blade he swiped at the nearest of the upreaching black spikes, not even aiming, just lashing out at its sharp spiral. The blade struck with a resounding *clang*, the sound of an axe on an anvil, and he lost his grip; the pygmy sword ricocheted into the thicket, embedding itself in the darkness.

Moving slowly, impossibly slowly, a spark undulated away from a deep scratch in the spike, fizzing and arcing with gentle grace as if its motion had been captured and dissected into a million component pieces. Jonah watched in wonder as it broke apart into a diverging cloud of lesser sparks, each of which gradually dimmed until they were all lost bar one, which drifted like a tiny feather to land between his feet, where it too finally died.

With infinite care he reached out his hand and grasped the black spike and there was . . .

. . . light in the trees, in the taiga . . . a wave of light moving across the land, baptizing all in its path . . . a sky filled with dark clouds . . . hot rain . . . something rising up through the

ground towards him . . . something coursing through his body, pulling . . .

. . . his hand away and crying out loud.

Running his hands down his body Jonah reassured himself that he was all right. Like a scarce-remembered dream the vision faded swiftly. Not so the knowledge it had brought.

'A memory rod,' he murmured. 'Here in the forest, not locked away beneath Stone's skin where it should be.'

Looking around, it dawned on him that all the spikes looked the same, and that the tree from which they sprouted looked the same, that everywhere he looked loomed hard black coils. Memory rods, twisted out of true as they had been in the Threshold. His prison cell was made of nothing less than the collected memories of the living minds of the world. Within these rods, which ran through Stone as steel bars run through concrete, was the past and the future, and, for Jonah at least, the gateway to both.

'You cannot contain me, Grandfather Tree!' cried Jonah, his frustration turning abruptly to triumph. 'Do you not know who I am? Your barricades of memories might be enough to keep out dryads and faeries, but I am no faery! I am a man, and I have the power to move what no man else can move. I have already touched the memory rods and looked into their heart. *And I alone can change them!* Now let me through, or I will take your barricade and twist it and break it until it is so much mangled wreckage. Then where will you be without your precious shield, when the dryads come rushing through to claim your forest for their own?'

He stood there, panting, while his words bounced around the cathedral. For a second or two he thought nothing would happen, then a familiar voice rumbled behind him.

'I know who you are, Jonah Lightfoot. Your powers too are known to me. Your skill with the memory rods, it is rare. This I know, as I know that you are only the third to possess that power. The basilisks, makers of Stone, I exclude. Archan was the second.'

Jonah faltered, his momentum lost. 'How . . . how do you know these things?'

'I know because I was the first.'

Jonah turned slowly. Behind him the barriers had been lifted. Now there opened a long, leafy tunnel at the end of which stood a brilliantly illuminated clearing. It might have been a glade in an English wood, speckled with the endlessly falling light of a summer's day. In the centre of the clearing, too far away for him to make it out clearly, was a great stack of timber; it looked like an unlit bonfire.

'Come to the beacon,' called Grandfather Tree. His voice echoed the length of the corridor, beckoning. 'The time has come. The rest of my story shall I tell.'

As Jonah walked black thorn-bushes raised themselves up behind him, sealing him in.

4

Annie's Journal – Two

It's darker here than back home. I remember the Kansas stars, so big and white, and the trail of the Milky Way across the sky. The Big Dipper. When Rance was fast asleep – boy, did he ever sleep deeply! – I used to sneak out of the house and lie out on the ground with my blanket wrapped tight around me, listening to the crickets and imagining I could hear the crop growing. Lying there looking up into the night I could pretend I was floating far away. I pretended that if I turned my head to the side I wouldn't see the ground at all, just a great bowl of stars surrounding me and going on forever. Some nights I'd lie there until the stars started to fade and the black sky turned deep blue, and then I'd sneak back inside before Rance woke up. Heaven help me if he found me out of my bed in the night, and Heaven knew what he'd think I'd been up to. One time he caught me creeping in he damn near knocked me out. Called me a whore, said I'd spent the night in Leighton dancing with the hurdy-gurdies and romancing the latest stage-load of pilgrims headed out west. I wore a bruise on the side of my head for a week and it was a month or more before I dared to visit the stars again.

I can remember so clearly when I loved Rance. I don't remember the feeling itself, but I remember that it did happen and that it felt good. Strange, that I should have such a fond, strong memory of a man I ended up despising. I don't know if what I feel for Jonah is the same thing. It feels good, so maybe it is. Rance was strong, very tall. Jonah is different, softer and less certain, but I feel with him something I never felt with Rance. It's as if – as if he cares more about my pleasure than his own. That's amazing, when you think about it. He's so . . . English. Gentle. I think that back in Kansas I might have found his attention a bit irritating. I certainly never got it from Rance, even in the beginning. But here it's just perfect. He's kind and sweet. He scares me a bit when he gets intense. For all his English reserve he's a passionate man. Oh yes.

Is it proper to talk of such things in a journal such as this? It feels right – of what value is this book if I am not honest with it? I just hope nobody reads it till I'm long gone!

On Stone there are no stars at all. No moon either. Here the night sky is truly black. There is a kind of light around you though – I think it comes from the air. From the charm, I guess. It's comforting in its own way, like a blanket.

I'm on my own tonight. Kythe offered to sleep with me but I told her not to be so silly. I don't think she really meant it – she's happy with her own company these days. She's growing up. As for me, well, I've already gotten used to sleeping with Jonah. He knows I have bad dreams. I haven't told him about them (I pretend I can't remember anything from the night) but he knows about them all the same. That's why I'm still awake tonight, while Jonah and Gerent are up there in the forest. I'm afraid that if I go to sleep I'll dream again. Dream about her.

About Archan.

Oh dear God, maybe if I could write about her she'd

go away. But when I try there doesn't seem very much to say. Archan was an evil dragon, the last one left in the world. Some kind of spell made her immortal, long, long ago, but robbed her of her body at the same time. Made a kind of ghost out of her, you could say. Then, somehow she found her way to me. I guess it could have been anybody. I guess I was just plain unlucky. She got inside me and possessed my body like some wayward spirit. When Jonah and I crossed over on to Stone she was riding inside me, controlling me. Eventually she exchanged my body for another dragon's and I was free again. Then Jonah sent her spinning into Stone's past, chasing her own tail back to the beginning of eternity. With any luck she's stuck there for good.

So she's gone.

So why do I dream this dream? Oh she doesn't exactly appear in the dream, not exactly, it's not as if I can see her wings, it's not as if she's trying to burn me with her fire. The dream doesn't even take me anywhere I know, much less show her to me, the dream . . .

The dream begins with the ocean, this ocean. I'm swimming through the waves, fighting the pull of gravity. Then the water boils away leaving me stranded on a reef. I walk for miles until I come to an enormous bridge stretching across a canyon. The bridge is transparent, like it's made from glass. It looks thin and very fragile. I'm scared to step on it in case it breaks but I step out anyway, taking care not to fall because its surface is so slippery. I walk out, further and further until I'm halfway across. I look down and see the sky – the sky is all around me. The bridge is just floating in the air, with nothing to support it.

Then it starts to melt and I realize it's not made of glass at all. It's made of ice. I try to run but it's no good. My feet sink into the melting ice and soon I'm falling through freezing cold water. And all around me, though I can't

67

see her, I can smell her, taste her, hear her. She's laughing at me, at all of us. I can *taste* her.

It's her but it isn't her. She's there but not there. Archan.

Where are you?

It's later. Still very dark. The air glows just enough for me to write. No shadows, none at all, so strange.

Kythe came to me just now. I was dozing, not sleeping properly but just drifting. When I first saw her outside the niche I had to put my hand over my mouth to stop from screaming. With her long, horned head and her wings spread out she looked first like the devil and then like Archan. I thought I had fallen asleep and the dream had come back for me.

Then I recognized her. By the time she'd shouldered her way in and lain down next to me I'd calmed myself down again. The feel of her scales is nice – they're warm and soft, not at all hard like you'd expect. Leaning on them is kind of like leaning on bumpy leather.

It turns out that I'm not the only one having bad dreams. She couldn't remember hers (but then that's what I say to Jonah). I think she really has forgotten though – I don't think Kythe's capable of lying. I tried to comfort her, and it seemed to work. She's had dreams for the past three nights, and that's what bothers me the most.

Because so have I.

We both of us felt even less like sleeping after all that so we got to talking about Stone, mostly about the memory rods. This is Kythe's home, so she takes the weird geometry for granted – it's all she's known, though her dragon kin hand down tales from what they call the 'Old World' – what I think of as 'my world' or even 'the real world'. Although I have to say that the longer I spend on Stone the less real that world seems.

The memory rods are another matter. I still can't fully grasp what they mean. Jonah has patiently described them to me, over and over it seems, but I still don't really have a sense of how they work. It's easier for him – when he touches one of the rods he sees what lies inside it, the memories it contains. As for me and Kythe and most other mortals, they're just long, straight pipes buried deep inside Stone. They don't give anything away.

Their existence isn't common knowledge on Stone. Kythe knows no more about them than I do. All we know is what Jonah has told us, and most of what he knows he learned from poor Esh. I wish she was with us now. She died so valiantly, she guided us and saved us at the end.

What puzzles me is this: if the rods *do* store all the memories of every living thing on our Earth, right back from the earliest of past times right into the future, then is everything already written? Is it like saying God has already decided our destiny and we have no choice in our lives? If I were to journey upStone, into the future, I would find the memories of people who hadn't even been born when I lived on the Earth. Are they living their lives by some Stone-written manuscript, just characters on some enormous stage?

And what of me, what of all of us here and now? Are our memories being added to the reservoir of Stone, we who are actually *living* on Stone? Are we of the past or the future now, we who travel beyond the normal constraints of time?

And what does it mean when Jonah says he can change what the rods contain? If he changes the past does he also change the future? By God in Heaven, what power is it that can take one of those characters and write them off the stage altogether? That's what Jonah tried to do with Archan – in the words of Esh he tried to *make her gone*. It didn't quite work out that way, of course, and he ended up just spilling her back into eternity, but the will was there, and it was only Archan's own skill in manipulating the rods that thwarted Jonah.

There *must* be danger in it! Esh mentioned there was one other who'd been able to work the rods, but she didn't elaborate. 'Don't ask what happened to him,' she'd say in her usual mysterious way. 'Better you don't know.'

I've often wondered who he was.

So we talked, Kythe and I, talking round and round in circles, pouring out more questions than there were answers. I told her about the stars and the moon, and she was fascinated and kept asking more and more. She's only ever known these dark nights of Stone, so the idea of lights in the sky is enchanting to her.

'How big is this moon?' she asked. 'And why does it not fall out of the sky? Does it fly, like a dragon?'

I told her it didn't fly exactly, but it did spin around the world just like the sun, and it was no more likely to fall than Stone's own sun. This satisfied her, though she kept straying back to the subject.

At one point she asked me, 'If you could go back into your past, Annie, what is the one moment, the one memory *you* would change?'

I thought hard, but couldn't think of a reply, so I asked Kythe the same question. She frowned and answered, 'I'm not sure. But . . . I have an idea.'

She wouldn't say any more. She's changed in the few short weeks since we met her. She's not the mere dragon-child we first met – her gaze is more distant, more intense.

We're going to try and get some sleep now.

It's later.

Still dark. Heard a crash outside the cave. Something falling on to the ledge I think. Going to look, both of us.

5

Beacon

It might indeed have been an English glade. Here were *real* trees, familiar trees, rising from an undulating bed of bracken and fallen needles. A dense pine forest filled with scent and sound: the whisper of the needles, the companionable chatter of unseen birds, the rush of the wind moving like waves through the ocean. Bark of a thousand shades of grey and silver, anything but black; fern and holly and a far-off splash of bluebells. Ground – horizontal and reassuringly solid, like the ground back home. It was only by looking up that the illusion was broken for beyond the treetops, where the scene promised blue sky painted with brilliant white clouds, there was only darkness. But Jonah had only to lower his head once more and the magic was complete. His mind told him this had all been fabricated, just as the hanging boats had been fabricated; his heart informed him he was home.

'Taiga,' croaked the lesky's voice, startlingly close. It sounded much thinner than it had before, but more *real*. Jonah turned and looked at Grandfather Tree.

At first it was hard to make him out, as it had been hard to see his face in the tree trunk. Rising before Jonah, in the middle of the dappled glade, was the beacon, a timber pyramid some twelve feet high. None of the logs or branches comprising it had been recently cut: those that were not rotting had petrified and resembled the fossils Jonah had been used to handling in his old life. It was grey and shabby; decay seemed to waft around it in visible shrouds. From its black interior came a thick stench of pine and hops and putrefying flesh.

Grandfather Tree was caged halfway up the pyramid, curled up with his head bowed down and his back hunched over. He had a man's torso, but where his legs should have been was a tail of tattered ivy. His spindly arms were as grey as the mesh of branches with which they were entwined; in places the branches actually penetrated his body in the same way that the trees had pierced the ships. Gnarled fingers clutched spiky twigs, or perhaps it was the other way round. His hair was a spray of silver knotted hopelessly with clumps of lichen; his face was . . . his face was made of liquid.

Grandfather Tree's face rose from a collar of thorns; it appeared to be made of thick green sap. His beard was a cascade of the same gelatinous fluid, flowing yet not flowing, alive with moving currents yet somehow resisting gravity's drag. His eyes were deep green whirlpools; his mouth was a spinning void from which sprouted a bewildering array of brambles and berries. These brambles trailed around liquid cheeks and met behind his head where they knotted themselves into his silver mane.

Haunted eyes followed Jonah's every move as he inched closer, simultaneously fascinated and repelled, and from the gaping, twirling mouth came more words.

'My appearance, it bothers you? Ye, it should. I can barely look on it myself these days. It too will end soon.'

'You look to be in a great deal of pain,' faltered Jonah. The fossil-body twitched inside its wooden cage, sending ripples across Grandfather Tree's face.

'Pain? Ye, there's pain in here with me. But it's one of the tortures I can choose to ignore, if I have the strength.

72

Others have come and they're less easy to evade.'

'Who put you here? Was it the dryads? Have they been lying to me, and is the truth that they have already overthrown you and placed you in this prison?'

To his amazement the lesky began to laugh heartily. But with the mirth came a rictus of pain. As the laughter subsided, a tremor ran through the corner of the lesky's mouth, closing it a fraction and crushing a cluster of tiny red berries. Juice like fresh blood mingled with the green sap of his chin, turning it to brown.

'Ah me, but you amuse me, Jonah. Now tell: what do you see beyond the trees?'

Jonah looked into the depths of the pine woods beyond the clearing. 'I don't know what you mean.'

'Look hard!'

He did so, and this time he saw a movement, a distant fluttering that might have been a bird or squirrel, but which he knew was not. 'The dryads!' he exclaimed.

'They circle my prison but they can't enter. This much they have told you?' Jonah nodded. 'Well then, your questions I will answer. Your first?'

For a moment Jonah was lost for words. Again he thought of the *Bonaventure*, plunging out of the forest base before careering down the dreadful slope of Stone. 'The ships. How did you make them? By which I mean how do you know of such things at all? The ships come from an era very close to my own, yet we are far from the place where Stone connects to that era. The ships come from upStone, from your future, Grandfather Tree; how do you come to have knowledge of them?'

'Ah! The question strikes at the heart of it! A wise place to start then. Sculpting is very least of my powers, yet all that remains to me now. The forest yields to the lesky, and the lesky bends the forest to his will. Wood lives, and all that lives can be made to change. I simply change it into something beautiful.'

'A sculptor! But why choose ships? Why choose what you have never known?'

'Jonah Lightfoot! Are you not an adept? I am like you. *I can travel the memory rods too!* To your future I have been on many occasions, as to my own and countless other pasts. I've ridden the aeons over countless years. Through history itself I've been a voyager. The ships you saw are just one small part of my collection. Both with and against the flow of the river of time did I swim. As might you, Jonah Lightfoot, as might you.'

'So what happened? You speak of your travels in the past tense. Why are you trapped here like this when once you had such power?'

'Because, like you, I confused power with freedom. I was intoxicated! My first days on Stone, imagine them! My roots broke through and brought me out on to a new world. Yet as my roots connected me to this world's soil so they connected me to something even greater: the memory rods themselves! No sooner had Grandfather Tree arrived than he was a god. Freedom he had, freedom to use Stone's store of memories to travel, to learn, to experience past and future events. Such wonders he saw, such wonders!

'Deeper and deeper into the rods my roots fused themselves. Further and further I journeyed. Upon each return I resculpted my forest into the likeness of what I'd seen. A souvenir, you might call it. Ye, this forest has been many things in its time. Once I made a mass of dragon nests; another time a coral reef. Always replicas of things others had made. That's why your age, the age of the natural faeries, became so fascinating for me. Of all the sculptors you were the most audacious. Such things I retrieved from your eras! Thumping machines and mighty weapons, minuscule structures woven from the tiniest particles. The ships, they are feeble by comparison to some I have made. But my strength dwindles and my memory grows short. And I can no longer travel the rods, of course. No longer do I share Stone's memories; now I have only my own.'

This last statement was uttered in such a low, sad tone that a shudder ran the length of Jonah's spine. A glance into the forest confirmed that the dryads were becoming more agitated; sudden flashes marked their faces as they darted through the undergrowth, ever seeking a way through the lesky's supernatural defences.

'The dryads lack imagination,' Grandfather Tree went on. Solid beads of green sap crystallized in the ripples beneath his eyes, and Jonah wondered if they were tears. 'They live in the trees but do they care for them? Pah! They guard them but their jealousy is driven by fear, not by love. They hate change, and they fear it. Me, I make things for my own pleasure and tear them down when I grow bored with them. Life is change. This they can't abide. Trees are trees, they say, and that's all. But that is not all! Trees are everything to the leskies, and the leskies are everything to the trees. This the dryads will never understand. Do *you* understand?'

'I think so. But if the dryads did not put you in this prison, then who did?'

A great storm fell upon Stone when Grandfather Tree arrived. A wind like a hurricane descended from the unreachable heights and tore away living things which had survived on Stone's torturous slope for countless years. Much was lost to the abyss, but despite the turmoil Grandfather Tree was rooted deep, though he had been here but a day. He withstood the storm, and soon he had made a new forest to rival the great taiga of the old continent east of the Spine. His trees flourished, and their roots bit deep into the hidden memory rods of Stone, which is also called Amara.

The storm was an omen, for the instant Grandfather

Tree broke through, Stone saw the coming threat. This vast world existing in a secret space barely a memory-width beyond eternity knew from that day forward it was doomed.

For in its own, ponderous way, Stone is alive and aware of its own existence. And it is haunted.

Roaming its network of hidden rods are the dislocated memories of the six immortal creatures who built it – the basilisks. Gone now, having bequeathed their immortality to the dragon-witch Archan, they still have influence in the rods' tenuous realm. Weak these ghosts may be, but they have long awaited the coming of the adepts, the ones with the power to change Stone forever. And to bring its great wall tumbling down.

The first would come alone. The harbinger. This first adept would quickly learn to tap the rods for knowledge. He would drink from the well but do nothing to taint the source, a passive observer wanting nothing more than to record his travels and build his own store of memories.

But the others, the two who would come together, it was they who would bring the real peril. He with his eyes turned up into the skies of possibility and she with her eyes cast forever down, into the impossible depths of Stone's well. He for the flying force of good and she for the endless fall of evil. It was they for whom the basilisks kept particular watch, and so they overlooked the first one, the harbinger.

They completely underestimated the powers of Grandfather Tree.

For thousands of years, if years can be measured on Stone's timeless wall, the forest thrived. Grandfather Tree soon learned to journey through the memory rods – after all, were they not merely extensions of his own elaborate root system? He travelled far and wide, both downStone and upStone, crossing even the dreadful turbulence of the Thresholds in his quest for new experiences. And in all that time he sought only to witness and remember, to bring back and sculpt.

Then one day he found a particular moment of history embedded into one of the rods. It was only a small moment, but it caught his attention none the less.

A large sea-creature, its hide a striking black-and-white, surged beneath a frozen sea. It soared upwards, breaking through a thin cloud of drifting ice and blowing a stream of vapour into the cold sky, then dived towards an undersea cliff. Having reached the cliff it broke for the surface again, rolling sideways and splashing down on to the pack-ice with a tremendous crash. It did this over and over again, and before long Grandfather Tree noticed the object of its concern: another, smaller beast stranded on a distant ice-floe, apparently unreachable. Plaintive cries echoed through the Arctic air as the two creatures called to each other. Each time the orca came to the surface its stranded calf was a little further away.

Grandfather Tree could sense the mother's agony. But more than that, he could see what it, in its confusion, could not see: a thin breach in the barrier wall through which it might force its way and thus reach the calf. Without thinking, he pressed forward into the memory and forced open the narrow gap. For an instant he feared he had miscalculated, and that the wretched beast would drown pinioned in a tunnel too narrow to squeeze through. With a desperate lunge of its tail it finally passed through the wall and emerged on the other side, where it surfaced to find itself within a few strokes of the calf. Its momentum carried it forward, crashing into and tipping over the drifting floe and spilling the little orca into the sea.

Grandfather Tree withdrew, the orcas' eerie duet resounding in his mind as he sped back along the memory rods towards the taiga. By the time he reached home he was racked with emotion: pride at what he had done, terror at the power he evidently possessed.

'I changed the memory!' he bellowed into the silent forest.

But something was waiting for him. The six basilisk ghosts set themselves in a ring around Grandfather Tree.

. . . *You have altered the proper flow of the river of time*, the largest of them intoned. Its words were not really words; they swept into Grandfather Tree's mind like sudden winter. Six phantom serpents, slowly closing the circle towards him.

. . . *The power is not yours to command*, added a second.

. . . *Memory is history. You have touched what it is forbidden to touch, and you shall pay the penalty!*

They took a skein of memory rods and wove them into a stack shaped like a pyramid. Then they took Grandfather Tree himself, condensing him from the wood through which he swam until he took his proper form, the form into which all his race were born and in which they existed only briefly before they dissolved into the trees. Limbs rolled themselves from clusters of knotted bark, streamers of sap congealed into a head, plaited leaves wrapped round upon themselves to form a pumping heart. Slowly the ancient lesky lost his aethereality, only to be locked in a crude and physical shell. Then, to make his bindings doubly effective, that shell was woven back into the trees through which he had formerly travelled, prohibiting all physical movement. And though the trees of the taiga were still his to command, he could no more traverse the memory rod network again than he could raise an arm or wink an eye. With the imprisonment came pain, and a hundred other tortures the worst of which was the loss of his ability to *voyage*.

It was in this state that the basilisk ghosts left the harbinger. Already the time had come to prepare for the greater peril: the coming of the two adepts whose abilities would mean real mischief . . . and ultimate doom.

Grandfather Tree worked hard to regain his powers. Never again did he voyage through the memory rods, but his hold on the taiga grew strong once more. This then became his only comfort: that he could still sculpt, and with a mind full of remembrances from his travels through the many ages of Stone, there was much that he could make from the loyal trees. The dryads, fearful that the basilisks would return, waited some time before daring to approach his prison cell; fortunately this gave Grandfather Tree enough time to build his defensive shield.

And so the siege began.

Jonah felt very much indeed like the occupant of a besieged castle. Beyond the outer perimeter of pine trees the dryads had massed into two distinct groups. They were not bothering to hide any more; he could see their sinuous bodies swaying rhythmically in the broken light, could see their long arms beckoning him, their hands stroking each other's bodies in a self-consciously lewd display. Quite what was keeping them at bay he could not tell, but he was sure it had something to do with the black spikes – the half-rods which had impeded his own progress earlier. Their voices, deep and seductive, floated across the clearing.

'When I used the memory rods,' he said to the lesky when his story was told, 'I was forced to view the past through the eyes of another, one of the participants in the scene. On one occasion I was in the body of a child, on another a tiny bird. The sensation was . . . singular. When I entered one of my own memories, I naturally looked out through my own eyes. But I sense this is not how it was for you.'

'It is not, Jonah. Rod is rod and root is root. Alone I travelled, and when I entered a memory I entered it alone. Were you to travel by way of my roots, you would find the same: a ghost would you be, attached to nothing but yourself.'

'But a ghost with power, it would seem. You say you changed the memory. Well, I too made a change, or at least I believe I did.'

'This much you told me. You drew a book from a moment in your own past.'

'The book . . . yes, the book was Darwin's *On the Origin of Species*. I took it from a memory of the day I saw my father and brother die; I was just eight years old. But what I do not understand is this: if I *removed* the book from the past, then my eight-year-old self cannot have possessed it after that moment. Yet I *did* possess it, I know I did. I carried it with me like a talisman. I brought it with me to Krakatoa, and only lost it when the volcano erupted. I left it on the beach with my clothes. So did I simply make a copy of it? In removing it from history, did I in fact create an identical book while leaving the original behind?'

'The power of creation! It is said to be beyond all mortal beings,' growled Grandfather Tree. 'Even the forces of charm can't create but can only transform.'

'Yet I *did* create things! I drew one of Archan's scales out of the past and brought it on to Stone. *And when I went back for a second time the scale was still there!* I took it again, so that I had now brought *two* scales with me. The first I embedded into Archan's back, the second I gave to the faery queen who fled with it, carrying it far downStone and hauling Archan after her like iron to a magnet. The scales were inextricably linked, you see. The pursuit continues still for all I know. That was the way I found to make Archan gone.'

'In that case you didn't actually *change* the memories. You copied them.'

'I do not know. I suppose I could travel back to those

80

times again, to see if the book lies still in the mud beside the Crystal Palace even though I know it exists here on Stone as well – it lies now in the cave I share with Annie. Or if the Arctic ice still holds a single, white scale, while two identical scales are locked in a desperate pursuit heading closer to the dawn of eternity.'

'So? Why don't you seek the answer?'

Jonah pounded his head with the flat of his hand. 'Because I am scared of the rods, Grandfather Tree! Even more so now that I see what happens to those who subvert their power! Perhaps you are all the proof I need that I did *not* make any changes, that I *did* create duplicates of book and scale, leaving the master patterns safe in their place in history. For if that was not the case, would I not already have been called before the court of the basilisk ghosts, and set in my own prison cell for my acts of treason?'

'All facts become riddles where the rods are concerned. But I believe your power – and that of Archan – is of many orders greater than my own. I believe you are beyond the jurisdiction of the basilisks now; I don't believe there is anything they can to do stop you. I believe, Jonah, you are rewriting the rules of the game.'

'If they cannot stop me, then nor can they stop Archan.'

'Nor her.'

'*Is* she gone, do you think?'

'The basilisks, they held a belief. It was this: *nothing goes.*'

Jonah sat heavily on the carpet of needles. One of the groups of dryads had moved round to the opposite side of the clearing; now the two groups were facing each other. Their cries had degenerated into cat-calls and long, screeching wails. He tried to shut them out, trusting in Grandfather Tree's defences to keep the weird creatures away.

'What are you thinking about, Jonah?'

'I was thinking about coincidence. I was thinking about how I was dreaming of travelling across the ocean when suddenly a boat fell out of the forest. It is too astonishing for words! And when I ventured into the forest I found enough ships to fulfil a thousand such dreams.' He shuffled forward and faced Grandfather Tree earnestly. 'Could the ships you have made sail on the ocean?'

'Most of the vessels you saw are badly decayed,' the lesky answered sadly. 'And I make a thing only once; never do I make repairs. And even were they whole, they would not survive the vertical sea. Bound deep with charm is its water. Only a ship that understands the ebb and flow of magic can make headway through such treacherous currents. For Stone's ocean we would need a Bark.'

Jonah fancied he saw a glint of light in Grandfather Tree's whirlpool eyes. 'A Bark?'

'When the basilisks had completed their task of constructing Stone, they spent many aeons journeying across its face. They wished perhaps to contemplate their labours. Sometimes they travelled using charm, sometimes they employed more whimsical means. When they came to the vertical sea, they made themselves a Bark. A ship it is, not unlike the ships you know from your world, but shaped so as to ride the upturned waves.'

'You have seen one?' interrupted Jonah enthusiastically. 'Do you know where we might find one? Or could you build us one?'

Grandfather Tree paused. His tortured face seemed to contract in upon itself, as if he were consulting some inner source of knowledge. A snail the size of Jonah's fist, its shell coloured brilliant gold, swam along his briar-bound lip before disappearing inside his mouth. 'Ye, I know where one lies.'

'Can you tell me where it is?' Jonah could not keep his voice from trembling. Did he dare to believe there was a way out of this dead-end? The romantic notion of sailing across Stone's sea with Annie in his arms filled him with excitement.

'Near the water's edge it is.' Grandfather Tree's voice was trembling too. 'There is a place where the taiga reaches to the ocean. That is where you will find the Bark.'

'Will she sail? What I mean to say is, will she *float*?'

'Float he will. As to whether he may sail . . . beyond my ability to guess.'

Jonah was only half-listening. 'Such coincidence,' he said again. 'That I should have found you.'

'Stone enjoys coincidence. That's its game.'

A dryad howl echoed like the cry of a wolf through the glade. A familiar feeling returned to Jonah, that he was moving across the face of Stone as a chess piece moves across the board. Somewhere behind hidden ranks prowled the white queen, evil and immortal.

'Do we move, or are we moved?'

But Grandfather Tree had no reply. His inert form seemed to have turned in upon itself like a flower closing its petals against the sun, though he appeared anything but relaxed. Rather, Jonah imagined, he had the look of someone preparing for action.

In contrast, the activity of the dryads increased steadily. Their energy showed no bounds: now they were dancing a wild, primitive dance in the underbrush, barely fifty yards from where Jonah sat contemplating Grandfather Tree's silently screaming visage.

Something the lesky had said had stuck in his mind like a fishbone:

He for the flying force of good.

Was he, Jonah, the good man? *She for the endless fall of evil*. He had little doubt that Archan was evil, but was

83

he any different, any less immune to corruption? It was said that power corrupted – what he possessed was surely the ultimate power.

'Jonah.' The lesky's voice was an almost inaudible whisper. 'What do you hear?'

Jonah listened. It was hard to hear anything above the screeching of the dryads, but he fancied he could make out a distant crashing. 'What is it?' he whispered back.

'My work, falling.'

'The ships? Have the dryads set more of them loose?'

Suddenly, shockingly, Grandfather Tree shook his head. A fine spray of yellow-green sap soaked the ground before the beacon. 'No!' he gargled. 'What you saw – the *Bonaventure* – the beginning of the end.'

'Then the dryads have won!'

The lesky was still again, but now the mouth was grinning, forcing the brambles deep into Grandfather Tree's liquid cheeks. 'Leave me be,' he chuckled. 'Busy I am. But . . . be ready.'

The lesky trembled erratically for about an hour, like a man having a fit. Jonah paced the clearing, pressing back the tide of fatigue that had for some time been threatening to roll over him; he did not dare sleep for fear that the dryads would break through and attack him. All the same, sleep began to lull him, and he was forced to pinch himself repeatedly to keep it at bay.

Then, suddenly, Grandfather Tree opened his eyes and bellowed,

'Run! Run and don't look behind you! I'll be there to guide you when I can. The lower edge of the taiga – just follow it downStone until you reach the sea. That's where you'll find the Bark!'

There was an awesome tearing sound right next to Jonah's ear. He whirled, sleep forgotten, to see a great swathe cut through the barricade. It bled into hazy orange light. The dryads were scurrying to and fro in confusion: the channel had neatly bisected the gap between the two groups, effectively cutting them off from each other. Individuals from both groups charged the channel but were thrown back by invisible defences.

'But . . . why?'

'The taiga is falling. Everything's coming down. Do you want to come down with it?'

'No, but . . .'

'THEN RUN!!'

Grandfather Tree's bellow struck Jonah an actual physical blow, hurling him twenty feet across the clearing. He landed sprawling in a spray of bracken, his chest throbbing as he laboured for breath. 'But my friends!' he wheezed.

'I've already told them. It's all I can do. Now go, or you will surely die!'

Sunlight poured across Jonah's face, a welcome flood of heat. Scrambling to his feet he ran for his life.

In no time at all he was through the barricade and out into the vertical forest. He sprinted along narrow boughs and leaped treacherous chasms, mindful of the danger yet powerless to slow his flight. Something had infiltrated his body and was pumping his muscles – charm perhaps, or the simple primal imperative to flee. A low branch swiped at his head; he ducked, half-stumbled, picked himself up, carried on, a little slower now. Presently he stopped, bent double to catch his breath.

No sooner had he stopped than a wooden face rose up out of the bark between his feet. It was the face of Grandfather Tree. Gaping open its jaws it exposed long black tusks with which it snapped at Jonah's feet. 'Run!' it growled, eyeing him with predatory glee. He stared back uncertainly, then shrugged off all doubt as the dryads howled close behind. Their chilling wolf-cries galvanized him into action. 'Run!' repeated the lesky-face.

'They're after your sap too! They'll kill you, Jonah, but not before they've sucked you dry!'

Something obscured the sun: it was smoke, thick and black. With no idea where it had come from he plunged into it, praying that the meandering trunk along which he was running did not make a sudden change of direction or simply fall away into nothing. Behind him the dryads shrieked in premature triumph, then moaned in horror as they too were enveloped by the smoke.

'Lesky!' Jonah heard one of them scream. 'Oh you demon! You've set the forest! Oh how you'll pay for this!'

Set the forest?

He emerged from the smoke gasping for breath and covered with cinders. An orange glare washed around his feet.

Below him the entire forest was ablaze.

The smoke seemed to disorientate the dryads, slowing them down sufficiently for Jonah to increase his lead. Still there was no time to spare. The trees were thinner now, and it was harder for him to make safe progress downStone; he imagined that for the fluid bodies of the dryads it would make little difference. There was no time to consider what lay ahead, what he might do if and when he reached this strange vessel of the basilisks, this *Bark*. He was just running: running from the dryads, running from the unpredictable lesky, running from the fire.

'Up then in,' came a muffled voice from somewhere ahead. Was it the lesky? It spoke again but he could not make out the words; they sounded like birds' wings, the melodic wheeze of wood pigeons taking to the air. In: in towards Stone, which meant to his right. Slowing all the while (his run had become a desperate clambering as the branches thinned dangerously) he obeyed, hoping it was not some ruse of the dryads. Strands of white flesh fell about him in a rain; looking up he saw hundreds of twin-worms thrashing through the branches as they came apart in the heat.

Presently he reached a platform of thick trunks, ancient black trees thrusting in uncompromising fashion out into the sky. And there *was* the sky, unseen for so long but clearly visible now to his left. On his right rose the craggy wall of the beach. He had reached the narrow downStone end of the forest. The familiar spicy aroma of Stone's magical air was tainted with salt; the ocean was near.

The trunks were laid out ahead of him like a Canadian logjam, great prone cylinders spaced only inches apart. He took them at a run, holding his arms wide as he sprang from one trunk to the next. A shower of leaves fell directly in front of him; for an instant the leaves were caught in a whirlwind that whipped them into the shape of a grimacing face. 'Careful now!' laughed Grandfather Tree. 'You wouldn't want to fall, not when you're so close!'

'I've done all the falling I care for already,' muttered Jonah, lashing out at the leaves as he thundered past. They danced away mischievously.

He allowed himself a surge of triumph as the foliage thinned dramatically before him. Clusters of branches peeled back to reveal the brilliant glow of the waiting sea. Gasping for breath, realizing belatedly that he had run himself almost to the point of exhaustion, Jonah pulled back with his hand pressed hard against his rib-cage. Wearily he cleared the final gap and stood on the last tree of the taiga before the ocean. There was a commotion behind: the sinewy sound of the dryads as they swarmed towards him, wrapped with the sinister crackle of the fire.

Swiftly he took in the view. The sea to his right, a silver-blue wall undulating in the morning light, stretched into infinite haze. The distant vertex, Jonah's proof of Stone's convexity, was for the moment invisible.

The sky to his left was striped in a stunning contrast of white and blue, ribbons of vapour riding the descending wind. Between the edge of the forest and the sea was a short stretch of dark cliff, ruptured at the point where the tree on which he stood had burst through the surface. One of Stone's dizzying shifts of scale swept through him as he again perceived the forest as a set of gigantic coat-hooks projecting from cracked plaster, himself as a reckless insect crawling across them. He had to reach out and grab a branch to steady himself.

Far into the distance the ocean's mighty curtain swayed rhythmically back and forth. The narrow cliff bounded the sea like a precipitous breakwater; waves broke across its surface, the spray succumbing to gravity the instant it left the charmed influence of the sea's environs and cascading into Stone's waiting depths. Far below jutted the cranes and derricks of the miniature dockyard only Gerent had ventured near.

There was no sign of a ship.

'Grandfather Tree!' Jonah bellowed, spinning round to face the glowering patchwork of the forest interior. Dense smoke was boiling out of the trees towards him; already he could taste the acrid fumes. 'Where is it? Where is the Bark?'

No response. In desperation he scanned the surface of the sea. Chunks of driftwood bobbed here and there. Twenty yards off-shore he could just see something breaching the waves like an upturned whale, its surface crusty and barnacled. Clouds of seaweed swirled, driven by the strong downward current. No ship, no sign of the lesky and certainly no sign of his friends.

He was about to cry out again when Grandfather Tree's face formed from a floating slick of sap. The slick was moored to the breakwater by flexible green strings.

'Trust me. They will come. You must swim to the Bark.'

'Swim? But ... but where is it? All I can see is wreckage.'

'The Bark may not look as he might, but he is anything but wrecked. You have to trust me.'

'Do I have any choice?'

'Look behind you.'

He turned to see one of the taiga's mighty trees ablaze and crashing to its doom. A huge cluster of knots had blown up like a crate of fireworks, showering the undergrowth with sparks and clots of charcoal. The forest interior was lost behind a wall of smoke, through which the leering faces of the dryads were already beginning to emerge.

They moved with long, steady strokes of their evergreen tails, now sinking into the heat-swollen trees, now accelerating forwards with sudden speed. Their fishforms seemed utterly out of place in this sylvan nightmare of fire and timber; their eyes glowed with hatred.

'You cannot hide, you cannot run,' they were chanting. Several of them had gnawed away their lips with their razor teeth; bright red blood drizzled on to their breasts. One was chewing on the severed arm of another, who raced on seemingly oblivious to her misfortune. Two of the dryads glanced against each other, merged into one many-limbed entity, separated. Repelled, Jonah found he could not look away.

'Listen not to them!' The lesky's voice buzzed at him but he brushed it away, a pesky fly. 'Enchant you they will!'

'Come into our midst,' howled the nearest of the dryads. Was she one of those he had spoken with? He could not remember. Her face was beautiful, her red hair like a mane. He took a step towards her. Why had he come here? 'Let us take you in. Let us teach you our ways. Serve us and we will serve you.' Wolf-words, impossible to resist. He opened his arms to her; she was barely ten feet away. She accelerated towards him.

'Jonah! Jonah Lightfoot! What the hell are you doing talking to those whores?'

The voice came from nowhere, then he was lifted off his feet.

The lead dryad slashed at him with a hand that had suddenly grown claws like splinters. They sliced the air inches from his face. She fell away, and for the first time he was aware of something gripping him tightly about the waist. Twisting his neck round he found himself looking into the long horse-face of Kythe.

'I may only be a dragon,' she panted, 'but I know trouble when I see it.'

She was back-thrusting her wings frantically, drawing them both clear of the forest while casting around for somewhere to land. Jonah knew from experience that she was not strong enough to hold him for any length of time and he steeled himself for the impact.

Annie! It was Annie's voice!

'Annie where are you?'

'Where the hell do you think I am, Jonah? Waiting here for you, that's where!'

The breakwater was deserted. As he searched, Kythe carried him past it and over the sea itself. It was then that she began to lose her grip. 'I'm sorry, Jonah!' she moaned. 'I'll drop you close to the . . .'

She did not finish what she was saying. Swooping within a few feet of the breaking waves she tried in vain to keep hold of Jonah but failed. Her tail unravelled and he slithered from its coils, falling for several yards before finally fetching up against the inclined plane of the sea. He hit with a tremendous splash.

He immediately lost all sense of direction. All his senses – his eyes, the balancing organs in his ears – told him that he was hanging over Stone's abyss, yet somehow the water held him. He was a fly embedded in a wall of wet plaster.

'I'm sorry,' called Kythe. 'I'd try and pick you out but you'll be all soggy now. I'm scared I'd let you fall even further.'

'It's all right, Kythe,' he spluttered. 'I can swim from here.' He paused, instinctively treading water though he suspected there was no need to do so. 'At least, I can if I know where it is I'm supposed to go.'

'Over here, you damned English idiot!'

'Annie!'

There she was, perched precariously atop the upturned whale-shape he had dismissed earlier. Gerent was just behind her, waving him on with short, stabbing movements of his arm.

Another shift in perception. The sea not a sea at all, but a waterfall lazily descending. The Bark a hemisphere of weathered granite protruding from the face of the waterfall, defying both gravity and the constant crash of the water. His companions balanced atop the rock, reaching for him as he swam salmon-like up the waterfall's façade.

Jonah struck out for the wreck, adopting a weird side-stroke that felt quite unnatural but seemed to propel him up through the waves with reasonable efficiency. He was a strong swimmer, having spent many a summer's day dipping in the lake on Lily's father's farm, and he climbed the short distance to the Bark in good time. Behind him the dryads had already reached the last tree on which, moments before, he had been standing like an imbecile.

'I don't know what happened to me back there,' he gasped as Annie and Gerent helped him climb out of the water. His feet found purchase on the limpet-like creatures adhering to the convex side of the wreck; as soon as he gained the relative safety of its upper curve he embraced Annie. She kissed him warmly, tears filling her eyes.

'They were trying to trick you,' she said.

'They nearly succeeded,' added Gerent.

'How did you get here so quickly? Did Grandfather Tree come to you?'

'Enough questions!' barked Gerent. 'We're in danger! Look!'

The wreck was drifting closer to the shore, where the dryads were beginning to lower themselves on to the breakwater, using the many cracks in its face to gain purchase.

'They're not giving up,' said Annie.

Kythe, who had remained airborne all this time, was trying valiantly to put the dryads off by swooping and buzzing them, but they slashed at her with their claws. After one very near miss her friends warned her off.

'Leave us be!' Jonah bellowed at the dryads, who were massing now at the water's edge, splinter-claws lodged in the breakwater like ice-axes. 'You have your forest! Let us go on our way!'

A chorus of jeers and screams erupted from the pack. Several of the dryads shouted more coherently, but their words overlapped and all sense was lost. Nevertheless it sounded thoroughly abusive.

'Do they fear the water?' wondered Gerent.

'They hate to be out of reach of their precious trees,' Jonah replied. 'Perhaps they fear being swept away. At least where they are they can regain the forest whenever they choose. If the fire leaves anything behind, that is.'

'Something always survives,' Annie commented. 'You'd think they could swim – they look a bit like mermaids. Vicious ones at that.'

'Vicious indeed,' agreed Jonah. He slammed his fist on to the barnacle-encrusted hull of the Bark. 'Damnation! What sort of vessel is this, that we are forced to perch here like monkeys? Is there no way to stop it drifting towards the shore?'

'We got here just before you did, my darling. There's a ledge back here – that's why you didn't see us. We were kind of hoping you'd have the answers. You or that damned wooden-face.'

'Grandfather Tree! You've seen him? Of course, he said he had sent you a message! What happened, tell me?'

'Kythe and I were dozing when we heard a crash outside the cave. We were scared as hell but we went outside anyway. Turned out to be a branch fallen from the forest. I was about to kick it over the edge – didn't want to trip over it in the morning – when I'll be damned if it didn't sprout a face and start talking!'

'What did he say?'

'Well, that's the crazy part. First of all it said we were to make our way up here, gave us real specific directions too. I told it not to be crazy, then I thought to myself, "What in tarnation am I doing talking to a *tree*?" But then it brought me up short. It asked me if I wanted to find the Aqueduct.'

'The what?'

'The Aqueduct. It's a dream I've been having, Jonah. A scary dream. I think it means something. I think it's something to do with Archan. But there wasn't any time to think about it because then the face turned to Kythe and asked her a question too. It asked her if she was ready to go home. Kythe started crying, and it was only afterwards that she told me that's what *she'd* been dreaming about the last three nights, about a hole opening up in Stone, a way leading back into our world, Jonah, a way to get back home!'

Jonah felt the breath of Kythe's wings against the back of his neck and turned to see her hovering very close to him. 'It's really true,' she said softly. 'There really is a way back. I've seen it, Jonah, I really have. And the tree-face said it could take us there.'

'The last thing it told us,' Annie went on, 'was that we had to do what it said or you would die. For better or worse, I believed it. Then Gerent arrived and the face just dissolved back into the branch. We called and shouted but it didn't come out again. Gerent told us about what happened in the forest. He was – still is – suspicious of the face, what did you call it? Grandfather Tree? But we had to come. Because of the dreams, Jonah, and because of you. Then they just flew me up between them, Kythe and Gerent, along with some of our things. It was tough on them; they flew hard.'

The half-sunk ship had drifted to within a few yards of the dryads. One of them, urged on by her siblings, coiled her tail like a spring and leaped the gap between breakwater and Bark. Long claws punctured the rounded hull, releasing a clear, sticky resin. There was a loud and dreadful sound, like a tooth being drawn. Her spiky tail thrashed in the water as she tried to haul herself up. 'Eat you,' she was screaming at Jonah. 'Love you! Eat you!'

Annie stood. Wearing the striped leggings she had plundered from the *Bonaventure*'s cargo and with her lips curled back in a snarl, Jonah thought she looked like a tiger. She drew back her right leg and planted a kick squarely on the jaw of the floundering dryad, propelling it clean out of the water and into the waiting sky. Its pink and green body whiplashed from side to side as it fell, performing grotesque contortions that would have broken the back of any human. Its sisters fell silent, watching it plummet towards one of the dockside cranes far, far below. By the time it struck the crane's shattered jib it was little more than a speck of dust lost in the immensity of the abyss.

'Who's next?' growled Annie, flexing her fingers.

The hull of the Bark suddenly moved beneath Jonah's feet. The familiar face of Grandfather Tree emerged from its salt-caked surface and grinned. 'I'm late. Please accept my apologies.'

'How do we sail this thing?' snapped Jonah. He did not have to wait for an answer.

From the skyward side of the hull there sprouted a sapling. It grew sideways at lightning speed, a tapering mast, perfectly straight and smooth, extending horizontally like a finger pointing at the clouds. As it lengthened it extended secondary runners out to either side, until it resembled a skeletal leaf vibrating gently in the falling wind.

'Charm-sail,' explained Grandfather Tree with a note of triumph. 'Hold tight!'

The mast rotated so as to present the narrow leading edge of the sail to the falling wind. At once beads of golden liquid condensed on the gossamer-thin spars and struts. The Bark lurched once, then accelerated smoothly away from the breakwater. Waves crested at what had become its bow. Behind them, diminishing rapidly, the dryads howled out their fury. The three passengers clung to the exterior of the weather-beaten craft, which still seemed little more than a gigantic buoy adrift in this strange, vertical ocean, while Kythe flew gleefully in its wake.

'Hurrah!' the young dragon shouted. 'Faster, faster!'

Already the dryads were a thin patch of colour on the even thinner line of the breakwater, their screams quite inaudible by now. The forest behind them, thoroughly ablaze, was pumping acres of thick black smoke into the sky, but even that was soon consumed by the terrifying scale of Stone. As the mighty taiga grew smaller and smaller, so Amara seemed to swell around it, an enormous world of a wall. And then Amara itself, or at least its solid face, was nothing but a narrow band of grey and brown balanced at ten degrees from the vertical on the distant upStone vertex. It lingered on this upturned horizon for what seemed an age before finally slipping around the curve of Stone and disappearing out of sight.

Only the vast, falling ocean remained.

6

Bark

North looked out over the Dead Wall, the top of which was by now looking decidedly ragged. The battlements had been ravaged on several occasions, weakening the defensive line. The interior was littered with the fallen, a broken square of tombstone shapes staring up into the light. The western part of the North Wall, the entire West Wall and much of the South was gone: the ramparts of the Live Wall had fallen, only to be reassembled far out on the battlefield in poor mimicry of their original splendour. The new patterns they formed there were beautiful but futile. Divided, the Live Wall had lost both strength and purpose, and now it was only a matter of time. An end was near, though none yet dared guess on whom fortune would smile.

Giving nothing away, North returned his attention to the symbols before him: a veritable forest of bamboo, a faceless dragon and the relentless southern wind, which had been with him from the beginning. How was it that he had come so far and achieved so little? In the beginning the odds had seemed good, but now, so late in the day, the symbols were no longer the friends they had once been. Implacable, of course inscrutable, they stared back and defied him to put them to work. Mercenaries all, their fighting days were over.

At last West moved. North hardly dared look as the long shadow of her arm fell across the remains of the Live Wall. A new tombstone appeared in the square, and North could not believe his luck.

'Kong!' he pronounced with a flourish, picking the nine-bamboo from where West had just placed it amid the discards and adding it to the three identical tiles in his hand. Having presented these four tiles face-up on the table before him, he took another tile from the Dead Wall. It was worthless to him – the staring eye of one-circle – and he discarded it at once. He was back in the game, but West already had a Calling Hand and, sure enough, she gleefully swept up the rejected one-circle.

'*Ma-chong!*' cried Annie triumphantly, laying out a two-and three-circle to accompany the newly claimed loner.

'I am fated when I play from the North,' grumbled Jonah as they tallied the points and discovered that Annie's lead was practically unassailable.

'You can huff and puff all you want,' she chided, 'but I won that fair and square. Not that there mayn't be a little bit of Western luck thrown in. What do you say, Grandfather?'

'You play the game well, Annie. And better every time. Soon it is me you will beat.'

'I'm beating you already, in case you hadn't noticed.'

'There is time. Always there is time.'

'I'll believe it when I see it!'

The tiles clacked like bones against Grandfather Tree's ebony fingers as he scooped them across the table. As East Wind, or Leader, for the next hand, he was responsible for organizing the next shuffle, after which the process of Wall-building would begin afresh. 'Gerent,' he said. 'First you should be to wash the tiles.'

Gerent rubbed his eyes then stood slowly, stretching his arms high above his head; his spine crackled briskly. 'Forgive me,' he said, 'but I can play no more.'

'Oh, stay a while, Gerent,' Annie pleaded. 'You're only fifteen points behind Grandfather. You're a natural at this game, you know you are.'

'It is enjoyable, but I am simply tired. The scores are tallied; we can resume tomorrow.'

'Jonah! Make him stay!'

But Jonah just snorted. 'If you think I am about to pass up an opportunity to bring an end to this evening's sorry proceedings, young lady, you are sadly mistaken. A night's rest and reflection is just what I need to prepare myself for further conflict. I'm glad to say this game of *ma-chong* is over for now.'

With a petulant lip Annie gathered up the tiles and stacked them back into their wooden box, tucking them into the crevices between the other things that lived in there: her oil paints, the little jars of linseed oil and turpentine, the shreds of rag. She paused before shutting the lid again, peering into the minute, self-contained artist's studio. The magical light by which they had been playing the game sent slivers of gold into its deepest recesses; the longer she looked the brighter the interior became, as if the light, once inside, could find no way to escape.

Her painting equipment shared its home with one hundred and forty-four small, ivory tiles, each one of which bore a Chinese *ma-chong* symbol on its front face. On the reverse of some she had painted the most intricate miniature scenes. Landscapes and seascapes, views from around the world, the old world, not the world of Stone. Scenes through which Annie had passed on her long journey west across the Rockies and out across the Pacific, the journey that had brought her eventually to Krakatoa, and at last to Stone. Sunset in the Painted Desert; nightfall on Galapagos; the brilliant blue of the terrestrial ocean. Captured memories, changeless and exquisite, like jewels, shining now in the light of a floating globe of charm the workings of which she could not even begin to fathom.

Beautiful though the paintings were, at first they made it quite impossible to play the game. On the back of one tile, for instance – the Red Dragon – was her rendering of the Javanese coast. Even face-down the tile was instantly identifiable and, as a playing piece, utterly useless.

Though she had had the rules explained to her by the old Chinese man who had given her the box so long ago in San Francisco, Annie had never actually played the game. Nor had she ever expected to. Nobody she met had ever heard of it, and since it required four players and boasted a set of elaborate rules she quickly forgot, she decided to use the tiles as ready-made cameos. Which was what the Chinese man must have intended all along, she realized belatedly. Had he not manufactured the little brass stand into which she was able to clip a tile ready for painting? In which case why not give her a set of completely blank tiles, rather than the hand-crafted, and presumably quite valuable, *ma-chong* set? It had not seemed strange at the time, or rather it had not seemed out of place during a period in Annie's life when, on the run from a violent husband, *everything* had been strange. The scenes of Colorado and the Rockies she had painted from memory; soon she started to paint from life and all thought of ever playing the game slipped away.

Grandfather Tree changed all that. As soon as he learned Annie had the tiles he was in raptures. 'I made a set once. But not as beautiful as this! Play we must!' His green eyes alive with excitement he contrived a charm that he described as an *elementary glamour*. 'The thinnest gloss of charm! Enough to make them blanks again. Enough for us to play the game!'

His enthusiasm was infectious, and his intimate knowledge of the rules invaluable. The glamour he devised effectively masked Annie's paintings without erasing them and so he was able to set about teaching them the game he knew as *Mah-Jongg*, the wonders of which he had discovered during one of his many jaunts into what was effectively Jonah's and Annie's future.

'I cannot understand why I never heard of it, or why my father never played it,' Jonah wondered when the lesky first proposed they play. 'He was fanatical about chess and draughts, and a ferocious card player. He would have adored *ma-chong*.'

'The game was scarcely known in your time,' replied Grandfather Tree. 'A curiosity, it is. An infant in the body of a king.'

Under his instructions the four of them – Jonah, Annie, Gerent and the lesky himself – seated themselves in the Bark's lowest chamber, in which he had extruded a table especially for this purpose. A floating charm, a wavering bead of light about the size of an orange, scattered a golden glow across the immaculately polished surface. In the centre of the table a large knot, its almost-face razed flat by whatever magical smoothing process the lesky had employed, stared shrewdly out of the wood, its almost-eyes seeming to track the movements of the players.

An elaborate ritual of dice-throws and tile-shuffling (or *washing*) determined which of them would begin the game as East wind, after which each player built a long wall of tiles, eighteen long and two high, which they pushed together to create a square. A city rampart enclosing a precious and empty space. A dice throw then determined where the square Wall was to be split to create the seven-tile-wide Dead Wall and the much larger Live Wall, from which each of them drew the requisite number of tiles to make up their hands – thirteen each for the North, South and West winds, fourteen for the East, whose first play would be to discard the extra tile. The rules seemed complex and alien, until Jonah suddenly cried out, 'Bamboo, Circle and Character! Of course! Hearts, diamonds, clubs and spades! There are only three but they are suits all the same!'

Annie grinned, sharing his revelation. Gerent was there ahead of them, but then he had already remarked on *ma-chong*'s similarity to a game his father had played using painted bones. Even with the added complexity of dragons and winds, flowers and seasons, *ma-chong* was transformed from an Oriental mystery into an elegant battle of wits, an exotic cousin of whist and half a dozen card games both she and Jonah remembered from their former lives. They played *ma-chong* every night thereafter and now, five nights later, they were playing it still.

'Leave the glamour tonight,' said Annie, running a finger over the smoothly stacked tiles. 'I know the pictures well enough. Covering something up doesn't make it go away.' She pressed her hand to her mouth, stifling a yawn.

'You are tired,' proclaimed Grandfather Tree, cracking his knuckles with a sound like knots exploding on a fire. Slowly he began to fold his gnarled body back into the chair from which he sprouted. 'Leave you I shall. Good night.'

Jonah and Annie watched as the lesky contracted himself into the seat of the chair. He looked much as he had on the beacon: a wooden skeleton strung through with vines and knots, his face a great bead of sap into which were moulded the features of a tired old elf, framed by a brisk silver mane. As for his bearing, that was very different. On the beacon, in his prison of branches, he had seemed near to death, and in dreadful pain. But now . . . he still seemed frail, but there was fresh vitality. Watching him melt into the chair was like watching an elaborate piece of driftwood consumed by a dark lake.

'He has great strength,' Jonah said as the topmost strands of Grandfather Tree's mane dissolved into the smooth wood.

'He saved us sure enough,' replied Annie.

'He saved himself. That must have been much, much harder.'

'Why didn't he try to escape earlier, I wonder.'

'Perhaps he did not have a reason.'

They were standing hip to hip, Jonah's arm wrapped unselfconsciously around Annie's waist. Light spun across the table-top as the floating charm bobbed in the air-current from the door. Like the table, and like all the other rooms in the Bark, the room they now referred to as the Games Room was circular, a compact cylinder of wood scooped from the long tube of the strange vessel's interior. As in a lighthouse the rooms were stacked one above the other. But unlike a lighthouse there were no stairs. Inside the Bark you did not have to climb from room to room, for although gravity still held sway within the rooms, in the Shaft it was banished altogether.

Gerent was outside the doorway, floating in the Shaft, the narrow thoroughfare running the entire height of the Bark. It was dark out there. The only light came from the hovering charm within the room; Gerent's face seemed to be made of shadows. He regarded the two of them for what seemed to Jonah an age, his eyes quite invisible. 'I shall go out on deck, I think,' he said, just as he said every night after their game. 'I may talk to the dragon for a while. I wish you both gentle dreams.' He tapped his toe on the narrow ledge just beyond the door, propelling himself slowly up into the darkness like a marionette removed from the stage of a toy theatre.

'He is very sad still,' Jonah sighed.

'I don't know. Tonight he's different. Something's changed.'

'His mind was not on the game,' agreed Jonah. He laughed. 'But then neither was mine.'

'I can guess what your mind *was* on!'

He closed his eyes as she turned his body and buried

102

her face in the hollow at the base of his neck. Aroused by her scent, the way it blended with the pine-musk of the dimly lit chamber, he held her tight and wondered at the strangeness of it all. Not the world of Stone, strange though it was, nor its singular ocean, but how one of Queen Victoria's Englishmen came to be embracing a woman from the American pioneer trail. He chuckled, amused that he should find this odd, that he should still imagine their backgrounds to be so different, despite all they had been through. By Stone's mighty standards they were practically neighbours.

'I hope that comment was not intended to be suggestive.'

'And why not, Englishman?'

'Because it is simply not proper for a lady.'

'Hey, did I ever say I was proper? Besides, I've not heard you complaining yet.' The corners of her mouth curved mischievously, she took his hand and placed it on her breast then, the instant he increased the pressure of his own accord pulled it gently away again. 'Still, maybe you're right. Maybe we shouldn't be acting like this, not while there's things to be done.'

Jonah tried to pull her close again as she turned slightly away. He felt lost without the touch of her body against his own. She yielded, rewarding him with a kiss that surprised him with its passion. The fire so swiftly damped rekindled just as fast. What had got into her tonight? She broke away abruptly, touching her fingers against his cheeks, scrutinizing his eyes.

'I love you, Jonah Lightfoot,' she blurted, her voice hoarse. 'By God I do.' Suddenly she looked terrified.

'I know. I love you too.'

'No! Listen to me!' Her hands were clutching at him with something approaching desperation. She kissed him again, a brief, wet blow. 'Jonah, I love you! I love you more than I ever loved Rance, *and he was my husband*!

Still is, God forgive me. All I want in this new world is you. All this, this *magic* is nothing. *We* have the magic here, now, nothing else matters, just us, you and me. It's *ours*!' Her intensity was unnerving; Jonah could not remember ever feeling so aroused. 'Don't ever forget that, Jonah, not ever!'

'I won't,' he gasped. 'But . . .'

'Don't ask me now. I'll tell you later. There's something . . . I'll tell you later.' Annie dropped her head; droplets of perspiration had gathered on her forehead and upper lip. She sighed as Jonah stroked them away. 'You should go to Gerent now.'

He blinked, puzzled. 'What? Gerent? I don't understand.'

Lifting her head, struggling visibly to bring herself back under control, Annie smiled disarmingly. 'Because I think he wants to talk to you.'

Confused, a little afraid though he had no idea why, Jonah protested. She ushered him to the door of the chamber. 'Go,' she whispered. 'He's all right. I just think he needs you. Just like I'll need you later,' she added mischievously. She kissed him again, clutching at his shoulder as she held him close. When they parted she was breathing hard. 'Don't take too long,' she whispered.

As he rose between the close walls of the Shaft Jonah looked down to see her face staring up at him, pale where Gerent's had been dark. Her eyes were shining, as if they had been filled with a magic that could do nothing but spill itself out into the air in search of something to touch.

The spherical bulb on to which they had all clung when Grandfather Tree had first piloted the Bark away from the forest still projected clear of the waves. The greater part of the Bark still resided behind the water.

This vessel of the basilisks indeed resembled a lighthouse in its overall size and shape, although it lacked the tapering form of its terrestrial counterpart. What glimpses Jonah had gained of the exterior of its massive cylindrical form, slipping smoothly along behind the waves like the disembodied head of a hammerhead shark, had revealed little – a long, curving back, a surface heavily scored and gnarled like the trunk of an ancient tree. It was the leviathan in which they rode, and if the lesky who was their pilot knew its secrets he was not telling.

The barnacle-encrusted conning tower stuck out like an afterthought about halfway down the Bark's length, it and its spindly charm-sail being all that stood proud of the water. Emerging into the open air from the hatch in the top of the conning tower, Jonah felt momentarily displaced. Wind struck him, knocking him off balance. Unlike Gerent, he did not come out here often: for some reason he found it harder to accept Stone's upturned geometry when it was demonstrated by all this water. It was one thing to be crawling along a gigantic wall, quite another to be speeding through an ocean turned on its end, forever on the point of crashing down into the clutches of gravity. His mind had tried many ways to resolve the image; tonight it came up with the story of Moses. How must the Egyptians have felt beneath the descending shadow of the Red Sea, knowing they were prey to an entire ocean?

Jonah thought he knew.

By night the spectacle was no less strange. The ocean phosphoresced. Yellow light moved through the deeps, stretching to the surface in long mobile tendrils like octopus-arms. Patterns ebbed and flowed within the light, rippling, fanning, spiralling and exploding out through the wave-tops where they broke into the air, condensing into shining droplets that might have been clear water or pure light. The instant the droplets left the magical field keeping the ocean upright they winked out. The sail was illuminated too, a spindly cobweb set with beads of golden dew, but all else was dark, totally dark. The night-time air-glow Annie had once found so comforting was gone; now there was just the light and the shadow, with nothing between.

And the Bark moved fast, at least thirty knots by Jonah's best guess. The wind it made was strong enough to turn Jonah's hair into a red banner, streaming out behind him. It flattened his clothes and made him gasp.

Aquatic aurora, he mused as he watched a cloud of brilliant yellow particles expand behind the submerged silhouette of the Bark. They moved like a million flaming wasps, swooping through the Bark's wake to erupt all around him, insect-magic, swarming charm dying into the night, hauled upStone into their slipstream.

Gingerly, leaning into the wind, he made his way down the precarious sphere of the conning tower to where Gerent sat wedged against the sail. The mast creaked and moved, and the Neolithic man's body moved against it in an easy rhythm. He looked immensely comfortable. Taking care not to slip on the damp wood Jonah sat himself down on a narrow shelf at the other side of the slender mast.

'Down there,' said Gerent at length, finally breaking the silence. 'Tell me what you see.'

Jonah leaned forward as far as he dared (unreal though the surroundings seemed, his sense of vertigo was particularly strong tonight) and looked down to where the Neolithic was pointing. Here, on the open sea, the air was clearer than he had ever known it on Stone: by day the distant vertex was clearly visible, and the view down into the abyss was breathtaking. By night, the abstract patterns of phosphorescence created an ever-changing display, as if the gods had taken it into their heads to paint the ocean but simply could not agree on the composition. The tremendous depth of the view merely amplified the confusion.

But was it all confusion? Was it simply random sprays of light? As he stared at the distant spot on the ocean surface many miles below them, watching the yellow patterns flower and wilt, he began to see a regularity behind the randomness. The more he stared the clearer it became.

'Tell me what you see,' repeated Gerent, 'so that I know I have not prompted you.'

'I'm not sure, but I think . . . yes, I believe I can see a line of some kind. As though a strong current is flowing from right to left – upStone, in other words – but in a narrow band only, and it is drawing the trails of light with it.' He broke off, suppressing a chuckle.

'What is it?'

'Nothing really. My mother used to make a tart with apples and an iced crust. On top of the crust she would pipe thin lines of jam. Then she would take a knife and drag it through the lines of jam – at right angles to them, do you see? Naturally the lines became distorted, dragged off their proper course. This phenomenon reminds me of the patterns they made. What could it mean?'

'Perhaps nothing, perhaps much. Do you recall how the dragon and I have both spoken about how hard it is to climb on Stone? Or to fall for that matter.'

'Not hard to fall, surely!'

Gerent laughed. 'In one way no, but in another it is almost impossible. When Frey killed Malya, when I leaped on to his back to take my revenge and we fell together, very far, I experienced many strange sensations. As if my mind was coming adrift from my body, as if my thoughts were slowing, thickening somehow. A feeling of growing pain, with only agony to come. It was only these wings that saved me.' He stroked them, the dragon-scale wings fabricated by Frey, and which had now passed to Gerent in a way so intimate even their maker could not have imagined it. 'You fell once too. Did you not feel something of the sort?'

'Something, yes. And Kythe has described similar feelings. Her dragon lore speaks of such a thing,' agreed Jonah. He had never heard Gerent speak so matter-of-factly about the death of Malya, nor did he ever recall seeing him so at ease with his magical wings.

'It is a truth of Stone. And there, down there where the yellow light turns aside, perhaps we see the proof of it.'

Jonah looked again, assessing the Neolithic man's words. The light was being deflected, certainly, but by what? 'Is there a barrier then, down there? Are you saying that one can only travel so far either up or down before one is repelled?'

'It is possible. But this is no stranger than what Kythe tells us about the sky. Remember how she describes it: if she flies outwards, away from Stone, when she gets far out into the sky the air turns her round without her realizing and she finds herself heading back the way she came. The sky *twists*, Lightfoot. Maybe all Stone is twisted too.'

Jonah leaned closer against the mast, wrapping one arm around it. The longer he spent out here the more vulnerable he felt. 'You have been thinking hard about this.'

'I have spent a lot of time in thought these past days,' replied Gerent. 'I hope I have not been bad company.'

'Oh, my dear man! You are grieving for the loss of the woman you loved. You have every right to be gloomy!'

'Perhaps. My father would have agreed with you, but I am not so sure. Anyway, my mind is clearer tonight than it has been for a long time, longer than you might imagine. Clear enough for me to begin to see through at least a few of Stone's glamours.'

He turned to face Jonah, his expression alive and earnest. 'Now, let us talk again about the true shape of Stone!'

And so they did. Lacking pen and paper, or even a convenient stretch of sand in which to scratch their thoughts, they sketched diagrams in the air. To Jonah's delight, they discovered that if they dipped their fingers into the golden beads on the sail could draw trails of light right in front of their eyes. The trails were tenuous, and lasted only a few seconds before fading to nothing, but by working fast they managed to find enlightenment when words were not enough.

They began by reiterating Jonah's theory about the conical structure of Stone.

'You are right about this, I can feel that you are!' asserted Gerent with such confidence that Jonah was quite taken aback. 'Stone's wall, the outer surface across which we crawl like insects, is the sloping side of an enormous cone. On this we are agreed?' Jonah nodded, enjoying Gerent's enthusiasm. 'But it is not enough to consider only the outer surface of Stone – we have to remember what lies behind the skin.'

'The memory rods!' Jonah shivered. He *had* forgotten. He had never even considered the place of the rods within the geometry he had so gaily extrapolated.

'Yes, the memory rods. We know that they run horizontally beneath the skin, buried in the substance of Stone itself. But I ask you this, Lightfoot, because I cannot answer it for myself: are the rods truly horizontal? Do they lie absolutely true?'

'Why yes . . . I mean, I think so. In every chamber I have seen where the rods have been exposed they simply run from one side to the other, right through the cavity, as straight and true as railway tracks. Except in the Threshold of course, but then the Threshold was . . . well, it was different.' He broke off with a shudder as he remembered the mass of knots into which the rods had congealed. 'It was an awful place,' he concluded lamely.

'Awful indeed. But I am not talking about the Threshold – I think that place had its own rules, don't you agree? I'm talking about the rest of Stone, about *most* of Stone, where the rods simply run their course upStone, carrying the memories of the world from the past into the future. *Are* the rods level? Think about it!'

Try though he did, Jonah could no more match Gerent's enthusiasm than he could grasp his point. He felt his mind straying back to Annie, who was surely awaiting him inside the Bark.

'Gerent, I am sorry, but I do not see . . .'

'Ah, but you shall see. Oh ye, see you shall, and very well!'

Grandfather Tree's face coalesced in the deck beneath them, a flattened elf-face barely visible in the eerie light.

Gerent rounded on the lesky, his eyes bright. 'You know, lesky! You understand me, is it not so?'

A mouth glistening with sap grinned wide, exposing rows of teeth like tangled briars. 'Ye indeed, never-king.' A laugh came, harsh and mocking.

'Do they lie straight?'

Silence, then the answer Gerent wanted to hear: 'No!'

Jonah closed his eyes and remembered his first hours on Stone . . .

A long, dark tunnel, oval in section. At its far end a splinter of light. Annie in my arms, except I do not yet know she is really Archan. All around me are the rods. Their slim black pipes emerge from the curved wall to my right, cross the space and plunge into the wall to my left. Matching barriers, hundreds of them, beneath which I must duck and over which I must climb. They seem to pulse with life, and I do not dare touch them.

I walk for miles.

When I am past them I look back. All is dark, except faint lines of daylight reflected from the gloss of countless horizontal lines. All of them lie in perfect order. Each one is as flat and true as the ground on which Atlas stood.

Except . . .

He looked at Gerent with dawning wonder. 'Grandfather Tree is right. The memory rods *are* inclined. By God they are! It is very slight – it could not possibly be observed by the naked eye – but I know it to be true! The rods are lower on the downStone side than they are on the upStone, by the merest fraction – if you were to follow a memory rod on its journey upStone you would gradually rise as you proceeded around the curve of Stone, which means . . .' He paused, his heart pounding, his head light. 'Which means that the memory rods are wrapped around Stone like the thread on a woodscrew!'

'Woodscrew!' echoed the lesky, his face a spinning gyre. 'To many places have I been. UpStone and downStone, and something of the shape of Stone I know. Mark it well, faeries. Mark it well.'

Spinning still, he screwed himself away out of sight.

'Has he been listening to us all this time?' wondered Jonah.

'It matters not.' Gerent was staring down again at the distant perturbation in the patterns of light. 'A spiralling thread. And movement is only permitted *along* the thread, not *across* it. That is why you cannot fall too far without suffering, and if you fall too far across the thread . . . I think you die.'

Jonah checked himself. Despite the testimony of Grandfather Tree they were racing ahead of themselves, constructing wild hypotheses based on nothing but speculation. Deep inside however, far beneath the veneer of intellect and reason, the animal part of him on whose back he rode whenever he entered the other-world of the memory rods recognized the scent of truth, and growled its approval. Was it important to know the shape of Stone? He believed it was, and a single look at Gerent told him the Neolithic believed it too.

'A spiral thread,' he whispered, gazing to his right: downStone where, hidden beneath the waves, the memory rods were even now spinning their way backwards through time. Then he looked the opposite way: upStone, the direction from which they had come. Then he looked straight up. Somewhere up there, if he and Gerent were right about this, was the tip of the cone. The screw's sharp point.

The place where the future finally came to an end.

'Where do the memories go from there?' he said, his voice loud and harsh above the gentle slap of the waves against the side of the Bark.

They talked on for a while, but with growing reluctance. After revelation came shock, a kind of delayed reappraisal of the sheer immensity of Stone, the meaning of its incomprehensible cargo. Their words grew dull, pressed down by the weight of reality.

All the memories of all the worlds were entombed here, gathered and sifted and spun into ebony rods spiralling their way up the face of a gigantic needle. The lives of humans and animals, of creatures with charm and those without, the infinite lives that had been and would be across all time, even into the future. Memories that were made long, long ago, and those that were yet to pass. Memories made solid, histories encapsulated, saved forever in Stone's precious amber.

And clinging to the curve of that needle, fighting their way across a tiny fraction of its circumference, they journeyed, and with what hope? That they would reach an ending? That they would find their way home?

Have I done all that is required of me here? Jonah asked

the black sky. *Archan was the enemy – it was she who came to threaten Stone. Now that she has been banished, is my work complete? If so, why do I feel unfulfilled?*

Where do I go from here?

But the sky had no answers for him. He stood up, holding tight to the swaying mast. Gerent did not move. 'I'm sorry about Malya,' Jonah said at last.

'Thank you,' answered the Neolithic. 'She is gone from Stone but not from my heart. I am beginning to understand something of what that means now. She lives within me still, you see, and that brings me comfort. In a small way she lives still.'

Jonah was about to tell him that he was brave, but the words did not seem right. The words had abandoned them finally, it seemed. 'Good night, Gerent,' he offered as he made his way back to the hatch.

'Good night, Lightfoot.'

Glancing back across the rounded deck just before he closed the hatch, Jonah was presented with a striking view of the Neolithic man crouched by the mast, his face bright with the golden light from the sail, a spray of yellow fireworks cascading through the air behind him, the great ocean-fall of Stone bisecting the view behind it all.

Going backwards, he thought. *Going down.*

Annie was no longer in the Games Room. Jonah kicked at the floor, ascending through the Shaft to the next room up. Smooth walls slipped past in silence, fine-grained and polished like mirrors. The Shaft was as tight as a chimney, wide enough for only one person at a time, and Jonah liked to be in and out of it as quickly as possible.

The room above the Games Room was Gerent's, though he spent little enough time in it. A cursory look confirmed it was empty, not that he would have expected to find either Annie or Grandfather Tree in here. As for

Kythe, she had not alighted on the Bark in all their time at sea.

Gerent's room was spartan in the extreme. A hard disc of a floor, a small pile of weapons lying against the curved wall – a long and short sword, another grapnel and a leather pouch Jonah knew to be filled with a variety of beachcombed objects: chunks of glass, shaped stones and all manner of tiny metal artefacts, all plundered from the miniature dockside. The bed, which was rarely used, was nothing more than a brace of furs spread on the floor, taken from two of the three-horned goats they had successfully hunted soon after their arrival on the beach ledges.

Next up was the room he shared with Annie. The lesky had extruded a bed for them, a rough, blockish affair filling half the available space. The dark wood from which it was made was pliable, even slightly springy, but it was still a coverless wooden bed and not especially comfortable. It had been made, like the table in the Games Room, over the course of an hour; it had been pure magic to watch the furniture gradually form itself out of the blank slate of the floor. It had taken most of the first day for the lesky to mould the rooms themselves – during which time the rest of the passengers stayed out on deck – but once he had completed that first task the rest seemed to come more easily.

'I have the measure of these basilisks now!' he announced proudly, pressing his face up through the hull. 'I only wish I had the time and charm to do more.'

There was, he explained, a limit to what he could do with the Bark. The basilisk vessel had been moored in its decommissioned state for many aeons, and many of the control systems its former owners had originally used had long since petrified inside its wooden flesh. 'Charm alone makes it what the basilisks intended. Without charm, a mere branch it is.'

Grandfather Tree's ability to wield charm was, he said, enough to get the Bark moving, and to resculpt its interior enough to afford at least a modicum of comfort for its human passengers. Kythe, for her own reasons, elected to stay in the air for the duration of the voyage, despite the concerns of her friends that she would get tired.

'There's more magic in the air here than anything I've seen before!' she protested exuberantly. 'I feel like I could fly forever!'

When they finally ventured into the Bark's new interior they found five rooms, one stacked on top of another, with the weightless Shaft connecting them all. The bottom-most chamber, intended as a hold for anything they might find along the way, quickly became the recreation area. Above that were the two bedrooms, and above those were a washroom and the communal top chamber, which Annie christened the Saloon. It was here that they spent much of their time during the day, for it was the only room with a window – a window, of course, looking out into the water. As for Grandfather Tree, he did not need his own quarters, residing as he did within the fabric of the vessel itself.

'Through the Bark I swim, as once I swam through the taiga. It's a little like home, a little. Cramped, however. Given time, I could sculpt you more: pillows and pictures and books. Things from your futures to make you amazed. But the Bark-stuff is hard to mould, full of old magic set in its ways. What I've done – it will be enough. The voyage will not last forever.'

Five days on, making in excess of thirty knots through an untroubled sea, Jonah was beginning to wonder just how true that last statement was.

Looking into his and Annie's room it occurred to him that they, like Gerent, had gathered artefacts to which they clung with something close to fanaticism. There beside the bed was Annie's painting box, closed up now, with its strange cargo of gaming tiles and oil paints. On the bed his own talisman: the first edition of Darwin's *On the Origin of Species*, the book he had drawn across the boundaries between the worlds, the book he had lost on the beach of Krakatoa and rediscovered in the landscape of his own memories as they flowed like liquid through Stone's hidden rods. And on the floor, the trunk made of Samsonite that had been flung from the wreck of the *Bonaventure*, and which Kythe had carried to the Bark on the day the forest caught fire. What urge was it to hoard in this way, to cling to material things the moment they became familiar? Clearly an ancient one, if it was displayed not only in humans from the nineteenth century AD but also in their companion from six thousand years earlier.

Six thousand years, thought Jonah. *Just two hundred generations*.

'It is no time at all,' he murmured, leaving the empty room behind.

Both the washroom and the Saloon were deserted too. The internal shutters were drawn over the latter's window, shutting off the view of the ocean depths. He was glad: he had seen enough water for one night. Now all he craved was Annie's embrace.

A pair of flickering light charms resting on one of the rough benches rose suddenly into the air as if startled from sleep.

'It's all right,' he sighed. 'I'm going.' The shimmering orbs bobbed uncertainly for a few seconds then lowered themselves gently to rest once more. Grandfather Tree had assured him that the floating charms were not actually alive; Jonah was not so sure.

'Annie!' he called. This was crazy – the Bark was much too small to get lost in. He checked the rooms again, just in case she had fallen asleep in the shadows somewhere, but without success. He was about to go out on deck again when he stopped.

Halfway up the Shaft was a little vestibule, in the outer wall of which was set the external deck hatch. To the left of this was a second hatch, oval and very small. Grandfather Tree had advised them not to use it, since it led to the hollow space inside the conning tower, in which was stored the raw charm gathered by the sail. The Bark's hull mechanisms drew on this reservoir of charm in order to create the forward movement of the vessel – airborne magic converted effortlessly into sea-borne speed. While the charm was not exactly dangerous, he explained, its effects might be disorientating.

'Like a stiff draught of whisky?' Annie had joked.

'Like giving up control of your mind,' Grandfather Tree had answered. Annie's mouth had shut with a snap – that was one experience she did not care to repeat.

'Think I'll stick with the whisky,' she said. 'Any chance you could make us a still?'

None of them had ventured in, nor even bothered to try the small hatch, as far as Jonah knew. But now, as he floated in the vestibule (which lacked gravity in the same way as the rest of the Shaft), he saw the dust motes scattered in the air around its seam. Closer inspection revealed it was not quite closed – one side was standing proud by a quarter of an inch. Someone had opened it recently.

'Annie?' He grasped the lumpy handle – like the bulbous head of a walking stick – and pulled. There was no lock; the oval hatch was simply a tight fit. A puff of air folded dust across his hands as he drew the hatch out on a single, complicated hinge. Fully extended it resembled a flattened claw, perhaps belonging to some weird crustacean, balanced on multiple elbow-joints. From inside the reservoir there came a thick golden glow, throbbing to a fast pulse. He slipped inside.

'Annie?'

She materialized from the fog with the silence of an owl, arms spread wide like wings. Free from the pull of gravity, her tanned body revolved slowly in the spacious interior, absorbing the light and throwing it back tenfold. She was aflame.

Drifting past Jonah she pulled the hatch shut then, with a lithe twisting motion, spun herself round and kicked lightly off the curved wall. Her arms gathered him up as she went past and they began slowly to spiral together. He felt her legs lock around his hips, her hands snake the shirt over his head and discard it like a shed skin. By the time they bounced against the far wall their only clothing was the sheen of charm crackling across their flesh. He kissed her hard, a rebuke for the game of hide-and-seek she had led him on, an acknowledgement of the degree to which it had excited him. At last she pulled away, fixing him with her gaze.

'I've never felt so dangerous,' she gasped. Jonah frowned, then smiled, then laughed. She pouted. 'Don't laugh. Laughing's what Rance used to do if ever I suggested we . . . you know. We only ever did it on his terms, at his time. Whenever I wanted it he was never interested. It was part of his power over me, I guess. I loved him for it at first, when I didn't know better, when I was still grateful to him for noticing me at all. But then he started coming at me with his fists, and I started to think maybe it's better not to be noticed. Maybe it's better just to hide yourself away, make a place that only you know about, where nobody can hurt you, even if they're hurting you.'

'You mean the place inside your mind, don't you, Annie? You told me you used to retreat there whenever your husband beat you. And that is where you retreated when Archan possessed your body. Your secret room at the top of the castle tower.'

They were spinning imperceptibly now, moving at a leisurely rate back across the open chamber. Soft sparks trailed down Jonah's back, their touch like feathers.

'I want to let you in there, Jonah. When I said I felt dangerous, I meant dangerous to myself. I hate that place now. It's a place where weak women go when they don't know any better.'

'That is not true. You were never weak.'

'It's a place for weaklings,' she repeated vehemently. 'And I ain't weak no more, Jonah. Not now I've got you.'

'Oh, Annie. I am not your strength. Your strength comes from within you. Do you not see that?'

'Maybe. But it's my love for you that makes me strong. Oh God, I know that like I've never known a truth before.'

'Is this what you wanted to tell me earlier? The depth of your love?'

She looked away, contradictory expressions competing on her face. 'Yes. No. Yes, Jonah, yes of course I love you, like I never loved Rance. You know that. But it's more than that. It's like . . . like being with Rance was a *good* thing. Like when you've had a nightmare, but now the sun's rising and it's only because of the nightmare that you really appreciate the light. That's what loving you is like, Jonah. It's like seeing the sunrise.'

Particles of raw magic splashed into her hair, drawing it out into a halo. The air flashed, spilling colours like paint. She pressed her hands into the nape of his neck and kissed him just as fervently as he had kissed her. Charm had glued their bodies together; Jonah could not imagine ever breaking the spell.

'I don't ever want to leave Stone,' Annie blurted. 'God forgive me, Jonah, but I feel at home here.' Her eyes were shocked wide, seeking his approval.

'I do not see any way we could go back.'

'Even if we could I wouldn't want to. We're *here* now,

119

Jonah, you and me, and we're together and that's enough. We were meant to come here, Esh told us that as if we didn't know it ourselves, and now this is *our* place. *Our* home, Jonah. Our home together.'

'Yes,' he sighed, daunted by her passion, overwhelmed by the depth of his own feelings for her. 'Yes, my love.'

'I don't want to ever leave you.' Her voice grew muffled as she buried her face in his neck.

'You shan't, dear Annie. Nothing shall ever take you from me again. Nothing in this world.'

A cocoon of light enshrouded their mingled bodies, pulsing to the beat of their matched heartbeats, quickening its pace as they quickened theirs, turning from gold to silver then brilliant white, pouring its energy out until the whole chamber was filled with incandescence, moving to a human rhythm. All sense of what lay at the centre of the cocoon was lost, all that remained was its measure, its pulse. And even when that pulse finally slowed the incandescence lingered, just as the sky stays light for a time after the sun has closed its eye, reluctant to give back what is beautiful.

'Tell me about your dreams, Annie.'

Revolving slowly, their tangled bodies or the chamber, he could not tell.

'I'm dreaming what lies ahead. I know that now. At the end of the voyage. I'm dreaming about it every night. When we've sailed far enough downStone we'll reach the Aqueduct. Kythe thinks it leads back to our world. Maybe it does, I don't know. Even if there is a way back, I don't think it's a way for the likes of us. I don't think we'll find anything on the Aqueduct but a heap of trouble. It's made of glass, but it's made of ice too, kind of. That means it's fragile, but it also makes it the strongest thing on Stone – no, I know that doesn't make sense, but that's what the dream's telling me: the Aqueduct's strength is in its weakness. That's what we have to remember when we step out across it. It's the only place we can hope to stand against what's coming our way.'

'What is coming our way, Annie my dear?'

She looked wretched.

'Trouble, my darling Jonah. Big trouble.'

Streamers of charm became fluttering cobwebs, tender filaments unwrapping themselves from emptiness. The net they cast was cold and uninviting and before long Annie began to shiver.

'Here, let us find your clothes. Are you cold?'

'I hope so.'

Jonah was still puzzling over this answer when he heard her small cry of pain.

'What is it?' he called urgently, wallowing through the chilly, magic-laden air to where she was clinging to a folded section of wall.

'Ow! Just stuck myself on that damned thing!' She was nursing her right hand, sucking angrily at the palm. With her good hand she indicated a tiny spike protruding from the wall, only a matter of half an inch or so.

'Are you hurt? I mean are you badly hurt?' He felt flustered, out of control.

'No. Only a pin-prick.' She gave him a wan smile. 'Look, it's stopped bleeding already.'

He wrapped her in his arms again, only to have her push him away, her smile breaking into a dazzling grin. 'Don't start all that again, Jonah Lightfoot. Let's get under some warm covers first.'

'You Americans, you are all the same. You should try one of our good old English winters – then you would know the meaning of the word "cold". I remember one year in particular . . .'

'I can leave you here jawing all night, or you can come with me. It's a fair choice.'

121

'Well, let me consider that for a moment or two.'

'Or I could take my custom elsewhere.'

'That will not be necessary. I have made my choice.'

'Maybe I've changed my mind.'

'Unlikely.'

'You flatter yourself.'

'It's true.' Jonah let himself fall into her dark, laughing eyes. 'Oh yes. I think that between us we have indeed discovered what is true.'

'You coming?'

'Of course.'

Regaining weight at the threshold of their bedroom was like waking from a dream, when sobriety floods night's impossible landscape. They moved together beneath the furs, flightless once more, aware that it was only the floor that prevented them from beginning the slow and endless fall.

7

Voyage

She tracked the movement in the ocean downStone, the vast presence swelling periodically against the surface. Occasionally it broke clear, but always when it was so far distant that she could see no detail, nothing but a vast grey hump. A shoal-shadow, a dense belly coasting up and down behind the waves a long way ahead, leading them on across the falling sea.

But she was sure to keep the black speck of the Bark constantly within her sight too: she had no desire to catch up with the shoal-shadow. While she adored the freedom of the sky she did not want to stray far from her companions. It was loneliness she feared; after all, she was only a child.

Kythe swung sideways towards the ocean surface, enjoying the hot splash of charm-rich air against her new dorsal spines and the vibrating backs of her wings. Two wing-widths from the waves she pulled level, skimming the surface, cheating the suction threatening at any breath to pull her in and behind the water. A long dragon shadow chased her, its pursuit futile. She laughed, revelling in the sheer sport, and dreamed of times long ago, when the skies of the old world had been filled with dragons.

*   *   *

The crystalline stronghold in which Kythe had been raised had been a prison. She realized this now, just as she realized that many of Stone's inhabitants lived their lives in retreat. The dragons who had cared for her – and who cared for her still, no doubt – had loved her truly, but they had been driven by an underlying terror she was only just beginning to comprehend.

Infants were rare on Stone, where charm was constantly leaking through from the old world. Tainted charm, on the back of which rode a plague, the same plague of infertility which had ravaged so many charmed creatures in the years leading up to the turning of the world. Most of Stone's inhabitants were affected to some degree, dragons and humans included. Gerent's tribe had held youth in the highest esteem, so rare were children among their number; the same was true of the dragon clan to which Kythe had once belonged. Like Gerent, she had been matched to an eligible partner, the only other available youngster. Unlike Gerent, she had not loved her chosen mate. And so she had left, a child who, though loved, was alone.

Kythe and Annie had discussed the relative ages of humans and dragons at some length during the time they had spent together on the beach. While Stone had only days by which to measure time – no months, no years, no seasons of any kind – they had concluded, after much calculation, that the young dragon was somewhere between six and eight years old. 'We'll call you seven,' Annie had proclaimed. 'It's a lucky number where I come from.' This pleased Kythe. However, Kythe's demeanour seemed more appropriate to an older human child: Annie placed her nearer to ten or eleven on the human scale.

'Even so,' Annie sighed, 'without years to go on it's all guesswork.'

'Tell me about years again. I didn't really understand it the first time.'

*   *   *

Freedom and fear, these two things were Kythe's whole world as she soared in the magical down-draught of Stone's infinite sky. Fear that she really was on her own, that she could never now go back to her home; freedom, because at last she could fly as her ancestors had flown.

The air was *alive* with charm. It clung to her scales like a breathing skin. She could feel it pulsating there; the sensation was at once dreadful and marvellous. Intoxicating. Two days into the voyage, as the Bark raced through the wave-crests at her side, she knew she would not alight until she reached solid ground on the far side of the ocean, if then. The sensation of flying, no, of *bathing* in such fabulously concentrated charm was impossible to give up. She felt no weariness, no sense of hunger, no desire to rest her wings. Sometimes it seemed as though it were not she flying at all, but rather the days themselves flying backwards past her wings, that it was time itself that would grow weary with the effort, that she herself could fly on and on into eternity.

The sea towered, an enormous wall of water at her right wing. As she peered into the ocean depths her thoughts were drawn inexorably back to what Jonah called the 'time-line'.

'The golden age of charm,' she whispered to herself, imagining the history lying parallel to this part of Stone. If a threshold were to open up now, affording her a view into that age, what might she see? 'The golden glow of charm, the skies filled with charmed dragons. Everywhere colour and light. And beautiful, beautiful dragons.'

Her first attempts at shape-changing were hesitant. Afterwards she glanced around her, acutely embarrassed. Later, having shaken off her misgivings, she tentatively injected a stream of charm into her tail, extending its length by half. Focusing her attention on the dragon shadow rippling beside her across the broken surface of the sea, she did the same to her wings, thrilling to the

125

sight of the shadow's wings expanding until they were twice their former size.

Then she lost her nerve and reversed the effects.

Then, having returned her body to normal, she sent charm back into her wings again, making them grow just a little bit. Hardly anything really.

Over the next few days she grew bolder with the experiments. The charm made her aware of her body in ways she had never been before. Where once she had been vaguely conscious of the beating of her heart in her breast, now she could feel the swish of blood – *charm-filled blood* – through every vein, the creasing of her wing membranes as they embraced the air currents, swift-contracting muscles bending her limbs, flexing her torso. She felt stronger, leaner, *older*.

She tried spikes on her flanks and down her spine, finally compromising on a thin line of flexible spines halfway down her back, nestled between her wings. Her wings she made first gold, then silver, then transparent. This last choice she liked immensely: the refraction of the Stonescape through their sheer membranes was a constant source of delight. Her face she did not alter, but she did make long, round-tipped horns jut from the back of her head.

She turned her tail into a spiral.

She made ivory blades from her claws.

She turned her scales into reflections of the sky, so that she could not be seen.

The spectre of Archan hovered briefly, reminding her of the dangers of loving oneself too much. Archan had taken the art of body-sculpture to the extreme, deleting limbs and eyes in favour of a flawless, serpentine form. The memory of that pale, dreadful shape brought Kythe up short. She straightened her tail, retracted her claws and returned her scales to their former orange hue.

But she kept the horns, and in the end she simply

126

could not bear to lose those beautiful, transparent wings.

There's nothing wrong, she reassured herself. *Once upon a time, all charmed dragons did this. It was just the way things were.*

Just a child dressing up as a princess, with a child's love of life, a child's denial of mortality, her simple belief in truth and light.

And a child's nightmares.

Like Annie's, Kythe's dreams came every night. Sleeping on the wing like a great seafaring bird, she cried tears through closed eyes as the ocean reached out groping tentacles and dragged her behind its waves. Teeth formed from breaking foam, the water thickened to jelly, holding her fast and filling her throat, her eyes. Blind and choking she wrestled with this liquid enemy until she could hold her breath no longer and, screaming silently into the blue emptiness, she opened her eyes to oblivion.

Death was both welcome and terrible. Yet just before it claimed her she saw something else, something solid beyond the void. Colours set in vivid contrast to the grey and blue of Stone and sky, Stone and sea: green and yellow, brilliant sunlight flooding the depths of a forest. The soft orange of fire. A wind that blew not down but *across*.

A pure white orb floating in the daylight sky. The moon.

Is there a way back to the old world? she asked herself each time she awoke with her wings shaking and her neck coiled back in painful spasm. *Back to the world of charmed dragons, the world of magic and chivalry?*

More importantly, if there was a way, could she take it?

Ahead, behind the deep waters lying far downStone, the mysterious shadow billowed, beckoning the voyagers on.

* * *

127

Jonah could not remember a happier time. Love illuminated his heart, connecting him to Annie with invisible threads of light. Just as welcome as the passion was the intimate school of discovery as they learned more and more about each other, as they shared their memories in more depth than they ever had before.

In telling his past Jonah rediscovered things he had long forgotten: childhood adventures with his brother Albert, the castles they built from smooth wooden bricks; the vast cellar of the gloomy house his parents had owned on the Kent coast before moving to London when Jonah was five. Countless moments, some important, many trivial, all brought alive by the dialogue.

Annie could not forget her dreams. She described the Aqueduct to Jonah over and over again, told him how it tasted of Archan, how the immortal dragon dominated her sleeping hours.

'You'll laugh at me,' she scolded, trying herself to make light of it.

'No, I will not. When we launched this ship of the basilisks I was thinking for the most part of escape. There was the prospect of adventure again, of continuing our journey across Stone. But I believe there is more to this voyage than I ever imagined. And I believe that you, Annie my love, know exactly where we are going.'

'Yes. Yes, Jonah, I guess I do.'

He held her tight. 'But wherever this bridge of glass may be, Archan will not be there. She is gone, my dearest one. I made her gone.'

In the night, Annie was sometimes gone from his side. He would lie half-awake, conscious of the emptiness beneath the covers, and she would slip back in, aware that her absence had disturbed him.

'Bad dreams?' he would murmur, curving himself into the crook of her body.

'They wake me and I have to walk for a while,'

she would reply. 'Don't worry. I'm never gone long.'

They spent hours in the Saloon, cuddled together in front of the wide, curved window. Its underwater view was increasingly captivating to Jonah, particularly at night when yellow fire ran through the deeps.

Furthermore the ocean was filled with magical life. Skeletal, phosphorescent eels, wide-finned rays with human hands tucked beneath their streamlined bodies, galloping horses trailing tenuous gills behind their manes. Charmed creatures, alien ancestors bearing only the faintest echoes of the future world from which the watching humans came. Sometimes they came up to the window and peered in at the two strange creatures staring out at them, their mouths working silently against the transparent membrane.

Once a mermaid passed within a few yards of the Bark, her face pale and sad. Her grey tail was ragged, her short hair knotted with kelp, and she swam with an awkward, lop-sided stroke, as though she were carrying an old wound. Pitiful though she was Jonah felt no sympathy for her: she reminded him all too vividly of the dryads.

Against this spellbinding backdrop Jonah told Annie all about Lily, his first love; he learned in detail about the long journey Annie had endured across the eastern plains of Kansas before the wagon train reached Leighton, learned about her early years with her parents on the banks of the Mississippi. Between them they unearthed stories that as individuals they had forgotten; it was like bringing the past to life.

They had to make a conscious effort to spend time with their companions, and invariably it was Annie who cajoled the naturally solitary Jonah into being sociable. Grandfather Tree was discreet, but seemed to sense when they wanted his company and appeared accordingly, thrusting his gnarled face out of a wall or floor surface and leering at them.

'You should get some rest!' he might say, or, 'When you've finished, then I'll come back,' regardless of what they might have been doing at the time. His manner was relaxed, and he seemed to enjoy in particular the nightly games of Mah-Jongg, which were becoming more competitive the longer the voyage went on. Sometimes the lesky joined them in the Saloon, commenting dryly on the antics of the creatures outside.

'I wouldn't trust those claws,' he warned, pointing out a yellow lobster the size of a sheep. Seconds later a gigantic mouth closed around the unfortunate crustacean, followed by an explosion of bubbles through which they could just make out a pair of glowing eyes and a single, razor-edged fin.

Gerent, who spent most of his time on deck, had cheered up considerably, and was pleased to demonstrate his latest pastime: making nets. Using lengths of rope extruded from the hull by Grandfather Tree (a feat demanding a tremendous expenditure of energy and outrageous amounts of charm, the lesky proudly proclaimed), he had knotted together enough pieces to clad the entire conning tower, as a result of which they could now clamber all over the exposed sphere without fear of falling. Gerent and Annie devised a circuit around the hull's exterior and so they were able to hold races, passing the time and exercising their bodies into the bargain. Jonah joined in occasionally, but never felt entirely comfortable hanging upside-down off a few threads of rope with all of Stone's ocean laid out beneath him. Annie on the other hand loved it, proving herself as nimble as a monkey and usually able to beat either of her male companions.

One day, when the three of them were resting in the sunshine, slung like baby kangaroos in a pouch of netting on the hull's outermost curve, Gerent disentangled himself and without warning jumped out into the sky. Jonah cried out, forgetting the Neolithic man's wings.

Twin triangles of black and red unfurled and buoyed Gerent in the charm-rich air. Slowly, beating his wings with long, smooth strokes, he surveyed the sky.

'Kythe!' he shouted, waving to a bird-shape far away. Eventually, after much gesticulating, he managed to attract her attention.

'Hello!' she gasped as she swooped in, breathless and excited. 'Oh, you're flying ever so well, Gerent. Are you getting used to the wings at last?'

Gerent nodded. 'Do you know, Kythe, I believe I am.'

'You look different,' said Annie, appraising Kythe's new spines and transparent wings. The dragon-child's face glowed deep orange and she looked away, flustered.

'Oh, er, yes. It's just charm, you know, I mean I was just . . . you know,' she concluded lamely.

'It's all right, Kythe,' laughed Annie. 'Enjoy yourself. So long as we know you're safe, that's all. Just don't go too far ahead.'

Kythe threw a quick glance downStone. Jonah thought he saw a tremor pass down her body, but it might have been the wind. 'No,' she said quietly. 'No, I'll stay close.'

After that she flew past the Bark more frequently, and often Gerent was there in the sky to meet her. He did little more than keep pace with the speeding vessel, flying a straight and simple line and refusing to be goaded into performing aerobatics with the excitable young dragon. Yet with every day that passed Jonah saw him grow more assured; he even thought Gerent's wings had grown a little larger since they had set out – was that possible? One look at Kythe's resculpted body assured him it was, but did the Neolithic know it was happening to him too?

Between them, Gerent and Grandfather Tree strengthened the kangaroo-pouch. The lesky stretched thin girders from the hull, announcing his growing skill at manipulating the Bark's tough hide. 'The heartwood I still have trouble with. But the Bark's bark – now that I'll conquer!'

Gerent wove netting around the structure, providing plenty of places for hands to grip, and soon the simple sling had become a solid nest projecting some five feet clear of the conning tower. Everyone enjoyed it in the nest, well away from the waves and with an unparalleled view of the falling ocean. With thinner, lighter nets Gerent managed to trawl for fish, catching an astonishing variety, from which Grandfather Tree selected those most likely to be appetizing.

'Though if you're poisoned,' he warned jovially, 'it's not me you're to blame!'

Everything tasted good, and Jonah found he could not imagine anything magical being poisonous, least of all the iridescent fish drawn from Stone's sea by a Neolithic fisherman.

And so, despite the unearthly surroundings, they slipped into routine: mornings in the nest helping Gerent with his catch, the hot part of the day watching the ocean through the Saloon window, lazy afternoons, evenings back on deck again, having shouted conversations with Kythe or just relaxing in the springy comfort of the nest, before ending the day with a boisterous game of Mah-Jongg. Days flowed past like the wind, merging seamlessly so that, were it not for Jonah's careful tally, they would surely have lost all track of time.

On the nineteenth day the sky changed from its indomitable, white-streaked blue to a glowering grey. DownStone it was almost black. For the first time since their arrival on Stone, it looked as though they were going to hit some seriously bad weather.

*　　*　　*

'You have told me of storms, Lightfoot. I always thought you were exaggerating: you would say, "spinning a yarn". But now I begin to wonder. Is this a storm, do you think?'

Gerent was standing in the nest, gazing keenly downStone, the wind tossing his long, blonde hair across his shoulders. His beard, unlike Jonah's red mane, was still sparse. The labour of making and fitting the nets had built muscle on to his lean frame and even his Nordic complexion, after weeks in the sunshine, was showing signs of a tan. Jonah glanced down at his own pale skin and wondered if he should not have spent a little more time on deck.

His wings rode the air like flags.

By God, the man looks magnificent!

'A storm? Yes, I rather think it is, Gerent.'

It had rained only once that Jonah could remember, the day they had first arrived on the beach. But that had been only a shower, a literal sprinkling of magic. Nothing like this.

The sky to their left was pure cobalt blue and devoid of the usual streamers of cloud; ahead the story was quite different. The entire vertex had been swallowed by shadow, an iron bar clinging to Stone's precipitous slope. Its outer edge feathered softly into the blue but the inner part, the part hugging the ocean's surface, was hard and angry. Even though it was a long way off Jonah sensed violent movement in the cloud-base. Soon he saw faint arcs of blue-white as lightning stabbed at the water. The black cloud extended both up and down as far as he could see: there was no hope of going around it.

'Grandfather Tree,' he called. 'What if we slow down? Come to that, we could stop altogether and try to outrun it by heading back the way we have come. We would lose a day or two but it must blow itself out sooner or later.'

'It must?' said Annie caustically. 'Don't bet on it, Jonah.'

'Lightfoot is right,' said Gerent. 'We must at least stop rather than plunging headlong into such a monster. Lesky! Stop the Bark.' They waited, hearing nothing but the crash of the waves and the creak of charm in the mast. 'Lesky? I command you to stop the Bark!'

Jonah, irritated by Gerent's imperious manner, raised his eyebrows at Annie: it seemed a storm had descended upon their Neolithic friend. But Annie just looked away.

After a moment the lesky appeared, extending a head, shoulders and torso out of the hull. As ever, his skin gleamed like ebony, the same flexible, wooden man-shape they had grown so used to seeing in the most unlikely corners of the vessel. He raised a branch-like arm and tugged reflexively at one pointed ear. His mouth, which normally he kept clear of new growth, was full of twigs, muffling his voice.

'Forgive me. Did I hear you right?'

Gerent scowled. 'If you heard me demand that you stop the vessel then yes, you did hear me correctly. Now stop wasting time and do as I say.'

Grandfather Tree raised one craggy eyebrow and tapped his chin with his finger. 'By the taiga! Such impatience. And so rude!'

Gerent turned away, struggling to control his temper, then turned back and said through gritted teeth. 'I apologize for the tone of my voice, but not for the urgency of my request.'

'Request? A demand it was.'

'Grandfather Tree,' snapped Annie, 'he's said he's sorry. Now will you please just pull in the reins?'

The lesky considered this for a long moment, during which time Gerent's face turned bright pink. Annie put her hand on the Neolithic man's forearm and shook her head almost imperceptibly, her eyes fixed on the wooden figure. At last the lesky let out a long, pine-scented breath. 'Alas! I have to disappoint you. It seems I can't do as you ask. The Bark – it's no longer under my control. Sculpt it I can; steer it I can't. Its own course is it running now. Where we might wish to be matters not at all. We are, you might say, at its whim.'

'Its *whim*!' exploded Gerent, lunging towards the lesky. Annie restrained him with difficulty.

'Calm yourself,' the lesky smiled. 'Journey's end is just one small part of what is after all a journey. Is there not value in every day we travel? Do we make it valid only by reaching a conclusion? Seeds on the wind, that's what we are, my friends. Seeds on the wind.'

'Then we should take our chances in the sky!' cursed Gerent. His hair billowed wildly in the gale.

'Yourselves you may please! My part I've said. If that's your choice then take it, if your mind's your own. Me, I'm going nowhere. You have the choice, if you're foolish enough to make it!'

In a fountain of bark shards Grandfather Tree drilled his way back inside, leaving a coarse knot in the hull's outer surface. Where he had been, Gerent's net was shredded.

Jonah rounded on Gerent. 'Why must you argue with him?' he demanded. 'I thought we were content with each other's company. We should be travelling companions, not adversaries.'

'I do not trust the lesky,' glowered the Neolithic.

'Your temper will be your undoing. Indeed, it will be all our undoing if you are not careful.'

'Grandfather has a temper too,' put in Annie. Her arms were folded across her chest, her lips were tight. 'And while you two bicker that storm's getting closer.'

'But did you not hear what the lesky said?' demanded Jonah. 'We have no control. We must ride this storm out: we have no choice.'

'There is always choice, despite what the lesky says,' said Gerent.

'We have no choice,' Jonah repeated. 'It is only a storm – if we are battened down safely below decks then it may do us little harm. This vessel is filled with charm after all. Come, we should all get under cover now. That cloud has already deepened – I fancy it is approaching us at considerable speed.' Rapidly he scaled the netting. Holding on to the mast with one hand he reached out the other for Annie. 'Come, let me lift you up.'

She gazed up at him, her hair blown into a dark mane. 'Give me a moment.'

'No! Come now, we have only a few moments as it is.'

'Then let me take one of them now.'

'For Heaven's sake, what is the matter with you, Annie? Just come inside.'

'I will. In a moment. But first I've got to speak with Gerent.' Her eyes filled his vision, indomitable eyes.

'Then speak! I can wait!' Jonah was trembling, more with frustration than anger. The cloud was noticeably bigger and where the lightning struck the sea the water was boiling.

'Alone.'

Jonah curled his outstretched hand into a fist and thumped the mast with it. 'Oh, very well! Whatever you wish! But don't blame me if you are both washed overboard! I do not imagine there are many desert islands in this particular stretch of ocean!' Turning with what he hoped was a dramatic flourish he flung himself through the hatch and into weightlessness.

The storm be damned, he fumed. *All of them be damned!*

Instead of retreating to his and Annie's chamber he ascended to the Saloon.

'Grandfather Tree?' he whispered, loitering in the doorway. There was no sound, nor any sign of the lesky.

The room was empty of light charms, leaving only the soft glitter of the water outside for illumination. Jonah walked up to the window and flattened his palms against the warm glass. The sea was deep blue-green, veined with broad ribbons of light and shade, a peaceful realm of strong currents and slow time. It was hard to imagine there was a storm on the way.

He jumped, startled, as a cloud of seaweed trailed past just inches from his face. It revolved, exposing the face of the mermaid he had seen days before. She drifted past and then, with a lunge of her tattered tail, caught up with the Bark, carefully matching her speed to that of the basilisk craft.

To his surprise, Jonah saw that her tail was not the tail of a fish at all. Rather her hindquarters resembled those of a seal, mottled grey with a pair of flippers at the very end. Minute bubbles adhered to close-knit fur like trails of silver. She raised entirely human hands, touching her palms against Jonah's, with only the glass to keep them apart.

This close he could see every detail of her face. She had the same slender features of the dryads, the same full lips; her hair was short and grey, like the fur on her tail.

But it was her eyes that haunted him. Dark-ringed, deep jade, they stared into his soul, pleading.

'How can I help you?' he murmured, his lips brushing against the glass. 'Do you need my help?' She did not react, just swam and stared. *Those eyes!* 'What is your name?'

The writhing of her tail was hypnotic. She removed first one hand, then the other from the glass, then placed them back in position. This time Jonah noticed she had one finger missing on her left hand. The wound was old and smooth, healed clean; the missing finger was the one on which, were she human, she might have worn a wedding band. Her eyes tracked his gaze as he registered her loss, then closed. Abruptly the movement in her tail ceased and the wake of the Bark sucked her away. Her fingers slipped away, leaving faint trails on the window.

'What is your name?' repeated Jonah, his breath misting against the glass despite its warmth. Then he remembered a Scottish word.

Selkie. Seal-woman.

The floor of the Saloon trembled beneath his feet. He was suddenly convinced he had been standing there for hours.

'Grandfather Tree!' he shouted, running his hands down his face. He felt dazed, only half-awake.

Quickly he checked the rooms. Surely Annie and Gerent had come in from the deck by now – but how much time had actually passed? What spell had the selkie cast over him? A cursory glance into each room confirmed they were all empty. He paused beside the charm reservoir and gingerly pulled open the hatch.

Turbulent noise erupted, electrical thumps and thin, whining screeches. Blue light clawed its way through the aperture. Jonah had a brief glimpse of roiling motion and stabs of lightning. There was nobody in there.

'Annie! Gerent!' he yelled into the interior storm. Something exploded inside the reservoir, showering him with sparks. 'Damn it all, where are you?'

There was another explosion. He decided to search the deck.

At first the deck hatch would not open. Fear came, a bitter taste in his mouth, as he imagined Annie fallen across the hatch on the outside. Anxiously he bent his shoulder against the wooden disc, bracing his legs against the curved wall of the tiny, weightless vestibule. The hatch resisted his efforts for a second or two then gave way with a gasp, throwing him out into a tangle of netting.

The gale tore at his clothes and hair, roaring

abominably, cramming its way behind his body in an attempt to prise him clear of the hull. Instinctively his hands bound themselves into the net while his feet flailed outwards. Rain lashed him from all directions, a constant explosion inseparable from the ocean spray. The wind tugged harder, sucking his body away from the Bark.

Slowly he hauled himself back. The wind screamed in protest but was unable to hold him and finally relented, allowing him to wind his arms into the ropes and secure his position. Beside him the hatch flapped wildly. He was inside the storm.

Cautiously he raised his head and squinted into the hot and howling gale. The sky was a steel curtain; the sea was ferocious; rain cut sideways, barb-like. He could not see far – the distance had been swallowed up by darkness – yet all around him the deck was bathed with flickering light. Looking down he saw where it was coming from.

The mast beneath him, with its spider-web sail, was boiling with charm. Charm frothed along the strands of the web like angry dew, charm arced from sail to sky, charm billowed outwards in vast, glowing sheets. Yellow and gold and fire-red, deep blue and pure cold white, the discharges of magic lit up the immediate surroundings like a display of Chinese fireworks. Jonah ducked as an orange fireball careered past his head and buried itself in the sea. The familiar creaking of the mast had become a symphony, its movement that of a cat-o'-nine-tails.

'Annie!' he bellowed into the wind. 'Annie! Where are you? Gerent!'

There was no sign of either of them, but then from here, high up on the dome of the conning tower, he could see relatively little of the deck. Were they clinging on just out of sight, or had they been able to lash themselves to the nest? If so, how long had they been out here?

How long was I in the Saloon, watching the selkie?

Gingerly he freed one of his hands and groped along the netting, securing another handhold before inching his way around the hull's precipitous curve. This was bad enough in brilliant sunshine on a calm sea, but now the Bark was bucking beneath him and the air was filled with teeth. After an agonizing crawl he had worked his way down as far as the mast, but the charm was crawling all over it and he was loath to get too near. A fiery spear jabbed towards his face and he recoiled, losing one of his handholds and reeling back against the hard outer shell of the Bark. The unexpected impact shook both his feet free and suddenly he was hanging by one hand, surrounded by the deafening roar of tempest and charm.

Then the rope to which he was clinging unravelled and he fell.

With a resounding thump he landed on the broad shelf of the nest, began to roll towards the edge then caught himself. Above him the section of net to which he had been clinging, his only safe route back to the open hatch, unwound itself and was torn away by the gale. He was perched alone on a swaying, groaning shelf fixed precariously to the outside curve of the conning tower, with no trace of his companions to be seen.

They have been swept overboard!

Urges came: to bury himself in the waterlogged netting, to stand and beat his breast against the storm, to climb to the light-strewn mast and walk out along its length, heedless of the peril. What reason was there to go on if Annie was gone from his side?

A chunk of netting tore free from beneath the nest and was ripped apart by the wind. The sound was like that of tearing flesh.

Storm be damned! What if they are just round the corner? You have covered barely one quarter of the sphere, Jonah Lightfoot. Now get on and cover the rest!

Bunching the net in his fist he crab-walked to the side, checking the downStone face of the hull. Here the wind was strongest, the netting shredded almost to nothing. There was no sign of either Annie or Gerent. When he looked down Jonah could not see any netting strung around the underside of the sphere at all. If they had been clinging to the conning tower's underbelly, they were not there now.

Which left only the more sheltered upStone side. The place where, if they were clinging to the outside of the hull, they were most likely to survive.

Jonah circled round, his heart in his mouth. The rain hardened, grew more dense, closing down his vision. He saw shadows moving, felt his hopes lift, then saw they were only waves crashing against the hull. He had reached the upStone waterline. They were not here.

They were not anywhere on the Bark. They had gone.

A single thread of rope swung to and fro above his head, an unexpected lifeline leading back to the hatch. Could they have been climbing back up as he was climbing down? Had they simply missed each other? Jonah hardly dared believe it. He grabbed the rope, not caring whether it was able to take his weight or not, and was about to climb when he spotted something shining in the darkness near the water. It vanished, then reappeared: something sticking out of the hull on the waterline.

Reaching down he took hold of it and pulled. A wave gushed across his back, as if he were not already soaked by the rain. At first the thing did not yield then, slowly, it slid out of its hole with a sound like a tooth being drawn. As he pulled it clear, a tiny flash of light winked where the hull had been breached; a wave rose, and when it fell back he saw that the hole was gone.

Jonah held the thing up. It was long and thin, a sharp splinter that looked like wood and felt like steel. Recognition came twice, a weird doubling sensation.

It was the spike on which Annie had pricked the palm of her hand.

It was the broken-off nail of the dryad who had thrown herself after them during their escape from the forest.

As Jonah held it in his hand he could feel it throbbing, could see the busy lines of light shimmering within it, and he had no doubt that it was filled with malignancy. Resisting the urge to hurl it into the storm-tossed ocean, he tucked it carefully into his belt and began to ascend.

8

Roots

I don't know what to say.

I meant to see you, to talk to you, face to face. But when I saw you there, hands against the glass and that creature outside – I just couldn't. I'm sorry.

You're there at the window now, as I write this, and I'm thinking maybe you'll come in and surprise me. That's why I'm writing fast. That and the storm.

Jonah – I've fallen in love with Gerent. God, now I've written it it looks –

I'm sorry. Writing it down's the only way I can tell you. We're going now, Gerent and me, before the storm sets in. His wings are strong now, really strong. He can carry us both, outwards past the storm. Maybe we'll fly with Kythe for a while. He won't let me go, if you're worried.

Leaving you is the only way. I can't think right any more. I loved you – Jonah I know this hurts you but I have to tell it straight, now, it's my only chance and I want you to understand it, understand it all – I thought I could love you forever but I was wrong. I think maybe I do still love you, but –

Love's a bit like charm, you know. I used to swim in the scoop and wonder what the charm was doing to us. At first I even worried it was the magic that was making me love you, that the feelings weren't my own. Does that sound crazy? Then I thought the hell with it and loved you anyway. Now I know *the feelings were mine all along, even when I realized it was really Gerent I wanted to be with. Not you, dear sweet Jonah, not you.*

I don't know what made me realize. Maybe it was the magic after all, taking the scales from my eyes. Or maybe true love is stronger than charm. I don't know. All I know is I've done you a terrible wrong and all I can ask is your forgiveness. I know you don't owe it me.

So it's best we just go, I guess.

Stone's a big place, Jonah. We all know that, you better than any of us. Somewhere in this wilderness there's a place for us all. I've realized my place is with Gerent, but there's a place for you too, Jonah, there really is, I do believe that. And you must believe it too.

Good luck to you. Ride out the storm and go where the sea takes you.

Annie

The page had been torn hurriedly from her journal; its left-hand edge was ragged. The words were obsessively neat, belying the hurry in which they had surely been written.

I was standing in the Saloon, only yards away!

He looked around their room, feeling dazed. The Samsonite case was still there, as was their bed. The two books from the *Bonaventure* were gone, of course. So was Annie's painting box.

How could she have left it behind! The painting box, with its cargo of pigments and tiles and bottles of exotic oils and solvents, had come to symbolize the notion of *survival* for Jonah. It was the only thing they had brought through with them to Stone when Krakatoa had belched them out of the throat of the world. It had become a talisman representing not only their ability to survive in this alien realm but also Annie's ability to survive the prison Archan had made of her mind.

Archan! Annie was possessed by her for days on end! Could it be that the dragon has left some shred of evil in Annie's mind, some punishment for us both? Is it Archan's magic at work here?

Looking down he saw his hands had bunched into fists, crushing the letter. He threw it to the floor, where it lay like a rose. Then he remembered the splinter of wood.

The dryad's fingernail!

He retrieved it from his belt, taking care not to put his fingers anywhere near the wickedly sharp tip. It seemed to vibrate gently in the wavering light of the floating charm, yet to the touch it was hard and cold, like steel. It was nearly six inches long.

Examining it closely he could see the poisons circulating beneath its translucent skin.

Charm has indeed deceived you, Annie, but not in the way you thought. It is not the charm of Stone that has meddled with your emotions but that of the dryads.

Thinking about it he knew it had to be true. Until the day Annie had pricked herself on the dryad's fingernail, he was sure – no, God damn it, he knew! – Annie had loved him truly. Yes . . . afterwards had come the nights when he had woken to find her gone from the bed.

Everything fitted into place.

It was the final revenge of the dryads. Furious at Jonah's escape, they had sacrificed one of their number in the hope of working some mischief – and how they had succeeded!

Swarming across the devastation in his heart came jealousy of Gerent, but somehow he beat it back. It seemed all too familiar, and much too convenient. Perhaps the magic had been working on the Neolithic man too; perhaps none of them were in control of themselves any more.

Even me . . .

The thought was disturbing.

Looking at the splinter focused his mind, reminded him of the bitter anguish he was feeling, the massive, all-swallowing sense of loss. Some primitive part of him yearned to take the splinter and plunge it into his own hand, to see what magic it might wreak on him. Or into his heart, that the anguish might stop.

Instead he turned and drove it into the wall, where it stood trembling and humming like a tuning fork.

'Damn,' he whispered, tears splashing between his feet. 'Damn, damn.'

'A good time this is not,' came Grandfather Tree's voice, 'to ask for help?'

Jonah listened hard-faced as Grandfather Tree – manifesting himself as a mere approximation of a human head and torso, an urgent statue shooting from the floor – explained their predicament. There was, he reiterated, no way for him to steer the Bark. He had indeed lost all control of the basilisk vessel, which was now effectively adrift and at the mercy of the onrushing typhoon.

'Up to you it is, faery,' the statue intoned, its mouth a fixed grin sprouting quivering brambles.

'Up to me?!' exploded Jonah. He had listened and heard little of interest. So what if they were both to drown? Annie was gone! 'What do you expect me to do?'

'Steer the ship, Jonah Lightfoot!' the lesky bellowed, moving not an inch.

'How can I possibly?'

'I was able. Stronger you are.'

'Stronger? In case it had escaped your attention this ship has no bridge. There is neither wheel nor rudder, nor any crew to climb the rigging. Do you expect me to melt into the deck and swim through the hull like you? I am a man, not a faery, a fact which seems to have escaped the attention of far too many people of late!'

Grandfather Tree responded by throwing forth a pair of sinewy branches, which rapidly coalesced into vaguely human arms. 'My hands,' he commanded. 'Take them!' Fingers unfolded from the wood.

'Why?' Jonah thought he heard a distant detonation. His heart, he assumed, breaking.

Annie . . . where have you gone? Come back to me, please!

'Because there is nothing else to be done.'

Jonah took his hands.

Jerked forward like a mailbag snatched by a steam train.

Lesky fingers expand, envelop, their tips enlarging into bulbous foothills, nails like precipices, a landscape to be scaled but already it is moving too fast to survey, just a tide of motion as he slips through and into. The crack between nail and flesh, an alien cuticle splitting open a passage into a realm of sap and slow pulse, the movement growing ever more urgent yet always fluid; except for that initial jerk there has been only . . . flight . . . a rushing, windless flight spearing concentric rings spinning back through the years, spinning too fast to be counted, each its own calendar of seasons, each bearing witness to the rising and falling, the living and dying, the slow-breathing beat of the taiga, the forest, to the life of the lesky. Swimming – half-man, half-fish – through a wooden sea where each tide is a year and each year is a little death, spilling through the knots of winter frost and the endless fall of autumn and the ripe joy of summer and the swelling hope of spring, on and round and round in the eternal spiral at the centre of which rise the high roots of light and life. Growth; renewal; maypole years etched forever in the heartwood.

Soft splinters, their touch like snow.

Jonah swam through the body of the lesky.

Around him living wood flexed like flesh. His vision was simplified, a travelling grid of line and rings, a mathematical journey through another soul. The sound of sap was damp and thunderous, the mother's heart beyond the womb. Tides pressed him back but he surged on, driven not by his own efforts but by a simpler force, an inevitable, expanding movement into a greater world. A force like history.

The heartwood thickened; its flavour changed from pine to something older, something musty and faintly acidic. Ancient metal, coppery. The rings, cycling past like segments of a tunnel, glowed brilliant red then faded altogether. All sensation of movement ceased. Surrounding him was a rhythm, something beyond sound.

He could feel his body again. Fingers pressing their way into hot gloves, legs extended and tightly bound. His torso bound also, limiting his movement. Head filled with light. Eyes gaping, ears and mouth wide. Such smells! Senses overwhelmed. Finger-tips like fire.

Water!

He was swimming. His body was relaxed, neither kicking nor sculling, and he could see nothing but a rippling yellow curtain but he was swimming faster than any man had ever swum before. A magical fish – three pink goat-eyes startled into absurdity – thrashed aside just in time, spilling bubbles from its spiny mouth. A raft of weed and algae tore itself to shreds against his back. Jonah sped through the waves at thirty knots.

Daylight, and there was the typhoon!

There was the typhoon, and he was the Bark!

The selkie was there too, slicing through the peaks and leaping like a dolphin, matching his speed. The tangles were gone from her hair; her body was still old but it looked sleeker, less tattered. The fur on her tail shone like gunmetal.

Accelerating into the shadow of the cloud he moved ahead of her, watching her slip behind him (his vision was panoramic, 360 degrees) and launch herself out of the water towards the charm-laden mast. Grabbing the mast with both hands, tail trailing in the surf, she yelled, 'Behind the waves. Dive, Bark, dive!'

He obeyed because the demand was good. Bark instinct was

148

rising through him like sap and his judgement matched that of the selkie. As the typhoon bit sideways at the waterfall sea Jonah drew the Bark inwards, to the place he still thought of as underwater. The selkie came too, drawn in behind the waves, a half-human remora clinging to Jonah's wooden shark.

Lightning pierced the ocean in his wake but he was moving too fast. It fell away, frustrated electricity.

'I am the Bark!' he sang, pressing his way into every corner of the basilisk vessel.

Hurricane wind chewed the outer skin of the ocean, tearing it to shreds. The sea was shallow here; Bark-Jonah was navigating the narrow slice of salt water sandwiched between the typhoon and Stone. Stone: a drowned wall to his right, encrusted with giant shells and fabulous streamers of coral. The coral was flexible, tracking his motion with pores like eyes, multi-coloured and mysterious, aglow in the phosphorescent depths.

An eel the size of a railway carriage, its back serrated, its mouth a shocked hollow filled with jewels. From its belly jutted a spear made of gold. It was gone in an instant, swallowed by the shadow of the storm.

A school of flattened creatures unlike anything Jonah had seen before. Their bodies were square, almost geometrically perfect, and they moved with the serenity of manta rays. Electricity crackled between them, binding the shoal in a brilliant lattice.

A blue flame, burning from nowhere in the dark and sultry water.

A thousand charmed swimmers, each new species an affront to nature, a miracle of life.

Bark-Jonah explored his new body from within, alert to the strangeness of this rigid basilisk flesh. Human sight had evolved into a kind of omniscient vision, sound into a range-finding super-sense. Unidentifiable data tugged at him, seeking a way into his perceptions, desperate to squeeze beyond the ancient basilisk filters and enter the living meat of his mind.

Lightning that was more than lightning slashed the ocean, barring his way. Bark-Jonah rolled, lashed a whip of charm *about the darting fire and turned it easily aside. More lightning came; he evaded it all and sped on, increasing his speed beside the shaking darkness of the typhoon.*

He cried out soundlessly – it seemed the Bark had no voice. He prepared to swim like this forever.

The selkie intruded. Transmitting her thoughts? He could not tell. Communicating somehow though, magical contact.

. . . Slow down. Be cautious.

. . . I must get through the typhoon.

. . . You will. But you are not prepared for what lies beyond.

. . . What is that?

. . . Best that you come on Her unaware. That way you may see a weakness that has eluded others, if such a weakness exists. This is my purpose. But unaware does not mean reckless! Slow down!

Bark-Jonah obeyed, though it was hard. Bark was an unbroken stallion, built for speed. But Jonah reined it in, shedding knots and hugging the craggy wall of Stone, the better to avoid the lightning seeking him still in this ocean of charm.

Onward, flanking the typhoon, trapped between Stone and the angry sky, denizen of the sea. Swimming forever in a magical light.

Clean coloured light.

. . . Slow down.

The shadow to his left breaking apart, the muffled scream of the wind dissipating. Sunlight piercing the ocean once more, fading slowly to darkness as the water swallowed it. Wave-broken beams flickering all around, cathedral light.

. . . Slow down!

He stopped altogether, basking in the heat of the sun, feeling its radiance embrace the skin of the Bark as he pressed the conning tower clear of the waves again. The mast lapped at the falling, wind-borne charm; he felt its energy fill him instantly, a breathless draught of ambrosia.

Clear sky, with only a trace of the typhoon far, far behind him, upStone. The sheer vertex ahead, downStone. Choppiness ultimately obscuring the view up and down, despite his basilisk vision. A calm afternoon in the sea of Stone.

. . . You have outrun the typhoon. But the storm is far from over. Now you must face Her.

. . . Face who?

. . . You have no choice. But – maybe it is what you would choose anyway. Go now, the lesky is calling.

Something was tugging at Jonah, something harsh and unwelcome. Though he could hear nothing, he knew it was the sound of Grandfather Tree's voice, calling from nearby.

. . . What is your name?

. . . Ruane. Go now.

Movement, suddenly. A backwards flow, suction all around. Noiseless sounds thumping. Darkness.

Jonah opened human eyes, saw his own human hands clutching sticks of wood. He took a breath and gagged, spitting out a mouthful of salt water. His throat was sore, his eyes felt as if they had been underwater for a week. The coughing fit continued for several moments before he was able to bring it under control.

Though he tried to let go of the wooden sticks, they would not release him.

Looking up he saw the angry face of Grandfather Tree.

The lesky looked much as he had when Jonah had seen him upon the Beacon, a scrawny timber giant locked into the floor, his face a gelatinous pool of bright green sap impaled by brambles. He did not remember seeing such an expression of rage however. Twig fingers maintained their hold, splinters biting into his flesh.

'You dare!' Grandfather Tree was intoning, his voice old and damp; the words came out in a kind of furious gargle. 'You dare, you *faery!*'

His grip was strong, but that was the only part of

him that was. A dreadful palsy had overtaken his body, so that he was shaking uncontrollably from liquid head to bark-covered foot. Jonah suspected that if he planted one of his own feet on the lesky's chest, the ancient creature would shatter into kindling.

'What is it that I dare, Grandfather Tree?' He tried to keep his tone reasonable: though he was not exactly afraid, the lesky's grip on his hands was painful and he had no desire to lose any of his fingers.

To his amazement the lesky abruptly broke his grip and folded in half. The shaking transformed into a series of heaving sobs. As Jonah reached out a hand towards his trembling shoulders, the lesky rolled over on to his back and gazed up plaintively, like a dog that has been kicked and beaten. In that ancient face Jonah saw only pain and, despite the great and heavy shadow of age, the yearning of a child.

'Forgive me,' moaned Grandfather Tree.

Jonah considered this latest shift in mood. He had grown used to the lesky's tantrums, and had for some time suspected him to be, if not dishonest, then forthcoming with the truth only when it suited him. For every revelation — such as the confirmation of Stone's spiral shape, for instance – there were surely a thousand secrets still untold. Jonah's heart urged trust however, for basically he liked Grandfather Tree, frustrating and unreliable though he undoubtedly was.

But then he had trusted Annie too.

'Forgive you for what?' he replied tersely.

He thought those green pool eyes narrowed momentarily, but he could not be sure. What came out of the lesky's mouth sounded honest enough; it was certainly straightforward.

'Jealous of you I was. There was I, imprisoned by ghosts. Stripped of my powers I was. Helpless. Then along you came, more powerful than me in every way. More powerful to be, in the future. Revenge it was I wanted, that's all, dishonourable though it may be. Forgive me?'

'I may forgive you, if you would only tell me what it was you were trying to do to me just now.' Jonah had an idea but he wanted to hear it from the lesky's own mouth.

'I can no more escape my prison than you can escape your destiny. As much a prisoner am I as I ever was. The effort it took to move from tree to Bark – nearly killed me it did. Many years' preparation it took, and prepare for it I did, just as Archan long prepared to move from pole to equator in the old world. Escape it was that she wanted too, so perhaps we're not so different. Ha! Timing was good: I knew you were coming, you see!

'When I set the taiga and slipped from the Beacon – ah me! It felt so good! Those dryads didn't know what hit them! But all the time the basilisks were behind me, their ghosts, funnelling me back to where they wanted me. This time the Bark. As good a prison as before, if not so painful. Time dulls most things; pain too, a little.

'The illusion of control – that was brief. I did believe I could sail him, the Bark. At first. For a day I nearly did. Then Bark took charge and a passenger I became. Such are we all: passengers on a ship of ghosts.

'All that remained was to lure you in. When you were weak. Lure you in and trap you in here with me. Let you see the truth; let you share the pain; let you know the folly of those who try to defy the Deathless, the futility of standing in the face of eternity. The madness that awaits those who defy the endless round of Stone! Before you came the dream was mine, but now it is you who dares. I wanted you to fail, like me. I wanted you to despair, like me. I wanted you to suffer. And yet, and yet . . . you have not.

'You have not, Jonah. You have touched the memory rods of Amara and you have survived. You have faced the immortal dragon and you live still. And so I hate you all the more, because you have inflicted on me a wound more terrible than any the basilisks could manage: you have cut me with hope, Jonah. With hope it is that I bleed now, for again I *believe*. I believe you may be the one. What once I abhorred now I must love, though I abhor you still. Abhor because you are all that I am not; love, because you are the only one who can save me.'

'Without Annie at my side, I am not sure that I am ready to save anything. Not myself, not you, and certainly not Stone.'

'Ye. Gone she is. I am sorry.'

'So am I.'

'Was her love as true as you believed?'

Jonah sighed, pressed his hands against the back of his neck and stretched. His vertebrae crackled like dice. He sat cross-legged on the floor, leaning back against the low bed he had once shared with Annie West. Before him, Grandfather Tree was heaped like firewood, his limbs twisted and ill-matched; his deep eyes were alert though, dark green wells.

'My father loved legends almost as much as he loved games,' said Jonah. 'He loved many things, especially those with stories attached. He was a writer, a reporter for the newspapers. One of the stories he used to read to me and my brother Albert was Malory's "La Morte D'Arthur". I used to love the names so much ... Uther Pendragon and Launcelot and Galahad – and King Anguish, that name in particular used to fascinate me.'

'These names I know,' rumbled Grandfather Tree.

'You do? Oh yes, I forget what a traveller of history you are.'

'Story *is* history,' agreed the lesky gravely.

'Well, now I find myself recalling the tale of Sir Tristram, a knight of Cornwall who found himself escorting the beautiful lady Isoud home from her native Ireland so that she might marry his uncle, King Mark. On board

154

ship they both unwittingly drank a love potion prepared for Isoud and Mark by Isoud's gentlewomen. Tristram and Isoud's love bloomed but it was forbidden. They separated, journeying far apart, even marrying others along the way, but their love was never diminished.'

'You drank no potions, Jonah.'

'Annie pricked her hand!' retorted Jonah. 'It was a spell just the same, except Annie fell not into love but out of it. She sleeps now, like Beauty, except hers is a waking dream in which she believes she loves not me but Gerent. The evil charm of the dryads! A curse be upon them!'

'The needle – are you so sure it put her to sleep? Are you sure it did not wake her up?' murmured Grandfather Tree.

'Yes, I am sure! She would not have betrayed me this way! I know her too well. She loved me.'

'Ye. She did. But no longer, it seems.'

'Things can change.'

'Always.' The lesky yawned, revealing the cavernous, briar-filled interior of his mouth. 'So what do you plan?'

'I do not underst . . .'

'What are you going to do about it?' Grandfather Tree sounded exasperated but there was a fresh smile on his face. Again Jonah was amazed by the sudden swing of his mood. 'Sir Tristram – or any of Arthur's knights – would they have sat looking glum? No! Off they would have ridden, to win back their lady fair!'

'That is all very well in the storybooks, Grandfather Tree, but I am no knight and Arthur is just a story.'

'Story. History.' The lesky narrowed his eyes and growled. 'They are the same. Look at me; think of the dragon you have made your companion. Are we not real to you?' His smile became a leer. 'Shall I take you to Camelot? I know the way; I have been before.'

'No!' cried Jonah, louder than he had intended. He

155

went on more softly. 'No. If I go that way it will be by my own means, not as your passenger.'

'Please yourself. But you must do something. About Annie, I mean.'

Jonah stood up, sudden claustrophobia urging him to move. It seemed momentarily that the lesky had grown, had begun to surround him in fact, closing branches and fans of nettle about the place where he sat, forming a living cocoon from which he might never escape . . . He looked down to see the same dishevelled figure, that rude concoction of bark and broken twig inside which the tree-spirit was struggling to survive. Pity returned, calming his fear.

I have nothing to fear from this creature, he thought. *Yet I may have much to learn.*

'The memory rods,' Jonah pondered. Grandfather Tree nodded enthusiastically, apparently eager to please. 'You do not – or rather did not – use them in quite the same way as I, did you?'

'No indeed!' gushed the lesky.

'Tell me about it, please. Because I believe you did not need to touch Stone at all to gain access to the memory rods. Is that not true?'

'True it is. Story is history, as I have said. But what is at the heart of both? Root! *Root*, Jonah! And lesky has plenty of that!'

'Your roots were connected to the memory rods whether they touched them or not! That is what I felt in your forest, is it not? Those spikes protecting the beacon – they were the product of your, your *fusion* with the system of rods.'

'Ye, ye, ye! Of course! Memory is all root. That is what it comes to. And in all the taiga there was much root and much memory. Leskies know this better than most. Trees know the past, Jonah, and their leskies know it all the better.'

By now Jonah was pacing back and forth, his heart thumping. He could feel his mind beginning to drift from his body, his awareness drawing back into the Bark's waiting shell. Was it drifting of its own accord or was it being taken? If the latter, taken by whom, lesky or Bark? He discovered he did not care: he had the strength to resist both and maintain his own agenda. He was in control.

'And now?' he demanded, holding on to his thoughts as a child might hold the string of a kite. 'Can you reach the memory rods now? Can I?'

'Not me, not now. But Bark can. Bark has roots too. He can go anywhere. So can you, Jonah. So can you . . .'

The lesky's voice was growing fainter; the smile on his green face was broad. Triumph or simple pleasure? Again Jonah could neither tell nor care. If this were another of Grandfather Tree's traps let the jaws close: he would slip between them and emerge the other side, free to fly in the realm to which he had been born, the kingdom of the memory rods, the landscape of the past, history, story and root, free to fly, free to voyage, free to dive and climb and slide, free to change.

Free to change the past.

Free to change the world.

No sense of dislocation this time, just an unburdening of the soul, a release of body and gravity and air. A clean departure from the world of flesh and as clean an entry into Bark's ancient timbers. A world of wood, a world of root.

A world of memory.

As the sea is more flexible than the land so the roots were more flexible than the rods. Jonah entered the maze of history like a fish penetrating a coral reef. It was easy, effortless even. He snatched at moments, eavesdropped upon the world of charm as it existed long before his own time, when man was faery and magic was real, before the world turned . . .

*　　*　　*

157

Night. Strange stars, brighter and more colourful than those of Jonah's world, the constellations strange. The sky deep blue, not black; somehow Jonah knew that in this age the night was never fully dark, that this was a time filled with colour, even when there was no light.

The moon rose swiftly above a landscape of long grass and rolling hills. It was pale and yellow, its warm light soft against the sumptuous purple shadows. In the distance, halfway up a shallow slope, a small herd of tall animals grazed. Four-legged, white striped with silver, like slender zebras only zebras do not have horns and these creatures did: each had a single horn jutting from the centre of its forehead. Unicorns, more beautiful than Jonah could ever have imagined. Charm dripped from their pelts like dew; their eyes were old and wise. They were knowing, formidable; intelligent.

What am I? he wondered. His previous travels into history, unlike Grandfather Tree's, had required him to enter the body of someone – or something – that was present at the time. But what about here? Did he require a host in this far-off realm of charm?

He looked down at himself and saw nothing. There was brief panic as he raised his arms and still saw nothing. Quelling the fear he hurried to a pool of water lying nearby and stared into its depths. There was the palest of reflections: his own ghostly face, peering up at him through ancient waters.

This is different! I am voyaging like the lesky now! I am here, *really* here!

Jonah approached the unicorns and they scattered, though none seemed actually to see him. One of them ran straight through him, braying like a donkey, its voice unexpectedly coarse. They crested the hill and were gone, some sixth sense having alerted them to the presence of this interloper, this future ghost.

Another change! What have I done here already? By stampeding the unicorns, what havoc have I wreaked in the future of this world? This world which will become my world?

The moon coasted higher. A dark orange speck descended from the centre of its disc, widening and growing wings as it fell towards the world. It was a dragon, a massive, many-winged dragon with a neck curved high as the arch of heaven. He imagined that, were Kythe to have seen such a noble, savage beast, she would have felt as Jonah might have felt to see Thor himself stride out across the mountains and smite a pass clear through them with his hammer.

He lingered a moment longer, watching awestruck as a trail of smaller dragons followed in the wake of this glorious queen of serpents. There was no doubt in his mind as to where they were coming from.

'My god,' he said aloud in a thin ghost-voice, 'there are dragons on the moon.'

A moment of discontinuity, as a hot wind scattered both him and his thoughts across the aeons. Immeasurable moments passed. Seasons not of years but of epochs; the harvest of species.

Lives tumbled around him, blown like weeds. Multiple viewpoints, glimpses of ancient lives seen through strange eyes. Many seemed to cycle over and over, each repetition spawning subtle changes, growth like the branches of a tree.

You can go anywhere, Jonah Lightfoot! Anywhere at all!

Grandfather Tree's voice echoed around him as he tumbled. Reaching out, he grasped a truth from the wind.

I no longer need to touch the rods!

And it was true. Entering the fabric of the Bark had liberated him somehow, advanced his skills. Now he was free to navigate the rods whenever he pleased, regardless of where he was. Now he was truly more powerful than Grandfather Tree.

Now he, Jonah Lightfoot, relied on nothing.

But is that really true? Might it not be that the Bark is generating the power I need to achieve this feat? It is a basilisk construction after all. Might it not be simply supplying me with the means to make contact?

Yet the power felt as though it belonged to him. He could feel it in his veins like fire. It felt like something he had learned. And like something he would never forget.

No matter: whatever its source the power was real. And he intended to use it.

The harvest . . .

Jonah flew beside the vast slope of Stone. A golden cliff, a shining precipice undulating like an ocean in the falling wind, sped past. Blue sky to his left, paling to the distant vertex where it met a glowering line of orange partially cloaked in a thin black haze. The familiar angles of the Stonescape, the individual features strange.

Things were wrong here – shadows, perspective. The orange and black of the distance made no sense, the clouds were not falling properly. He raised his hand before his eyes and saw nothing: he was still a ghost, then. Ghost or not he could taste the air. Cool and sweet, stiff with pollen, not the air of Amara at all . . .

Spreading his wings like a bird, Jonah rolled. Before him the upright vertex of Stone rolled with him until it was laid out horizontally like the edge of a tablecloth, an unbroken line marred only by an enigmatic black smudge. A horizon. The clouds were not falling at all but ploughing from right to left in an alien sky that was so familiar. The ocean of gold was a field stretching as far as he could see. Corn, a thousand miles of it.

It was not Stone but the world, his world.

He wept invisible tears: though he had dreamed of Earth no dream could match this reality. There was truth here, however flexible a commodity that may have been in the realm of memory. There was an honesty that would not be denied and he revelled in it.

He knew at once where he was, specifically, and why he had come here. Memory is personal, he thought, smiling an invisible smile. However much I may believe myself to be

160

in control of my emotions and animal urges, still I ride the unbridled ape.

No more substantial than a ghost, Jonah Lightfoot soared above the vast and rolling plains of Kansas.

Turning his back on the far-off horizon, he slowed his rate of flight and descended to ground level. The corn was high, astonishingly so. Ears swayed six inches above the top of his head, their voices as ghostly as his presence here.

Jonah walked through the cornfield – literally through the stalks – following his nose. The sun informed him of his compass bearing: due east, in a direction he could not help but think of as upStone.

At first the only sound was the susurration of the corn, a soft insistent hiss. Soon he heard something less soothing, a hard metallic sound, rhythmic in its way but altogether brutal. The sound of the blacksmith at his forge, perhaps. It grew louder, muffled only a little by the corn, so penetrating was it. Then, abruptly, Jonah emerged into clear air.

To either side of a gap some twenty yards wide, the cornfields ran as parallel as railway lines. Or should that not be railroad tracks? *he corrected himself. The ground was bare earth, rutted and scattered sparsely with hay. It was like a corridor cut through the prairie, running to infinity to the south, ending abruptly just a few yards to the north.*

Nearby a pair of oxen stood patiently, chewing the cud. Behind them loomed a frightening machine, all wheels and blades. A reaping apparatus, Jonah assumed.

Just beyond the northern end of the corridor the ground rose in a shallow dome, beyond which Jonah could just make out the pitch of a roof; a thin trail of smoke was drifting to the east. Before the dome was a black hole in the ground. It was from this hole that the metallic sound was rising.

His curiosity aroused, Jonah made his way up to the hole. The oxen behind him seemed oblivious to his presence, making not the slightest move. The hole was rough-edged and deep; he could see movement at the bottom, which was very far away.

A knotted rope, staked into the hard soil, was clearly the only way up and down. Beside it was a ball of coarse linen that might have been a rolled-up shirt.

Abruptly the ringing noise ceased and the rope started to twitch. He stood back, though there was no need, as a big man squeezed his way out of what could only have been a well. He was of prodigious height – six feet and six inches, Jonah estimated – and thick with muscle. Stripped to the waist, the man gleamed with sweat. Attached to his belt was a second rope; hauling on this he drew a basket full of rock chips out of the hole. Wedged into one of the knots holding the basket to the rope was a pick-axe.

He knew who the man was even before the gruff voice shouted it past his shoulder. Nevertheless to hear it spoken came as a shock.

'Rance West! You still wastin' your days in the ground?'

Rance – for that was who the big man was – picked up his shirt and used it to wipe the sweat from his face before shaking it open and hoisting it on to his wide shoulders.

Rance West. Annie's husband!

He appraised the man whom Annie had described as being both violent and possessive. Here was a man who had tracked his wife's movements like a gaoler, and who had beaten her whenever he considered her to have broken one of his many rules. Once he had struck her so hard in the stomach that she had bled for days. That one blow, Annie was convinced, was the reason she had never borne him a child.

That fact had made him mad too, and so he had found even more reasons to use his fists on her.

When speaking of her years with Rance, Annie had always spoken quietly and reasonably. In fact, Jonah could not recall her ever expressing any bitterness about those times. There was sadness, certainly, and occasionally anger, but also . . . a kind of longing. Not for the abuse, most assuredly not, but for what they had once had together, and for what might have been. What should have been.

Regarding Rance now, Jonah felt momentarily wrong-footed. Despite Annie's refusal to condemn her husband, he had never managed to conjure anything but loathing for a man he had visualized as a veritable beast in human guise. Yet, confronted by the man himself, he found Rance easy to look upon.

His face was broad and open, honest and without guile. Sandy hair flapped in unruly fashion in the brisk Kansas breeze, making him seem barely a man at all, more like a boy. Blue eyes gazed out of that face not with aggression but with reservation. He looked . . .

He looks gentle!

Dazed, a little confused, Jonah stepped aside just in time to avoid Rance as he advanced. Ghost he might have been, and affable Rance might have appeared, but he had no desire to get any closer than he had to.

The man who had called Rance's name stood his ground as the tall man approached. He had emerged from the cornfield behind the oxen, which were clearly his: he had patted them both in proprietorial fashion as he made his way past. Much shorter than Rance, he was shaped rather like a barrel, with bandy legs and a massive stomach that looked not so much fat as solid. A thick mat of grey beard covered much of his leathery face, reaching almost up to his eyes. His clothes were clean but heavily worn, as though he washed regularly but never bothered to take them off while doing so. In his eye was the gleam of a buzzard.

'Want your field back, boy?' the old man called with a grin. Revealed was a vivid cluster of yellow teeth. 'Could be your lucky day.'

'One of these days, Clayman, you'll wish you never offered.' His voice: surprisingly soft. Jonah watched Rance's right hand clench and unclench, shaking all the while.

Clayman's grin became a laugh, a raucous sound that bounced back off the surrounding walls of corn. Then his humour vanished as quickly as it had come and the buzzard was back. 'Can't resist, can you, boy? What'll you wager today?

That sorry house of yours, made of shit? Or how about that little wife? I could use her, yessir!'

'I made a mistake,' growled Rance, looming over the old man. Barely two yards separated them now. Jonah was fascinated: surely Clayman was no match for Annie's bull of a husband? *'Let's settle it now, if we must. Man to man.'*

'Will the boy never learn?' shouted Clayman, spreading his arms like a showman as he addressed the listening corn. *'Wasn't your last whippin' enough? You've had enough chances. What makes you think you'll beat me this time?'*

'I'll beat you,' muttered Rance, holding that buzzard gaze.

'What'll it be then? I'm in the mind for a wager again. Now let's see. Seein' as how you lost your field to me last year, how would it be if we bet the same field again? North Field, I'm offerin', boy, and the first two acres west of Knife Edge Field. Winner takes it all!'

'I've got nothing to put up.'

'Just your fists'll do, boy!'

Clayman stared at Rance for a moment, than turned and spat on the ground. *'Devil take you!'* he jeered, then spun round and punched him hard in the belly.

Rance folded in half and fell to his knees, whereupon the old man drew back his boot and kicked him in the side of his head. Rance landed like a meal-sack; Jonah could hear the tinkle of Clayman's spur as it spun frantically on his heel. He thought for a minute that Rance had been knocked unconscious, but then he sprang to his feet, blood trickling from his left ear. Clayman watched him in glee.

Hiding behind raised fists, Rance darted forwards with sudden speed and succeeded in landing a blow on Clayman's shoulder. The old man rocked back but did not so much as stumble; low-set and round he would be almost impossible to knock over. Just as fast Clayman ran in and made contact with his opponent's stomach again.

Rance sagged momentarily then flew back with a veritable torrent of blows, forcing the old man back until he was almost

164

swallowed by the corn. Blood sprayed from Clayman's nose, his eyes rolled in their sockets. He stopped, grasped Clayman by the throat and raised his fist to deliver the final blow. Then, incredibly, one of the oxen lurched forwards and butted Rance in the side, just below his ribs. At the same time the big man trod in a pat of the same beast's dung and fell flat on his back, striking the back of his head on a flat stone. Clayman, bleeding and swearing, followed up the beast's blow with a kick to Rance's ribs, then staggered backwards dizzily, claiming victory in a desperate, cracked voice.

'Too bad, boy!' he croaked. 'You could've been a man of land again! But you ain't never gettin' it back, and if you . . .'

Clayman stopped and sniffed the air, wiping the blood away from his nose to facilitate the operation. Jonah had to suppress a laugh, so broad a pantomime did the old man present as he raised his face and snorted, turning this way and that in an effort to locate . . . what? While Rance picked himself up from the dust Jonah found himself craning his neck in an effort to make out the source of Clayman's unease. Then he remembered he was a ghost here and simply levitated his way above the level of the corn.

He smelt it at the same time as he saw it: a vast curtain of smoke pouring upwards from a brilliant orange glow. It was the smudge he had observed hugging the horizon upon his arrival; now it was much, much nearer.

'Prairie fire!' Clayman squawked. Now he sounded like a buzzard. Screaming abuse at the two oxen he rapidly unhitched them from the reaping machine and urged them away down the alley. He could afford to lose neither beast nor machine to the fire, Jonah guessed, but his apparent concern for the animals was strangely touching. Clayman and his oxen turned a hidden corner and were gone.

By now Rance was marching back to the well, seemingly unaffected by the extraordinary defeat. He looked indomitable, even heroic, and Jonah wondered how Clayman had ever beaten him. He hurled the stone chips from the basket into the corn growing in the nearest of Clayman's fields (by now Jonah had deduced that all the corn he had seen so far belonged to the belligerent old man) and slung the ropes over his shoulder. He trudged to the top of the rock dome, a point high enough for him to see the extent of the fire. Jonah followed and stood with him, staring into the west.

The whole of the field through which Jonah had walked – North Field itself, he guessed – was ablaze. The fire, though burning furiously, had clearly defined extents to both the north and the south.

All at once Jonah understood the function of the alley in which the fight had taken place: it was a fire-break. Wondering where Rance and Annie's crops were, if indeed they had any since Rance had gambled away his land, he swung his gaze round.

On the other side of the rock dome, perhaps a hundred yards north of Clayman's cornfields, was the Wests' house. Smoke from its tilted chimney still scrawled a grey line across the thick blue sky. The house looked slumped and ill-kept, its walls the same mossy green as the ground from which it sprouted like a squared-off tuber. To either side rose fields bearing the same corn as Old Man Clayman's, except this crop was barely half as high and brown instead of gold.

If this was Annie's home, *Jonah thought*, then it is no wonder she ran away. What a dreadful place!

Then he checked himself, looked further than the shabby house and the dying corn, looked out again to the broad green horizon and the glorious sky. The land rolled like a tide that had been charmed to a standstill; the sky's infinite bowl was alive with cloud, an entire world of space and light beyond the reach of mortal man yet close enough to fill his heart with longing. Jonah found he was suddenly, agonizingly homesick for Stone.

'What a big, beautiful land,' he said, his ghost-voice no louder than the beat of a butterfly's wing.

Rance was halfway to the house, walking tall. Catching him

up, Jonah saw that the building was made not out of wood as he had imagined but sod, bricks of dense earth dug from the ground and laid diligently one atop the other. If the house had been here for some years – as it presumably had – then it had obviously been constructed with some care. Its dilapidated condition was, perhaps, more to do with the inferiority of the building materials than lack of maintenance.

Then the door opened and Annie stepped out.

Jonah's heart doubled in both size and weight, threatening to plunge from his breast altogether. It was Annie, indeed, but a much younger Annie than the one he knew. He wondered what year it was and found that he knew already: it was 1874, two years after the grasshopper plague, the story of which Annie had recounted to him on several occasions, and nine years before he and Annie would first meet on the shore of Krakatoa. That would make her just . . .

'. . . eighteen years old,' he whispered.

Yet she looked older than his Annie. Her eyes were under-scored with dark shadows, her body was thin beneath the rough apron she wore. But worse: behind her eyes there was not the bold and spirited woman he had loved but someone downtrodden and faithless. Someone living without hope and without love.

Worse still: he found himself despising her for being like this.

He looked deeper into her eyes and saw that she was not to be trusted.

As Rance West strode towards her, sliding the belt free from the loops in his trousers and curling the end into his fist, as Annie pressed herself back against the sod wall and tracked his inexorable approach with wide, hurting eyes, Jonah found himself wondering if she had not brought all this upon herself.

'Did you betray him as you betrayed me!' he shouted, spilling his heart out not through his breast but through his mouth. Neither of them could hear him of course, but . . . did Annie flinch then? Or was she merely responding to her husband's *shadow as it fell across her face? 'Is that why he hits you, Annie? Does he think you deserve to feel the same pain you have inflicted upon him? That you inflicted upon me?'*

Rance raised the belt, but Jonah could no more bear to watch than he could bear the dreadful torrent of emotions the scene had unleashed. He hated her! He was appalled by his reaction, appalled that he could feel anything but outrage at Rance's behaviour and sympathy for the abused and hopelessly obedient Annie, appalled at the prospect that he might be no better than Rance West himself, that he could be present at such a scene and do nothing to prevent it.

But I could prevent it, could I not? Is this not just a memory, and are not all memories like clay to be worked by the hands of the sculptor?

Spinning upwards into the vast Kansas sky, leaving the sod house and its tiny human drama behind, soaring above the line of the fire as it bore down on Old Man Clayman's smart timber residence in its plush setting of gold, Jonah examined his glassy, ghostly hands and wrestled again with both the ethics and the practicalities of changing the past.

If I save her now will she ever leave, and so will we ever meet and so will I ever have loved her? Yet I have loved her so what could I possibly do that could change that fact? If I do this thing will the hate I feel now turn to love again? Can I ever forgive her for what she has done to me, to Rance?

A single pebble creating a thousand ripples. In changing one memory he would change them all. Such was the peril of the memory rods.

Amara's strength was that it resisted change; tiny alterations were possible that would shape lives but not necessarily alter the broader sweep of history. This much Jonah understood, not from any gained knowledge but from a deeper, primal understanding of the nature of time as manipulated by Stone, an understanding afforded only by his special status as an adept of the rods. However, the skill lay in recognizing which changes were tiny enough to be absorbed . . . and which would have a more devastating effect.

Early on in his encounters with the rods, Jonah had been presented with the opportunity to change the day on which his father and brother had died. To save their lives. He had chosen not to. Still he found occasion to wonder if that decision had damned him, even though he could still choose to return and perform the miracle he had not dared to the first time around.

He fled into the sky now because he did not believe he could be so strong a second time. Faced with the sight of Rance whipping Annie with a leather belt, he would not be able to stop himself from tearing that memory to pieces, twisting past events so that Rance had been killed in the brawl with Clayman, or that he had never been born at all.

Or so that Annie had been punished every day instead of every week.

It was in his power to do such things, and the knowledge was terrifying.

So into the air he flew, letting the fields of Kansas sink below him as he tried to outpace the tangle of his thoughts. His grip on this moment had already begun to slip and other memories, other places were trying to take its place. His limbs felt stiff, as though they were made of wood, and his mouth was filling up with the taste of salt water.

A voice rolled in like the prairie fire. He recognized it at once as Grandfather Tree's, but at first he could not make out what the lesky was saying.

The words, when deciphered, struck a blow as hard as that which had knocked out Rance. They stayed with him as he plunged into unconsciousness.

So obvious, was his last thought before darkness swallowed him. Why did I not perceive this before?

What Grandfather Tree said was, 'Memory is not absolute, Jonah Lightfoot. It is personal. This you must realize. And if it is personal, then it is biased. It is coloured. It is tainted. It can

169

deceive! *So, when you are navigating the rods, an important question you must ask yourself:*
   ' ''Whose memory is this?'' '

9

Goddess

The deck of the Bark had been ravaged. Not one of Gerent's nets remained, and the patina of barnacles and scale had been scoured away by storm and sea. The hull, though still intact and quite watertight, now bore deep grooves and a series of ruts like great stab-wounds, as though the wind had grown claws and tried to prise the occupants from the vessel like a snail from its shell.

The sea and sky, by contrast, were blank and uniform, and in such perfect balance that Jonah could not decide which was reflecting which. Utterly cloudless and as smooth as the water it flanked, the sky might have been a second wall of water, an immaculate mirror of Stone's remarkable ocean.

"'And the waters were a wall unto them on their right hand, and on their left,'" he spoke into the gently falling wind.

A mote of dust materialized in the vastness of the sky, grew wings, drew nearer. Jonah watched it approach from his perch beside the deck hatch, occasionally casting his eyes downStone towards the immense shadow drifting there behind the waves.

The Bark was still moving downStone, but slowly now. Charm trickled through the spider-web sail; the only disruption in the sea was the gentle wake of the basilisk ship. UpStone, only recently arrived in the sky, the warm sun of Stone coasted out along its invisible track.

It was a beautiful morning.

Kythe had much news. Jonah listened eagerly as she regaled him with her account of the storm, as experienced from her vantage far out in the sky. From there she had, in Earthly terms, been above the clouds; on Stone, 'above' translated simply into 'beyond'.

'It was like looking out across another ocean,' she gushed, spreading her new translucent wings wide for dramatic effect. 'Only this ocean was black and angry and full of flashing lights. What was the name you used for it? Lighting?'

'Lightning,' Jonah corrected, amused by the dragon's childish sense of wonder, her simple enthusiasm for something so dreadful.

'Lightning! Yes, that was it. Anyway, I made sure to keep well out of the way and it was mostly trapped inside the clouds, but even so the lightning sometimes stabbed out into the sky. It never came too near to me, even though it did scare me a bit.'

She paused and lowered her head, her eyes wide. Perched on the Bark's mast like some giant bird of paradise, she looked resplendent with her brilliant orange scales, gossamer wings and shimmering spines. Stray charm streamed over her body, running down the leading edges of her wings like dew and pooling against her flanks. Jonah thought she looked older and larger and most comprehensively *alive*.

'Do you feel different, Kythe? You look different to me.'

'Oh yes! Yes, Jonah, I do! It's the charm, of course: I can feel it doing things to me. Can't you feel it doing things to you too?'

'I do not know, Kythe. But . . . yes, I suspect the charm is changing me just as it is changing you.'

Kythe shifted nervously from one clawed foot to the other.

'I saw them,' she blurted.

Jonah nodded, unsurprised. The news was not unexpected, nor did it stir him. His heart was numb. 'Did you speak to them?'

'No. They were too far away. Not too far for me to recognize them, of course. Gerent's wings looked enormous! Jonah, he looked spectacular . . .' Her voice trailed away and she looked stricken. 'Oh, I mean . . . oh dear.'

'Go on, Kythe,' Jonah said gently.

'Well, I saw them flying near to the clouds, much nearer than me, but safe enough, as far as I could tell. I was afraid of going that near but Gerent seemed to know what he was doing. Annie was holding on around his waist – I think they'd made a sort of sling, though it was hard to see from that distance. At first I couldn't imagine what had happened – I thought maybe you were dead! Then I saw them . . . oh, I'm sorry Jonah, but I saw them, you know, kissing.'

Jonah stared past her into the infinite blue, testing his reaction, such as it was. His heart felt as empty as the sky.

Turning his gaze downStone, he extended a finger towards the ominous shadow in the sea.

'And that?' he asked. 'Did you see that too, Kythe?'

She nodded, trembling.

'Do you know what it is?'

'No. When the storm was passed I carried on flying downStone. I was far out into the sky by then and I couldn't see the Bark any more. I could see that shadow still, climbing up behind the waves, but I couldn't make out what it was and I didn't want to get any nearer to it than I'd got to the storm. I felt scared and alone and all

I could think of doing was to keep on flying. The charm felt even stronger after the storm – I could feel it right through my body – so I just went on and on and on.'

'Until?'

She fixed him with young dragon eyes and an old, knowing gaze. 'Until I reached the other side, Jonah!'

At this Jonah sat upright, his heart racing. Part of him was able to wonder that he should feel more emotion at this news than at the sighting of Annie and Gerent; but it was a small part only, and one quite overwhelmed by the prospect of an end to this fateful voyage. 'The other side! Do you mean that you have seen the opposite shore of this damnable ocean, Kythe?'

'I've done more than that, Jonah: I've landed there!'

'Then what is it like? How far away is it? Is it a land? Is it like the parts of Stone we have already travelled, or does it hold wonders the like of which we have not yet seen?'

'So many questions!' laughed Kythe, fluttering her wings so that spirals of charm spun from their tips like Catherine-wheels. 'I didn't stay there long, Jonah, but I can tell you that it's a very peculiar place. I've never seen anything quite like it. It looks like a wall of ice but it's all curved and half-melted and it's not cold. There are things inside it too, trapped inside it, things like shells, and there are lots of tunnels half in and half out of the water. Oh, and there's a tremendous whirlpool right near the shore. I'd stay well away from that if I were you!'

'A wall of ice, yet not ice,' pondered Jonah, recalling Annie's dream. 'Did you see anything resembling a bridge, Kythe?'

'No, but I didn't fly far across the ice wall before I turned back. The wind was getting stronger and gustier and the surface of Stone was ... kind of bulging and stretched. I was getting scared again so I turned back and came looking for you.'

'And I am very glad that you did so, Kythe, and that you found me.' The young dragon looked away, suddenly troubled. 'Kythe, whatever is the matter?'

'Oh, I don't know. Yes, I do: I'm *lonely*, Jonah. Here I am in a fabulous charm-filled sky, flying just as dragons were always meant to fly, with wings filled with magic. This is what it must have been like back in the old world, in the glorious golden age of charm, when great leaders like Halcyon and Destater ruled from mighty dragon citadels. Can you imagine those days? I can – I've dreamed of them all my life. And now here I am flying in just such a sky, expanding my wings, growing more and more strong with every charm-laden breath I take . . . and I'm alone.'

'I know of no way to return you to your family.'

'I don't want to go back to my family! I want to go back to the world I've never known. I want to go back to that golden age, Jonah! I want to see a sky alive with fire and the shining hides of a thousand golden dragons. Jonah, I want to go home!'

She stopped abruptly, panting hard.

'Golden ages are not always what they seem,' Jonah said gently.

'I know that. But I want to find that out for myself.' She paused, a wistful smile on her face. 'And I would dearly love to see the moon, Jonah. I think it is that more than anything that captivates me.'

The Bark lurched beneath them, almost tipping Kythe from the mast. Her wings unfurled gracefully for balance, throwing glittering charm across Jonah; its touch felt like the fall of tiny embers, or snowflakes.

'What was that?' she quavered.

Jonah did not answer: he was inspecting his skin where the sparks of magic had struck. At length he turned his attention to the water: the sea was growing choppy, though the wind was still practically non-existent. Looking downStone, he was not surprised to see that the shadow had drawn a little nearer.

It seemed unimportant.

His encounter with the past had left him drained. As he lay back against the Bark's round hull, basking in both the warm morning sun and the heat radiating from Kythe's body, he tried to recall the moment when he had seen Annie emerge from the Kansas sod house. It was difficult – the memory was elusive – and even when he managed it he could not revive the feelings. The emotion had simply gone away.

The contempt, the anger, the conviction that she was untrustworthy, a betrayer, a woman who deserved to be punished.

The emotion has left me because it was never mine in the first place. It was his – Rance West's.

'What is it, Jonah?'

And so he told her about the Kansas memory, about the loathing he had felt for the woman he loved, about the confusion that had subsequently descended upon him, about how he had hauled himself away from the scene of Rance beating Annie like a dragon taking flight, soaring back over the fire-break, over the corn, back to the waiting world of Stone and sea . . .

'You see,' he concluded, 'all this time I have been aware of my ability to travel through time by way of the memory rods, and all this time I have believed that the past is fixed and immutable – unless such an adept as myself should come along and change it, of course. How foolish of me to believe such a thing, and how utterly wrong I have been! History is not what is written but what is experienced, and to experience an event is to personalize it. Not until now did I realize that for every event in history, past or future, there are a thousand memories. A million, or perhaps a number that cannot be counted. All of them different. All of them true.

'History holds many truths. Some appear quite at odds with each other, such as the fossil record which tells me that there was never such a creature as a dragon, set against the plain fact of your existence. You and I share an ancestral world, but the histories which brought us here do not agree. They contradict one another, yet they are equally valid. They are incompatible. *Yet they are both true.*

'Then, on a smaller scale, there are individual memories. My own memory of the day my father died in the grounds of the Crystal Palace, for instance, crushed beneath a fallen concrete dinosaur. An absurd death, it seems to me now; at the time it was like witnessing the hand of God. What might I see were I to view that scene again, this time through the eyes of my father? Or my poor brother Albert, who died with him? Would it differ so greatly, would I find a new truth? Would I find that my memory of the event – the memory of an eight-year-old boy – is confused, inaccurate? Wrong? Do you see, Kythe, do you see? Where is the truth in all this, in all of history? How can we ever know what really happened? Annie told me that Rance became unbalanced during the year of the grasshopper plague, but perhaps Rance was quite sane. Might it not have been Annie who lost her mind? Perhaps Rance beat Annie because she was unfaithful to him, as she has been unfaithful to me. How can I know, Kythe, whom can I believe? Do you see? It was *Rance's* memory of the day of the prairie fire. That's why I felt all those awful things: because *he* felt them. What if I were to go back and watch the same thing through the eyes of another? Through ... through Annie's...' He stopped: the idea was shocking, an intruder inside his mind.

'Jonah, you're trembling.'

He buried his head in his hands. 'The idea scares me. What if I find that the feelings were my own after all?'

The Bark lurched for the second time, more gently, and a dripping face appeared over the curve of the hull. Jonah looked up in amazement.

'You! The selkie,' he exclaimed.

'Hello, Jonah,' she replied.

Her voice was old and deep. She herself was old, something he had known all along but which became more apparent the further she pulled herself on to the deck. Out of the water, her pale skin was dull, tinged with a drab, grey hue. Water clung listlessly to her seal-tail and lingered in her short, grey hair. Her face, though not heavily lined, bore the weight of long care; it was, however, quite beautiful.

'H-hello,' he responded. Slowly and with considerable effort – as though it were at great cost that she left the water at all – she shambled to his side, clutching with her hands and thrusting with her tail and showing none of the grace with which Jonah had seen her swim.

At first she seemed as sad as when he had first set eyes on her; then he realized the frown on her face was one of simple concentration, for as soon as she flopped down next to him her face relaxed into a radiant smile. Young eyes shining in a worn face, a face into which any man might fall . . .

'Ruane,' he murmured, recalling her name at last.

The selkie curled her seal-tail forwards and clasped it in her hands. The motion was smooth and unhurried, and vividly demonstrated her non-human anatomy. Somehow Jonah had imagined there were legs concealed beneath that dense grey fur, as though she were nothing but a costumed performer in some gay West End revue; but to see that tail flex in a fashion not even the most limber contortionist could have managed was to prove her alien origins once and for all. She waited, as if she

were aware that Jonah needed time to compose himself;
all the while those jade eyes tracked him from beneath
dark brows.

'You are sad,' she said at last, when she deemed it
appropriate to speak. 'That is to be expected, if the
woman you love has gone.'

'How do you know that?' Jonah demanded. The
encounter was at once dreamlike and agonizingly real.
He could see every filament of the selkie's hair, every
droplet beaded on her waterproof pelt.

'I saw you together through the eye of the Bark. You
looked out at me. Now you are alone and your face has
become sad. Am I wrong in my presumption?'

'The eye of the . . . oh, the window.' Jonah gazed into
her eyes, then sorrowfully shook his head. 'No, no, you
are not wrong.' Awkwardly he reached out his hand. 'I
should be thanking you. Did you not assist me in the
storm? It certainly felt as though you were guiding me.'

'I was there,' she agreed demurely, her face creasing
into a smile. She placed her hand in his. 'And I am pleased
that you remembered my name.'

Kythe had begun to squirm around on the mast, clearly
uncomfortable. Ruane turned to look at her, shielding
her eyes from the sun's glare. 'Hello, dragon,' she called.
'What is your name?'

Kythe told her, relaxing again now that she been
included. Shuffling along the mast towards the place
where it was rooted in the hull, she listened eagerly as
Jonah and the selkie talked.

'What happened to your finger?' Jonah was asking,
He was still holding Ruane's left hand and the gap left
by the missing ring finger was plain to see; the scar was
smooth and neat, almost surgical.

'All the selkie women are branded in this way,' she
explained. 'It is strange for me to have to tell you this,
so fundamental is the knowledge, but I must remind

myself that you are not of Amara, and many of the things I know are not known to you. There is much I wish to tell you, Jonah, and I hope you will trust the truth of it.'

'Truth?' replied Jonah. 'Well, I will do my best, Ruane. That is all I can promise you.'

'Yes. But you asked me about my finger, and I have told you little enough . . .' But she got no further before the Bark shook violently. It sank sideways into the water as though something were pressing it towards Stone, then bobbed outwards like a cork submerged and suddenly released. Before he realized what was happening Jonah found his arms flung around Ruane's shoulders, while the flippers at the end of her tail were entwined in his legs; their touch was soft and warm. The embrace was entirely functional, as they struggled to keep themselves from being thrown overboard, however the proximity of her flesh, however strange the form, was arresting.

Kythe lost her grip altogether and was flung quite free of the mast. 'I'll stick to the sky, thank you very much!' she called, cycling her wings in the charm-laden air. 'I'll come aboard again when you've learned to steer that thing properly.'

'It is not my doing, Kythe, I can assure you.' Carefully he disentangled himself from the selkie's embrace and established a better position for them both, close enough to the mast so that they could hold on to it should another surge come.

'It is Her!' cried Ruane, pointing dramatically down-Stone. 'She comes!'

A wave was speeding towards the Bark, a thick band of water like a terrestrial roller turned on end. Foam was cascading from its breaking edge, showering out beyond the limit of the attractive power keeping the ocean tipped sideways and falling in a fine, turbulent mist. Beside the wave, behind the translucent blue of the water, came the shadow.

'Who is she?' Jonah shouted over the steady crescendo. 'What is it?'

'She is Rata Kadul, Queen of the Sea! The Ocean Goddess!'

The velocity at which the wave was approaching drained Jonah of all feeling. It was like Krakatoa all over again: vast quantities of material propelled through space at impossible speed, a tidal wave large enough to swat a continent. Perception shifting uncontrollably (now it seemed the wave was not rushing towards him at all but remaining still and simply growing wider), he scrambled numbly towards the hatch, gaining its sanctuary seconds before the Bark began to roll outwards along the wave's precipitous leading edge.

Scant inches behind him as he tumbled through the hatch was Ruane.

'I won't leave you again, Kythe!' he shouted past a blur of seal-skin. Paper-thin wings glowed in the sunlight, hauling her away.

'I'm not going anywhere!' came the dragon's cry. 'Just shut the hatch, Jonah!'

An enormous curtain of blue-green wiped away the sky, its far edge fluttering like white fire. Kythe was eclipsed; Ruane beat Jonah to the hatch by a fraction of a second, slamming it shut just as the wall of water crashed against it. The Bark revolved, the sudden motion ejecting human and selkie out into the weightless Shaft where they bounced and rebounded as the long chamber spun in stately fashion around them. A pair of light-charms rattled high up in the Shaft, painting the confusion with erratic strokes.

Jonah shouted for Grandfather Tree but there was no sign of him. All he could do was draw up his knees and try to protect his head with his hands as best he could. It was like riding a carousel in an earthquake.

Any moment now, he thought, *my stomach will leave my body by way of my mouth.*

181

The rotations began to slow, then subsided to a gentle rocking, a sensation which Jonah, having spent many months on a barque between England and Java, found rather comfortable. He opened his eyes to find Ruane floating nearby, her tail flexing as though she were still underwater.

'I suppose this does not feel unnatural for you,' he blurted. 'What I mean to say is, I believe this floating sensation to be a little like swimming.'

'A little.' She gave him a wan smile.

'Oh dear! Are you . . . what I mean is, should we get you back into the water? Can you breathe? Well, of course you can breathe, but . . .'

'Calm yourself, Jonah. I breathe the air just as you do; I am no fish. I can survive well enough in the open air, though not indefinitely. A selkie's skin will dry out if left too long without water, but many days would have to pass before that happened. Relax: I am not in danger.'

Something thumped against the hull, the sound dense and blurred.

'I am not so certain,' commented Jonah.

Ruane moved through the air seemingly without effort, half-swimming, half-flying. She grabbed at Jonah's hand, tugging him towards the entrance to one of the bedrooms.

'Come. Is this the way to the Bark's eye? The window?'

'Next floor.'

The Saloon was dark, the window screened over. There were no light-charms in here, nor did the ones from the Shaft follow them in. Jonah called for the lesky again, but again there was no response.

'Can you open his eye?' Ruane's voice was soft and low. She heaved herself across the floor towards the shuttered window.

'What will we see out there?'

'Can you?'

He sighed. 'I can pilot the Bark, so I am sure I can find a way to throw open the windows.'

It was surprisingly easy. No sooner had he knelt on the hard floor, preparing to force his hands *into* the wood in search of the appropriate trigger, than he felt his senses begin to mingle with those of the Bark again. Just as with the memory rods, he no longer needed to touch the Bark to control it.

As a corner of his mind became one with a corner of the Bark, he sensed a fleeting movement, a sudden whiff of pine. *Grandfather Tree!* The lesky was still in there, skulking through the fabric of the Bark, for some reason unwilling to present himself. *Perhaps he is afraid of what is out there.*

Or perhaps he was concocting another scheme, another betrayal.

No matter. Jonah would deal with him if necessary. But now, he too was concerned with what was out there. He instructed the Bark to open the window shield.

Ocean light flooded in, yellow-green and luminous and fragmented by a thousand dancing ripples. The pattern of the waves on the tilted ocean surface turned the sunlight into questing beams, probing the depths like torches in mist. The water was thick, visibility poor.

Ruane slithered up to the window, her head and shoulders raised up to form a human silhouette against the underwater panorama. She looked tiny against the vast body of the sea.

Something filled the sea.

It grew from the distant murk, at first a flat shape, an indeterminate profile cut from board. Then, as it passed through the flickering sunbeams it seemed to inflate, to acquire solidity. The beams splayed across its surface, hesitantly describing its form.

A great wave passed down the length of the shape and it moved downwards, rolling over like a barrel as it both plunged and advanced, drawing still closer yet dropping below the level of the window. Jonah had the impression that it was not only immense but immensely variegated, smothered with texture and secondary forms, not so much a shape as a collection of shapes, a planet with a million satellites in tow. Huge and grey and utterly unstoppable.

A vortex twisted past the window, alive with bubbles and strands of weed. The thing, whatever it was, had disappeared from view.

The bubbles broke apart, leaving the gentlest turbulence.

Jonah had just joined Ruane at the window, and was leaning over in an effort to see where the thing had gone, when it returned; its slow approach and sudden dive had been the preamble to its grand entrance.

'Quickly!' hissed Ruane. 'Can you make more eyes?'

'More eyes? Oh, I see. Yes, of course.'

'Open the Bark up, Jonah. Now is your chance to look upon the Goddess. It is your best chance to understand Her, for nothing I say could describe Her to you as well as your own eyes.'

Drawing in his breath he reached once more under the skin of the Bark and tugged *thus* . . . and the walls and roof of the Saloon turned transparent.

They both cried out, human and selkie, and Jonah reached out a dizzy hand to reassure himself that the window was still there, that there were windows all around them in fact, for it seemed to him that he was standing quite exposed on a circular platform, with nothing between him and Stone's vast ocean.

But there was no time to wonder at this, for the Goddess was here.

She rose upwards from where she had dived beneath the Bark, moving with the momentum of a continent adrift on the aeons. Her head was sleek and broadly human, with a tangled mane of pale grey hair. It was elongated, streamlined in fact, and Jonah was reminded of the profiles he had seen of Egyptian women who as babies had had their heads bound with cloth so as to alter the shape of their skulls. Her face was light of skin and fair of feature and her eyes were closed, and She was a giant.

It took thirty seconds or more for Her head to pass through Jonah's field of view, from the knot of hair at Her crown to the elfin point of Her chin; it was, he guessed, a hundred yards high. His mind, always ready to count, reminded him of the ratio of head size to total height in a typical human adult.

She would measure nearly half a mile from head to toe, were She human . . .

There was plenty of opportunity to contemplate these astonishing statistics. Now Her neck was arching past, and here Jonah saw signs of the heavy texture he had sensed before. Tendon-lines, thick as factory chimneys, were scaled with growths and corals; pink sponges swarmed in the hollow at the base of Her throat. Around Her neck was slung a slim blue rope, to which were attached thousands of tiny pink shapes. Jonah could not make out what they were through the obscuring tangles of Her hair. Shoals of tiny silver fish darted like shooting stars in Her shadow.

As She rose She rolled. Her shoulder lifted into view, a round mountain crazed with limpets and long, searching worms. Now they were looking across Her back. Here the flesh was livid red, alive with motion; Her spine was a thoroughfare for countless species, few of which Jonah recognized, even after so many days spent adrift on this magical sea. Squid with too many arms, shellfish crackling with electricity, tigers with fins . . . there were too many to count. This was no creature, no individual – this was a *land*!

The Goddess's back went on forever. Jonah could feel pressure against his forehead, then realized he had fallen forward against the invisible window, unable to support his own weight any longer. With the realization his legs buckled and he sank to where Ruane lay on the floor.

'Are you all right, Jonah?' she asked gently. 'Are you amazed?'

'Yes, Ruane. I am amazed.'

In the downStone direction the sea was no longer visible: the Goddess occupied one half of the entire world. Moreover, She appeared to be growing as she presented more and more of herself to their perusal; or was She simply drawing yet nearer? Jonah could not tell. He was becoming disorientated.

Now he could not see Her skin at all. Her lower body was a little like that of a gigantic whale, heavily encrusted with barnacles and indeterminate growths, crags, humps, finned outgrowths and deep craters, a whale or perhaps a moon . . . it was all blurring together, and Jonah was about to turn away, to try to find a handhold for his mind as it slipped towards hysteria, when he saw the first of the tethers.

A thin strand of blue hemp, just like the cord She carried about her neck, was embedded in the coarse flesh of the Goddess. It shone against the drab and broken hide like a line of fire. Jonah craned forwards, trying to see the other end.

It came into view quickly enough; it was tied around the waist of a selkie.

She was very like Ruane, younger and a little plumper but clearly of the same species, possibly even the same family. Her jade eyes opened wide as she saw Ruane and Jonah looking out at her. Ruane yelped, a sharp sound exactly like a seal. He saw that the tethered selkie had a missing finger too.

'Why does she not free herself?' he asked, but he saw the answer even before Ruane could speak.

The blue rope was not knotted – it had actually been fused to the selkie's flesh. To free herself she would have to shed her skin.

'Few of us escape,' Ruane mourned, touching her own waist. Jonah could see no marks there, no sign of a wound or even a scar. He saved his questions for later; for now all he could do was look. 'Look – here are the others.'

They appeared then, all of them, a hundred selkies and then a hundred more, and then yet more still, a never-ending stream of semi-human forms both male and female, each held captive by a single thread of blue notched into the hide of the Goddess. They should have been sad, their faces downcast, these prisoners of the deep, but when he looked closer he saw not a gaol but a community.

There was laughter and joy, sadness too to be sure, but in no great measure. There were selkies deep in conversation, gesticulating to each other in an elaborate sign-language; there were selkies embracing in friendship and passion and all points between; selkies swam and selkies even slept. Grey selkie bodies thronged the currents thrown out in the wake of the Goddess, united and for the most part uninhibited by the web of blue that defined the parameters of their prison.

'Is this . . . is this your *home*?' stammered Jonah, goggling as a fresh crowd of selkie prisoners was hauled past the transparent bubble protecting their viewing platform. Some kind of wrestling contest was going on in the midst of this group: an audience was clustered round a pair of males who were busily trying to squeeze the air out of each other's lungs. The crowd was gesticulating wildly, urging their favourites on with frantic hand signals. 'But how do they breathe?'

Ruane regarded him balefully. 'At regular intervals the Goddess comes to the surface.' She paused, allowing the import of this to sink in. Then she continued, 'If She is displeased She waits a little longer between breaths.'

'I imagine She can hold her breath rather longer than the average selkie?' ventured Jonah. Ruane nodded, the mute confirmation more than sufficient to fill him with horror.

'However,' Ruane went on, 'genocide is not at the front of Her mind. It is a long time since She grew so angry, but even in those dark times She allowed some small number to survive. For what is a Goddess without Her worshippers?'

'What indeed?' echoed Jonah, watching as the crowds of selkies thinned and finally disappeared altogether. All that remained was the great, grey tail of the Goddess, growing ever more slender and ever more smooth until suddenly it flared into a pair of tremendous flukes, each the size of Trafalgar Square. They flexed, just once, knifing the ocean, then they too were gone. All that remained was Her enormous silhouette, receding into the dense green above their heads, flattening back into two dimensions as it rose out of the sunbeams and into the high and distant shade.

'*Is* it a prison?' Jonah asked when the Goddess had finally vanished. 'And if it is, can you tell me how you came to escape? I gained the impression your fellow selkies are not unhappy with their situation. Do they crave freedom as I presume you did?'

Ruane stared through the towering sunbeams. 'These days there are few who realize they are not free, nor do they even understand the concept of freedom. Rata Kadul is our Goddess; She is our provider and our world. To believe in a world beyond Rata Kadul is blasphemy.'

'Then you are an outcast?'

'Yes. But what I am gives me purpose, for my people

are imprisoned. Rata Kadul has become a tyrant, a monster. She no longer heeds the laws She once obeyed. She no longer cares. She must be brought down.'

Jonah waved his hand at the immense green dome of the ocean. 'How long have the selkies lived in this way?'

'Ever since they came to Amara, many generations ago. Legend tells of a time in the old world when the sea boiled and our forefathers were dragged through into the falling ocean of Amara. The legend is old and worn, but we know it to be true.

'The charm of Amara is strong, stronger than it ever was in the old world, but it is mixed with the threads of charm that spill across from the old world from time to time. This charm is twisted, filled with malice and strange intentions. Some say it carries a plague of infertility. Cailin, the largest of the selkies who came through, was caught by this broken magic and turned into a giant. She was the first Goddess, and she was strong and good.

'She took a tax from the other selkies and bound them to Her, driving spikes into her tail so that She might be reminded of the pain they felt at their lost freedom. In return She gathered about her a mighty crop of life from which the selkies might draw a constant harvest. Cailin became Rata Kadul, Goddess of the Ocean, giant of the sea and benefactor of all the creatures of the deep. Her reign lasts for one thousand days then She withers and another grows to take Her place. To be chosen as the next Goddess is the greatest honour.'

'"A mighty crop of life",' echoed Jonah, pressing his hand against the window. 'She is like a living garden, then. Why, there is practically an entire coral reef alive on Her back! But what is this tax you speak of . . . oh, the necklace! I have just realized what it is made of!'

Silently Ruane raised her left hand and spread out her thumb and three fingers.

'Rata Kadul takes a finger from each new-born selkie

female as a sign of fealty. To begin with the act was purely symbolic, but the broken charm wove its way into the law and made it a requirement of succession.'

'I do not understand.'

'In early times, any female selkie had the potential to succeed the failing Goddess; the choice was made at random at the whim of the charm. Now however, only a selkie with all her fingers intact is permitted to rise to the throne.' She looked earnestly into Jonah's eyes. '*This* Goddess, *this* Rata Kadul, has now reigned for more than one thousand days, and still She takes a finger from every new-born. As long as She continues to do so, as long as She will not allow a natural successor to arise, She will never be overthrown.'

'Are the selkies unhappy?' asked Jonah cautiously. 'Forgive me, but I did not sense misery in your community, nor was I aware of undue hardship. The present Rata Kadul may be greedy, perhaps even afraid to lose Her position of power, but is She really the tyrant you say She is?'

Ruane closed her eyes and said nothing.

'I should close the window,' suggested Jonah.

'No. Leave it as it is. Please.'

He stepped away from the selkie, pressing his temples with his fists. All at once he felt lost and alone, a castaway washed up on a far and alien shore. A shore where 'closing the window' did not mean what it meant in South London. A shore where mermaids swam and gods were fleshy giants, where a man did not need to eat for nutrition, only out of habit, where magic was a real power, and an unpredictable puppeteer.

Where love falls prey to charm.

Yet, had he not started to belong here? Had he not, when first setting eyes on the remembered fields of Kansas, perceived them as tilted into the upright plane of Stone? Had it not taken a conscious effort of will to remind himself that the Earth, his home, was not tall but wide? That on Earth it was much harder to fall than it was on Amara.

He thought of Kythe, of her description of the ocean's far shore; he yearned to be on dry land again, however strange its appearance.

I have drifted for too long. It is time to walk again.

Leaving Ruane huddled against the window, peering upwards in search of her Goddess, he wandered out into the Shaft. Stepping from the normal gravity of the Saloon into its weightlessness was like taking flight.

The two light charms tumbled like eager puppies towards him but he shooed them away; reluctantly they retired to the games room where they sulked, spilling the faintest yellow glow across the lowest levels of the Shaft. Curling up, tucking his knees up into his arms, Jonah floated in the vertical passageway with his eyes closed and his mind full. He knew that with the lightest touch he could take control of the Bark again and steer it to a safe berth. He could avoid the Goddess, maybe even outpace Her, make a landing . . .

But what then?

Find Annie. Make her mine.

The Bark was calling him but he ignored its voice for the time being. He was a natural creature: not a faery but an ape. It was not his place to wield charm. Leave that for the lesky. Suddenly he felt altogether *human*. He longed simply to stand on the ocean's shore and breathe in the warm, spicy air of Stone. Never mind that it was laced with charm: he felt strong enough to resist that now, to take in what he needed to live but to reject the rest, the insidious magic that tried to twist his thoughts and emotions, just as it had twisted Annie's. There were things he wanted from the Bark – not least information – but they could wait.

His spirit lifted. *If Annie has reached the shore already, then perhaps she too has seen the truth and rejected the charm. Perhaps she awaits me even now!*

It was a thrilling idea. Unwrapping his limbs he pushed himself off the curved wall of the Shaft towards the Saloon; he surged over the lip at the edge of the floor like a whale beaching itself.

The sea was like a huge fluid sky, painted with pale light. With the window now a panoramic dome, it felt less like entering a room and more like reaching the top of a tower. *Like the roof of a lighthouse*, he smiled to himself, remembering the layout of the Bark. He almost expected to feel wind in his face.

Spreading his arms wide he turned a full circle, gazing out into Stone's gigantic ocean.

The Goddess was rising again. He turned to face Her.

She moved more slowly now, Her rope-thick hair coiling and uncoiling as it ascended, as if it had a life of its own. Eventually, after what seemed an eternity, Her brow came into view, a smooth cliff overhanging the deep shadows of Her eyes. Her eyes were closed, just as they had been before.

As they drew level with Jonah and Ruane, Her eyes opened. Ruane said nothing. Jonah stared in disbelief; he had seen these eyes before. Slowly his stomach began to turn over and over.

The eyes of Rata Kadul were mirrors, pure and feature-less, like chrome.

10

Annie's Journal – Three

I had hoped I'd be able to write in this journal while we were flying. That proved impossible – hardly surprising, I guess! So I need to catch up with events.

It was soon after we got past the storm that we reached the shore, if you can call it a shore. The ocean comes to a stop against a big wall of what looks like ice. It isn't ice, as we found out soon enough, more like glass, only with a rough surface, rough enough to walk on without slipping. I can't tell if it's just a coating, a layer covering Stone, or if this is actually what Stone is made of here. I know one thing – it's damn weird.

We call it *glice*. Crazy name, but it's stuck.

We'd not landed five minutes when Archan appeared.

I knew it was her even before she opened her eyes. The body was different of course – some giant of the ocean, half-woman and half-whale as near as I could tell – but I could taste her in the air. God, I could feel her scratching at my *mind*!

Then she opened her eyes and I knew for sure she was back.

It's not the same as it was before though, not quite. I don't think Archan's actually inside the whale-woman like she was inside me, and then inside that dragon giant Torus. I can sense her close by, but not *that* close. No, I think Archan herself is still a long way away, but somehow she's managed to hook a snare into this whalewoman's mind and she's yanking on it with all her might. Pulling the strings, you might say. The whale-woman moves slow, like she's drugged. Not that I'd know what she moves like normally, of course. But I *know* Archan's behind this! I've drunk in so much of Stone's damned magic I can feel things like I could never feel things before! And Archan was pulling my strings once, so I guess I know the signs.

So there we were, stood on that great cliff of glice, looking back over the ocean we'd just crossed, when a woman's face the size of Clayman's best cornfield lifted out of the waves. We couldn't move, even Gerent was rooted to the spot. She looked at us with those evil mirror-eyes, then she had us in her hand.

That was the only time she moved fast. I swear I didn't even see it. One minute her hand was in the water, the next it was all around us, a fist clenched almost shut. Fast as magic, which is probably what it was. Next thing we knew the fist opened and we were falling into a hole in the glice. Gerent tried to open his wings but it was like a funnel, it just kept narrowing until I thought we'd get stuck like pigs in a barrel. Eventually we popped through and dropped into a cave. I slipped forward and nearly carried on falling down another hole in the floor, but Gerent grabbed me and stopped me before I went. He figured we'd fallen far enough already.

Gerent's tried to fly out several times since then but it's just too tight – he can't keep his wings open at the narrowest point and the glice is too slippery to get purchase. We've been dropped into the bottom of an hourglass, me and my winged friend. I just hope Archan doesn't start dumping sand down on top of us.

As soon as we realized we couldn't get out through the roof we took a look at the hole in the floor. It's a pit, not very big, maybe ten feet across, which makes it half the width of the cave. The sides and edges are curved and it's filled nearly to the brim with water.

In the water are hundreds of creatures, little monsters in fact. At first I thought they were crabs, but they're not.

Each one is about a foot long, with more legs than God would ever have granted it. I tried counting them and lost count at thirteen pairs. They're always moving, you see, so it's hard to keep track. Instead of claws they've got little harpoons – that's the best way I can describe them – little harpoons that look sharp as needles. They stab them at each other when they get cross. Tiny sparks flash in the water when they make contact.

They're called juruas, at least, we're pretty sure they are. The whale-woman spoke to us, you see, just before she let us fall. She said,

'Stay out of the water and the juruas will not harm you.'

That's all. Mind you, it was enough. Her face was very close to us when she said it and her voice was like all the thunder you ever heard rolled up and sealed into a gigantic kettle. Her breath stank too – damp wood and rotting seaweed. I thought I was going to throw up but I held it down somehow.

So, the juruas turned out to be evil-looking crabs with needles for claws. To be avoided at all cost.

But there's more to them than meets the eye. They're transparent, like glass, or like *glice* to be exact. You can see their insides – all weird squirming tubes and tiny points of light. And this pool they thrash about in, it's really a kind of nursery.

It was Gerent who saw it first – by God he sees so much! Jonah gets obsessed with counting things, as if cataloguing is the same as comprehending. Gerent's different – he sits back and watches, takes it all in and learns

195

from what he sees. He's so sharp it can be a little bit frightening. Anyway, he was looking down at the edge of the pool where a couple of the juruas were jousting, half in and half out of the water, and saw that one of them was only half there. It had a front half but its hindquarters were buried in the glice of the pit wall, or rather its hindquarters weren't actually there at all. As he watched, the jurua slowly emerged from the glice.

He watched it being born.

No sooner had it popped out than its opponent stabbed it through the middle. All the juruas surrounding it immediately turned and fell on it, tearing it to pieces until there was nothing left.

Gerent called me over and we watched together, fascinated and horrified at the same time. We reckon a new jurua is born every minute or so and about half of them survive. At any one time there's usually one of them being eaten or dismembered or just plain bullied, new-born or not. It's like watching a pit full of piranhas – there's times when the water's seething, all froth and bubbles and practically nothing visible under the surface.

And it was Gerent, of course, who made the connection. 'They must be a breed of Ypoth,' he said at last. 'A degenerate breed at that.'

I agreed. Just as the Ypoth are made of black Stonestuff, so the juruas are made from glice. He was right when he said degenerate though – this is the branch of the family you never invite round, about as far removed as you could get from Esh, the noble and intelligent Ypoth who was our companion for a while here on Stone. But if the Ypoth are the caretakers of Stone, the ones who fix the damage when a threshold punches its way through from our world, then what do these critters do? What purpose do they serve?

We figured that with a thriving new jurua appearing every couple of minutes, before long the pool should be full to bursting. Only it wasn't then and isn't now – even as I write this it's still full, but not spilling over.

All we can think is the pool leads down and out to sea. Under all those fighting crabs there must be an underwater tunnel. The pool is the place where the juruas enter the world, or hatch or get born or whatever damn thing it is that breathes life into them. As soon as they've got their bearings they turn tail and dive for the ocean, leaving room for the next batch. Not that knowing this helps us any. I'd no more stick my foot in that water than I would offer my hand to a grizzly.

So, no way up and no way down. In short, no way out.

I watched Gerent working at the hole in the ceiling for a while. He's found a new determination I think. Before now he was prone to bouts of melancholy – God knows he's every right to be sad after Malya's death – but that seems to be changing. Jonah thinks he's a pessimist at heart, without any sense of his own worth. Born to a king who wanted a warrior son and was given an intellectual.

But I believe Gerent is beginning to accept who he is, to walk out of his father's long shadow. And the voyage has put muscles on him. Brains or no brains, he's a handsome man!

I know I should look back over what I wrote before, back on the beach. I know I would be shocked to see the contradictions. Once I loved Jonah with a passion like nothing I'd felt for a long time, maybe not ever. Now I find myself with feelings of love for Gerent. It's different, gentler somehow. With Jonah and me it was – I don't know, *frantic*. Leastways that's how I felt. Underneath the passion there was a kind of desperation. I know I felt it and I think Jonah felt it too, though I don't know if he'd admit it. I still love him, I think, but I've got this weird feeling about it.

My love for Jonah is real enough. But so is my love

for Gerent. That has to be wrong, but how can it be when both feelings are *true*? Some people reckon choice is a luxury. I say it's a curse.

Writing the note to Jonah was, well, harder than climbing the Rockies. Harder than anything I've done.

Not as hard as reading it, I guess.

As I stood there with the pen and paper in my hand, wondering what to write, it seemed there was no such thing as truth, no such thing as *me*. Choosing between Gerent and Jonah was like – like choosing which one to shoot. The damned pen even started to feel like a pistol. I thought of Jonah and thought of passion. I thought of Gerent and remembered holding hands in Stone's starless night.

Remembered romance.

Was that my choice? Romance or passion? Did I deserve either?

Then I caught sight of my painting box lying open on the floor and a wonderful calm came across me.

I knelt down and picked out one of the tiles. It bore the symbol of the North Wind, and it seemed to me the marks were people, one a little taller than the other, a man and a woman dancing in each other's arms.

It was such a simple image, and it seemed so solid there in my hand. So *true*. The North Wind.

I dug into my heart and found what I believed. Therefore what is true for me.

I love Gerent more.

There is nothing more to say.

I put the tile back, picked up the box and left.

I still believe it, I do. Yes, I'm sure it must be the truth. It must be.

There are things embedded in the glice.

They look like seashells, giant conches. The smallest one is as big as my fist, and some are nearly as big as a beer barrel. Like the glice and the juruas, they're transparent – I guess that's why we didn't notice them at first. You have to move your head from side to side to catch their outlines. I caught Gerent doing it a few minutes ago and just had to laugh. He did look funny!

One of the shells is sticking partly out of the wall, like the jurua that was being born, only the shell doesn't show any signs of coming any further out. In fact, I get the feeling it's been jammed in there, that they've all been jammed in there. The juruas are keen to get out of the glice – the shells are just staying put.

We've both tried to pull this one shell out, but it's wedged tight. It's smooth too, so you can't get a grip on it. Just one more thing we can't do in this damned hole!

It's another prison cell, of course, only this time I'm not on my own. I can't imagine any company better than Gerent. He's gentle and considerate, and happy to talk and happy to listen, which is the part most folk find hardest of all. Part of me wants never to leave.

Part of me wants desperately to be rescued.

Jonah's coming, I'm sure of that. He wanted to rescue me before, when I was Archan's puppet. I think he was disappointed he was never able to. Yes, he's on his way.

But he'll want to do more than rescue me this time. This time, he'll want to win me back.

11

Ghosts

Teeth like rotten ivory towers, vast and yellowed, climbed up over the roof of the Bark, sliding beneath it until it was enclosed. A shadow the colour of twilight, the size of a world, loomed.

Sudden explosions of bubbles, each bubble a cosmos, alive with light and inner form.

Complex patterns struck through the shadow by the light of the sun as it coursed through the bubble-streams, touching the darkness ahead just enough to make a mystery of it.

The Bark pitched forwards, crashed against a wall of bubbles and was knocked back. A sound like an army hammering at the door, trying to break in. They were rocked this way and that, while outside the onslaught continued, a constant barrage of pops and rumbles and deep, jarring impacts. The window was useless, the view a kaleidoscope of light and ever-breaking spheres.

Then they were through the turbulence and into the shadow. The Bark rotated jerkily until they were facing backwards, looking back past the two rows of towers. One row jutted up from darkness, a city skyline; the other hung suspended like a series of gigantic stalactites. Beyond them . . . *between* them . . . was the ocean from which they had come.

200

Slowly the teeth began to close.

'Oh dear God, we are in Her mouth!' exclaimed Jonah. Ruane looked up at him with hard jade eyes and said nothing.

There was more turbulence, strangely gentle this time, as the two rows of teeth closed upon their wake. The resulting darkness was total but for a few streamers of phosphorescent weed swept up in the current. But their feeble glow faded quickly as they were torn apart and before long there was nothing at all to see. Apart from the occasional lurch they might just as well have been buried beneath the mud of the sea bed, or floating free in a starless night.

Ruane remained silent. Jonah was relieved: he could think of nothing to say to this weird woman of the sea. Her tale felt more than strange – it felt completely alien to him. The fate of the selkies seemed remote and irrelevant, utterly unconnected to whatever quests he might yet have to pursue. Yet she had helped him through the storm, so did he not owe her a debt of gratitude? His conscience informed him that he did, but he was beginning to think there was no place for conscience on Stone. Only survival.

The survival of the fittest.

'There is nothing to see. In the throat of the Goddess we are. Close the window.'

It was typical of Grandfather Tree to show his face when the drama had died down, Jonah thought. The lesky's legless body rose through the floor as if from the grave. His undertaker's tone befitted the sombre mood of his entrance.

'Why do you not close the window yourself?' suggested Jonah. 'Can you no longer manipulate even the Bark's simplest functions?'

'Well you know that I cannot,' growled the lesky, his face taut and grey. 'Yours he is now, the Bark. I hope you will be happy together.'

'It still permits you to roam its interior,' observed Jonah. 'Perhaps you are not as helpless as you would have me believe.'

'Do you not trust my word?'

'My trust has been greatly tested over recent days, Grandfather Tree, and there has been precious little proof that you are any more to be trusted than the rest of my companions!'

'Bitter words, Jonah. A sure way to lose companions, to speak of them like that. Not to mention friends.'

'What do you want with me?'

The lesky's face was inscrutable. 'I was going to say "companionship", but now . . . I'm not so sure. Farewell!'

With a sound like a wood-saw he duck-dived into the floor. Jonah watched his departure with a mixture of resentment and regret. Was he indeed to lose all his companions, one by one?

Outside all remained black. Even now they must be descending into the guts of the Goddess. Swallowed whole. What fate lay in the bowels of this awesome creature, and what hope of survival?

'On one thing I do agree with you, Grandfather Tree,' he said firmly. 'The window needs closing.'

Crouching down, Jonah focused his attention on the invisible barrier of charm separating him from the inner workings of the Bark. In his mind the barrier acquired solidity: there hung before him a screen of willow branches, green and vibrant. Leaves parted as he pushed his arm through the gently moving curtain and touched the charm beyond.

Silently the window turned opaque, solidifying into a densely woven dome. He sighed, pausing briefly to savour the sensation of being one with the Bark, of the powers at his command. Ruane was watching him; he must look odd, he considered, squatting in the centre of the floor with one arm raised and his eyes half-closed.

Still, she seemed very distant. Everything seemed distant in fact: the gloomy surroundings of the Saloon, the still-rippling patch of floor into which Grandfather Tree had disappeared, the dark weave of the domed ceiling.

Extending his other arm he passed completely through the leaves and into the Bark.

Charm enfolded him, a green sea the texture of syrup. A shape swam at his side as he abandoned his physical shell: Grandfather Tree, vital and alert in his native environment. Jonah's irritation with the lesky melted away and they swam together for a time, dodging the slow currents of the Bark's internal ocean.

'They know you are coming,' said the lesky as he plunged into a lazily turning whirlpool. 'They know everything.'

'That is what I hoped,' Jonah replied.

The whirlpool became a tunnel, turning first this way then that. The green light thinned then abruptly turned vivid red. Nebulous colour condensed to interconnecting strands, a shining web of light . . .

Jonah and Grandfather Tree emerged into the presence of the six basilisk ghosts.

They lay in a circle, these once immortal beasts, looking just as Jonah remembered them from his previous encounter. Pale, scaly flesh. Squat, legless bodies, propelled by muscular tails and elaborate arms. Claws and eyes of silver.

Yet they were not real.

The basilisks it was who had built Stone – or Amara, to give it its proper name – as a vault for all the memories of the world. Including memories of the basilisks themselves.

Thus, when the unthinkable happened and the basilisks finally perished, some record of them survived in the fabric of Stone. Ghosts in the wall.

One of the six lumbered forwards like a clumsy spider, poisonous breath condensing before it and raining on to the web to which it clung. Its voice crossed the web to where Jonah stood, entering his perception not through his ears but his feet . . .

. . . *Geiss would bid you welcome, faery. You have done well.*

. . . *Have I? If you mean I have done well in vanquishing Archan, I disagree. It seems she is harder to get rid of than even you imagined. She is here, now – in the Goddess!*

. . . *Underestimation is not a basilisk weakness. Archan is strong. Nevertheless, you have done well. As your powers grow the possibility of ultimate success increases.*

. . . *Then you did know I would fail! When you told me to 'make Archan gone', you knew it was a fool's errand. She is immortal, and whatever fate I might have devised for her still she would always have found a way to elude it. You should have found yourselves a proper dragon-slayer!*

. . . *Your ally, the faery queen, has indeed been unsuccessful in her quest. And it may also be true that there is no pit deep enough to hold Archan. Nevertheless, the Deathless would have considered success a possibility. The Deathless had a saying: 'Everything changes'.*

. . . *I thought that what you believed was, 'Nothing goes'.*

. . . *The two are compatible. But we debate trivialities. More important topics remain, not least your education. You have heard mention of the Aqueduct, though you know not what it is, and you have some notion of what lies beyond the ocean. You are beginning to consider more deeply the nature of the memories stored in Amara's rods. You have learned that Archan is not vanquished and that, in an atmosphere of charm, there is little that can be trusted or considered true. All these splinters of knowledge are part of the tree you must climb and comprehend. If you cannot do this then Archan will prevail and Amara will fall indeed, along with the world you once considered your own.*

Jonah stared at the creature, wrestling with the

knowledge that this was not a basilisk at all but the *memory* of a basilisk, reconstructed and articulated like a puppet by the hidden machinery of Stone. The basilisks themselves were long dead and this gave him hope, for once the basilisks had been immortal, yet in the end they had died. Given this fact, Archan, though immortal, was not invincible.

. . . Tell me what I must know. And what I must do.

The basilisk lurched forward, its metal eyes glistening. It looked eager, more lively than the one Jonah had spoken with before. What had been the name of that one? Bak? *Bacht.*

. . . Geiss would tell of glory and valour, but the others would counsel caution and wisdom before impetuous action. Therefore Geiss, were it alive, would demonstrate the predicament in which you find yourself with a parable. The parable it would use is doubly convenient because it deals with specifically faery concerns – it would crave forgiveness – with specifically human *concerns, the nature of which may not only edify but incite.*

Jonah was about to ask the ghostly creature to repeat this in rather plainer fashion but already the creature was going on.

. . . In short, you will be shown a memory with which you are already familiar, in another form at least. Heed it well, for it bears on your situation.

The ghost of Geiss bowed its ugly face and closed its forbidding eyes. Beneath its claws the web glowed an even brighter red, then the mesh flew apart and Jonah was pulled through it by unseen hands. He was falling, briefly, then everything turned to gold . . .

. . . corn that was just as high as he remembered it, the day just as clean and clear. After the thick spice of Stone the air tasted gloriously pure. Kansas sky embraced the heavens, a blue cosmos so high and wide it might have been set at the very edge of the universe; etched across its face was a scripture of cloud

so detailed even the wisest scholar would take a lifetime to decipher it. In that epiphanous moment Jonah believed the world of his birth to be just as mighty as the world of Stone, if not mightier, for its many wonders had been arrived at not by cynical construction but by a miraculous process of evolution.

Something was touching his lips and he jumped involuntarily, startled, only to discover it was his own hand raised to his mouth in wonder. Looking to his right he saw Annie standing not two paces distant in the doorway of her sod-built house, her own hand raised in an identical gesture. They lowered their hands simultaneously, and lowered their eyes from the enormity of the sky.

'Annie!' he blurted, but of course she did not hear him. Once more it was he who was the ghost, and though he knew he could make her hear him if he tried hard enough, he also knew that was not the reason he was here. He was here not to make contact but to observe. And to learn.

He followed Annie out of the house and up the path over the ridge of land. She scanned the smoke-blackened horizon apprehensively, then stopped as she saw Rance and Clayman fighting in the corn-alley.

Rance was bent double, Clayman's left hand firmly entwined in the collar of his sweat-soaked shirt. With his free hand the old farmer was raining blow after blow upon the young man's head; Rance for his part showed no signs of retaliating whatsoever. After a minute or two of this Clayman let Rance drop, kicked him once in the belly for good measure, then strode off towards his oxen. Rance did not move as his adversary spotted the approach of the prairie fire and frantically led the oxen back towards his homestead, abandoning the threshing machine in the gap between the two cornfields.

By and by Rance came round. By the time he was raising himself shakily to his feet, Annie was running back to the house. Clearly she did not want Rance to know that she had just witnessed his shattering defeat at the hands of a man three times his age. Closing the door quietly behind her she quickly scattered some linen across the table to make it look as if she were in the middle of sorting through it, then took several deep breaths and returned to the door.

Beside the jamb was a small circular mirror. Much of the silver was gone from around the edge but the reflection it threw back was fair. She appraised herself, patting her hair to no great effect. Then she stuck her tongue out, took another deep breath and opened the door.

Rance was halfway down the path, limping noticeably, his face torn and bruised.

'Oh my dear, look at you!' cried Annie, darting forward. He growled and pulled away. Then he started to unlace his belt.

Jonah heard his own teeth grinding together and wondered that the teeth of a ghost could make such a noise. This was the point at which he had abandoned the first version of the memory, unwilling as he had been to witness Rance whipping the woman he, Jonah, loved. Nor did he wish to see it this time, but he was here at the whim of the basilisks and did not believe he could leave until they chose to release him.

In an effort to distract his racing mind he considered the differences between this sequence of events and the one he had observed before. This, he was certain, was Annie's version of the story, and it amused him to compare her memory of the fight with Rance's own, in which he had lost to Clayman only by virtue of an unfortunate slip in some ox dung! According to Annie, Rance had not even landed a punch: he had been utterly outclassed.

And it was while Jonah contemplated this crucial difference that the story diverged once more.

'Put that away, Rance West,' Annie barked. 'There's no time!'

Jonah saw murder in Rance's eyes; he knew then that the big man was capable of killing Annie and that had she not left him when she did she would not have lived to see her thirtieth year. He also understood that this retaliation of Annie's was uncharacteristic, not to say unprecedented. And he could only imagine how she must have paid later, when the drama of the day was over.

For she was pointing past his head towards the tower of smoke billowing above the corn. 'Prairie fire!' she cried. 'Not a second to lose, Rance. Let's get movin'!'

'Let it burn!' he growled, snatching at her arm as she brushed past him. His fingers gripped so tight Jonah could almost see the bruises developing as he held her. 'Fire-break'll do its work.'

'That's just it! It won't.'

'What're you talkin' 'bout, woman!' His voice was sullen now, like a child who cannot have his own way.

'Come see!'

He did not relinquish his grip so she hauled him, still clutching her upper arm, all the way to the top of the rise, from where they could see clear across Clayman's fields. Jonah followed them and saw that the flames were barely a hundred yards short of the alley between the two nearest fields.

He also saw why Annie was so concerned. He suspected that she, like Rance, would not shed too many tears were Clayman's crops to be destroyed. Even if North Field burned to the ground it was far enough from the Wests' property for the fire to do them no harm. However, if the fire were to jump across to the next field then the Wests were in trouble. Knife Edge Field bordered directly on to their own meagre crop, with only a shallow ditch to separate them, a ditch that appeared to be filled with dry and broken ... and eminently combustible ... scraps of timber.

Under normal circumstances the fire-break would have prevented the flames from travelling from North to Knife Edge. But in his panic Clayman had left the threshing machine neatly bridging the gap between the two fields. In a flash Jonah imagined the fire reaching the edge of North Field, finding its way to the wooden chassis of the thresher and using it as a stepping stone into the next field, from which it could spread at least to the next of Clayman's fire-breaks but also, and more *importantly for the Wests, across the wood-filled ditch and on to their own land.*

'If we don't get that damned thresher moved,' Annie was shouting, *'everything we own's going up in smoke!'*

Jonah felt grudging admiration for Rance West as the big man, clearly still dazed from the fight, loped clumsily down the opposite slope to the alley. Annie was close on his heels. Jonah thought her dark hair, streaming back over her shoulders, was more beautiful and perilous even than the approaching fire. Grunting with the effort, Rance set his shoulder between the traces and heaved. The machine did not budge.

'Wheel-brake!' he growled and Annie leaped up to the seat and disengaged the lever.

He bent again and this time the thresher rocked most of the way out of the rut into which its wheels had settled. Jumping nimbly down again Annie joined him. Jonah felt touched, humbled even, by the sight of husband and wife straining their bodies to save their land and home. It was a primal scene, an intensely human *scene stripped of all but the most essential elements.* Suffer or die, *the scene said to him,* yet there is glory in suffering.

By now the flames had consumed even the mighty sky. Smoke and hard pellets of blackened corn swirled past, making it hard for Annie and Rance to breathe. Jonah found he could taste the smoke but was otherwise unaffected. The noise of the fire was daunting, a crescendo of cracks and rumbles over a spiralling roar.

With an animal moan the threshing machine rolled forwards, scything its way into the opposite wall of corn and burying itself unceremoniously in Knife Edge Field. Both Annie and Rance fell to the ground; Annie was up almost at once, dragging her husband clear of the first whip-cracks of fire as they lashed out from between the doomed stalks of North Field.

They sat there, fear and flame painting their faces red, but the prairie fire came no further. The bridge removed, the fire-break did its work and the rest of Clayman's land – not to mention the Wests' entire homestead – was saved.

Jonah felt his awareness pulling back from the scene, as if he were taking flight. The fire transformed into a web of red light and with a painful, jarring transition he was back among the basilisk ghosts.

. . . He did beat her, did he not? Later, I imagine, after the excitement was over.

. . . The memory continues. You are free to experience other parts of it as you wish. But for now that is all you need to observe; that is all the lesson requires.

. . . If you showed me that scene to teach me that Stone holds many memories of an event, and that each memory is tainted by the prejudice of the person through which it has been recorded, then you are teaching me nothing I do not already know. That was Annie's memory; what I perceived before was Rance's. Somewhere between the two is what we might consider to be the truth.

. . . Part of the lesson is to confirm what you already know. For example: regard this shape.

The ghost-basilisk raised one of its forearms and extended a silvery claw. The claw stuck out sideways from its wrist, and was rotated so that it stuck straight up like a congratulatory thumb. It was a perfect cone.

. . . It is the shape of Stone, Geiss. Is that not so?

. . . It is so. You deduced this fact by your own measurements, which is a notable feat. The memory rods describe a spiral path around and up the narrowing circumference of Amara, until they reach the apex. But we are not concerned with the apex but the base, or rather its absence. When you sent Archan in pursuit of the faery queen you sent her backwards through time – here on Amara that equates to the direction you know as downStone. *Thus she travelled down and around the thread, following the ever-widening spiral of the rods as they unwind their way into eternity.*

. . . Then Stone does go on forever? Jonah jumped to hear Grandfather Tree speak. He had forgotten about the lesky, who was loitering some yards behind him.

. . . Once it did, Lesky. But no more. As soon as Archan caught the faery queen she wasted no time. She commenced the destruction of Amara.

. . . Its destruction!? Jonah blurted. *But how can she do such a thing? And if she has started then why do we not know about it? Is there anything we can do to stop it?*

. . . She has started and we do know about it. How else would it be possible to inform you? Jonah could not tell if the basilisk was demonstrating exasperation or developing a sense of humour. If the latter, he judged, some honing was needed. *Archan is capable of anything, and it may very well be that there is nothing any creature, alive or dead, can do to stop her. But the attempt must be made and you, as has already been made clear to you, are the best placed to succeed.*

. . . It is a heavy burden for any man.

. . . Heavy indeed.

. . . Tell me then the nature of this destruction, and what one man can possibly do to stop it.

. . . Imagine the moment in the past, far downStone, where Archan finally caught up with the faery queen. Imagine that moment now, human. Put yourself into the mind of the dragon.

Closing his eyes, Jonah found it was easy. He smelt the wrathful excitement as Archan closed in on her diminutive quarry, the hound on the heels of the fox. The blinding speed, the final spurt and the long, long skid across the aeons as she shed her monumental velocity in a shower of charm and triumph. Coming to a halt, assessing how far she had descended into history, how far back up the thread she must go.

Smiling as she decided the manner of her return.

. . . How is she coming? What is she bringing with her that can possibly do damage to Stone?

. . . That is not known. But do not doubt that she comes, and

211

*that with her she brings doom. That is why you are here, in
this place. That is why you must understand what it is that
lies beyond the ocean, and especially the function of the Aqueduct. Amara was designed with destruction in mind, and places
were constructed that will not yield to doom, whatever its
nature. Archan can be stopped, but there are few places where
this is possible. You are near to one such place.*

Jonah felt something like a firework light up his mind.

*. . . A fire-break! You are talking about a fire-break! Is that
what this Aqueduct is, something lying in Archan's path?
Is it a line of water to quench her fire? If so, why do you
need me?*

*. . . There is indeed a fire-break, but it is not the Aqueduct.
The fire-break is deep enough and wide enough to stop anything
coming upStone. Anything, including Archan. But there is
something lying across the fire-break: a threshing machine, if
you prefer to continue the analogy of the prairie fire. That is
what the Aqueduct is. It is Archan's hope and our despair.
And you must demolish it!*

The ghost of Geiss continued to talk for some time but
it was already clear to Jonah that it actually knew very
little. The longer it spoke the more he sensed its desperation – or rather the desperation of whatever force it
was that kept these basilisk puppets mobile. There was
much that this force knew, clearly, but even more of
which it was entirely ignorant. It was a sobering thought,
that even such a mighty edifice as Stone was ultimately
vulnerable.

It is coming apart, he thought to himself as he turned
away from the web of red light. *Stone has stood for a very
long time, perhaps for all eternity, but now it is starting to
come apart at the seams.*

The curtain of leaves delivered him back into the
Saloon. Ruane was waiting anxiously, half-reaching for
him as though anxious to speak, nervous to touch.

'I hope I did not scare you,' Jonah said. He could hear his own heartbeat in his ears, its humanity eerie. 'Was I gone for very long?'

Ruane looked puzzled. 'Gone? But you have been nowhere, Jonah. I watched you crouch and reach out your arm, then you closed your eyes and opened them again. It took a mere breath. I was concerned because I was suddenly afraid: it was as if I could taste fear in the air itself. It was a very unusual feeling.'

'There is much we should fear, Ruane, not least the monster whose belly surrounds us. We have to find a way to escape – she wants us dead. Or rather she wants me dead, and has little concern for anyone else who gets in her way, you included.'

'You know what has happened to the Goddess, do you not? Why She has turned away from the selkies?'

'Yes, I do. It is a long story, but I think I must tell it to you.'

So Jonah told Ruane a little of his tale, and told her especially about Archan, who would stop at nothing on her quest to rule eternity. 'She seeks to destroy things simply because she can. She inherited the state of immortality from the basilisks when they died – or it might be said that she stole it – and I believe that the knowledge that she will live forever is slowly driving her mad. She has been immortal for over one million years, and she spent most of that time encased in Arctic ice, powerless to do anything but absorb the slow leaks of charm that finally permitted her to free herself. A million years! Now she is free she is full of anger. I thought I had defeated her, but it seems my relief was premature. Even as we speak she is making her way back from far downStone, her anger no doubt many times multiplied.'

'If she is so far away,' asked Ruane, 'how is it that she is in the Goddess?'

'I do not know. All I can imagine is that some trick of

charm is allowing her to control your Goddess. She is no stranger to controlling the minds of others.'

'And she is doing this to stop you?'

'I believe so. Not only does she bear me a grudge – and *that* is a mighty understatement! – but she knows I am still a threat to her. If this Aqueduct can be thrown down, then she can be stopped. And I am the only one who can throw it down. Therefore she wants me dead.'

'Then she has surely succeeded. We are consumed indeed.'

'Not necessarily. Grandfather Tree!'

The lesky appeared at once, as though he had been awaiting the call. Jonah supposed that he probably had. He looked different, smoother and less gnarled, like a highly polished version of what he had been before.

'I've been listening. Out you must get, that much is true. The Bark cannot survive in this place. Already it begins to disintegrate.'

'I believe you can help us.'

'I believe so to. But quick we must be. Time outpaces us.'

Jonah turned to Ruane. 'We must get out of the Bark. The lesky can help us to escape. But we must do it now.'

Jade eyes wide, Ruane nodded. Clearly she did not understand what was about to happen; Jonah had only a vague idea himself, but there was a green fire in the lesky's hollow eyes. It seemed Grandfather Tree had a plan. Ruane's eyes grew wider still as they made their way hurriedly to the hatch, stopping only once to collect two things from Jonah's room: Darwin's *On the Origin of Species* and the dryad's fingernail. The former he tucked inside his shirt; the latter he lodged securely in his belt.

'We cannot go out there!' she exclaimed, pulling away from the hatch.

'We are not,' answered Jonah. 'We are going in here.'

So saying he pulled at the smaller of the doors, the

one leading into the charm reservoir. The chamber was dark and gloomy, a daunting cave from which an icy draught blew. It was, Jonah considered, very different to the warm, electric place into which Annie had once enticed him. He ushered the selkie in first, then followed, closing the hatch firmly behind him; Grandfather Tree simply flowed through the wall and reappeared on the other side.

With the hatch closed a faint blue glow was discernible, like shadowless moonlight. All was quiet.

Jonah waved his hand like a conjurer and the walls turned transparent.

If they had doubted Grandfather Tree's urgency the scene outside the Bark was enough to make up their minds on the spot. Their vessel was half-submerged in a sea of acid, the surface of which was boiling like a pan on a stove. A dense mist obscured the distance; the foreground was a confusion of lurid mist and exploding bubbles. The outer surface of the window was growing dull as the acid began to etch its way in: it seemed even the construction materials of the basilisks were no match for Rata Kadul's digestive juices.

'Can you still sculpt the exterior of the Bark?' demanded Jonah. 'Is that what you intend to do?'

'Would I be here otherwise?' retorted Grandfather Tree. 'While we talk, the Bark weakens and my powers diminish!'

They glared at each other, then Jonah's gaze softened. 'But what of you, Grandfather Tree? I do not wish to abandon you here.'

'You worry about me. Don't!'

'I want you to come too.'

'Not possible.' The lesky's voice was deteriorating as his mouth filled up with brambles. 'Listen, Jonah. This thing the basilisks will permit me to do: they will permit me to sculpt the Bark one last time. You would say I have a choice – to stay or come – but you know there is no choice. I am lesky: I can live only in the taiga. Even this Bark is inadequate. I do not have enough control to survive. For you it would be like life in a straitjacket.'

'Is that not at least life? And were you not a prisoner in your taiga when I found you?'

'But still free to move and sculpt! Not here! The basilisks will not permit it! Jonah, my successor you are. I was only ever your herald. You must do all that I could not: work the memory rods, save Amara! Now behold Grandfather Tree's final work. And remember: just before you reach the water, take a deep breath!'

Halfway up one of the rounded walls a spiralling pattern formed. The wall shook momentarily, then stretched outwards. Moving to the side, Jonah was afforded a startling view of the lesky's creation as it sprouted out from the Bark's transparent conning tower: it was a slender tree trunk, devoid of branches but barbed with razor-like fins. Watching it grow through the curved window was like watching a tree grow from the vantage of a worm.

As it grew – extending from the Bark under the lesky's control just as the mast had done so many days before – it shed its magical light across the turbulent sea of acid. Jonah watched its progress as it approached the far boundary of Rata Kadul's cavernous stomach.

The light illuminated vast rolls of translucent flesh. It looked less like a gut and more like the surface of a monstrous brain. And it rippled, shiny and flexible and undeniably alive. Bubbling acid poured down the convoluted wall. Jonah resisted the urge to turn away, simultaneously fascinated and repelled.

Now the spike at the tip of the tree made contact with the lining of this gigantic stomach. For an instant the flesh resisted, then the tree penetrated. Scarlet fluid poured from the wound, mingling with the freely flowing acid.

'Go now,' urged Grandfather Tree. 'Any minute the pain will be felt.'

Ruane still looked confused, until Jonah pointed out the hole in the opaque part of the wall leading directly into the new tree's hollow interior: the tunnel that would take them straight through the Goddess's abdomen and out into the water beyond.

'It is an escape tunnel,' he explained. 'Even the most secure of prisons has been known to possess one or two of these.'

With a doubtful expression she slithered inside and began to crawl. Just before following her Jonah turned to Grandfather Tree, who was lodged in the floor immediately below the tunnel entrance. It was a curious sight, seeing this wooden half-man emerging from transparency – like seeing a materialization, or some exotic fakir's trick.

'As soon as I am through I will take control of the Bark again. I may be able to draw it out. And you with it, Grandfather Tree.'

The green eyes were tight shut, the face contorted in concentration. This was the lesky, Jonah reminded himself, who had given up hope of ever controlling the Bark again, even on this comparatively superficial level.

Grandfather Tree nodded almost imperceptibly.

Jonah threw himself into the hollow tree trunk, glad to be enclosed in darkness again, to be rid of the disconcerting view of the whale-woman's interior. Some way ahead he could just see the swaying rump of the selkie; soon, as the darkness became total, he could not see even that.

He tried not to think as he crawled, tried not to visualize the dreadful cutting action as the knife-sharp tree trunk sliced its way out through the belly of the Goddess. He could, he knew, control the growth and progress of the trunk himself. But that would take a lot of energy and all his attention, and he needed both if he were to make it through before the Goddess noticed what was happening to Her.

Light poured into the tunnel; in close pursuit was a tidal wave. The first took Jonah completely by surprise, giving him only a second or two to take the deepest breath he could before the wall of water struck, knocking him several yards back in his tracks. Floundering and gasping, he struck out with his flailing hands and made contact with something warm and soft: a pair of flippers, Ruane's. His fingers clenched and suddenly he was moving forwards again, being towed out of the tunnel like a ship from its berth. Rata Kadul's abdomen, seen from a more proper exterior viewpoint now, was a vast plain. Ahead, beams of sunlight and a symphony of ripples marked the outer surface of the sea and the promise of life-giving air. The surface was no more than ten yards distant; holding on to Ruane's tail with one hand Jonah paddled with the other while the breath turned to lead in his lungs.

They had gone no more than two yards when Jonah felt a burning around his waist and a sudden, sharp tug. He stopped dead in the water; Ruane's fur-covered tail flippers were torn from his grasp. Thrashing both his arms and legs, giving in to panic, he clutched at his waist only to find a rope there. He looked down.

A thick blue cord had wound itself around his middle, sealing itself into an unbreakable loop without even a hint of a knot. The same type of cord that bound the selkies to the body of Rata Kadul. He, like them, was now Her prisoner.

Unlike them, he could hold his breath for no longer than a minute. As the last of the air spurted from between his lips and he prepared to inhale Stone's warm ocean waters – as he prepared, in fact, to drown – he turned to look at the wound the lesky's tree had made in the flank of the Goddess. Perhaps it had delivered a fatal blow, and at least a small part of Archan's presence had been banished from Stone.

All he could see was a pin-prick in Rata Kadul's thick grey skin, a tiny hole through which he could not imagine having squeezed. Even as he watched through blurring eyes it was beginning to heal over and the cloud of silt and blood that had leaked from it was dispersing rapidly into the waters. The severed tip of the lesky's tree, its end torn and scored with acid-marks, turned end over end in the eddies. He could neither see the Bark nor sense it in his thoughts. The door had closed.

He had managed to do no more than exchange being consumed for being drowned. Archan had conquered him after all. And she was not even here.

He could feel the square pressure of the book beneath his shirt; the knowledge that Darwin was getting soaked made him inexpressibly sad.

Opening his mouth, he took in the water.

12

Surface

Above him swam exotic fish, their long, languid bodies like those of mermaids. They spiralled down towards him, talking in silent voices as they cocked their beautiful heads towards him. The nearer they drew the less like fish they seemed, the more human, the more female. One of them flashed close enough to brush her tail against his thighs then disappeared in a stream of darting blue bubbles. Her touch was like the softest moleskin. Another reached sinuous arms behind her head and grasped the tip of her tail, spinning herself into a perfect circle that drew a vortex in the water. The first mermaid reappeared, floated above him momentarily then kissed him back to sleep.

When he woke he was still being kissed. The mermaid's face soared over him like a huge kite; for a moment he lost all sense of scale and believed it to be the face of Rata Kadul. Then the features resolved into neither Goddess nor mermaid but selkie: Ruane's face. It was drawn, heavy with concern, and the kiss it delivered was filled with live-giving air.

Their lips parted and Ruane slipped away, leaving Jonah spinning through sunbeams. The flat belly of the Goddess rotated lazily beneath him; the blue rope still connected him like an umbilical cord to a point on Her waist, near to where pale skin melted into dark whale-fur. Looking the other way he saw a white halo expand around Ruane's shadowy form as she broke the surface, then she was returning to deliver another kiss of life. Three more times she did this before a change in the light informed him that Rata Kadul herself was drawing near. Her gigantic body shone as it approached the ocean's surface; all around Jonah selkies were appearing, thrown into activity by the imminent surfacing of their Goddess. He held Ruane's breath in his lungs, hardly daring to believe he would shortly be breathing for himself again. The giant's body was very close now, pressing against him like a vast, advancing wall. Fast-moving currents whipped past, threatening to beat him against Her, but again Ruane was there, guiding him through the turmoil. At the instant he felt the skin of the Goddess pushing against his back the sea parted before him and he was painted with the light of the sun and Stone's warm, flowing air.

No sooner did he escape drowning than he awoke to the danger of gravity. The Goddess continued to breach the waves, moving not upwards of course but sideways, and pressing her living cargo out into the sky. As the spray around him began to fall Jonah grasped the rope with both hands, preparing himself . . .

It was less a fall than a slide, and a short-lived slide at that. He had slithered only a few yards down the slope of Rata Kadul's belly when the rope snapped tight about his waist, bringing him up short. To either side selkies were already clambering back up Her worn and pitted hide, anxious to gain the relative comfort of the shallow upper slope of Her flank. Jonah joined them, casting his gaze round for Ruane, who had disappeared.

As well as Malory, Jonah's father had often read to him from Swift, and he could very well imagine how the Lilliputians might have felt as they swarmed over Gulliver's gargantuan form. Even the ropes were reminiscent of that fantastic tale, except this time it was the Lilliputians who were bound by the giant.

Rata Kadul was basking in the afternoon sunshine, a whale-woman coasting through a vertical sea. Drifting with Her head pointing directly downStone, She had exposed Her face and the front half of Her torso to the open air, effectively turning Her flank into a curving shelf on to which the selkie population had already thrown itself, making the most of this opportunity to breathe freely in warm air. Jonah continued to climb until the slope was only a few degrees then threw himself on to his back and stared out into the sky, trying to forget that this island on which he was beached was alive.

Trying to forget that Archan was somewhere inside it.

A shadow obscured the sun. Raising himself on to his elbows Jonah looked up into the face of an old selkie male. Jade eyes, just like Ruane's, regarded him with humour.

'A faery without wings. Well, Ruane was at least half right.'

'Completely right, Tam.' Ruane herself, climbing to meet them, corrected the old selkie, who bobbed his head in a non-committal way. Ruane flashed Jonah a brief smile. 'This is my brother, Tam. You can trust him, but do not expect him to go out of his way to help you. Or to do anything at all, for that matter.'

Tam adopted a wounded expression. 'You bite deep, Ruane.'

'Nothing personal, Tam. Apathy is a selkie disease. You are not alone in having contracted it.'

The banter continued and Jonah decided it was largely good-natured. 'You said "apathy", Ruane,' he interrupted, 'and I see evidence of it. Tam, do you not acknowledge that you are enslaved?'

'We are not slaves,' said Tam with a broad smile. 'We are worshippers.'

'But the one does not demand the other. What kind of Goddess denies her worshippers the basic right of freedom?'

'It is the way of things. The way of the sea. You are a faery: you would not understand.'

'Oh, Tam!' Ruane scolded. 'It is not the way of things and you know it! Our ancestors did not live like this. Once we were free, and we can be free again if only you and all the others would get up off your furry backsides and make a stand!'

Tam shrugged and continued to smile the same, infuriating smile. Jonah gazed around at the rest of the slope: selkies were everywhere, many of them sprawled in the afternoon sunshine, some picking through the pools of water left in the many crevices scarring Rata Kadul's hide, beach-combing. The scene was remarkably peaceful, even idyllic. *Yet why not live like this?* he asked himself. *If they are happy, who am I to question what they do?*

'Are there many others like you, Ruane?' he asked. 'Selkies who wish for something more than this life?'

'Some. Not many,' she added reluctantly. 'But that is not the point, Jonah! It is wrong, simply wrong to be a slave! You must know that! Please, I need your help.'

The sun was crawling sideways towards the vertex, illuminating the distant hills of the Goddess's bosom, the soft angles of her exposed face. Looking along the flowing deck of this living vessel he was struck with the sheer pastoral beauty of the scene. The low orange light, the relaxed poses of the selkies, the steady wash of the waves above his head all conspired to calm his spirit. He felt both light-headed and dull of thought, as though he had been administered a mild anaesthetic.

With an effort he turned his mind to his quest. Beyond Her head, obscuring the vertex, was a thick line of light: the coast! The Goddess had brought them within sight of land and was drawing closer to shore all the time. His pulse quickened, but still he felt . . . *slowed*.

'I have thought for some time,' he said carefully, 'that Stone's charm has an ill effect on the spirit of man – or on the spirit of all creatures for that matter. What I mean to say is that you selkies are not unusual in displaying what you, Ruane, refer to as "apathy". The same trait was evident in the clan of my Neolithic companion, Gerent, and also in the dragon colony we encountered. With a few exceptions, both were devoid of adventurers, of individuals willing to experiment or even to learn. Something about Stone, some malicious combination of magic and magnitude, perhaps, works to subdue curiosity. In short, when you come to Stone you are likely to lose all ambition, all desire to challenge what you see. I sense the same process at work here, though I must confess,' he rubbed his brow, trying to press away the headache that was developing behind his eyes, 'it seems exaggerated.'

Ruane's eyes were wide as she listened; Jonah sensed she was hungry for news of the wider world beyond this ocean, that he was more than just a stranger to her: he was a messenger. 'What you say explains a great deal, Jonah! It may be that the presence of Rata Kadul intensifies this magic of which you speak. The selkies are encased in a shroud of indifference. Now all becomes clear: were we to distance ourselves from the Goddess then Her power over us would diminish, yet it is that very power that prevents us from distancing ourselves! A neat trap, would you not say so, Tam?'

The non-committal shrug. The smile.

'It is only a hypothesis, Ruane,' said Jonah. 'I really know nothing about your people. Do not rely on my deductions.'

'It is the truth, Jonah! Do you not know it when you hear it?'

*   *   *

Jonah walked upStone with Ruane along what he could not stop thinking of as a shore; at least, he walked while she crawled. With her seal-like hindquarters she was certainly clumsy out of the water, but was able to match his pace so long as he did not walk too fast. Together they descended the ridged slope of Her ribcage and strolled along the softly curved valley floor that was Her flank, moving in the direction of Her tail. To their right Her belly swelled outwards into the sky before rolling away like a fleshy alp; the ocean was a wall of water to their left, the actual waterline perhaps fifty yards away up a shallow rise. There were fewer selkies here in the valley – the mountain of Rata Kadul's torso cast an immense shadow and the air was noticeably cooler. Stone's eternally falling wind still pressed against Jonah's head, but it was weaker than he remembered it.

His clothes – and Darwin's book – had dried quickly in the sunshine. He allowed his bare feet to scuff the ground. Yet this was not ground but skin, he reminded himself. Pale and translucent, Her hide was divided into irregular tiles varying in size from a few feet across to tens of yards. White flakes and strands of seaweed were clustered in the cracks between the cells – or were they scales? It was altogether unearthly. Jonah brought the back of his hand close to his face and examined his own epidermis, trying to imagine how that would seem were he a flea or some small parasite crawling across it. Similar to the surface over which he was walking, he supposed. Rata Kadul's torso was quite hairless however, much to his relief: he had had enough of forests for the time being.

The blue rope trailed behind him but, rather than impeding his progress, it moved with him; though its root remained embedded in the Goddess's skin it slid along behind him, permanently connected but free to move wherever he led it.

Stopping to look up at the gravity-defying ocean, he

recalled his impression of the Goddess when he had first seen Her behind the waves. She had been surrounded by living things, a veritable ark. There was no sign of those things now; apart from a scattering of selkies lining the ribs behind them, all was deserted.

He was about to ask Ruane about this when he remembered how the Goddess had rotated in the water. Once Her face had gone past they had spent most of their time looking at her back.

'Her cargo of sea-beasts,' he asked, his voice loud against the steady lapping of the waves, 'they reside along Her spine, do they not? I remember the appearance of Her flesh was very different there; I seem to recall it looked red and swollen, even disfigured.'

'That is right. As I explained to you, Rata Kadul supports a mighty crop of life. She keeps her underbelly largely clear of growth, for the convenience of the selkies. Her back, however, is a different matter. There She moderates Her control, allowing a wide variety of living things to flourish: weeds and worms, corals, sponges, kelps and kelpies, flatfish and reels and many other denizens of the sea. This is our farm. This is what the juruas hunger for whenever the Goddess approaches the shore.'

'Juruas? What are they?'

'Little monsters.'

She would not be drawn further. They ambled on, soon reaching the bottom of the slope. Dusk filled the vale like an enormous liquid shadow.

'Tell me, Ruane, how is it that you alone out of all your people have escaped? What happened to the rope that Rata Kadul bound around your waist, and why does she continue to tolerate your presence?'

'The Goddess is short-sighted. She perceives the selkies as a population, not as a group of individuals. This, I think, is your salvation, Jonah.'

'Yes, I had wondered about that. Archan, through

the medium of the Goddess, undoubtedly believes me to be consumed. This was clearly her intention: to have me consumed and destroyed. If Rata Kadul is unaware of my escape from her belly (and I suspect that even Grandfather Tree's onslaught was but a pin-prick to her, a trivial ailment to be all but ignored) then her eyes may have turned from me altogether. Her present indolence is evidence of this, for if Archan believed me still to be alive then surely she would have instructed her puppet to continue the pursuit. And if what you say is true, then the Goddess has already forgotten that I existed, if she was ever aware of it in the first place.'

'As to the riddle of my binding rope,' Ruane went on, 'the answer is simple: I never had one. When a selkie child is born – an all too infrequent occurrence – it is taken immediately by the juruas to the mouth of the Goddess, where the Goddess's holy teeth remove the third finger of the left hand, a delicate operation for such mighty obelisks, you will agree; the teeth are honed with charm, of course, making their accuracy unparalleled. The necklace of fingers you have already seen, and you also understand the reason for the amputation.'

Jonah nodded. 'The suppression of the tendency of a female selkie to grow into a new Goddess. Yes, you have already explained this to me, and it reminds me suddenly of a colony of bees, where the ruling queen prevents the emergence of a new queen by using special scents. What the queen bee achieves by potions and philtres your Goddess achieves by wielding charm. But I still do not understand why you are not captive.'

'I was taken to Rata Kadul's mouth at exactly the same time as another infant; I believe we had been born within a few breaths of each other. The ropes, as you have witnessed, are extruded spontaneously from the skin of the Goddess but not, I believe, by an act of will on Her part. Rather their emergence is a reflex, a response to an untethered selkie presence. As soon as our fingers had been removed, two ropes snaked towards us, but they became entangled due to a freak current and both struck the other child simultaneously. You may see her still roaming the weed-beds, with her twin tethers. The event apparently confused whatever system the ropes use to track which selkie is tethered and which is not, and as we have discussed Rata Kadul herself does not see me, and so since that day I have been able to swim quite freely among my people, the rest of whom remain prisoners. It has given me a unique perspective.'

They walked on, slowly climbing out of the valley and up the steep slope leading to Her pelvic bone. Her skin grew steadily rougher the higher they climbed, and soon the occasional dark grey hair was visible, sprouting like a sapling from between two scale-cells. Jonah's tether, ten yards of smooth blue rope, followed him obediently, a constant reminder of his predicament.

'Can anything cut the tethers?' he asked, knowing the answer.

'Some have tried. There is no tool we know that can even scratch them. But I believe there is a way.'

Together they crested the hill and turned to look downStone at the sunset. The sky had turned orange while they had been in the valley's shadow; the sun was now a glorious yellow ball hugging the coast. Clouds were pouring down from high above, turning to fragments as they dashed themselves against some invisible current of air. It was more beautiful than any sunset Jonah had yet seen on Stone, though he fancied he had seen even more spectacular ones back on the Earth. The thought felt like a betrayal, and for a moment he struggled to remember which place was really his home.

He looked in the opposite direction, taking in the view of Rata Kadul's tail. A dark grey meadow extended for a quarter of a mile down a gently undulating slope; it was formed from dense growths of wiry hair, each strand about as high as Jonah's shoulder. Walking through it, he supposed, would be a little like walking through a vast field of corn . . .

The hair-meadow descended towards the narrower part of Her tail where a pair of whale-flukes flared like massive triangular sails. He watched them lazily stroking the surface of the water, barely raising a ripple as they slipped first into the sea then out. He remembered the steel fish he and Gerent had found in the lesky's sculpture garden and imagined that craft being driven not by a propeller but by mechanical fins, a scientific reconstruction of an organic motor. Surely in the future of man such marvels would be commonplace?

Tipping his head to the side he tried to convert the view into a horizontal Earthly scene. He could not: everything was wrong, from the angle of the light to the direction of the water cascading off the constantly moving flukes. He closed his eyes, no longer willing to contemplate the alien richness of the vista.

Music came to him on the breeze. Its tender melody reminded him of reeds and rushes, an oboe blowing mournfully on the banks of a river, a blade of grass vibrating in the last breaths of a dying day. He thought it must be the sound of the wind in the meadow, an ocean-sound infiltrating the giant crop. Its soft lament enhanced his melancholy and he opened his eyes to find tears spilling out on to his cheeks.

The sun was disappearing. The hair-meadow was no longer grey but orange and blue, alight with the evening. Beside him Ruane had reared up on her tail; stanced thus she was as tall as him, a fact that took him quite by surprise. Her attenuated shadow reached almost to the tip of Rata Kadul's tail.

'Can you see them?' she said excitedly. Not waiting

for his answer she jabbed a finger towards the forest. 'There. Beyond that patch of shadow.'

Jonah could see nothing in the darkness towards which she was pointing, but he was sure the song had grown louder. A deeper reed had joined the melody, under-pinning it with a powerful undulating bass. Ruane was trembling.

'What is it?' he asked. 'What is this music? Are there selkies out there, playing on exotic instruments?'

'Oh no, not selkies.'

Now he glimpsed a movement further down the slope. The sun had gone. The sky had deepened to a heavy royal purple and he could sense the black of night plunging towards him from far upStone, from the future.

A head appeared from the uppermost hairs of the meadow, too remote for Jonah to resolve anything but its outline. Long and thin, atop a sinuous neck, it looked like nothing so much as a pair of scissors balanced at the end of a hose. As he watched its scissor-mouth opened, revealing a dextrous tongue that lashed into the forest then back to the creature's mouth. Just before it dis-appeared again Jonah saw a blur of red at its tip: some-thing it had snatched from the foliage.

'What is it?' he whispered.

'It is what I brought you here to see,' Ruane murmured in reply. 'This is the creature in which lies our hope for salvation. It is more soaked in charm than any other we know: it absorbs magic with every breath it takes yet most of that charm is never released. The death of these beasts is a beautiful and perilous sight, for when their bodies fail a lifetime's charm is set free in a single moment. I have spent a lot of time with them, and I know their ways. I trust them and believe they trust me. And I want you to meet them too.'

'What are they called?'

'They are the Shifters, and this is just one of their many forms.'

'Is it them you were thinking of when you said you believed you knew a way to release your tethers? Do they hold the key to your prison?'

'I hope so, Jonah. I hope so.'

She led him into the field of hair. His initial concern that his own tether would become fouled on the dense growth proved unfounded: it tracked his movements unerringly, never once becoming tangled no matter how much their course meandered. There was a path of sorts, one seldom trodden and increasingly littered the deeper they went: stranded crustaceans fought their way through heaps of seaweed, fish caught unawares by the breaching of the Goddess gulped stupidly at the air that would shortly kill them. It was like a beach caught by an unexpected and cataclysmic tide.

They descended the slope of Rata Kadul's tail while the darkness thickened around them. Tiny insects chirped in the open sky to their right, their long legs aglow like the tails of fire-flies; they looked like sparks dancing in the twilight, each insect a multiple light source.

'What will happen to me if She decides to submerge again?' demanded Jonah abruptly, voicing the fear that had been with him ever since they had returned to the air.

'It is unlikely now, tonight at least. Rata Kadul has been swimming hard for many days now and She needs to rest. She will not consider the deep until tomorrow afternoon at the earliest, and perhaps not even until the day after. You are safe for a time.'

'Hmm. But what then?'

'That is one reason we are here, Jonah.'

A head reared up in front of them, pirouetting so that it stared directly into Jonah's eyes. Poised like a cobra about to strike, it towered twice as high as a man. In that moment of shocked silence, with a pair of bright yellow eyes staring down at him from that knife-like visage, he could feel his heart trying to explode out of his chest. The Shifter's mouth gaped open to reveal multiple lines of teeth like a shark's; its breath smelt of fish, old and rank; far back in a cavernous throat its tongue writhed like a caged python. Jonah stood his ground, but he was shaking from head to foot, jaw clenched, unable to articulate his sudden terror.

Some distance behind it, three identical heads ascended, staring down as imperiously as the first.

With a smooth gliding motion Ruane placed herself between Jonah and the looming Shifter. To his astonishment she pressed first her hands then her face against the base of its neck and murmured to it in low, soothing tones. Soon he realized she was not talking: she was singing.

The Shifter responded at once, coiling its neck so as to bring its pointed head down to their level. Its face floated before Jonah's, yellow eyes partly veiled by translucent membranes, generous mouth parted enough to show the first line of teeth; it almost seemed to be smiling at him. Its skin was pale yellow and smooth like silk.

Then, abruptly, it changed shape.

Its long neck contracted almost to nothing while a pair of human shoulders rose up either side of it. The head flattened then grew round. Jonah watched in astonishment as it rearranged its anatomy before his eyes. Hooves raised themselves from where they had been hidden in the Goddess's hair, melting into hands as they did so; the translucent eyelids turned opaque then cleared to transparency, revealing eyes that were human in all but the yellow hue of their irises, gazing back into his own; teeth rolled from its gums and out of its mouth altogether on to its chin, where they wove themselves into a wiry beard.

Stage by stage, piece by piece, the Shifter transformed itself into a man.

Only a few seconds had passed before its three companions underwent the same metamorphosis. The trio of giants stretched their arms solemnly above their heads, then disappeared into the undergrowth again.

The first Shifter towered over them, a veritable Goliath. Though its shape had changed out of all recognition its overall bulk had not; it still wore the same buttery skin, smooth and eminently flexible. Ruane, who had pulled away during the transformation, drew close again and laid her head against the giant's midriff.

'It is good to see you again, Lawal,' she said. 'Do you remember me?'

'Of course,' rumbled the Shifter. 'You are Ruane. You are a selkie. You are my friend.'

'He does not always remember,' said Ruane to Jonah in what amounted to a stage whisper. 'Sometimes I have to remind him of everything – how we met, what my name is, how we are friends and that it would not be polite for him to try to kill me.'

'Does he try that often?' asked Jonah, nervously glancing at the giant's grim visage, made even grimmer by the paucity of the light.

She shrugged. 'Not as often as he used to, so I suppose he is learning.'

'Are the Shifters of low intelligence then?' enquired Jonah. He immediately regretted what he had seen as a reasonable and innocent question when Lawal's yellow paw of a hand grasped him about the neck and lifted him high enough that his toes were scrabbling to maintain contact with the ground. The giant's fishy breath exploded over his face like a grenade, and the low growl in his throat was equally reminiscent of artillery.

'Enough!' cried Ruane, tugging at the Shifter's massive arm. 'Lawal! Let him go, please. He is ignorant of your ways and did not mean to offend you. Please, give him a chance to apologize and then we can help him to understand.'

'Why should he understand?' grunted Lawal. 'Why did you bring him at all?'

'Because he can help us, Lawal. He can help you – he can help us all.'

The Shifter's dark moon-face glared at Jonah for a moment or two longer, then he relented and lowered him to the ground.

'Th-thank you, Ruane,' Jonah coughed, rubbing his throat. 'I am truly sorry, Lawal. Please forgive me for jumping to an inappropriate conclusion, and pray tell me if there is any way I can make amends.'

'Well,' said Lawal, addressing Ruane after a moment's consideration, 'your friend is polite. And my age vexes me. But can he help?'

'With your permission, Lawal, I will tell him what we know, and what we have guessed to be true. Jonah – are you ready for a story?'

Jonah sighed. 'I have heard many stories recently, Ruane, but none from lips as fair as yours.'

'Nightfall is time for tales,' put in Lawal. 'That much I recall.'

'This is a story from the home-world we all share,' began Ruane. 'Some of it is known, some of it is deduced from our shared knowledge, some of it is pure guesswork. Much of it, I believe, is true . . .

'It was a world of charm. Across its face, life was drawn in a few mighty strokes. Undisputed lords of all were the fire-born trolls, whose heads cleaved the sky as they strode from one continent to the next, carving the landscape with their bare hands. Next in line of power were the faeries. As different from the trolls as night is from day, the faeries were the first and greatest of the aethereals, insubstantial spirit-beings who took on solid forms only once in every hundred years. Later, but not much later, came the dragons.

'As well as the trolls there were lesser colossi: the giants of earth and salt and ice and stone, but they were really pale imitations of the trolls whose forms they mimicked. As for the faeries, they were alone and uncontested in the aethereal realm.

'And these were all the creatures there were. Life was abundant but there was no diversity. Until the day the faeries made war on each other.

'The war lasted for only one day. The reasons for the conflict have long since been forgotten, but it is known that two opposing factions met on a battlefield belonging to a third and there occurred the most dreadful carnage imaginable. Faeries were slaughtered in their millions on this one day when all faeries were corporeal . . . and thus able to die. And so the race that had once been known as the Gentle Ones saw a shadow fall across its otherwise peaceful history, and some of its oldest and wisest ministers pledged that such bloodshed would never happen again.

'Looking beyond the complex political machinations by which the war had been engendered, these faery ministers considered *insularity* to be the single key factor behind the violence. Faeries were, they said, too much alike. There was, they said, too little scope for individuals to express themselves. Their society was, in short, stagnant.

'So they decided to do something about it.

'Having stolen shape-changing charms from the giants (who had possessed this knowledge for aeons) the ruling faeries waited another hundred years until all faeries adopted bodies once more, then they set to work.

'It happened quickly: by the evening of that fateful day three-quarters of the faery population had lost their wings. Many of them saw their legs fuse together into a tail, capable of propelling them variously through water, wood, rock and a range of more exotic elements. All of those whose bodies were changed by the carefully scattered charm found that they were no longer wholly aethereal: when the sun rose the next day they were trapped in their new bodies.

'In one stroke the faery ruling class had decimated its population, ridding itself of its most rebellious fraction. In doing so it had created a wealth of new races, all of whom, in time, spread across the globe.

'Though there was much celebration among the remaining faeries, many said afterwards that it was the beginning of the end of the aethereals. Some even muttered that the cynical actions of the faery elite had accelerated – if not actually brought about – the fall of charm and a premature Turning. Their days were now haunted by fears of the future, and inside even their aethereal forms they could feel the heavy calcium that was slowly turning to bone. Soon they would have skeletons, and then it was only a matter of time before they too would be trapped in the physical world, forced to fend for themselves against the twin forces of nature and mortality, neither of which had troubled them unduly before.

'As for their strange offspring, they thrived, for a time at least. Some even clawed their way back into the realm of the aether, using their bodies merely as a means of connecting with the physical world. Eventually they too were swamped by nature's savage tide, but before that sad day they lived their lives in all the far corners of the world: the nymphs and the dryads, the sprites and the selkies, the peris and the leskies and all the spirits of the land and its many sons. They soon learned to enjoy the freedom of the natural world, and just as quickly forgot the complex shape-changing magic that had brought them there, though they remained jealous and wary of the faeries. And though they were kin, those ties of blood were also forgotten and they lived as different races live: together yet alone in a world of infinite variety.'

'Darwin would have smiled,' commented Jonah as Ruane paused in her telling of the tale. She and Lawal looked at him blankly. 'Charles Darwin proposed the theory of evolution by natural selection. The faeries ended up practising a distinctly *unnatural* selection – some might even say "unholy" – but achieved a similar result: a great diversity of species.'

'What they did must have seemed cruel at the time,' said Ruane. 'But without the cull my people would not exist.'

'This does explain something I have found puzzling, namely the many similarities between the selkies and the dryads, and even Grandfather Tree for that matter. You all have tails instead of legs, but your torsos are largely human. Or rather I should say largely *faery*. The dryads and the lesky swim through wood while you swim through water. The common origin of your species is clear to see now that I know something of your history.'

'And yours, Jonah, for your race is descended from the faeries too. We are kin, you and I.'

'I still find it hard to adapt my view of the past. You see, I was brought up to believe in Darwin's Theory of Evolution, not faery tales describing charm and the turning of the world!' He shook his head; he knew only too well that the world possessed many conflicting histories, all of which might – or might not – be true. Yet his heart balked at the suggestion that to be human was not all it seemed.

Lawal moved suddenly, scratching at the back of his neck with one immense paw. As he did so his arm elongated, becoming a curved knot of muscle quite unlike any mode of anatomy Jonah had ever seen before. The light was almost gone, making it hard to see his face, but Jonah was sure his features were becoming blurred.

'And what about you, Lawal?' he asked. 'Were your ancestors part of this great faery cull?'

'I . . .' the giant creature wiped its face with one distorted arm. When the arm fell again most of its features were gone; it was like looking at an unformed clay bust, abandoned by the sculptor after only an hour's work. 'I do not recall.'

'The Shifters were indeed one product of the cull,' said Ruane, giving her huge companion a reassuring pat on the leg. 'Perhaps the saddest. Or so it is assumed, since the Shifters themselves remember nothing of the event. Most of the other victims – my ancestors included – received sufficient of the shape-changing charm to alter their bodies once and once only. It is said that the race of Shifters comprises those faeries who received an abnormally high dose; they were never able to fix their final form as the rest of the new species were. The Shifters change their shape, usually by an act of will, sometimes spontaneously. Moments of high emotion are particularly powerful triggers. They are good mimics of other species, and tend to copy any new shape they see. Hence Lawal's attempt to copy you, Jonah. They cannot alter their overall bulk, of course, so even his best effort has created a giant. Nor can they alter the colour and texture of their skin without a colossal waste of charm.'

'Forgive me, but I do not understand why you consider this to be sad. Is it not a wondrous gift, to be able to change one's form thus? Why, one day you could dive to the deepest ocean, the next you could sprout wings and explore the heavens! Is this not the most miraculous gift?'

Lawal shook his head. 'It might be,' he acknowledged. 'But Shifters do not remember well. Many memories . . . gone. But there is one we must retrieve.'

'And what is that?' Jonah asked.

'The memory of what we really look like.'

The darkness was complete but for the phosphorescence of the ocean and the sparkling of the fire-flies. In this faint glow Jonah saw Lawal's form change again: a long neck extruded, carrying the same scissor-shaped head he had seen first. The man-shape melted into a squat body bearing four stout legs and a long serpentine tail. It was like no animal of Earth; nor, apparently, was it the natural form of the Shifter.

'Does your wish have any meaning?' he asked carefully. 'Forgive me, but if the faeries created you as ever-changing beings, of what value is the knowledge of your first form? Would not the first Shifters have looked much like the dryads and the selkies, given what we already know? We can surely make a reasonable guess that the natural Shifter form comprises a faery body and a fish-like tail, and by extrapolation . . .'

'That is not enough!' It was odd to hear the same, gruff voice emerging from that slender head, balanced now many feet above. 'We must know! There is a source. There is a beginning, but it is lost in distant memory.'

Lawal's angry breath clouded round Jonah again, its stench overwhelming. A confusion of animal noises broiled in his throat: the growl of a wolf, the scream of a hawk, the rattle of a snake.

'You can retrieve it for them, Jonah,' announced Ruane, turning on him with her eyes shining.

'Me? I . . . is that what you want of me, Ruane? Do you want me to enter the memory rods in search of this elusive primal form of the Shifters? That much I can do, if I can but summon the energy. But how does this help you?'

'I have made a deal with Lawal. If I can supply him with the knowledge his people crave – with your help, of course – then he will give me his charm when he dies.' Jonah was about to interrupt but she pressed on regardless, her tone urgent. 'I believe the enormous amounts of charm Lawal has absorbed through his life will be sufficient to cut the tethers, if the magic can only be directed at the crucial moment. Lawal is dying – at most he has only a few days to live – but he is not so weak that he cannot make a bargain.'

Jonah shook his head. 'Ruane, how can you be sure of any of this? How can you possibly know what effect this explosion of charm might have; and what use, forgive me again, is the forgotten knowledge to one who is about to die?'

'Death comes to all, faery,' growled Lawal. 'One moment's knowledge outweighs a lifetime's ignorance.'

'Nor will the knowledge be his alone!'

Jonah jumped at the sound of a new voice. Looking up he saw not three but a multitude of scissor-heads. They swayed like trees.

'There are many of us,' the new voice continued. Many mouths were chewing on whatever passed for Shifter supper, and there was no way to gauge which one was speaking. 'We are new to the world of Stone but we are no strangers to charm. If we can repossess the knowledge we have misplaced there is a chance we can liberate the magic that makes us its slave. We absorb charm but we cannot wield it. It is our hope that in rediscovering our true shape we will rediscover the ability to forge spells, to weave magic as our ancestors did. To be ourselves. It is a noble thing Lawal has pledged to do, and we salute him for it.'

Looking Ruane in the eye, Jonah said, 'And what of me? If I do this thing, and if your people are freed, what will you do for me?'

'I will thank you, Jonah. But you are a prisoner too; it may be that this is not only our hope but yours too. The only one you have.'

'I need to think. I need to be alone.'

'We will walk together back to the breast of the Goddess, then I will leave you.'

'Goodbye, Lawal,' said Jonah. The Shifter dipped his weird head; his companions echoed the gesture, then retreated into the night.

The tether lay in a coil at Jonah's side. Ahead, the sky was a featureless curtain of black; behind him was a wall of gentle ocean noise. All was peaceful. In the distance, very faintly, he could still hear the song of the Shifters.

He had used the memory rods enough now to be confident of his navigation skills. And he had proved that he could travel through Stone's store of memories without needing actually to touch the rods; having touched them once, the link was made for good. He could sense them now at the periphery of his awareness, their presence curiously like the distant singing of the Shifters, something heard rather than seen. Not for the first time he imagined the rows of rods as a musical stave, the score of the aeons carrying notes struck by the passing of innumerable lives.

The music of the spheres . . .

The Shifter wish was, in theory, easily granted. Yet he was troubled. His visits to Rance's and Annie's Kansas memories had proved to him the unreliability of the memory rods as a source of truth. And what were the Shifters seeking if not the truth? Was that something he could realistically promise them?

Would they know if what I told them was wrong?

But he would know.

As for Ruane's plan, he considered it at best desperation and at worst lunacy. She could no more predict the effect the dying Shifter's charm would have on the tethers than he could – always assuming it could be appropriately directed in the first place. And who was to say Lawal really was dying – or if he was, how long it might take? About that side of the arrangement he had the gravest doubts.

Still, the story of the Shifters and their forgotten shape captivated him. Somewhere inside he knew he was going to do this.

Something disturbed the fire-fly glow, something large moving through the air. The insect-shapes scattered, revealing a dragon: Kythe, swooping towards him from the darkness of the night sky.

For the second time that night Jonah felt tears running down his cheeks. He marvelled at the loyalty, the simple *friendship* of this marvellous creature, and stood with arms outstretched.

'You do keep coming back for more!' he shouted as she flared her wings into a stalling attitude. He watched in awe as she dropped her speed from thirty or forty knots to a virtual standstill in the time it took him to take a breath. Light as thistledown she dropped on to the skin of the Goddess, a broad smile on her long, dragon face.

'My, it's good to see you, Jonah!' she exclaimed, wrapping her wings around him enthusiastically. It was like being parcelled up in sailcloth. 'When I saw the mouth of this awful beast closing round the Bark I thought I'd never see you again. But here you are! I'm so glad you're all right – you are all right, aren't you?'

'Yes, Kythe, I am. Apart from this cursed rope, that is. And you?'

'Okay. I've been thinking a lot.'

Kythe frowned when she saw the tether. When Jonah had explained its purpose she tried to bite her way through it, even managing to channel a little charm into her jaw to provide an extra edge to her already sharp teeth. When she withdrew the rope was not even marked.

'Gosh! It's strong stuff. I'm sorry, Jonah, but I think you're stuck here for a while.'

'Maybe I am, but I'm glad you are here with me!'

'You'll be even gladder when I tell you my news!'

Jonah raised an eyebrow then, realizing the gesture would be lost in the dark, asked the excited Kythe to elaborate.

'I found them, Jonah! Annie and Gerent! They're stuck in the ice-stuff on the far shore – some sort of cave they can't get out of. I landed and we shouted to each other through the entrance hole, and they asked if you were all right and I said I wasn't sure, and they said a whale-woman had put them there but that she was really Archan – is that true, Jonah? Is it really her we're sitting on? – and they said I ought to fly back and find out if you really were all right or not and Annie sort of half-laughed and half-cried and said, "Jonah inside a whale!" in a strange voice but Gerent and I didn't understand. So I told them to stay where they were and they said they couldn't very well go anywhere else and by that time it was getting dark and now here I am!'

Jonah rubbed his chin; his mouth was dry. They were imprisoned as surely as he was, but they were close by and that thought gave him hope. The end of the voyage was within sight. If only he could find a way to break the tether . . .

'Uh-oh,' whimpered Kythe. 'I think something's happening!'

Something indeed was happening: Rata Kadul was pitching beneath their feet like a fishing boat in a squall. Yet the wind was still moderate and the waves inconsequential. Jonah started to breathe quickly and deeply in an effort to saturate his lungs with oxygen, a technique he had learned watching young boys diving off the Javanese coast. The Goddess was undoubtedly preparing to submerge.

The pitching continued for only a few seconds before ceasing as abruptly as it had begun. A shudder passed beneath them like an earth tremor chasing a storm, then all was still again.

Stiller, Jonah realized, than it had ever been before.

From somewhere deep behind the waves something vast emitted a bleak and muffled groan.

Then Jonah felt the tether tighten briefly around his waist before twitching, just once, and falling away. He watched incredulous as the blue rope was drawn back into Rata Kadul's skin, slithering into a hidden pore with increasing speed until finally, with an audible 'pop', it disappeared altogether.

He was free.

13

Annie's Journal – Four

I'm writing in almost complete darkness, so if this is illegible I'm sorry. The only light is coming from the jurua pit, and that's little enough. But I've got to get this down, and down fast. I think things are getting a little crazy.

It started about ten minutes ago. It'd been dark for maybe an hour, and we'd only just gotten used to the weird light coming from the bodies of the new-born juruas (they glow a bit when they first emerge from the glice – it looks like they've got little blue candle flames inside them, the light of creation or some damn thing). We'd settled down to try and get some sleep, and I think Gerent managed to doze, when suddenly this weird noise woke us up. It was like a scream, far away but incredibly clear. It was eerie, like seeing someone a mile down the street and still being able to read their expression.

Then the juruas went crazy.

I think I described the pit as being like a bowl full of piranhas – I'd read back and check but I can hardly see. Well, now it's like someone took those piranhas and pumped them full of firewater. They started jumping out of the water and for a minute we thought they were coming for us, but they just dived straight back into the fray. They're tearing each other apart trying to dig their way down the well. They're dying by the hundreds but they're being born by the hundreds too – the whole process just got speeded up. Something's got them riled, that's for sure.

I'm going to . . .

I just had to pull Gerent back from the edge. He'd gotten too close, crouched down on his hands and knees to get a better look because he said he thought they were slowing down. One of them slashed at his face and I had to practically knock him over to save him. Damn fool.

Got a close look at the jurua. Wish I hadn't.

They've got *faces*. Their bodies are round, like transparent plates, and they've got all these scrabbling crab's legs underneath, each one with so many joints it's more like a tentacle than a leg, and you can hear the joints clicking so as it moves it sounds like whipcracks. Oh, and did I say they had two long needles instead of claws? Well this one had *six* long needles sticking out from underneath its shell in two sets of three, all sliding in and out like evil little pistons. And in between the two sets of needles was a tiny face, like a bat's face made of glass, all squashed and evil.

It clung to the edge of the pit, looked at each of us in turn, then spun round and jumped back into the arena. A second later we saw it ripped to shreds. Its body flew apart like broken glass, and when the pieces struck the glice walls of the pit they hissed like fat on a griddle.

Before all this started I was going to write about Kythe's visit. Her shadow fell across the hole in the roof and at first I thought Archan had come back, but then I heard Kythe's voice. I was overjoyed, it was so good to hear her again!

She tried to get down to us but there was no way she was going to fit through that hole. I couldn't see her very well, but she seemed different somehow – bigger or some damn thing.

She told us that Jonah and the Bark had been swallowed by the whale-woman. I was caught between laughter and horror. I mean, has the whole world gone crazy now? Or the whole of this world at least. I can't accept that he might be gone. Gerent says the same but I can't help thinking he wouldn't be too sorry if Jonah were dead. I guess it would make things . . . simpler.

Dear God I hope he's alive. I pray there's enough magic tied up in that boat to punch a way out of that whale-woman's belly. But if it really is Archan behind it all she won't stop until she knows he's dead.

I wonder if she'll come back for me then.

It's slowing, thank God. The jurua birth-rate's slowed to a fraction of what it was when we got here. The level of bodies is going down too. It's actually going down as I write this. I shan't be sorry to see the back of them, that's for damn certain.

The first hint of daylight. Gerent's telling me to stop writing but I want to finish this. The juruas are gone. Not long after I wrote the last entry they stopped emerging from the glice altogether, and a few minutes after that they all disappeared down into wherever it is the pit leads to. We were left in total darkness – it really was black, blacker than anything I've known. Back home even the darkest nights are kind, with moonlight and starlight. I held Gerent close to me all night, and we kissed and even when we were kissing I couldn't see his face.

It was scary at first. On top of the darkness the silence was unfamiliar, after the din the juruas had been making all day. I was sat alone, trembling just a little, when something touched my thigh. I bit my tongue trying to stop the scream but of course it was only Gerent. He was

247

frightened too. He touched me some more, and in the pitch black it was – oh God, it was not what a lady should be writing about, even a rough-necked Kansas girl like me! I couldn't see him at all, only feel him.

Later we both got to trust the silence, and to believe the juruas weren't coming back. We both slept until the morning light woke us up.

The first thing we did was look down into the pit. Gerent was all for jumping in and taking a look but I told him not to be so stupid! It's very like a funnel, only it curves away as it narrows so you can't actually see what's around the corner. There could be anything, I told him. Even if there isn't a jurua posse waiting there for one of us to try it, chances are it narrows so much we'd never get through anyway – what we can see is tight enough and it looks like it only gets tighter.

And the sides of the pit are steep and slippery, so once you were down there you'd never get back up again.

I talked him out of it, thank God. I'm surprised he even considered it. He's usually more level-headed than that.

Personally I don't think there are any juruas down there – I can't hear anything and they're not the quietest of beasts. All the same, there's no more chance of escape that way than there is through the roof.

Still at least it's quiet.

I can't help thinking Jonah's going to come and rescue me soon.

Had another go at prising one of the shells out of the glice.

Gerent found one just below the lip of the pit, one we hadn't been able to get at while the juruas had been in there. It was beautiful, like a conch. More than half of it was poking out and he managed to get his fingers into one of the spirals. He pulled and pulled but it wouldn't budge.

Then I had an idea. Taking his place I got hold of the shell and turned it. It moved at once. I twisted it right out of the glice, just like taking out a screw from a wall. Gerent looked cross – he likes to work things like that out for himself and gets moody when someone gets the better of him. I kissed him and he softened up quick enough.

He sat down against the wall and I sat down in his lap, my back against his chest. It's our favourite way to be close. We examined the shell, me holding it up and him looking over my shoulder.

Just like everything else in this hourglass of a prison it was hard and transparent. Gerent pointed out a scratch running round the inside of the spiral, like a flaw in a crystal. I said it looked like a diamond, which it did. And that was all. No matter how hard we looked at it, it was just a glass shell.

Gerent was about to toss it into the pit when I asked for it back.

'Let's listen to the sea before we throw it away,' I said, and held it up to my ear.

But it wasn't the sea I heard inside that shell, it was a voice. Impossibly far away yet quite clear. Crystal clear, in fact. And though I knew her only through what Jonah had told me, I knew straight away who it was.

It was the faery queen.

14

Exodus

'And the waters were a wall unto them on their right hand, and on their left.'

Jonah spoke into a rising wind, with the sun plunging out into the sky directly before him, the ocean a wall on his left hand. Standing on Rata Kadul's shoulder was a little like standing on the dome of St Paul's Cathedral, and getting up there had been as perilous as climbing to the top of that mighty edifice. The view made it worthwhile, however.

The entire body of the Goddess was laid before him like a statue miraculously floating in the ocean. All the way back along Her body selkies were waking to their new state of freedom; there were clusters of activity, selkies deep in conversation; minor scuffles had broken out in places; many were wandering aimlessly, looking dazed; some of them returning to the water, swimming upwards through the descending waves in an effort to reach Her trailing left arm, a peninsula pointing into nothing but empty ocean. Some were looking downStone in the direction of Rata Kadul's head, which from their vantage they would not actually be able to see. They would be able to see him clearly, exposed as he was on the rounded crest of Her shoulder.

But Jonah was not concerned with the selkies: he was looking for the Bark.

Earlier, while it was still dark, Jonah and Kythe had puzzled over the disappearance of the tethers. Kythe suspected trickery but Jonah was not so sure.

'Grandfather Tree! What if he has managed to turn the Bark against the Goddess from the inside! What if he has injured the Goddess somehow, found a way to subvert her magic?' But could the lesky actually cut his way out? 'Kythe? I hardly dare to ask you this, but . . . well, you have grown your wings to a spectacular length and you seem to be much stronger these days than ever you were . . .' He broke off, embarrassed.

The young dragon peered at him quizzically in the darkness, then grinned. 'Oh, you want to know if I can carry you any further than I could before! Do you know what – I think I could probably carry you all the way to the shore. In fact, I'll take you to the other side of Stone if you like!'

'Thank you, Kythe. The shore will be quite far enough. But not just yet, I fancy. Could you take me somewhere a little nearer to begin with?'

It was surprisingly comfortable on Kythe's back. His only experience of flying with the dragon had been under extreme duress: usually being snatched from certain death during an untimely fall. She had saved his life on more than one occasion; he could feel his debt of gratitude weighing like a comfortable chain around his neck.

'Do let me know if I hurt you.'

'You won't hurt me, Jonah! I've changed a lot, you'll see!'

Indeed she had. By Jonah's best reckoning she was twice as big as she used to be; clearly she had used charm of an order far beyond the basic shape-changing spell of the Shifters. Her gauzy wings spanned at least thirty feet

251

and looked more than capable of lifting their combined weight. He held on tight nevertheless.

There was a natural saddle just behind her head, a single broad scale free of the short, flexible spines adorning the rest of her back. It was almost as though she had put it there on purpose . . . His hands dropped naturally on to the horns flaring from the back of her head; though he did not exert any pressure, when she turned her head it felt as if he were doing the steering.

'Are you ready?' she asked brightly when he had finally stopped shuffling his backside.

'As ready as I will ever be, Kythe. If you get tired, or feel you cannot carry me any more . . .'

'Then I'll drop you over the side. Stop fussing, Jonah! Just enjoy the ride!'

She turned, dipped her head and slid gracefully down the slope of Rata Kadul's belly. Within a few seconds they were airborne, and to Jonah it was like entering yet another new world.

He had been out here in the sky before, naturally. The dragon giant Torus had lived on a floating island several miles out from the surface of Stone, an island to which Frey's magic wings – the same wings that were now fused to Gerent's back – had carried Jonah and his companions. And once he had fallen through this same sky, an event he tried to put to the back of his mind just at the moment. But this . . . this was different. This was breathtaking!

Kythe was riding the air like a giant eagle. The combination of body-sculpting and constant practice had made her a remarkable flier, and she could not resist showing off a little. She swooped low under the body of Rata Kadul, below the shadow of Her overhanging breast and into the concavity of Her flank. Then she rolled – fast enough to cut lines of vapour from the air but not so suddenly as to compromise Jonah's grip – and ascended past the sleeping selkies and up towards the open ocean.

Then she pulled away from Stone altogether, retreating into the limitless sky until the sea was a remote, blue-black canvas, the Goddess a driftwood doll embedded in its weave. DownStone, the coast was just visible as a dim, near-vertical band, much nearer than it had been the previous day; upStone there was only the sea and the incipient brightness of the pre-dawn sky.

'Kythe! You are a marvel! If this is what it was like in your golden age, then I would visit it with you without hesitation!'

'I've been practising hard! I hope you don't think my wings are too . . . you know, I wouldn't want you to think I was a show-off.'

'You are growing up, Kythe. And it seems that it is in the nature of charm to give creatures a helping hand in that respect, if they choose to take it.'

'Oh, I just love the sky. I feel like I could fly for ever and ever!'

'As I am certain you could! But right at this moment I would like to take a closer look at the Goddess, if I may.'

'Haven't you got close enough already? I mean, you were actually inside her, Jonah.'

'Her face, Kythe. Take me in so that I can see her face.'

She needed no urging to indulge in some spectacular flying. Tumbling downwards, directly in their path, was a feathery ribbon of cloud. It broadened as they approached, obscuring their view of the sea altogether. Kythe careered into it with a whoop of delight.

Immediately they were surrounded by hot, damp vapour; it felt to Jonah like walking into a steam bath, except the steam in this bath was speeding past them at a velocity in excess of fifty knots. He shut his eyes and held tight on to Kythe's horns.

When he opened his eyes they were still in the cloud.

'Kythe?'

'It's all right, Jonah! We're nowhere near Her yet.'

'I come from a place called London, which is famous for its fogs. This is thicker than one of London's best pea-soupers, Kythe. I must confess to be a little . . .'

'Don't worry!'

Visibility returned. The fog unpeeled and there was the ocean, a vast wall of water filling the world from top to bottom and plunging towards them like a juggernaut.

'Now I know how the Egyptians felt!' exclaimed Jonah, ducking his head beneath the low crest at the back of Kythe's skull. Sudden acceleration thrust him down into the saddle as his dragon steed wheeled in a tight, spiralling turn that brought her wingtips mere yards from the waves. No sooner had she pulled back from the sea than the sagging flukes of the Goddess's tail loomed. Man and dragon slipped between them with only a breath or two to spare.

The organic landscape of Rata Kadul's body rolled past, its contours dizzyingly close. Peering around the side of Kythe's head Jonah was unsurprised to see a huge grin on her face. He could not help smiling in sympathy.

Kythe swooped close to the hemispherical mound of Her shoulder – the exact spot where Jonah would later be standing to watch the dawn – and then they were over Her neck. The macabre necklace of selkie fingers was strewn below them, laced with foam from the breaking waves. Slowing now, Kythe slipped gull-like into the rising thermal beneath Her chin; the sudden buoyancy was exhilarating, like a fairground ride.

The skin of Her face was remarkably smooth, as fine as marble. Passing close to Her closed lips Jonah suppressed a shudder; the memory of being swallowed was still vivid.

Kythe pulled away a little as they neared Her eyes, evidently sharing Jonah's apprehension. They had fallen silent: being this close to the face of such a monster was sobering. Jonah felt strangely alone despite his close contact with the dragon: for a moment there was just him and the sky, and the Goddess.

Her eyes were open. They stared unseeing past the hovering dragon and her human passenger, not the blank chrome Jonah had been expecting. The eyes of the Goddess had changed: they were entirely human, apart from the massive scale, their irises the same jade as Ruane's. They did not move, nor did the eyelids blink or even twitch.

Archan had departed.

And Rata Kadul was dead.

'But it cannot be so! Rata Kadul cannot die before a new Goddess has risen to take Her place. The selkies and all the denizens of the Goddess's realm must be allowed to move from the old Goddess to the new. She cannot be dead – it is not in the way of things.'

Jonah could not remember seeing Ruane so emotionally charged. Having joined him on Rata Kadul's shoulder she could see for herself the lifelessness of the body that was her home. Seeing was very different from accepting, however.

'But there is no new Goddess, Ruane. Rata Kadul is dead. At last you have what you dreamed of: your people free and able to make their own choices.'

'But this is . . . this has never happened in living memory. Where shall we live?'

She was growing increasingly agitated, casting her gaze around wildly. Jonah placed his hand on her shoulder. 'Ruane, you can live anywhere. You are free.'

She stung him with tear-filled eyes. 'But we need the Goddess! The freedom I wished for was freedom beneath Her benevolent gaze, to live as we have always lived but untethered. To be subjects and not slaves.'

'Listen to me. Even before Rata Kadul's death Archan

had already subverted the cycle by which the Goddesses replace themselves, simply by prolonging the life of Rata Kadul and preventing the emergence of a natural successor. Indeed, she may have broken the cycle altogether. You must prepare yourselves for the possibility that none of your people will ever again make the transition from selkie to Goddess. Freedom means more than even you imagined, Ruane.'

Jonah looked towards the coast, now only a few miles distant. Glassy cliffs, ablaze in the morning sunshine, formed a wide, near-vertical bar of light towards which the body of Rata Kadul and her living cargo were being carried by an invisible current.

'It looks as though we will be taken to the shore,' he commented. 'Perhaps you will find somewhere there to live, or at least to rest while you discuss what has happened to you.'

But Ruane was not listening. 'I cannot believe She has died. Damn your lesky friend and his meddling. He has killed her from within, poisoned her with his forest magic!' She stopped and stared at the shining cliffs. 'Oh, by the Goddess! The juruas!'

If she had been agitated before, now she was terrified. Thrashing her tail like a fish just landed she beat her hands against Jonah's breast. Kythe, who was circling close by, listening to what snatches of the conversation she could take from the wind, dived to his rescue. Reassuring the young dragon that he was in no danger, Jonah managed to manhandle the writhing selkie into Kythe's firm embrace. Between them they bound her with arm and wing until her energy was spent, after which she stopped struggling and simply sobbed.

Eventually she had no strength even to weep. Kythe unfolded her wings and allowed the selkie to fall into Jonah's arms. They fell awkwardly on to the soft deck of Rata Kadul's skin and sat staring into the vivid blue sky.

'Tell me about the juruas,' said Jonah quietly, after what he judged to be a suitable pause.

'The Goddess is more than a mere provider: She is a protector too. What you have seen, it is only part of what She does for the selkies and all Her children. She loves us, and would not see us come to harm.'

Jonah was about to take issue with this, recalling the necklace of fingers, but he thought better of it.

'As you know,' Ruane continued, 'the body of the Goddess is our home, our farm, the submersible island on which we live our lives, selkies and Shifters and . . . but I have given you lists already. All of us together; a community in constant motion.

'But we are not without our enemies. Occasionally the Goddess grapples with the other giants of the ocean: the serpent lords and the kraken. She always wins, for she is mighty with charm and they are physical beasts, unskilled in the lore of magic. Then there are the juruas.

'The juruas are spawned not in the sea but at its edge. The edge of the sea is a dangerous place; it is not to be trusted. Nor are the juruas. They swarm in the shallow waters near the shore and detest all those who draw near, including the Goddess. They are the guardians of the coast and they will let no creature pass.'

Ruane's words triggered something in Jonah's head but a question chased the thought away before it had properly formed. 'What brings the Goddess to the shore at all, if it is such a place of danger?'

'At the edge of the sea the food is good. One visit alone can yield a bounteous crop of reef. The deep ocean is almost barren, Jonah – only at its edges, or on such living islands as Rata Kadul – does life sustain its grip on Amara. You of all people must know that Amara places little value on the life that clings to its surface. When She visits the shore, the Goddess will uproot whatever reef she can find and return to the sea with it wound around Her body. The reef contains all that is needed to sustain Her for many hundreds of days.'

'Forgive me, but is your definition of the term "reef" the same as mine?'

'I do not know what you understand by the word, but on Amara a reef is an extended mass of flexible coral, like an enormous tether. The coral supports a wealth of life just like Rata Kadul, but it is not sentient as She is. The Goddess can prise a reef from the seabed and wear it like a garment. As soon as it is picked the reef and all it contains begins to die, but there are always more reefs. The juruas live near the reefs. They are small creatures but they number in the millions and this is their great strength. But Rata Kadul absorbs the charm of the reef and can withstand them – She even flaunts Herself in front of them, knowing that they can harm neither Her nor those She protects. As long as She is alive, the juruas are no threat.'

'What current is it that takes us towards the shore?' demanded Jonah. 'Is there anything we can do to prevent Her body from crashing against those cliffs?' He could see a commotion in the water where the cliff met the sea. It might just have been waves, but he fancied it was turbulence caused by something just below the surface – an army of tiny creatures, perhaps, preparing for a battle . . .

'There is a gap in the cliff,' answered Ruane. Her eyes too were fixed on the turbulence. 'It is hidden behind the water but it makes a whirlpool. The whirlpool is huge, Jonah, bigger even than the Goddess. If you throw something into the sea near the whirlpool it is sucked in, never to be seen again. Some say it passes through the cliffs and emerges on the other side, into another ocean just like this one. Others say it is stolen away by the juruas and taken to another world.'

'She's right, Jonah,' quavered Kythe, darting in on the

wind. 'I saw this whirlpool too, don't you remember?'

'I remember only too well, Kythe, and it seems that the body of Rata Kadul will be its next sacrifice. Ruane, your people must be urged to abandon this floating cadaver and take their chances in the open sea.'

'But the juruas will eat them alive!'

'And if they remain here they will surely be drowned!'

Tears returned to Ruane's eyes as she spread her arms as if to embrace the distant selkies. 'Then you tell them, Jonah! Do you think they will listen to me, when they have ignored me my whole life? Do you think they care for anything more than the food they eat today and the sport they will enjoy tomorrow?'

She flung herself away from him, looking back defiantly as she landed heavily on the slope of Rata Kadul's upper arm. Jonah watched her crawl away, head held high, and wondered at the plague of apathy infecting this world of Stone.

'Gerent's people, your dragon community, these wretched selkies, they are all the same!' he cried out to Kythe as she circled over his head. 'What must be done to rouse the inhabitants of Stone, to make them realize that their world is just as real as any other, that there are battles to be fought here and prizes to be won? That the events that go on here *matter*, and that they too can make a difference! That it *behoves* them to make a difference, or at least to try! I am tired of defeatism, Kythe, and I am tired of the way in which people's lives here are not judged to be their own. Do they wish to live or die? Will they not face this world of Stone, will they not look it in the eye and take up the gauntlet it has thrown down before them? Will they not live?'

'Bravo!' cheered Kythe. 'But it is not me you have to convince, Jonah. And there is something else that's worrying me: are you so sure it's Grandfather Tree who finished off the Goddess?'

Jonah frowned. 'I . . . well, do you have a better explanation?'

'A different one. What if it was Archan?'

'Archan? But she was trying to keep the Goddess alive, even after her official term of office was over. It was Archan who closed those mighty jaws around me, not Rata Kadul.'

'Exactly! And once that was done, and Archan thought you were dead, she didn't need the Goddess any more. So she left, killing Her in the process.'

'Abandoned ship and set fire to the rigging,' whispered Jonah. 'By God, Kythe, how right you must be! And how foolish of me not to see it! As soon as Archan let go of the strings, the Goddess fell to the ground.' He shuddered, remembering a time not so distant when it was Annie who had been the marionette. 'Oh dear – this means that the Bark is almost certainly destroyed after all, and Grandfather Tree is dead too.'

'But what about Archan?'

'I must believe what the basilisk ghosts have told me, that Archan is returning from the past with the means to bring Stone down, and that beyond those cliffs of glass is the only place where she can be stopped. I must face her on the Aqueduct, Kythe, and it may be that my only weapon against Archan is her belief that I am destroyed.'

Kythe lashed her tail and snorted. 'I think you'd do better with a sharp sword.'

Years before, Jonah had spent a series of idyllic summers on a farm in Kent. Lily, the farmer's daughter, had introduced him to many things, and their young love had been Jonah's most precious secret; one of the things they did not feel the need to keep secret was the time they spent with the horses. Lily's father had owned two mares, one chestnut and one grey, and she had spent many hours trying to teach Jonah the rudiments of horsemanship.

She rode bareback, legs astride the horse like a man; Jonah could not even maintain his position on a stationary horse without a saddle. He felt clumsy and inadequate, he despised everything about the experience, from the danger of the fall (how he chuckled at that now) to the smell of the animals. But Lily was a natural and desperately wanted him to share her enjoyment. So, for her sake – and not unmindful of his own pride – he persisted, masking his distress.

He never told her how much he hated taking the saddle, and though she teased him about his lack of aptitude she never guessed his true feelings. It was the first time in his life that he understood how love and deception can ride side by side. One on a chestnut mare, one on a grey.

Now, to his amazement, he felt quite at home astride Kythe's bony spine.

'Down there,' he urged, tugging at her horns. 'That's the biggest group.'

'Is Ruane with them?'

'That doesn't matter! Just take me down there, Kythe.'

He felt like one of Arthur's knights as his dragon mount brought him in low to hover above the heads of the astonished selkies. Their genuine surprise gave him a thrill of anticipation: perhaps they were capable of high emotion after all.

'Selkies of Rata Kadul!' he bellowed. 'A new life awaits you! Your Goddess is dead. Even now Her body is being borne towards the maelstrom. If you remain with Her, you too will die. If you take to the sea now you can still avoid the juruas that even now are swarming towards the corpse of the Goddess. Swim upStone: they will not stray far from the shore.'

Eyes of green and turquoise stared up at him, blank as glass.

'You are crazy!' a young female selkie cried. 'The Goddess cannot die.'

'The sea is not our home,' argued another, an older male. 'This is our home.'

'There is no food in the open ocean,' protested a third, speaking directly to Jonah.

'Of course there is food!' Jonah replied, fighting to be heard over the uproar. 'I have travelled from one edge of this sea to the other and seen a multitude of creatures along the way. But you do not need food, do you not know that? The air of Stone contains all that is needed to sustain life. Ruane told me how the Goddess harvested the reefs, but She valued them for something other than their value as a food; it was their charm in which She was interested.'

'Who are you to say that food has no value?' shouted the young female. 'What do you know of our ways, stranger?'

'Very little, I will admit.'

'What do you care? What do you want from us?'

'I want your help. I need your help. If you will let me help you escape, we can work together to save the world we share, the world of Stone.'

'Like I said – you're crazy!'

The female selkie, who looked like Ruane might have done when she was younger, turned her back on Jonah and stalked away through the crowd. The other selkies applauded her.

A fresh voice hailed him, one which he recognized: it was Ruane's brother, Tam.

'I know your name, Jonah, but I do not know you. Nor do you know us. Of course we understand the power of the air: if we do not eat, we do not die. But we *do* eat. We eat because that is what we do, and if we do not eat then we are not what we are. We eat as we swim, as we love one another, as we tend our gardens. Are there not things you do simply because you do them, Jonah? Do you not love, for instance?'

The question caught Jonah unawares and it was a moment before he could answer.

'Forgive me,' he said, 'but as you say, I am ignorant of your ways. But you cannot ignore the peril you are undoubtedly in. Nothing can remain the same forever. If you want there to be a race of selkies in the future you must be prepared to adapt. This is Stone's most subtle charm: that it robs its people of the will to adapt. By doing that, it renders them passive, no longer a threat to its integrity.

'But now there is a new threat, a very real one. A dragon is coming this way, a monster the like of which has never been seen before. A new kind of goddess, you might say. And unless she is opposed she will wipe out everything in her path. I am ready to stand in her way; are you prepared to stand with me?'

Selkie eyes stared at him in disbelief and he knew it was useless. He marvelled that he had held their attention even for this long. One by one they turned away, leaving Kythe hovering over an empty field of flesh.

'Well,' she sighed at length, 'you did your best, Jonah. Did you mean it, when you said you needed their help?'

'Oh, Kythe, I do not know. It seemed the right thing to say. I suppose I thought that if I could present them with a purpose, something more inspiring than simply taking flight, then they might respond. I was wrong, of course.'

'Still, a little extra help wouldn't have come amiss, not where Archan's concerned. Shall we go then? There's no reason to stay around here if all they want to do is see the inside of a whirlpool.'

Jonah could not help thinking about Gerent's people, the Denneth, who had remained inside their castle while it had burned around them, not seeking escape even when it detached itself from Stone's wall and plummeted into the abyss. This was the appalling face of what he was coming to think of as the Disease of Amara. With a very few exceptions, there were no adventurers in this world!

Yet he was convinced the disease had more to do with local magic than with Stone itself. And given that Rata Kadul had been a powerful wielder of such charm, as her magic dispersed there was a chance that the disease would disperse too, at least among the selkies. Maybe they just needed a little more time.

'Can we go towards Her tail?' he asked.

'First the head and now the tail. Make up your mind, Jonah!'

It took less than a minute for Kythe to carry Jonah to the hair-meadow of Rata Kadul's tail. He leaned forward, peering over her shoulders as she soared over the sleek grey contours. Before long he saw what he was looking for: the steady movement of large creatures through the undergrowth.

Their buttery skin was unmistakable. Scissor-heads reared into the air, gazing at the dragon and her passenger. Then, without warning, the Shifters began to change shape.

One after the other they sprouted long, tapering wings. Retaining their long necks, they allowed their heads to widen in mimicry of Kythe's; serpentine tails lashed out like whips. The transformation moved through the herd like a wave as one by one the Shifters turned themselves into dragons.

No sooner had they changed than they spread their wings and took to the air.

'You have given them the means to escape,' said Jonah

in wonder. 'Quickly, Kythe, I do not want them to leave. Fly in close to the flock.'

New-formed wings lifted all around them; it was like flying into a storm of yellow blossoms. Jonah panicked briefly, unable to remember the name of the Shifter he had met the previous night. Then it came to him.

'Lawal! Lawal, are you here?'

Smooth yellow heads, each one uncannily like Kythe's, swivelled towards him. The flock parted, allowing them to fly through its midst; the Shifters closed up again as they passed, folding like liquid. Jonah scanned the flock, seeking an individual where all the individuals looked the same.

'Jonah?' The voice was familiar. *But might they not all sound alike too?* A dragon-shape sidled close beside them, eyes bright within scaly cowls. 'Have you decided?'

For a moment he had no idea what the Shifter was talking about; then he remembered their conversation, and his own promise to think about the plight of these weird creatures who could not remember their true shape.

'Decided? Yes, Lawal, I will help you if I can. I will use the memory rods to seek out the moment when your race was created, and I will try to bring you evidence of your original form.'

'That is good! What can Shifters do in return?'

Jonah hesitated. 'I had not planned to ask for anything in return, Lawal, but events have outpaced me. I do not wish to see the selkies destroyed by the charm that still enslaves them. I am seeking a way by which they may be taken safely to the shore.'

The flock was still dense around them: clearly the other Shifters were listening to their exchange, choosing not to disperse until an outcome was reached. He found this strangely touching.

'Selkies.' Lawal's flight-path grew erratic as he

pondered; the ability to grow wings did not apparently imbue their owners with great skill in flight. 'Juruas are quick. How many do you want to save?'

'All of them.'

'Yes, I see.' Lawal called out something Jonah could not decipher, whereupon a second Shifter rose out of the flock to join them. 'This is Meem. He is a great thinker and not near to death as I am.'

'I have an idea,' said Meem at once. 'Though it is dangerous. I cannot judge the chance of success.'

'Are you willing to try it?' asked Jonah doubtfully.

'You are willing to unlock the mystery of our past,' replied Meem in a matter-of-fact tone. 'Of course we are willing to try it.'

The attitude of the selkies had changed somewhat by the time Jonah and Kythe flew back over Rata Kadul's belly. They had gathered in an enormous group on the curving flank of the Goddess, evidently confused. A few had taken to the water but most lingered on their floating island.

'Listen to me, I beg you!' Jonah shouted, struggling to be heard over the sound of wind and wave, not to mention the noise of the crowd. Some of the selkies looked up as Kythe's shadow flashed across them, but he was not sure they had even heard his words.

Then he realized he did not need to speak.

Rata Kadul was rotating on the face of the ocean like the hand of a clock. The movement was slow but inexorable. As the line of her trunk moved steadily from horizontal to vertical, what had been a relatively flat plain of flesh was rapidly becoming a mountainside. Urging Kythe back out into the open sky, Jonah looked out on this latest turn of events in wonder.

To his left the whirlpool was clearly to be seen, a vast, dark cavity in the ocean. It looked as if Thor had taken

266

his hammer and struck the sea a mortal blow from which it had never recovered. There was a slow, seductive spinning at its periphery, accelerating to a dizzying blur at the centre. It revived memories of another whirlpool in Jonah's mind, the one that had brought him through to Stone in the first place, and he wondered if the selkie tales might be true, that here was another form of threshold, another route between the worlds.

Even more worrying than the whirlpool was the mass of foam barely a mile from the Goddess. Here the surface of the ocean was fractured by constant, frenzied activity: the juruas, swarming in their millions as they sped towards the prey that, after taunting them for so long, was finally theirs.

Time was running out.

Caught in the pull of the whirlpool, Rata Kadul was performing a slow pirouette in the water, rotating gracefully about Her middle until Her tail was pointing straight down, *Six o'clock*, Jonah thought dizzily. By this time the selkies were in uproar: those who had managed to cling on were doing so for dear life; those who had plunged into the sea were trying not only to avoid the still-revolving mass of their former Goddess but also to swim out of the path of the oncoming juruas. As far as Jonah could see, none had actually fallen from Her skin into the abyss but on Stone, as ever, that was always a danger.

The Goddess continued to rotate until She had more or less reversed Her original orientation – now She was heading, tail-first, directly towards the whirlpool.

Jonah watched with macabre fascination as the piranha-foam of the jurua shoal drew nearer to and then finally touched the grey flukes of Rata Kadul's lifeless tail.

If the sea had been foaming before, now it was positively boiling. The juruas ate through the first twenty yards of the flukes in a matter of seconds; it was like watching concentrated acid etch its way through a metal plate. Progress slowed a little as they proceeded along the length of Her tail (the higher up Her body they travelled the more meat there was) but they progressed none the less. At this rate Rata Kadul's body would be gone within thirty minutes.

The Shifters crowded out of the sky, a mighty flock of identical yellow dragons. Flying swiftly towards the part of Her flank to which most of the selkies were clinging, they barely slowed as they approached the water. Making contact with the sea in a series of almighty splashes, they changed shape once more.

Dragon shapes melted into bizarre composite forms, forms that Jonah recognized only by the sketchy descriptions Ruane had given him. Each Shifter transformed its body into an assemblage of thirty or more small, crystalline shapes that reminded Jonah of crabs made of yellow glass. Instead of claws, these crabs boasted long, whirring needles.

Before the astonished eyes of Jonah, Kythe and several hundred selkies, the Shifters turned themselves into juruas.

This done, the Shifters drew themselves together into a tight formation resembling, to Jonah's eyes, a lifebelt. Between them they created a ring of jurua bodies into the middle of which they urged the selkies to climb. Hesitant at first, the selkies seemed to understand rapidly what was required of them, and most of them complied.

It was a tremendous gamble, for they were relying not only on the juruas' inability to see beyond the protective ring to what was hidden inside, but also on the authenticity of the Shifters' mimicry of the jurua form. Kythe flew Jonah over the ring and between them they hustled as many of the remaining selkies as they could inside. Even now, with their Goddess being consumed yard by yard within plain sight of where they floundered, some of the selkies refused to move. Jonah hardened his heart and left them to their peril: if that was their choice there was nothing he could do.

Now the juruas had reached the wide pelvis of the Goddess. It was as if Her body were being fed into an invisible mincing machine; the notion made Jonah feel quite ill. The ring of imitation juruas broke away from Her flank scant seconds before the cold flesh was torn to shreds. Incredibly the marauding army ignored the life-belt in favour of the dead body and bit by bit the Shifters propelled the makeshift Ark in the direction of the shore.

So single-minded were the real juruas – or short-sighted – that they did not even slow as they ate their way across Rata Kadul's chest; if anything their velocity actually increased. Jonah and Kythe lingered, anxious to follow the progress of the Shifter raft but unable to tear their eyes from the incredible sight of the Goddess being consumed.

If the Bark was not destroyed before, then it surely is now, thought Jonah sadly.

Now only Her head remained, adrift in an aurora of hair. The juruas took it unceremoniously, consuming its lips, its fine cheeks, its eyes, still wide open at the last. By the time they had finished, the Shifter raft was passing directly below the whirlpool and fighting hard against the currents induced by it.

That was when the real juruas turned.

'They have smelt a rat!' exclaimed Jonah, tightening his grip on Kythe's horns. 'Dear God, if only there were something we could do!'

But there was nothing they could do except watch.

Spinning slowly, its tipped-up ring dwarfed by the whirlpool's massive circumference, the raft struggled in the relentless current. Froth exploded from every side as the Shifters thrashed their jurua bodies in desperation. Then, as the real juruas drew near, the Shifters gave up the pretence and transformed themselves once more. Pincers melted into fins and multiple bodies melted back into one; crustacean shells became sleek tails beating against the water. This latest incarnation of the Shifters was based on no animal Jonah had ever seen – superficially similar to an Earthly shark, each one bore a trio of serrated dorsal fins and a tail resembling that of a tadpole, greatly enlarged of course. The form was well chosen however, for the sudden thrust afforded by those powerful tails accelerated the entire ring formation briskly away from both the whirlpool and the juruas.

But it was a turn of speed the juruas proved more than capable of matching. Again the gap began to close.

Kythe rolled sideways towards the Shifter ring, and to his amazement Jonah spotted Ruane in the middle of the throng of selkies. She was watching their approach, and for a moment their eyes met. She mouthed something he could not read and then they were past. This close, the noise was deafening: a paddling, hissing scream backed by the roar of the whirlpool above them. Spray from the maelstrom poured down across the scene, a fine, warm rain.

A single Shifter broke away from the pack. Jonah watched in horror as it ducked behind the waves and resurfaced heading back towards the attacking force. Instinctively he knew it was Lawal.

'Closer, Kythe!' he bellowed in the dragon's ear.

Valiantly she brought them hard in against the ocean surface.

'Lawal!' The shark's head bent backwards in a way its anatomy should not have allowed. 'What are you doing? You will be killed!'

'I am dying. You know this. Shifters grow old and I am older than most. Ruane has told you how we die. Now witness it for yourself.'

It took Jonah a breath or two before he understood.

'My God! Kythe, take us away from here, right now!'

Instead of peeling away from the speeding Shifter, Kythe simply folded her wings and dropped, using her tail to angle them outwards along Stone's ten-degree slope. Together they slid down beside the sea, slowing only when Jonah tugged at Kythe's horns. She maintained a hovering position as they both craned their necks to see what was happening in the waters above them.

Lawal, now quite remote from the selkie-filled ring, accelerated into the front ranks of the jurua shoal. The crustaceans fell upon him like tiny motorized demons, stabbing at his buttery skin with gleaming needles. He lasted a split-second before succumbing to the irresistible onslaught.

Then he died, and in dying he set free all the charm his body had accumulated over the many years he had lived. In a single, soundless explosion, a lifetime's magic was unleashed.

Lawal's last conscious act, as he unleashed the charm, was to direct it forcibly into the heart of the jurua shoal, just as Ruane had once imagined he might direct it into the tethers. The effect was as devastating on the juruas as she had hoped it would be on the Goddess.

Lightning darted from one jurua to the next, an abrupt network of light. Glass bodies melted into the sea like crystals of ice. The turbulence of the shoal died away in an instant: one minute the juruas were there, the next there was nothing to be seen but a few final traces of fire-laced foam. The fire died quickly, leaving only the hiss of the bubbles.

The juruas had not just been repelled: they had been decimated.

The Shifter ring broke apart; it was far enough now from the whirlpool for the currents to pose no real threat. Shifters and selkies made their way as individuals to the shore, the former maintaining their shark-like appearance until one by one they reached the smooth glassy beach. Then, as they hauled themselves out of the surf, they assumed the forms they had worn the first time Jonah had seen them: large bodies and sharp scissorheads, clearly their body-shape of choice – or perhaps simply the current fashion.

The selkies too beached themselves on the shore, making no attempt to hide their relief at having reached a safe haven, whatever their feelings about the demise of the Goddess.

The beach itself was much as Kythe had described it to Jonah: a slab of some glassy material inclined at Stone's usual precipitous angle. Deep grooves had been cut horizontally into its surface, creating a series of convenient ledges on which both selkies and Shifters could rest. Some hundred yards inland from the waterline a row of cliffs stabbed outwards, an irregular wall of glass blocking the downStone view. Leaving the exhausted escapees to recover from their ordeal, Jonah bade Kythe fly towards the cliffs.

'Take me to the cell,' he said. 'Take me to where Annie and Gerent are being held prisoner. I am anxious to see them again.'

15

Ashore

Kythe stared at Jonah, her orange face shading to a deep, embarrassed red.

'I don't know why I didn't think of this,' she stammered. 'Oh, I can be so stupid sometimes!'

'No, Kythe, you are anything but stupid. Dragons are not tool-users as men are, so the idea would not come so naturally to one of your kind. Gerent would have thought of it eventually, but your earlier visit was very brief and he might not have appreciated the level of your skill.'

'This is nothing to do with tools – it's what my mother would call plain common sense!'

They were crouched together at the rim of the funnel into which Annie and Gerent had been dropped. The funnel, unlike the surrounding surface, was slippery and they made sure not to get too close. The glassy landscape rose behind them in a series of terraces, like gigantic crystal steps.

'Will you do it from the ground?'

'No. I feel safer in the air.'

Hesitantly she took off, beating her wings hard in the warm, falling wind, side-slipping until she was hovering over the centre of the funnel.

'There isn't as much charm here,' she called. 'It's

harder to fly. I just hope I can make my tail do what you suggested.'

Concentrating hard, she raised her head high and let her tail drop straight down towards the hole in the ground; she had to beat her wings hard in order to keep station. At first nothing happened, then, very slowly, beads of shining moisture appeared on her neck. Rolling down her back, they gathered into larger droplets and trickled on to her tail, where they were immediately absorbed.

Kythe's tail began to grow, lengthening and thinning as she poured more and more charm into its fibres. Jonah looked on in wonder: he had seen a lot of shape-changing recently, but there was something entrancing about seeing it performed by a creature he considered to be his friend.

Soon the young dragon's tail was dangling inside the bottleneck that prevented egress from the cell. It swayed to and fro as it grew longer, then abruptly snapped taut.

'They've got it!' she gasped. 'This is hard work, Jonah!'

'Keep going, Kythe,' he urged. 'The hard part is over.'

'That's easy for you to say!'

Clenching her jaw she pumped enthusiastically with her wings and by fits and starts rose higher into the air. Her grossly extended tail emerged inch by inch from the funnel; its progress was tantalizingly slow and it was as much as Jonah could do not to throw himself into the funnel and haul on it himself. Then he saw a pair of hands clutching the orange scales, followed by bare arms, a familiar face . . .

'Annie.' It was no more than a whisper, but she looked up as he said it. Her eyes skated away from his as soon as they had made contact, and he could not tell if she was embarrassed or indifferent.

Labouring now, Kythe swung Annie as gently as she could across to the edge of the funnel where Jonah helped guide her down to a soft landing. After a brief rest she returned to her station and set about retrieving Gerent.

Jonah stood awkwardly to one side as Annie pulled her hair away from her face and straightened her clothes. She looked tired, he thought, but that was hardly surprising. He had rehearsed this moment during the flight from the sea: in his mind Annie had been by turns apologetic and defiant, while he had assumed the noble air of a martyr. Already his expression was that of the wounded man, but when she looked up at him again he saw that the encounter was not going to follow his imagined manuscript.

'Jonah, you won't believe what we found down there! We thought they were just sea-shells at first but . . . goddamn, wait till Gerent gets out! He's carrying all the stuff. You just won't believe your ears!'

Here was the very same woman with whom he had fallen in love – was still in love. All notions of rebuking her fell away as he was faced with the simple yet unexpected fact that although everything had changed . . . everything was the same.

'Really?' he said weakly.

'Really! I just held it up so I could hear the sea and, well, you'll hear it for yourself. Oh, Jonah, I'm glad to see you again. Are you . . .' her hand came up to her mouth, as if she had only just realized what she was saying '. . . all right?'

'The last few days have been . . . harrowing. For a number of reasons. I . . . I found your letter.'

'Oh, that. Yes.' She looked away. 'I knew you'd come after me, Jonah. Oh, I don't mean that to sound as if, you know, as if I think I'm worth chasing. In fact I'm pretty sure I'm not. It's just, well, I just knew you'd come, that's all.'

'Well, yes, I have. And so here I am.'

'Yes, here you are.'

Not like the manuscript at all.

Kythe picked that moment to deliver Gerent from the funnel and deposit him at its lip. She sprawled on the ground next to him, her chest heaving.

Jonah regarded Gerent and found it impossible to summon any hatred. Here, however, was the caution he had been expecting in Annie: the Neolithic man was eyeing him warily, clearly uncertain as to whether he should approach or not. A dull headache pulsed at Jonah's temples, spreading slowly down behind his eyes and into his jaw.

Ignoring the pain and feeling a little like an automaton, Jonah marched across to Gerent and hugged him. He sensed rather than saw his friend's eyes meet Annie's behind his back. Pulling away, he held the Neolithic at arm's length.

'It's good to see you both.' He thought he meant it, but the words were still hard to say.

'It is good to see you too, Jonah,' replied Gerent, risking a smile. 'Thank you for coming to our rescue.'

'Kythe did all the hard work. I merely planned the campaign.'

Gerent was rummaging in a belt pouch. He was arrayed with a remarkable variety of bags and pouches, all slung around his person with straps and thongs. Jonah did not recall him having so much baggage on board the Bark, but then Gerent had always had a knack for picking things up; like the rest of his people, he was a born scavenger.

On his back, hanging between his wings, was Annie's beloved painting box. Jonah patted his own talismans to reassure himself they were still there: Darwin, beneath his shirt, and the dryad's nail wedged firmly under his belt.

'Here it is!' announced Gerent, withdrawing a large,

spiral shell from the pouch. Jonah took it and turned it over in his hands, commenting on its unearthly transparency.

'It's made of glice,' said Annie.

'I beg your pardon?' Some absurd urge made him want to count every strand of hair on her head.

'Glice,' she repeated with a toss of her head. She kicked the ground. 'This stuff. A cross between glass and ice: glice, get it? Everything's made of it round here: the cliffs, the ground, those damned juruas . . .'

'You saw juruas?'

'Saw them? We were practically their dinner! That cell down there's a kind of spawning ground for the little devils. There must've been thousands of them, millions even, popping out of the walls like corn on a griddle. They stopped coming in the end, thank God. There's none left now.'

'Really? When did they stop?'

'Couple of hours ago, I guess. Why? Did you see where they came out? Did they come out in the ocean like we thought?'

'Yes, you could say that. At least, I did not see where they came out but it was very clear where they were heading.'

He told them briefly about the Goddess, concluding with her final moments.

'It must have been a terrifying sight,' said Gerent.

'Kythe and I had what you might call a ringside seat,' Jonah agreed.

'It was her, wasn't it?' blurted Annie, taking Gerent's hand. Jonah tried to ignore the contact. 'I mean, it was A-Archan. Those eyes – you could never forget . . . it was *her*. What I mean is . . . it was her inside the whale-woman, and so now the whale-woman is dead . . . does that mean . . .' Her agony was palpable. Jonah shook his head sadly.

'I only wish it did mean that Archan were dead, but I am rather afraid it was Archan's retreat from the Goddess that caused Her death. By the time the juruas did their work Archan was long gone. But not gone for long, unfortunately. She is coming this way, Annie . . . I know this is not something you want to hear but it is the truth. Archan is coming this way. She has caught the faery queen and turned on her evil dragon heels to head back in this direction. I do not know how fast she can travel, but I think she will be here before very long. And she is going to be angry, angrier than she ever was before. And we are going to have to stand in her way.'

'I know. I knew all along, I think, but I just . . . I just wanted to hope. There's a side to this story you haven't heard yet, Jonah, though it sounds to me like you've put a lot of it together already. Do you want to hear it?'

'If you are ready to tell it.'

'Not me, Jonah.'

Taking his hand (the touch was like electricity) she guided the shell up to his ear. For a second or two he heard nothing but the hiss of the sea, then, very distant, he heard a tiny, familiar voice . . .

. . . *fragile here. It is more than I can do to keep myself intact now. Face her, stand in her way. Stop her, for only you can.*

I send a message from a world I thought I would never see again. It is a message to you, Jonah Lightfoot, and it brings simple, sad news: that I have failed in my quest.

We fled far downStone, Archan and I. I the hunted, she the huntress. As we travelled so I dwindled. Such was my destiny, as you well knew, and at the time I believed it would be my salvation. I was foolish; I was wrong. Forgive me.

Through many worlds we moved, I always just ahead, she always just behind. Her breath was ever hot on my heels. Through many memories, many pasts. From the world of charm we entered a world of metal, and then a world where the only living creature was a many-minded monster bent on destruction. It had a name, and as I flashed through its presence it seemed that its name was important, though I did not learn what it was. Remember that, Jonah, not for now but for the future.

Oh, Jonah! Why did you not describe to me the dazzling immensity of Stone? Perhaps you could not – I cannot express it to you now. There are worlds and worlds and worlds . . . each Turning is a single beat of the heart of the cosmos. I nearly drowned in the memories . . .

A world of shadowless light; a wholly inverted world of clinging eyes and rising rain; a world made of diamond, another of mist. In one world there existed nothing but speech; in another there were pools of love set deep into a desert of despair.

All these worlds, a million and more. A world where time ran slow. A million more . . .

Until finally I reached a world where time was not slow but altogether still.

Oh, I should have run on! Had I done so I might be running still. We will never know how long the hunt might have lasted.

But Jonah, did we ever truly believe it would last forever? As Archan will last forever?

I believed I had found the answer to the riddle in that world without time. Far downStone it lies, a version of our world from a billion Turnings past, a world where time exists but does not flow. A frozen world filled with life without breath, mind without thought, peace without love. I descended into that world, immersed myself into its icy grip.

I stopped running.

I thought I had her then. Whether she saw me or not, the scale would draw her to my side and she too would become entombed in the same prison of icy time. A fearful fate, I believed, for one who had already spent a million years trapped in ice of a more conventional kind. And a fitting one. For myself I was not concerned.

All this I believed.

As my thoughts started to congeal I managed to whisper something, a taunt:

'Come, Red Dragon. Come and join me. At last I have found us a tomb.'

The words moved like lead. Countless millennia passed before I had spoken them all, as my body gradually succumbed to timelessness.

Above my head hung the memory rod that had brought me into this forsaken place. It sang as Archan swept past, her entire awareness focused on me, on my chosen spot. Until that moment I had not realized how powerful she was, how astute . . . how invincible!

She skidded. I can think of no other way to describe it, nor can I explain how I am able to describe it, how I was able to perceive it from my . . . unusual perspective. She skidded through time, ploughing up the memory rod as she sank her claws into the aeons. I cannot say how many Turnings buckled before her as she shed her speed and turned to face me again, scrabbling at the skin of the rod. I cannot say what damage she must have done to ages past in that long, relentless slide. Nor can I describe the look on her face as she finally shifted her direction and began the steady climb upStone, back towards my hiding place, which I believed would shortly become her prison. But I can imagine that look only too well; it would surprise me if you could not imagine it too.

She struck me like an avalanche.

I was thrown entirely clear of that timeless place, but not before I let go the scale. I fell out of the world altogether, nor did I regain the sanctuary of the memory rods.

I do not know what happened to me, Jonah, or where I went. I simply . . . fell.

But I saw her as I fell. I saw her crash into the scale, saw the scale lock into place on her back, saw the fire return to her eyes, saw her slide on through the timeless world with such momentum that she was carried far upStone before she even began to slow, by which time she was flying free with wings spread and mouth agape, flying back upStone through the memory rod, free at last in Stone's realm of memories while I . . . while I despaired.

I do not know how long I fell. There was an aroma, dry and ancient. Tired. It was familiar yet I could not place it. Around me I seemed to sense a network of light, bright lines entwined both around and within me, and for a moment I thought I was inside the Maze of Covamere, which was once a mighty nexus of charm, but then I knew that I was in a place not of life but of death.

I struggled free and found myself falling through clean air towards a bed of soft grass.

The ground reached up for me and took me in.

I lay there for a hundred years, then opened my eyes and saw the moon and knew that I was home.

And I am here still.

When I woke, I saw that I had landed at the top of a cliff. I was whole again, that is to say I was back to my true size, as I was when I lived as a faery in the aether and in the world. Descending to the shore I found a mass of shells. Charm laced them, flowing among them like a living thing. Into each shell I will speak my tale, this tale. This will take another hundred years. With each word I speak, I will let a little more of myself go; when I have finished, there will be nothing of me left but the words inside the shells.

The shells will be taken by the sea. I have watched this sea for long enough to understand its moods. There is a whirlpool not far from the shore, and the currents will drag the shells under. I will no longer be here to see this happen, but happen it will. And the shells will find their way to you, Jonah. I know this, though I do not know how I know it, any more than I know how I was saved or what power it is that will finally bring the shells to you.

Tell Kythe that the moon is very beautiful. And tell her . . . tell her she must remember all the names.

I am weak. I am, at last, dying. I am alone in the earliest

days of charm, trapped in the past of the world in which I once was alive. I am fragile here; everything is fragile here. The trees on the cliff-top are shedding their leaves; the leaves are made of iron. It is more than I can do to keep myself intact now. Face her, stand in her way. Stop her, for only you can.

The message repeated like an echo, growing fainter each time, still just audible even when Jonah had removed the shell from his ear. Looking down he saw the other shells buried in the glice, thousands of them, perhaps millions.

'All these . . .' he said, waving his hand uncertainly. He raised an enquiring eyebrow.

'We got two more out of the glice,' replied Annie. 'You could hear the same story in both of them. I reckon that's true of all these shells, Jonah; I reckon your faery friend just sat on that beach and talked the years away.'

Jonah looked at Kythe, but her eyes were turned away, remote and thoughtful. He smiled grimly. 'Then all that remains is for us to find our way to the Aqueduct.'

Annie and Gerent both assailed him with questions, demanding to know what he had learned about their destination. Annie's interest was acute; after all, the Aqueduct was a place she had dreamed of without ever visiting, a place that filled her with both hope and fear.

'I know little enough,' admitted Jonah. 'I met with the basilisk ghosts again. They behaved differently to the first time: they seemed to be less sure of themselves and more forthcoming with information.' He smiled. 'Which is not to say they were not still aggravating and inscrutable. Nevertheless, I believe they are more reliant on us than ever to save their precious Stone. And of course, if we do not manage that feat then we and the worlds we love will perish too.

'The Aqueduct is a bridge, as its name suggests, a bridge lying across a gap in the great wall of Stone. This gap is not just a stretch of clear air, you must understand, *it is a gap in the very reality in which Stone exists*. There is nothing there, not even clean air, nor is there even a vacuum. There is . . . nothing. It is a fire-break, like the fire-breaks in the Kansas cornfields, Annie, set against the kind of fire that Archan is bringing this way. Nothing can cross it except by way of the Aqueduct, which is the means by which the memory rods themselves are carried across the divide. The Aqueduct is like that threshing machine, Annie, the one you and Rance had to push out of the way of the prairie fire. It is up to us to push the Aqueduct out of the way, and to make sure . . .'

His voice trailed away. Annie was staring at him with fists clenched, lips tight.

'The prairie fire! I never told you about the threshing machine, Jonah. I never told you anything about that day at all.'

Jonah's mouth worked but he found words hard to find.

'You've been into my past, haven't you? You've been down one of your precious memory rods and looked into my life! Damn you, you bastard! You've been inside my *mind*!'

'Annie . . . I . . .'

'How *could* you, Jonah? Ain't it enough I had Archan crawling round in my head? How d'you think it makes me feel, knowing you've been prying into my life? God-damn it, Jonah, what were you looking for? It's like . . . it's like you're a Peeping Tom or something. What did you expect to see – me and Rance, is that what you wanted to see? Or did you want to change things around? Make it all different and see what happened?' She paused, hands held against the sides of her head. 'Jesus, is that what you did? Did you change my life around, Jonah? Did you tamper with my memories?'

'No, of course not. Annie, I did not choose to go there.

In fact, the second time it was the basilisks who . . .'

'The *second* time?' She spun away in disgust. Gerent reached for her but she shoved him away and ran off across the glice; he threw Jonah a look that was hard to interpret: contempt or concern? Perhaps it was both.

Definitely not according to the manuscript, he thought.

For a while he thought he had lost her again, this time for good. Gerent pursued her, finally catching her at the foot of the nearest terrace of glice. Jonah watched, devoid of emotion, as Annie fell into the arms of the winged man, her shoulders heaving. Then Gerent swept her into the air, soaring higher and higher up the shallow slope of the terraces until they met the steeper wall of Stone.

Here Stone itself was made of rippled sheets of glice, and the reflection it returned of the tiny figures was like one from a circus Hall of Mirrors, warped and crazy. They flew close to it for a while, then struck out into the open sky.

Kythe, unusually, showed no desire to fly; however, she was more than keen to talk.

'Do you think it's the whirlpool, Jonah? Do you think that's what I've dreamed about? Is it a way back to our world?' She hesitated, her voice shaking. 'And what did she mean about the names?'

'I do not know, Kythe. In a way it was a whirlpool that brought me and Annie . . . and Archan . . . to Stone in the first place, though I believe it was the volcanic eruption of Krakatoa that actually bridged the gap between the worlds. Clearly the whirlpool in Stone's sea is in some way connected to a similar whirlpool back in our world – the faery queen used it to send the shells across. As to whether anything can travel in the opposite direction . . . oh Kythe, everything we have experienced on Stone so far suggests that these bridges allow travel in one direction only. And the whirlpool is most assuredly a treacherous place. Anyone entering it is more likely to be torn to pieces or simply drowned than to find their way home.'

'But our world is there, Jonah! It's close enough to touch! Can't you feel it?'

'If the world is there then it is the world of charm, Kythe, the world as it was long before I or any other man was born. It may be your world, but it is certainly not mine.'

Kythe nuzzled him, sensing his melancholy. But she was unable to disguise her own excitement. 'But . . . the world of charm, Jonah! The golden age of dragons! Wouldn't that be a sight to see? Wouldn't that be worth the risk?'

'Worth risking your life?'

'Aren't there some things it's worth risking *everything* for?'

Jonah tracked the motion of Annie and Gerent, their combined bodies a single black organism afloat in the reflected sky. Their chimera shadow sped across the glice terraces towards him: they were coming back.

'Did you change anything?'

'No, as I have already told you.'

'Jonah, we must be honest with each other.'

'Must we?'

'Don't be difficult! Of course we must.'

'If you say so.'

'Impossible man!'

'I changed nothing, Annie. The thought would never have entered my head.'

He had to glance away, for though he was indeed proud to have resisted the temptation to tinker with the events in Annie's past, he was ashamed that the temptation *had* come to him. He was even more ashamed about telling her it had not.

Far below, Kythe and Gerent had devised a gliding competition, taking great leaps into the air and seeing who could stay aloft longer without flapping their wings.

'Look, this isn't easy for me.'

'You left me, Annie. You did not even say goodbye. How do you expect me to feel?'

'I don't know. Upset, I guess. I'm sorry, Jonah, but . . . oh, I said it all in the letter. I told you how I felt, what had happened. I can't tell you any more than that. I don't understand it any more than you do but . . . it's how I feel. It's the truth.'

'The truth. Do you want to know the truth as I see it? We were in love with each other, as much in love as any couple ever has been. We were *happy*. And in the world I come from love is defined by nothing so much as by *loyalty*. I was prepared – as I am still prepared – to love you until my dying day, and I believed you felt the same way about me. But then you changed – not me, you. And the reason you changed is this!'

He brandished the dryad's fingernail like a scimitar. Annie flinched and he withdrew it swiftly, ashamed at having frightened her, pleased that he had at least provoked a reaction.

'What the hell is . . . ?' Recognition dawned before the words were out of her mouth. Trembling, she took the fingernail from him and held it up in the sunlight, turning it over and running her free hand along its length. At length she gave it back and fetched up a deep sigh. 'Well, I guess you're right about one thing. It did all change after I pricked my hand. But not the way you think. That's when I came to my senses, Jonah.'

'But how can you say such a thing! How can deciding not to love somebody be "coming to your senses"?'

'You think I *decided* not to love you? Is that what you think?'

'How can I know? I thought your heart was mine, and then you betrayed me!' They were glaring at each other, breathing hard. Jonah felt the fury inside his breast and fought to keep it at bay. It felt obscenely good, but it also felt like . . . *betrayal*. He looked away and muttered, 'Perhaps the ways of love are different in America.'

He saw his own fury reflected in her face as she grabbed his shoulder and shook him. 'You, you . . . God damn you, why do you have to be so *English*?! Do you think we're a bunch of savages? Do you think we only *pretend* to love each other? If you stopped to look around your precious London I'll bet you'd find more adulterers in a single street than in the whole state of Kansas. *I loved you*, Jonah Lightfoot, and maybe I still do, though God alone knows why after what you've said and done! It wasn't magic made me love you, I just did; it wasn't magic or some witch's finger made me turn to Gerent, I just did. It may not have been right or fair or honest but it's how I felt and what I did, and that's all I can say, and that's the simple truth of it!'

'But truth is only a matter of perception! The memory rods have taught me that. My journeys into your past have taught me that. When you move around an object the light changes and suddenly everything is different – suddenly you see the ugliness behind the beautiful façade, you see the beauty hidden within the rotting shell. The dryad worked evil magic on you, Annie, magic that switched off altogether the light by which you saw our love. You were left in darkness, and in that darkness you turned to Gerent. I do not blame you, or him. It is only natural he should turn to you too, given what he has experienced. But none of this changes the fact that our love still exists; you have merely forgotten that it is real.'

She shook her head; he watched her long hair move like water. 'You're wrong, Jonah. But I'll never convince you. You've even managed to kid yourself that nothing is real.'

'Oh, everything is real. It is just that very little of it is true!'

Her gaze then was so intense that he had to glance away. She calmed her breathing, which had grown fast and shallow, then seemed about to say something, then thought better of it. She laced her fingers together and took a deep breath.

'Do you need me to help you bring down the Aqueduct?'

The question took him by surprise. 'I . . . yes, I think I do. The basilisk ghosts told me I alone could do it, but I think I will need help, your help.' He thought hard, then added, 'I would like your help please, Annie. I want you to be with me there, to face Archan with me.'

'All right. You got me. I still can't stop dreaming about that damn place, so I might as well come along and see what all the fuss is about!'

Her humour was bitter but none the less welcome. Cautiously he reached out his hand to take hers as they descended the slope towards their companions, but she avoided the contact by spreading her arms wide, like a tightrope walker, to help her balance on the way down.

'I don't hate you, Jonah.'

Her voice carried forwards, directed not at him but the open sky.

By the time they reached them, Gerent and Kythe were leaning over the edge of the funnel, listening to the hissing noises rising from the interior.

'The juruas are back,' commented Gerent, pulling a face. 'Not as many as before, but the sound is growing steadily louder.' He reminded Jonah about what they had seen during their incarceration.

'This place must indeed be their spawning ground,'

said Jonah. 'And you are right: they may be distant cousins of the Ypoth. Ruane said something about the juruas being the "guardians of the shore"; at the time the phrase washed over me but now it brings to mind the dreadful guardians we found at the Threshold, and they too were a kind of Ypoth. They are all part of the same pattern – Ypoth, guardian and jurua – an army born of Stone with but one aim in mind: to protect it. Clearly the juruas are there to prevent any sea-borne assailants from reaching the Aqueduct.'

'Lucky for us we can fly straight past them,' suggested Annie.

'Lucky indeed.'

'We flying now?'

'Yes, but not to the Aqueduct, not just yet. There is someone I want to see first.'

They found the selkies spread over a wide stretch of shoreline some way below the glice cliffs which had looked so impressive from the sea. Here the weird landscape rolled gently in a series of folds that reminded Jonah of bedsheets. The association made him long for the scent of newly washed linen, the simple comfort of his old bed.

He had explained his obligation to the Shifters on the short flight to the folded shore, and his desire to meet with Ruane again, if only to wish her farewell.

'Mighty attached to this mermaid, ain't you?' teased Annie as they landed in a scooped-out vale of glice.

'She is not a mermaid,' Jonah snapped, regretting his sharp tone almost as much as the pink glow that was rising above his collar.

It took a while to find her: the selkies had scattered themselves over a considerable area, and those they asked for help were for the most part still dazed from their ordeal. There was no sign of the Shifters at all. Eventually Jonah spotted Tam, who was able to take them up over a smooth, glassy hummock to where Ruane sat watching the waves striking the soft line of the beach. She smiled as they approached.

'Hello, Jonah. These must be your friends.'

He made halting introductions, aware of the strangeness of his achingly polite English manner in these most unusual circumstances.

Selkie, meet dragon, his mind narrated as they traded names. *Dragon, selkie. Winged man, of course. Oh, and this is a woman. She was once possessed by a dragon, though. Me? Yes, you know me: I am just a man. Just a man.*

'I grew angry with you, Jonah,' Ruane continued when the formalities were dispensed with. 'I apologize. The shock . . . it was more than I can articulate. Watching the ocean is soothing. There is a great deal for selkies to think about now that the Goddess is dead.'

'Ruane, where are the Shifters?'

She waved her arm upwards. 'They stayed near the cliffs.'

Jonah gazed up at the overhanging cliffs of glice. Here was a landscape truly worthy of Stone: a mountain of weathered crystal adhering to the edge of a vertical ocean. It was unclimbable, and he could only begin to imagine how the selkies had got down here. Ruane must have sensed his puzzlement.

'We swam down, of course. We thought we ought to use the sea while it was still passable. Soon things will return to normal.'

As if in response to her words a commotion broke the surface of the sea a little way off-shore. As they watched, a pair of juruas leaped sideways out of the water and fell a quarter of a mile before striking the waves again.

'They're back,' shuddered Kythe.

'Yes,' Ruane agreed, 'and so for the time being we are trapped here.'

'At least you are alive,' said Jonah.

The selkie smiled. 'Yes. We are alive. And we are free. We are trapped, certainly, but we are free.'

'Then you are free to choose whether or not to join us in our quest!'

Ruane raised her eyebrows and put her head on one side. 'You have my attention.'

Jonah had become so used to flying that he thought nothing of sitting astride Kythe's back as she ascended through the tumbling air. Annie too looked comfortable in the improvised harness slung around Gerent's waist and shoulders.

The flight itself proved less than comfortable, however. The air currents were unpredictable beneath the swollen overhangs of glice. Partial vacuums jostled with pockets of high pressure, making flight a difficult and delicate business. Gerent handled it with great concentration; Kythe positively revelled in it, whooping as she dived through rotating streams of air and laughing as sheets of vapour dashed themselves against her wings.

'This is fantastic!' she cried. 'You really ought to get yourself some wings, Jonah. You don't know what you're missing!'

'I know I have been classed as a faery on more than one occasion, Kythe, but I am still, fundamentally, an ape. Apes can jump, they can even swing from tree to tree – but they cannot fly.'

He gripped Kythe's horns tightly and clenched his legs against the saddle-scale on her neck. Glancing across at Annie he saw she did not have such a luxury: slung as she was in front of Gerent she had nothing to hold on to at all. Instead her arms were spread wide in mimicry of the Neolithic's wings. It was a position of absolute trust.

Beneath him, Kythe chuckled. They bobbed upwards through pockets of air; Jonah's stomach turned over.

'Are we nearly there, do you think?' he asked.

The Shifters were in their dragon-forms, suspended upside-down by long claws from a ridge of glice running around the cliffs like a raised vein; in this attitude they looked like giant yellow bats. From time to time one of them would detach itself, swoop in towards the sea and snatch a fish from the waves, hunting like an osprey; for the most part they were still, basking in the noon sun.

Kythe and Gerent took up a difficult hovering position before the Shifters while Jonah scanned the line of identical faces.

'Meem!' called Jonah. 'Is Meem here?'

There was a flurry of movement, then one of the individuals nearest to them swivelled its long dragon face and said, 'You have come about your promise to Lawal?'

'Yes. That is a promise I will keep. I am a man of my word. But there is something I must do first, something more important. Important for you, as well as for me.'

'Are you going to save Amara?'

Jonah was taken aback. 'Do you know that it is in peril? If so, how?'

The Shifter performed a complex gesture that might have been a shrug. 'We are, more than most, creatures of charm. Lawal's sacrifice has proven to you the depth of charm we carry within us. Of course, most of the charm we carry is useless to us. That which is available is used either for shifting or *perception*. Perception is what some creatures call *charm-sense*: the ability to detect charm at work over great distances. Our perception is greater than that of any other creature. The basilisks, when they lived, might have possessed more; we shall never know.

'When we gather close together our perception is amplified still further, almost to the point where it becomes unbearable. When we grouped together to rescue the selkies, we sensed the doom you plan to confront,

Jonah. We sensed the onrushing fire, the advance of Red Dragon from far downStone. We sensed the destructive power at her command, the inevitability of her approach.

'We saw her coming, and we resolved to help you stand in her way.'

Again these giants had managed to surprise Jonah. He had come here with a desire to enlist them, expecting a resistance. Now here they were offering their services before he had even opened his mouth! But before he could offer his thanks, Meem confounded him once more. 'But . . . you made a promise to Lawal before he died. That promise has not yet been upheld. The time to uphold it is now.'

A gust of wind knocked Kythe downwards and left Jonah flailing for his grip. Eventually she regained her position in front of the inverted Meem, who had not altered his position so much as an inch.

'There is little time . . .' began Jonah. Then he stopped himself, thinking about how Lawal had sacrificed himself, not only for his own people but for the selkies too. He had been close to death, but he had still given his life. 'Very well. If I do what Lawal asked, will you come with us?'

'If you keep your promise, I will keep mine.'

'We will have to land, Kythe,' he whispered. 'I would prefer to be on solid ground for this.'

There was a ledge immediately above the overhang to which the Shifters were clinging. Kythe deposited Jonah there before returning to the sky; Gerent hovered nearby; still harnessed to the Neolithic, Annie watched Jonah intently.

He breathed deeply, savouring the familiar spice of Stone's tumbling air. The wind was strong, but not unbearably so. The glice rolled downStone like a frozen sea, and as he looked that way he imagined Archan racing towards him, a locomotive running at full speed along tracks made only of memories, her chrome eyes alive with hatred . . .

'Enough,' he muttered to himself, breaking off the vision.

Kneeling, pressing his hands flat against the glice, Jonah shut his eyes and imagined one of those memory rods before him now, imagined its ebony surface slick beneath his skin, the pulse of the life-forces within it. He let himself sink into the memory rod, feeling it rise around him like a tide, despatching his awareness in search of the moment when the Shifters were first created by the faery council, the brief moment when their shape was whole and new and right. The moment he had promised to Lawal.

The memory rod enfolded him. He turned to face upStone, knowing instinctively that he had already journeyed past that critical moment in faery history and that he would therefore have to backtrack, when suddenly . . .

. . . he was seized from behind and spun around to face downStone once more. Before him broiled the heat of a blast furnace. Struggling to pull himself free he pulled in the direction he wanted to go, but to no avail. Something had ensnared him and was pulling him gradually into the past. The fibres of the rod, slender stripes of memory carved through with thoughts and dreams and loves and losses, faces smiling and dying, long nights of peace and bloody days of war, spiralled past him as the unseen force accelerated him downStone. He fought against it, harder and harder, and the movement slowed a little. Desperately he tried to focus his mind on his task, on the birth of the Shifters: it did not matter very much where he was within the network of rods, since every rod connected to every other and so he should be able to find the moment he was looking for from here as well as anywhere. But past and future were blurred together; individual memories were drowned in a

stormy sea. It was like listening for a whisper while the orchestra played. He twisted, thrown this way and that, gradually losing control.

Like a wind-blown seed he tumbled downStone. Slowly he became aware of a roaring sound. His vision had narrowed to a tunnel: all he could see was an ever-expanding curtain of red at the centre of his field of view; his peripheral vision had gone completely, though he had the unsettling sensation that weird things were swarming there.

Archan appeared as if out of a mist.

A dragon skeleton. Long red bones articulated like the limbs of a marionette, an elongated skull in which two chrome eyes were set like metal gems. A flesh-less dragon, scale-less too but for the single, white diamond high up on her back: the one scale she had at last reclaimed from the faery queen. Her mouth was gaping and what looked like tiny black ants were crawling across her teeth.

Jonah could not see clearly: the mist lingered and he was still tumbling. The insect-shapes were forming from the memory rod, springing from its surface wherever it was touched by Archan's teeth. Sparks of charm scintillated inside her mouth, making it even harder to see, but it seemed to Jonah that when her teeth scraped against the inside of the rod, the rod broke apart.

He could see a ring of fresh black scales forming around the single white one, a dark growth like fungus.

Archan was eroding the memories of Stone and using them to make herself a new body. In her wake, the memory rod was crumbling into nothing.

Jonah tried to cry out but could make no sound. He noticed that Archan was drawing no nearer, though she was surely approaching him at some considerable speed, and he understood that what he was seeing was merely a projection. She was out there to be sure, but not quite this close, not yet. But soon, soon.

'You will not win!' he shouted. 'I will not let you win!'

Archan said nothing, just leered that skeleton grin and

steadily wore away at the precious memories of all the worlds that lay downStone. Steadily she took on new flesh, a new skin that was made from those memories. Memories she was slowly making her own.

'You are a thief!' Jonah said under his breath. 'Nothing but a common thief. And like all thieves you will be brought to justice!'

Grimacing with the sudden pain he threw himself sideways out of the rod, while at the same time hauling his mind back upStone, seeking in the split-second available to him the ledge of glice from which he had departed. Something rushed at him with dizzying speed: the whirlpool, the line of Shifters hanging from the glice, the warm . . .

. . . rays of the afternoon sun on the back of his neck.

Annie and Kythe were both calling to him; he raised a hand to show he was all right.

Meem rose like a ghost, blotting out the sun.

'You were successful?' he intoned, fighting to keep the excitement out of his voice. When Jonah shook his head the yellow dragon face rippled, momentarily losing its definition. Jonah imagined the Shifter to be made not of flesh and blood at all but liquid, a living broth for which solidity was merely a convenient way of interacting with this particular world.

'I am sorry, but Archan's presence in the network of memory rods – however far away she might be – makes it impossible for me to see anything other than what she wants me to see, which at the moment is her.'

A chilling sound came from Meem's throat, the same combination of animal predators he had heard from Lawal's. 'Then your promise is broken.'

'No, it is deferred.'

'Do you still plan to journey downStone?'

'Yes. Do you still plan to come with me?'

The Shifter pondered this, then said, 'I will come, and

Teget will come too. We will protect you, Jonah, for unless you survive your encounter with Red Dragon, Lawal will have died in vain.'

'If I do not survive, we will all be dead, Meem. Are you sure you are not simply joining me in order to keep an eye on me?'

'Think what you will. We will come.'

Jonah nodded, disturbed by what he had experienced inside the memory rod . . . and apprehensive about his two new travelling companions. He found it hard to accept them as allies, so transparent was their suspicion, though in their favour they had rescued the selkies from certain death.

'Meem, would you and Teget be prepared to carry some passengers?'

16

River

They had not flown far downStone before the landscape began to grow more complex. To begin with the glice had resembled a steep mountainside of blue ice. The smooth contours were broken occasionally by deep ravines, scars trailing diagonally through the glice like the claw-marks of some primitive god; inside several of these ravines they glimpsed large sloth-like creatures, their bodies vague beneath wiry grey fur. The sloths stared vacantly back at them with dull, incurious eyes.

Soon however the terrain speeding past on their right began to undulate more vigorously. The mountain threw out great arms of glice, globular spears reaching for the sun; part of the mountain high above them sagged downwards, producing a swollen belly that forced the fliers out into the sky. Beyond the belly loomed a series of growths like gigantic propeller blades, curved vanes that caught and turned the wind, creating a belt of ferocious air currents through which they flew only with the greatest difficulty.

'We must land soon!' shouted Gerent over the noise of the wind.

Jonah eyed the twisted terrain, looking in vain for anything resembling a safe place to land. He felt comfortable enough where he was; the leather satchel Gerent had given him made it easier to carry Darwin and the dryad's nail, his only two possessions in this world, with the exception of the clothes on his back. He wanted to fly on, to reach the Aqueduct and do whatever was required of him. Meanwhile the wind continued to buffet them, and even Kythe found it difficult to maintain her heading and altitude.

'He's right!' she yelled at last. 'We can't go on much further!'

'Can we not distance ourselves from the glice?' Jonah shouted into her ear. She shook her head.

'I've been here before, remember – well, not quite this far. I tried flying out and the sky just sent me spinning back in towards Stone again. The air's just wild here, Jonah, and there's nothing we can do about it.'

'More security,' he muttered, recalling the lethally high winds surrounding the Threshold. This was different – the wind was more unpredictable than powerful – but the end result was the same: if it got much worse it would become impossible to fly.

Eventually the two Shifters spotted a niche at the root of one of the glice vanes. An exploratory dive by Kythe established a safe approach through air that was almost calm, and one by one they landed.

Jonah was greatly relieved to be standing on something solid again, and said as much. Kythe pouted.

'I thought you enjoyed flying.'

'I do, Kythe. But that was just a little too exotic for my liking.'

There was nothing much to see here: the niche was little more than a flat area at the base of a projecting arm of glice. There was no vegetation of any kind, nor any form of wildlife. A cluster of smaller outcrops formed a cowl above this convenient landing platform, creating a cave-like shelter from which the wind was almost completely excluded.

Looking downStone, Jonah announced he could see through to the other side of the forest of glice outcrops. 'The air is remarkably clear,' he added. 'For the first time since my arrival on Stone I find myself looking through an atmosphere free of haze.'

'Free of charm, Jonah,' Gerent corrected him. 'We are leaving the magic behind now. That whirlpool: it was the Threshold marking another moment of Turning. We are all finding it difficult to fly now, and it is not just the wind.'

'Back beyond the age of magic,' mused Annie, settling herself into the crook of Gerent's arm. Jonah watched the winged man stroke her hair absently as he gazed into the sky. 'I wonder what's next? What came before the charm.'

'We know that already!' Jonah snapped. 'The faery queen told us in her message: something about a world of metal. But it is more important that we reach the Aqueduct itself than explore what lies beyond it.'

The others regarded him, expecting more, but he could think of nothing more to say.

'Well,' sighed Kythe. 'I can fly for a bit longer, but then we'll just have to start clambering.'

It was the Shifters who gave up first. Considerably less skilled in flight than either Kythe or Gerent, they furled their yellow wings less than a mile's distance downStone from the niche. Landing simultaneously – and clumsily – on the exposed tip of a broad shelf of glice, they deposited their selkie passengers and carefully made their way inwards to the relative shelter of the supporting wall, where they awaited their travelling companions. Kythe landed with a lurch that nearly threw Jonah from her back, but Gerent circled overhead, waving them on.

'There is a better place ahead!' he urged. Annie,

strapped in front of him, was nodding enthusiastically.

'Gerent's right. There's a hole in the glice – it looks like a way in. At least it'll be a proper shelter, and if it leads somewhere so much the better.'

Kythe, tired as she was, needed little persuasion, but the Shifters and the selkies were a different matter.

'We cannot fly even that short distance,' asserted Meem. 'We will put neither ourselves nor our passengers at unnecessary risk.'

You did that the moment you set out with us, thought Jonah, though he kept quiet.

Teget too remained silent. Indeed, he had not spoken a word since joining the expedition. Though he shared Meem's overall shape and size there was something about him that made Jonah uneasy. He was peculiarly *weighty*, and there was a dark look in his eye.

Gerent was clearly eager to fly on at least as far as the hole in the glice; it was only Annie's pleas that kept him hovering while the others made up their minds. Jonah too was keen to investigate, but was reluctant to break up the group so soon into the expedition. He scanned the glice wall between the platform they were on and the distant hole.

'There is a ledge of sorts,' he said dubiously, 'which appears to lead to the hole. But I cannot determine whether it is intact along its entire length.'

'We see it too,' agreed Meem. 'It will suffice. If problems present themselves . . . Shifters are resourceful.'

'Ruane, Tam?' Jonah turned to the selkies, who looked painfully small in this vertical landscape of ice-glass. He was suddenly aware of how far they were from their natural environment, and what a risk they were taking. *Like fish out of water*. He was aware too of the immense trust they were placing in the Shifters to carry them when they could not make their own way.

'Meem and Teget will look after us,' replied Ruane,

glancing quickly at her brother. He silently nodded his approval.

'Gerent and Kythe could take me and Annie across, then come back for you.'

'But then the Shifters would be alone. Neither of your friends could possibly carry their weight. No, we will stay with them. Together we will traverse the ledge, then meet you at the other side. We will not be separated for long.'

'We should not be separated at all.'

Ruane did not reply, simply looked up at Gerent loitering impatiently in the air above their heads. Jonah sighed.

'Very well. It should take you no more than an hour to reach the hole, assuming you encounter no serious difficulties along the way.' He looked out into the sky, where the sun was already past its noon extreme. 'Even if it takes you twice as long you should still make it before nightfall.'

'The Shifters will look after us,' repeated Ruane as Jonah resumed his position astride Kythe's neck. She was holding hands with her brother; despite their lined faces and grey hair they looked like two children – mer-children of course – ready for their first day at school.

As Kythe swooped in towards the hole Jonah was relieved to see its shape was quite different from the ravaged circle of the Threshold: this cavity was smooth-sided and quite regular in shape, clearly artificial. Six equal sides were joined seamlessly to create a tunnel penetrating the glice that was hexagonal in cross-section; as soon as they drew level with it he saw that it *was* a tunnel, extending into darkness within a hundred yards of the entrance. *Man-made*, he thought at first, then he amended that. *No, just* made. *And almost certainly* not *by the hand of man.*

Following Gerent and Annie into its maw he felt a thrill: might there be Ypoth here?

It was unlikely. Nevertheless, he was entering Stone again, which meant he was approaching the physical reality of the memory rods again; perhaps even approaching a place where they were exposed and vulnerable.

Stone did not allow its surface to be broken without good reason. He wondered what the reason was this time.

The hexagonal tunnel led them through blackness. Some trick of the walls amplified the wing-beats of both Gerent and Kythe so that they flew surrounded by echoes and soft, sea-wash rhythms. This sound intensified the deeper they flew, and when finally the air grew brighter around them they saw that the walls had closed in, halving the tunnel's diameter. Tiny lights studded the ceiling and floor, like stars. Directly ahead and impeding further progress was a dark grey wall, in the centre of which was set a massive, square hatch.

Jonah felt a momentary thrill. Beyond the hatch were the memory rods, he was certain! Moreover, he was coming to believe that if he could only make contact with the rods again – real, physical contact this time – he could throw off the grip Archan had on them and explore the realm of memories again without her interference.

I can keep my promise to the Shifters. Then I might be able to confront Archan herself a million miles downStone, before she even reaches this Aqueduct. I might succeed where the faery queen failed. I am the one she wants – with me before her she might yet abandon her orgy of destruction!

But he knew only too well that the memory rods were calling him as opium calls the addict. He knew he could not deny their siren voices any more than he could truly hope to turn Archan aside. He knew he was as much in their power as they were in his.

And he was afraid. For, once he was touching the memory rods again, he could not be certain where he might choose to go, or what he might choose to do.

The hatch was a curious amalgam of familiar and unfamiliar forms. Twenty feet on each side, it was made of what appeared to be irregular plates of iron held together by thick black rivets. It was huge and heavy and, to Jonah's eyes, remarkably *Victorian*. Its hinges however were pale, organic knuckles, and over to one side was coiled a handle made of the same pliable substance. Jonah had Kythe hover close enough for him to touch the handle; when he did so it yielded slightly beneath his fingers; he even fancied he felt a pulse beneath its fleshy exterior.

Looking back over his shoulder to where Gerent and Annie were holding station behind Kythe's fast-moving wings he called, 'Should we wait for the others?'

'Let us see what lies beyond!' barked Gerent without hesitation. 'If there are more tunnels within we will wait. There may simply be a safe place for us to wait . . . or something more interesting.'

The light in his eyes was unmistakable, and for the first time Jonah wondered if his Neolithic friend was here not simply as Annie's lover, not simply to satisfy his curiosity about how Stone's countless mechanisms worked, but for reasons of his own.

Jonah peered over Kythe's brow and into her eyes. She waggled her head in an indecipherable gesture that almost threw him overboard.

'Sorry, Jonah! But Gerent's right – let's take a peek!'

He grasped the handle, flinching a little at the unsettling fleshiness of it, then pulled. Instead of swinging towards him, as he had expected, the hatch folded up like an Oriental paper sculpture, each metal plate sliding behind its neighbour until no neighbours remained and the entire structure had consumed itself.

Kythe perched on the edge of the aperture like a gigantic albatross and together they peered in.

Jonah was disappointed: beyond the aperture was

nothing more than an empty chamber, hexagonal in section just like the tunnel; on the far wall was another hatch, more or less the same as the one he had just opened. The star-lights too were the same, but for their colour: they were bright green.

He visualized a succession of identical chambers receding into the heart of Stone. The purpose of such a chain he could not imagine, but then there was so much about Stone that made no sense, or at least concealed its true origins or purpose. Stone's basilisk architects, he decided, would have made formidable poker players.

'What do you reckon?' called Annie. 'Do we go on?'

'The chamber is merely a junction,' answered Gerent, boldly flying inside. 'Whatever there is to see here lies beyond the second door.'

Jonah scowled at him. 'How can you know that, Gerent?'

The winged man shrugged, causing his body to dip a little as he hovered near the green-starred ceiling. 'I know it. Come, Kythe, enter with us and let us see what there is to see.'

Obediently the dragon followed Gerent into the chamber. Jonah was about to argue for caution but his own curiosity was aroused: curiosity about Gerent's confidence as much as his own desire to investigate the tunnel system.

Space was limited in the chamber and Kythe was forced to land and tuck away her wings while Gerent and Annie floated up to the second hatch. He pulled on the handle just as Jonah had done, and smiled when the hatch did not unfold.

'Nothing is happening, Gerent,' said Jonah.

'It is. It is happening behind you, Lightfoot.'

He spun on Kythe's neck and watched the first hatch grinding silently shut behind them. Iron plates slipped into view from hidden corners of the air, materializing

305

as if by a conjuror's sleight of hand. The sprinkling of white light outside was eclipsed, leaving them bathed in green.

'Curse you, Gerent! You knew that was going to happen!'

'I guessed it might, Lightfoot. But I could not be sure.'

'You seem very sure to me . . .' He hesitated. The star-lights were flickering and there was a hissing sound. Annie glanced at him, clearly alarmed; her hands gripped Gerent's forearm tightly. Jonah began to feel an uncomfortable sensation in his ears and sinuses, and his eyes began to water.

'The pressure's rising!' blurted Kythe, ever sensitive to the behaviour of the air.

'We will be crushed!' cried Jonah, raising his hands to his ears.

But before he began to experience anything more than mild discomfort the hissing noise ceased. By exercising his jaw and inducing yawns Jonah was able to balance the pressure in his skull with that of the denser atmosphere. He was amused to feel Kythe doing the same thing beneath him; evidently there were some forms of behaviour that transcended the barriers between species.

No sooner had the hissing stopped than the hatch in front of them folded itself away with the same unlikely grace as its twin. A new sound intruded: the rushing roar of a waterfall. Immediately beyond the hatch-way was a wide iron platform formed from black plates riveted as roughly as the hatches themselves had been; Jonah hoped that it too was not designed to reduce itself to nothing. Gerent and Kythe landed side by side and let their passengers dismount, then together they advanced to the edge of the platform and looked out.

As a child, Jonah had been told tales by his uncle – who had brought him up after the tragic death of his father – about the sewers of London. A dinosaur enthusiast like his brother, Uncle Ward (born Edward) had regaled him with tales of forgotten prehistoric beasts roaming the vast network of underground tunnels. 'They are like cathedrals, some of these sewers,' Jonah could remember him enthusing. 'A city beneath a city, eh? What secrets they must hold, what secrets!'

The stories – one of which had included a memorable showdown between two hungry *Troödons* in a vaulted passageway below St Paul's – had been entertaining enough, but Jonah's interest had waned when he had realized his uncle did not regard them as fiction. Their prehistoric content had remained with him however, and memories of their grandeur came to him now as he gazed from the platform across the enormous cylindrical chamber.

It was a pipe, simply, a pipe half full of rushing water. The platform jutted out some ten feet above the torrent and extended – as did the pipe – as far as they could see both upstream to their right and downstream to their left. The curved walls and ceiling were plated and riveted, and studded with the familiar star-lights, these ones white.

The river was, Jonah judged, as wide as the Thames at Waterloo Bridge.

All this was remarkable enough, but what really caught their attention was the cluster of memory rods thrusting from the ceiling a short distance upstream (which was also upStone). They broke through the metal plates, many of which had dropped away altogether to reveal twisted black shapes above, a root-like mass of gnarled black tubes that looked as though it were in constant motion, even though it was utterly still.

'They look like the rods in the Threshold,' observed Annie.

Jonah nodded: the similarity had not escaped him either. The normal condition of the memory rods was smooth and uniform, their alignment with the thread-like grain of Stone as precise as railway lines. But some-times, in places where the barriers between Stone and the real world were thin, that uniformity broke down. This, though it was not a Threshold, was evidently just such a place.

On their way down to the river the memory rods twined themselves into a single, gigantic rope; by the time it reached the water this rope had lost its woven texture and was as smooth as any of the rods Jonah had encountered in his time here. Except with those he had been able to close his hand and feel his fingers meet his thumb, and this single memory rod was half the width of the pipe through which the river was flowing. At the point where it plunged beneath the waves it was nearly four hundred feet in diameter.

'The green chamber is a pressure seal,' announced Gerent. 'The air pressure is higher in here, perhaps to keep the river from rising, and the chamber is the means by which the air is locked inside.'

Jonah did not show that he was impressed by this deduction. 'I suppose you have also determined that this is the place where the memory rods join together, ready to cross the Aqueduct?'

'Of course. What we are looking at – this single, giant rod – is the amalgamation of all the individual rods lead-ing to this point. Where the world's memories are normally stored in many thousands of individual rods, here they are gathered into just one.'

They fell silent as they regarded with awe the mon-strous black rod. All the memories of their home-world were held in that one vessel! It did not *look* fragile – indeed it looked as though Mjolnir itself would not even have dented it – but its very uniqueness *made* it fragile. One cut and the thread would be broken, the ceaseless skein of memory would unravel and blister in eternity's glare. Here was the basilisks' greatest gamble: in thus concentrating the forces of memory they had hoped to protect them from ultimate destruction, but in doing so they also created a weak point, a tempting target for anyone with the power and will to bring the wall of Stone tumbling down.

'How far downstream is the Aqueduct, do you imagine?' Jonah wondered.

The winged man gazed into the star-lit depths of the pipe. 'Not far. The memories are vulnerable like this; they would not have been kept this way for any longer than was necessary.'

'I wonder what it looks like,' Kythe interjected. 'Annie – you've dreamed about it, but you never really told me what it looks like.'

Annie followed Gerent's gaze. One of his wings was poised over her head like a parasol, an unconscious gesture of protection. 'In my dreams it was just a bridge, a bridge made of ice – well, I guess I'd call it *glice* now.'

'It *is* a bridge,' asserted Jonah. 'A bridge strong enough to carry this monumental rod across the fire-break – and exactly what *that* looks like we cannot possibly predict. Unless, of course, you dreamed that too, Annie.'

She did not offer a response, instead throwing him a caustic look.

'But how can we get there?' Kythe went on. 'I suppose we could fly down this pipe . . . though I don't like the idea very much. We don't know what might be down there.'

'No, Kythe,' said Jonah, 'we do not know what lies down there. But it appears to me that there is no other way. If this giant memory rod does indeed lead to the Aqueduct, then we must follow it. We can fly no further outside; we must make our way as best we can on the inside now.'

'Jonah's right,' agreed Annie, coming over to Kythe

and stroking her forehead as she might have done a horse or steer. 'But look, there's stars all the way. We'll see danger long before we reach it. Don't worry.'

'All right,' Kythe gulped, looking unconvinced.

Gerent was crouched at the lip of the platform gazing down into the water. Jonah approached him, fascinated by a steady pulse in his wings, like a baby's heartbeat. The wings were very big now – at full span they looked to measure about sixteen feet, though the red and black scales from which they were made had thinned considerably and were partially fused together; Jonah thought they looked like a mosaic of silk. Like Kythe, Gerent had been building his wings with charm, and they had become glorious.

'You should go out to meet your friends,' the Neolithic man said without turning round.

'I? We should all go. It was folly to separate in the first place and we should remain together now.'

'No, Lightfoot, I shall stay.'

Jonah felt his fists clenching at his side and willed them to relax. 'What are you here for, Gerent? What do you want from this place?'

He thought his questions would be ignored, then Gerent slowly turned his head. To Jonah's surprise there were tears on his face. 'Please, just leave me here for a while. Go and meet the shape-changers and the seal-people. I will be here when you return, I promise.'

Both irritated and curious, Jonah returned to Annie and suggested she wait with Gerent while he and Kythe went back through the air-lock. To his surprise she refused.

'There's a lot Gerent hasn't got right in his head, Jonah. About Malya, you know? He loved her so much – they'd known each other since they were children – and to see her murdered by her own father in front of his eyes. Dear God, Jonah, can we even imagine what he is feeling?'

'He seems able to feel something for you,' Jonah snapped. Kythe was examining her claws closely, pretending not to hear.

'How dare you, Jonah Lightfoot! Yes, he feels something: he loves me, for God's sake! But that doesn't mean he's stopped loving Malya any more than I've stopped . . .' She bit her lower lip fast enough to stop her words and deep enough to draw blood.

'Loving *me*? Is that what you were going to say, that you still love *me*?!' Jonah was incredulous.

'Oh, *Jonah*! You see it all so damn clear, don't you? It's either day or night, nothing between. You can't see that I can love you both in different ways. And of course he still loves Malya: she was his first and only true love and I can never live up to her memory and that breaks my heart, but at the same time he loves me and I'll gladly give my broken heart to him to hold, if it means we can be together. Do you understand, Jonah? *Try* to understand, I beg you! Because I love you still, whatever you may think.'

'I do not know what to think any more, Annie. Perhaps you are right: for me there is either day or there is night. If that is true then you and Gerent are living between the two in a world I cannot comprehend, a world where nothing is certain – a world of endless twilight.'

'Or a world of coming dawn, Jonah.'

The roar of the river forced its way between them like a knife, as impenetrable as silence. A single tear from Annie's cheek splashed on to the iron at her feet and there was nothing more to say.

When they returned outside Jonah felt as though the sky were mocking his words. It fell into Stone's abyss, a thick purple tapestry down which fat, dark clouds were racing like vast drops of rain. *Twilight world*, he thought. *A fitting place for me to be, where all is change and nothing is secure.*

The Shifters were easy to see against the curved glice Stonescape. They had discarded their dragon-forms and now resembled enormous yellow caterpillars, complete with segmented bodies and multiple legs. On their backs, looking curiously out of scale, rode the semi-human selkies. As soon as she saw Jonah, Annie and Kythe appear, Ruane raised her arm and waved. Jonah fancied she was shouting something but the wind whipped her words away before they could be heard. Five minutes later Meem and Teget crawled into the lee of the tunnel entrance and flattened their bodies out, allowing their passengers to alight.

'I am sorry we took such a long time,' Ruane said, stretching out her long grey tail in an effort to remove a cramp, 'but the ledge was more precipitous than we had imagined.'

'It was practically a suicide mission!' added Tam with one eyebrow raised. 'Between the sudden drops and that appalling wind – it's a wonder we are here at all.'

'Well, I am glad you *are* all here,' replied Jonah. 'Come, let us go through before night falls.'

The Shifters were in ill humour after their precipitous journey and refused to change from their caterpillar forms, so they all proceeded on foot. Jonah explained in some detail what they had found at the end of the tunnel; the news was received without comment, other than Ruane's unenthusiastic 'At least you found us some water.'

'Alas,' said Jonah, 'I would not recommend swimming in this particular river – it is flowing at such speed even Rata Kadul Herself would not prevail against the current. No, I am afraid that you, Meem and Teget, may need to grow your wings again before very long.'

He experienced momentary panic when he thought the air-lock had ceased functioning. Then, with a shrill grinding sound the iron petals repeated their miraculous

Origami trick, admitting the motley group into the small chamber. It was with increased trepidation that he put the pressurization process into operation; even the hissing of the air sounded erratic, and he began to wonder if what the basilisks had built here was beginning at last to decay.

To his relief the second hatch peeled apart without crisis, releasing them on to the platform. Both selkies gasped when they saw the thundering river; the Shifters exchanged an inscrutable glance and settled down against the wall to rest.

There was no sign of Gerent.

Jonah hurried to the edge of the platform and looked over, immediately feeling foolish: there was nothing down there but water and if Gerent had fallen – or jumped – there would be no trace of him. He would however be the first of their party to reach the Aqueduct, though he would not be alive to appreciate the fact . . .

It was Annie who spotted him first: he was squatting on the giant memory rod, low down near the waterline, wings held low against the rod's slick black skin. As they watched, he bent his head against the rod so that his ear was touching it.

'What is he doing?' whispered Jonah.

'He ain't listening for buffalo, I know that much,' was Annie's response.

Gerent looked up sharply and spotted them. Hastily he took to the air and flew back to the platform, the sheepish look on his face clear to see as he drew near.

'I did not mean to alarm you,' he said to them all. After reassuring Annie with a quick embrace he turned to Jonah. 'Have you ever wondered, my friend, if the rods also store the memories that are made on Stone?'

Jonah blinked and wondered if evolution had not taken a backward step somewhere between him and this Neolithic prince. It had never occurred to him to ask that particular question, but now that it was asked he found it a compelling one.

'I have never been aware of Stone memories – all I have ever seen in the rods are memories of the real world.' He smiled, amused at this way of referring to their home-world, as if Stone were any less 'real'. 'But then I have never been looking for them. Why are you interested?'

'Some interesting possibilities are raised. Listen: so far you have explored only the memories of people from your world. Natives of Stone, like myself and Kythe, have been outside the boundaries of your travels. But if Stone *does* store its own memories, then you could look at anything: events from our journey across the ocean, for example. Even events from our future, Lightfoot.'

'I don't like the sound of that,' quavered Kythe. 'I don't think I want to know the future.'

'And you could change anything you found,' continued Gerent intently. 'Could you not?'

'Ye-es,' said Jonah carefully. 'But I am not sure that I would want to.'

'Why not?' demanded Gerent.

'When I looked into my own childhood I found myself reliving the death of my father and brother. I had to wrestle with the knowledge that I could step in and change what happened, could make them live for longer, perhaps even forever. But there is something fundamentally dangerous about the process of changing memories, Gerent, and that is why I have never actually done it; I have only ever retrieved things from the past, such as Archan's scale, or this copy of Darwin.' He tapped the satchel Gerent had given him. 'For example, if I had saved my father's life that day, my own past life would have been altered too: I would never have gone to live with my uncle; my brother would still be alive today;

314

and I might never have travelled to Java and hence never come to Stone, *and never gone back to change the past*. A contradiction would have been created, a division if you like, and however flexible the truth may be it cannot be divided.

'However, in that moment when I considered saving my father, it seemed to me that whatever changes I made would in fact be readily absorbed. The flow of time would ... readjust itself to accommodate the changes, and would do so in a way that caused the least overall disturbance to history, or to memory – in this discussion the two are interchangeable. So, on balance, I believe I *would* still have come to Java, even if I had changed my own past.

'But there were years to play with there. What if I were to make a change to the more recent past? What if I were to go back not years but days? Why not *minutes*? In that case there would be little or no opportunity for the river of time to alter its flow around whatever obstacles I put in its way. And if I made a big enough change ... what might it be? Yes, I know. What if I were to go back and force myself to step off a ledge and into the abyss? By killing myself, I would also *prevent* myself from killing myself. Do you see the conflict? Both truths cannot possibly exist at the same time.'

'That is a foolish example,' muttered Gerent, unimpressed.

'But it illustrates the principle. In any case, we have little enough time available to us, and certainly no time to be theorizing on the hidden wonders of Stone's vast store of memories. There will be time enough to debate these things later – if we can turn Archan aside. That is what we must focus our minds on now.'

Gerent fell silent, though Jonah knew the discussion was far from over. He noticed Annie regarding him quizzically.

'What is it?' he asked gently, for the look on her face reminded him of earlier, happier times.

'Nothing . . . oh, well, it's just I was thinking about what you said before. I thought you'd stopped believing in the truth.'

'That may be so. But I do not think Stone has.'

He watched Ruane and Tam as they fussed around the Shifters. The big, yellow beasts were sprawled against the wall, their bellies heaving as they drew in great draughts of air. The selkies were treating them as Jonah might have treated a pair of respected elders, grandparents perhaps, and it came to him that the Shifters were incredibly old. At the same time he felt a growing impatience, for he was keen to move on down the pipe, to reach the Aqueduct before Archan did.

He need not have worried, for no sooner had he made his way over to the selkies to enquire after their steeds than the Shifters raised themselves up and shook themselves like drenched dogs. Then, perfectly synchronized, they turned back into dragons.

'They tire quickly,' explained Ruane, 'but they recover quickly too.'

Jonah nodded, looking up at the sail-like wings that were overlapped above his head; it was like being beneath an enormous yellow marquee. Meem did indeed look refreshed and ready to go on; Teget simply glowered. Ruane, in stark contrast, looked haggard: deep grey rings underlined her eyes, which were dark and swollen; her hands were shaking and clots of fur had fallen from her tail.

'Ruane!' he exclaimed. 'I had not noticed – are you . . . you look dreadful!'

'I would have preferred a compliment.' She gave him a pained smile. 'But you describe me as I am.'

'You are sick. What can we do to help you?'

She sighed, the sound a soft rasp in her throat. 'Oh

316

Jonah, I have no idea. I feel . . . very tired. That is all. I am in no pain . . . I am simply exhausted.'

'You should stay here. More journeying will only make it worse.'

'No, I should like to see this Aqueduct. I am a creature of the water, after all, and it sounds . . . interesting.' Again the sad smile, revealing teeth that looked too big for her wasted gums.

Tam, who had been listening to this exchange, crawled over and helped Jonah lift Ruane on to Meem's back. Unlike his sister, he looked in fine health.

'She is determined,' Tam said. 'I have known her all my life, Jonah. She will not be turned aside.'

'What is wrong with her?' Jonah whispered, convinced both he and Ruane knew.

But Tam had nothing for him but a philosophical selkie shrug. 'Our mother used to say to us: "We think our lives are our own. But in fact the reverse is true – it is we who belong to our lives."' With an enigmatic smile he clambered on to Teget's back and said, 'Well, we are ready to go. Are you?'

Jonah was about to reply when he heard raised voices. Further down the platform Annie and Gerent were arguing; even from here he could see that Annie was shaking with rage. Though curiosity urged him to go over he loitered near the Shifters, unwilling to interfere yet desperate to know what was going on. He could not make out what they were saying, such was the blurring effect on words of the river's roar, but it was clear that neither of them was happy.

Suddenly, Annie slapped Gerent on the chest, a weak blow but demonstrative enough to make him back away almost to the lip of the platform; for a moment Jonah thought he would keep on walking backwards until he fell, but he stopped within two paces of the edge. Annie, her face bright red, stormed back towards where he stood. Ignoring him, she marched up to Teget's side and said to the Shifter, 'Can you carry two?'

'Annie, what on Earth is wrong?' asked Jonah, reaching for her. Her thunderous look was enough to stay his hand.

'I could ride with Ruane,' suggested Tam, raising an eyebrow at Jonah. 'She is not well and might appreciate the company. Meem?'

The Shifter silently nodded his dragon head and without further ado Tam slithered off Teget's back and climbed up to join his sister.

'Help me up please, Jonah,' said Annie, grasping the thick leading edge of Teget's wing. Cupping his hands he boosted her up and watched as she settled herself astride the base of the Shifter's neck, adopting much the same posture as Jonah did when riding Kythe. As he made to speak again she raised a hand and closed her eyes. 'Please, Jonah, not now. Maybe later.'

'If you must ride on one of the Shifters could you not have chosen Meem,' hissed Jonah, hoping Teget did not hear, 'rather than this surly beast?'

Looking down the platform Jonah saw that Gerent was already aloft, circling impatiently above the giant memory rod. Then Annie spurred Teget like a mustang and the Shifter took to the air, closely followed by Meem, who now bore both of the selkies.

Something pressed against the small of his back: it was Kythe's snout.

'We'd better get a move on, Jonah,' she said eagerly. 'We wouldn't want to be left behind.'

Watching the Shifters eclipse the red and black of Gerent's wings as the Neolithic man led the way down the starlit pipe, Jonah suspected that had already happened.

17

Annie's Journal – Five

God damn it why do men have to be so difficult?!

'Of course I love you,' he says, but he says it oh so carefully, like he's not really thinking about what he's saying at all but about something else altogether, and like if he really stopped to think about what he's saying then he wouldn't say it in the first place. He's got every right to be alone, of course he has, but why now, just when things are getting tough and we need to be together? I wouldn't mind so much if he'd got a good reason for not wanting me to fly with him any more, but he hasn't. Just mumbled something about having some 'difficult things to decide'. Wouldn't tell me what, of course. Is it any wonder I got so mad?

The worst of it is, now I feel guilty. Like I should have understood, given him the freedom without question. Truth of it is I'm scared of losing him. Maybe I got an idea how Jonah feels and didn't like it. And there's another reason to feel guilty. Does it really matter if Gerent wants some time to himself? If he says he loves me then I believe him; it's just – oh I don't know, there's just something else on his mind, something far bigger than the love we feel for each other.

I've left two men already in my life and now it looks

like this man's thinking of leaving me. Maybe it's what I deserve. A kind of poetic justice.

I've tried to look on the bright side, but all I can come up with is it's given me a chance to write in this damned journal again, not that I can raise much enthusiasm for that now. It passes the time and helps me think – or maybe it stops me thinking too hard. What chance is there that anyone's ever going to pick this up and read it? If I thought I'd get old and use it to help me reminisce that'd be something, but I think Archan's probably got us licked this time. I don't think I'll ever be an old lady – I don't think I'll ever have a rocking chair out on the porch and a glass of lemonade at my side.

It's a frightening thought, to know that soon you'll be dead. Though I wonder if it's even more frightening to be immortal. Only Archan knows the answer to that, but I don't think she'll be letting on. You probably think I've turned into a defeatist or a coward or something, but the way I see it is this: Archan's coming up on us like the biggest, fastest, meanest express train you ever saw in your life. Going so fast and furious she's tearing up the tracks behind her. And what are we doing? We're sauntering down the line towards her, with nothing in our hands but a few harsh words to throw at her fenders as she gets ready to crush us to pulp. Jonah knows what he needs to do – destroy the Aqueduct – but he's no idea how to go about it, or even what the damn thing looks like. He doesn't even know if it can be done at all.

I know I'm just mad at Gerent, and that's probably not really fair, and it's probably making me feel worse about everything. I've tried watching those little stars on the walls go by, trying to calm my nerves I guess, or watching the river seething below – the further downstream we go the worse it gets. It's like the worst rapids on the Colorado in places, real mean water, you know? It's comfortable on Teget's back, and it gives me room to write; it's great flying with Gerent – warm and intimate – but it gets a bit cramped after a while.

The pipe's going on forever. We all believed Gerent when he said it shouldn't be far to the Aqueduct, but it feels like an eternity. I guess on Stone's scale of things even a thousand miles is just a scratch, but it still feels like we've been flying forever. I've no idea if it's day or night outside – all we can see in here is the stars on the walls. They're beautiful though, small and white. Pure.

The thing that keeps coming back to me though is Rance. The first man I left. Ever since Jonah started talking about that day, the day of the prairie fire, I can't get him out of my head.

The thing of it is, I'm remembering good times. For so long, all I've been able to remember is the bad times, the times he used his fists on me, the years I spent in fear of the door opening and him returning from the fields and taking out his meanness on me in whatever way he saw fit. For so long I've cursed myself for having stayed as long as I did, for putting up with it all, but now I think I probably loved him all along.

That's scary, but it's true. He *was* a good man. I remember when we first set out in the wagons, all the family, and my daddy had already promised him my hand (sounds like a fairy story when you put it like that) and I was practically a child and he was older but still not old, still young and able to laugh and make me laugh. We did laugh a lot, then. And the first years on the prairie were good years, toiling under the sun, tanned nearly black by the wind, dancing naked round that old sod house in the middle of the night, whooping like Cherokees in a white man's rain dance. We thought up crazy names for our babies – those were the happy days when we thought we *would* have babies – and drew maps of the land and threw stones on to guess where we might dig a well, or drew charcoal battle plans right through the middle of old man Clayman's fields, giggling as we plotted invasions to snatch away his best soil. In those days the years were as big as the vast new land we'd planted ourselves in, and the future was as far away as the hidden hills. Little did we know those hills would throw such a storm our way.

Rance was changed by the grasshopper plague. I told Jonah it was the grasshoppers drove him crazy – not the millions in the sky but the single one he breathed into his lungs – but he'd been getting crazy for a long time before. By the time the plague came he must have dug ten wells or more. Not one of them had given us so much as a drop of water. God knows he worked hard – he started each new dig with even more enthusiasm than the last, but thinking back I reckon it wasn't really enthusiasm, more like panic. I think maybe he felt bad for letting me down – leastways that's how he saw it. Trouble was he couldn't say it to me so he just hit me with it instead.

The year after the plague the grasshoppers were still around and I said to him we should gather them up like old man Clayman. The little critters had been declared Public Enemy Number 1, would you believe, and Clayman, just like the rest of our bounty-hunting neighbours, was collecting a small fortune just for dragging a pair of wooden crates around his property and scooping them right up out of the crop. Not Rance. That didn't suit him at all, that wasn't what he'd come to Kansas for. So we slaved on, crops dwindling while our neighbours found ways to profit from the disaster. By the time the grasshoppers had been beaten back folks had pretty much bounced back. Except us.

After that he just got crazier, but the thing is I think it was all meant to tell me he loved me. It was all because he couldn't do what he most wanted to do – provide for me and the children I couldn't give him (never mind it was probably a punch from him that wiped that possibility out of our future).

On the day I walked out of Kansas I thought I hated him. Somehow I found my way to Salt Lake City without getting raped and murdered, then I found a stage headed for San Francisco and – well, I guess that was all just part of the same journey here, to Stone. And I think I've hated him pretty resolutely ever since.

But when Jonah talked about the prairie fire it was like a firework going off in my head. Not just because I was angry at Jonah for prying into my past but because he'd brought back a day I'd forgotten about completely. It was one of the few days Rance and I worked together, right by each other's side, worked as equals. And in the end I saved his life, saved both of us and our homestead. It was a terrible day, a day we saw all the land to the west of our little house consumed by fire, but it was a good day too. That night we lay under the stars together by the well he'd been digging, not saying much, not even touching, just breathing together.

Then he sat up. 'Do you hear that, Annie?' he said. He rarely called me by my name. We never had company, it was just him and me, so whenever he spoke I knew who was meant to listen. At first I couldn't hear anything, then I heard it: a tiny trickling sound I couldn't place, then I realized it was water at the bottom of our well. We shrieked and shouted thank you to the stars and the rain gods and the gods of the wells and all the gods we could think of, then we made love next to our new well, and it was warm and real and I *knew* he loved me, despite everything that had happened to us, despite everything he had done to me. I *knew* it.

It was a terrible, wonderful day, and a wonderful night, and I'd forced it out of my mind because it reminds me of things I cannot bear. That day and night we were in love again. The next morning he slipped and fell on his way down to the well, ripping the sleeve of his shirt. That night I was nursing a black eye and six weeks later I was heading west.

We've been flying fast and mostly in silence. I think Ruane's getting really sick. Tam keeps leaning over where she's laid on the Shifter's back and at first she kept pushing him away, but now she doesn't bother. He strokes her hair and talks to her, not that I can hear the words.

Gerent's been leading us all the way, but now he's dropping back to fly alongside Kythe. He keeps glancing across to Jonah as if he's about to say something, but so far they haven't exchanged a word.

There's an air of excitement now. We're all bunched together a bit more and wings are flapping harder. Travelling faster too, though we've no idea what we'll see when we get there. Heads are up where before they were mostly down.

Looking for the light at the end of the tunnel.

18

Return

The semi-circular patch of light was blinding. It reminded Jonah of his first day on Stone, when he had trekked through a black tunnel to emerge on to this world's endless precipice; then too the sky had appeared as a distant glow.

But is that the sky?

No indeed: geometry told him it was not. The true sky was away to his left, beyond the thickness of the pipe. Ahead was not sky but . . . *fire-break!*

He found himself clutching with excitement on to Kythe's horns, and had to force himself to slacken his grip. Below them the river was sleek, with barely a ripple breaking its mirror-surface. It was anything but still though; no mill-pond this, it was flowing at an astonishing speed towards the exit, a fact evidenced by the occasional fragment of debris – a sliver of wood, a strand of weed – caught in its flow. Beneath the reflections of stars and multi-hued wings lurked the massive swell of the memory rod.

Behind them was receding the black wall of the air-lock, big sister to the lock which had admitted them into the pipe in the first place. They had passed through without incident. Though it was larger, its riveted hatch operated in the same way, folding up to reveal a green-hued

interior space big enough to hold three steam loco-
motives. The river was channelled beneath the lock
through a row of enormous valves patched and joined
with slime-streaked flanges and bent tubes, plumbing
stolen from beneath a giant's washroom. The memory
rod too divided to follow the different streams, reassemb-
ling itself on the other side; here the scene was just the
same as the one they had left, except the air pressure
was lower and the water level higher.

And they could see the way out.

Gerent's wings passed in front of the light, growing
larger as he dropped his speed to draw closer to Kythe
and Jonah. Kythe dipped slightly, allowing Gerent to take
up a position just above Jonah's head.

The Neolithic man was bent almost double. Jonah was
about to ask if he was in pain when he straightened up
again. Light glanced off the knife Gerent was holding in
his right hand. Soundlessly his wings folded. He dropped
on to Kythe's back and threw his left arm around Jonah's
waist from behind. Jonah felt the touch of cold metal as
Gerent pressed the knife against his throat.

Still without saying a word, Gerent flexed his great
wings and lifted Jonah into the air.

Hard muscles gripped Jonah's midriff, muscles made
strong by charm. Charm-filled wings thumped the air.
Even Gerent's voice seemed alive with magic.

'Don't struggle, Lightfoot.' The words tolled like bells.

Jonah struggled to speak, at last managing to grunt,
'You have been soaking up charm . . . like Archan.'

'Try not to speak.'

'What have you become?'

'Only what I have always been. But stronger.'

His arm clamped tighter, digging under Jonah's ribs.
Below them their companions were looking up in con-
sternation; Jonah could see that Annie was shouting but
all he could hear was his own blood rasping in his ears.

His vision was painted red and the tunnel seemed narrower than before. Gerent shook him.

'Don't faint, Lightfoot – I need you awake!'

Jonah could feel his strength ebbing and decided that if he stood any chance of escape he would have to act now. Falling momentarily limp, he allowed his left leg to swing forward then brought it back with a crunch against Gerent's shin. His captor cried out and dropped with alarming speed towards Meem, who was flying close beneath them. Jonah saw the uplifted face of Tam as they plummeted towards him, then Meem's large yellow wing folded across his field of vision. Gerent lunged sideways to avoid the wing and continued to descend, only regaining his composure when he had fallen some distance below the Shifter.

Something was still falling though; it was several seconds before Jonah recognized the shape as Ruane. Gerent's close encounter with Meem had caused the Shifter to roll violently to the side, as a result of which the unconscious Ruane had been thrown completely clear. Glancing up, Jonah saw Tam's face again, anguished now and peering over the flank of his steed, watching as his sister fell into the river.

She made hardly a splash; indeed the water was moving so fast she seemed not so much to submerge as vanish altogether. Jonah searched in vain, knowing she must already be far downstream, if her body was even intact after the impact.

'Curse you!' cried Gerent. 'Now you have something else to mend!'

'I do not . . . understand,' croaked Jonah, his resolve gone. He was no longer feeling faint, but his body felt numb, except for the place where the knife was still touching his neck. It seemed that he was not held about the waist at all but suspended on that blade. 'What is it . . . that you want?'

Gerent did not speak for such a long time that Jonah thought he had fallen into a trance, or perhaps taken leave of his senses altogether. When he did speak it was only a single word, but a word that unlocked the puzzle entirely:

'Malya.'

. . . and Jonah understood what this was all about: Gerent's quest for knowledge about Stone, about the way it worked; his particular interest in the way it handled recent memories; the unfathomable depth of his grief . . . everything fell into place. Shifting his position just enough to make talking possible, Jonah said,

'You want me to . . . to go back. Is that it, Gerent? You want me to go back to the moment . . . when Frey killed Malya in front of us all. And you want me to change the memory. You want me to make it so that her death never happened. You want me to bring Malya back.'

Gerent's tears rolled down Jonah's cheeks. 'The reason you know this is because you are my friend, Lightfoot. That will always be so. Do not make me kill my friend.'

'Let me go and we can talk about this, we can . . .'

'No! No talking. Do it, Lightfoot! Do it now!'

The blade cut into Jonah's skin and he felt the first hot trickle of blood run down his neck. Instinctively he raised his head, but that only drew the skin taut and forced it even harder against the knife.

'But . . . you know what happened when I last tried to use the rods. Archan is in them . . . her presence is overwhelming. She must be defeated before we can even think of trying to . . .'

'I will only say "no" so many times!' Gerent's voice was bigger than a man's voice had any right to be. 'You will find a way past her, Lightfoot. I have waited long enough.'

'Then you must wait a little longer. If we do not reach the Aqueduct in time then all this will be worthless.'

'If Archan defeats us I want Malya to be with me at the end. I would not die alone, Lightfoot.'

Jonah swallowed, the essential movement embedding the knife a fraction of an inch deeper into his neck. 'You are not alone, Gerent. You have Annie.' He meant what he said, though he could not keep the bitterness from his voice. He spoke slowly, desperate to give himself as long as possible to think of a way out. But his mind would not turn itself to that task; instead he found himself anticipating using the rods again, imagining a way he might slip through Archan's net. Found himself yearning to do what Gerent had asked of him.

'If you kill me,' he said, 'then you will surely never see Malya again, and you will have lost a true friend. And when Archan comes you will see Annie taken too, and all of Stone brought down about your ears. Is that what you want, Gerent, my friend? Is that really what you came here for?'

'I no longer care. If you don't understand that you are a dead man. I know that if I wait until after you've defeated Archan you will find a good reason not to do this thing. You know it too. Did you not tell me of the moment when you returned to the memory of your own father's death? You didn't even save your own *father*, Lightfoot! Why should you do anything for poor Malya unless you're forced to?' Jonah felt Neolithic fingers tighten on the handle of the knife. 'Do it. Do it now!'

'He means it, Jonah.' It was Annie's voice, floating up like a miracle. He sensed rather than saw the Shifter, Teget, hovering directly beneath his feet, and he guessed that Annie had heard the entire conversation. 'Do as he says, while we still have time.' Her voice was harsh with emotion, and he wished he could see her face.

'I want Kythe to fly beneath us,' demanded Jonah.

'Why?' Gerent did not hide the suspicion in his voice.

'Because when I bring Malya back you will be carrying

not one person but two. I want some insurance against being dropped.' By now Kythe too was in earshot, Annie having immediately called her over. She took Teget's place beneath Jonah. 'Did you hear that, Kythe? You would not let me fall, would you?'

'I haven't yet.' It was a very small voice to be coming from such a large creature.

'Gerent. Take the knife away.'

'I don't know . . .'

'Do it, man! I am going to do as you ask, but I refuse to perform the task with a weapon at my neck!'

For a moment he thought he had pushed the prince too far, then the thin pressure of the blade relented. He allowed his head to drop a little, wincing at the sudden pain accompanying the movement. Blood held in check by the presence of the knife flowed freely for a moment before clotting, and his throat felt unnervingly fragile.

'If I cannot do it, I will tell you; you must trust me to tell you the truth.'

Gerent did not reply.

Jonah took a last look at the fire-break's distant light, then stared down, past Kythe's orange wings, at the sunken memory rod. It was clean and black and in fine focus, as if the water surrounding it were not even there. Already he could hear its music.

He held his hand out in front of the rod, imagining his fingers growing longer, extending right around the rod to meet behind it, take hold of it, a giant's grasp on eternity, and suddenly he was . . .

. . . *tumbling like a wind-blown seed as he was hurled downStone. Everywhere there was a roaring sound. Red bones gyrated within a red mist, while hulking shapes loomed on every side: the basilisk ghosts, watching his every move.*

She was watching him too, Archan, but whereas before she

had seemed omnipresent, now she was not so daunting. *Before, she had filled the unreal space within the rod like a piston in a cylinder but now ... now there were gaps – slight and occasional, to be sure, but gaps all the same.*

This is all rods in one, *thought Jonah triumphantly.* However much I could see before I can see everything now. And she cannot possibly be everywhere at once!

That was the truth of it, though the fear nagged at him that if she prevailed then she would *be everywhere. Forever.*

Something else struck him as he fought for control: she was slowing down! Archan, with all she had consumed weighing heavy inside her, was acquiring vast momentum. And perhaps too she was simply growing tired. Not that she would not reach the Aqueduct, but any sign of weakness was welcome, particularly now.

With the basilisk ghosts looking on impassively, Jonah turned his back on Archan and delved into the memories. It was like thrusting his fingers into ...

... warm, moist soil. But when he looked around he knew he was no longer on Stone.

A low sun poised above a yellow horizon, and a tribe of leather-skinned men and women wrapped in furs. A tusked monster that could only be a mammoth painting a mountainous shadow across the tundra.

Long ago, *he thought.* Too long, and the wrong world, except ...

Except these were *Malya's people, her ancestors. His aim had been true but Stone had deflected him. The memories he sought of Malya herself were near, he was sure of it, but Stone did not want them broken into.*

Heartened, he abandoned the Neolithic sunset and plunged into ...

... a mountain of fire. Screams and explosions. Nothing to see but black smoke, but still the right direction, still a moment

from the Denneth story, a moment to be used like a stepping stone on to . . .

. . . another time altogether. A later time, when serpent-headed ships plied the icy waters, their sails striped red and black, shields pinned to their hulls like dragon scales. Viking oars dipped and he knew he had come too far, he had missed the moment when the Denneth tribe had been drawn through to Stone, the day of the dark skies when the gap between the worlds had turned to dust and . . .

. . . suddenly there was a breakthrough! Pure blue light and an endless sky filled with falling clouds. A whole world turned on its side. Dazed, the Neolithics stepped through into the world of Stone, many believing they had died indeed and that this was not simply a new world but the next world. Jonah watched as these Stone Age pilgrims wandered out of history and into . . .

. . . memory.

Here they were at last! Stone moments. The self-perpetuating memories of Stone itself. Here were the places where the history of Stone was both recorded and ordained. Places within Stone yet apart from it, and when he saw where they were, he understood.

The Stone memories were inside the basilisk ghosts. Where Stone held the moments of the world, so its makers held the moments of Stone. Even in death, the Deathless could not forget how to remember.

Jonah swam between them, pale wraiths filled with infinite stories. They themselves were like the memory rods; in a way they had built Stone in their own image, thus behaving as all god-like creatures should.

Each time he had met with them they had been spilling over with memories but only now, as he actively searched, was he aware of it. Or perhaps, only now did they allow him to perceive it.

It was as easy to navigate the basilisk ghosts as it had become to navigate the rods. With Malya at the front of his mind he plunged into their phantom forms, narrowing his attention from the infinite sweep of their memories to the vast wall of Stone, to the dragons' crystal stronghold, to the wooden bridge upStone of the entrance, to the day they had arrived at the junction of bridge and ledge, to the moment when Frey had appeared, to the instant when . . .

. . . he turned to the sky and found himself looking straight into the eyes of Malya's father, Frey, shaman to the Neolithic tribe known as the Denneth.

Malya, beside him on the wooden decking, saw him at the same instant; she hissed and gripped Gerent's arm tight enough to make him flinch. Looking through his own eyes with fresh insight, reliving the scene exactly as he had experienced it the first time, Jonah saw the depth of the bond between them and wondered how he could ever have refused Gerent this chance.

Wondered how Annie could ever have believed that it was her Gerent wanted.

'So,' Frey announced, the leather harness to which his artificial wings were attached creaking as he maintained his hover. Small and lean, his naked body was encrusted with pale mud; dark pigment underscored his eyes and on his belly was painted a blue star. Jonah's attention kept straying back to his wings: he had grown so used to seeing Gerent with those same wings grafted into the flesh of his back that he had forgotten they had been constructed from stolen dragon scales and borrowed magic by Frey himself. 'You have decided to trespass after all . . .'

As Frey and Gerent traded verbal blows Jonah became aware of Annie behind him. She pressed her body close and whispered to him, and with a jolt he remembered this was not Annie at all but Archan.

Suddenly he wanted nothing more than to be out of this place. This had been a dreadful, fateful day, and to relive it was more than he could bear.

But can I do what Gerent asks?

He had already rejected the idea of actually changing the events of that day. He did not believe he could prevent Malya's death by revisiting the scene any more than he had been able on the day itself. He had something rather more subtle in mind.

It worked with Darwin, *he told himself.* There is no reason to suppose it will not work with Malya.

Stepping forward, away from Archan, he marched straight up to Malya and grasped her upper arms with both hands.

'Gerent loves you more than you will ever know,' *he whispered, his mouth brushing her ear as he did so. Then he fell out of the memory, pulling her with him.*

There was a long, keening scream and suddenly the six basilisk ghosts were surrounding him, claws upraised.

. . . What have you done? *one of them uttered.*

Or it might have been . . . It had to be done!

Then they melted into the redness of the mist and there was only Archan, bone-dragon Archan, bearing down on him. Of Malya he could see no sign, though he could still feel her arms within his grip. Shutting his eyes he pivoted inside the memory rod and spun himself . . .

. . . into a shaft of agonizing light. He had not left the decking at all! Malya was shaking herself free of his grip and Frey . . . Frey was bearing down on him with his lips curled back from his teeth. In his hand he held a tiny human skull, no bigger than a doll's; a cloud of vapour was pouring out of the air and into the minuscule eye sockets, which were ablaze as if a sun had been crammed inside the tiny cave of bone. Lightning looped itself around his neck, drawing tight like a fiery garrotte; already choking he fell to his knees and lifted his hands to his throat, feeling his fingers burned away as they entered the stream of crackling fire. Archan was beside him, staring down without expression, moving not a muscle as his whole body started to burn. On the other side Malya had fallen into the

arms of Gerent. He looked around for Kythe, then recalled that all this had happened before they had met her.

Except this never happened!

His breath altogether gone, Jonah collapsed on to the wooden ledge. His vision was split into three, an abstract conjunction of the grey of Stone, the blue of the sky and the red of the dragons' crystal home. The colours began to blur together, growing dark.

He had not come here to change history, yet he had managed to do so. What was different?

His vision gone, he understood. In returning to this memory, his own memory of the confrontation with Frey, he had entered his own body and forced it to perform an action it had not performed the first time around: he had grabbed hold of Malya. Frey, disapproving of Jonah's intervention, had simply attacked him. Jonah recalled the attack had taken place the first time too, but a little later on and at a level that was merely debilitating, not . . . lethal.

I took hold of her arms and erased myself from the past . . .

This was Jonah's final thought before he died.

19

Fire-Break

... What have you done?
  ... It had to be done!

The basilisk ghosts melted into the redness of the mist, leaving only bone-dragon Archan screaming through the years.

Spinning . . .

... all the way round to face Gerent. The screaming went on and when he opened his eyes again he saw it was Gerent who was screaming. They were facing each other, disconnected. Gerent's arm was no longer around his waist; he was about to fall.

Between them, her back to Gerent, was Malya.

'Take her!' he yelled as gravity claimed him. Gerent needed no further instruction; though his face was that of a man in a dream his arms whipped around Malya's chest and hugged her close. Pushed away by the act of throwing her into Gerent's arms, he fell.

He had fallen no more than ten feet before Kythe caught him. By that time he was already unconscious.

The screaming brought him round, only this time it was his own. His body was on fire, fire around his throat like a garrotte. Archan bearing down through red mist.

An intense awareness of his own hidden workings, his attention telescoping into himself as he sensed the spin of every atom within his body. Electron shells flashed like polished steel, microscopic ball bearings orbiting through his own inner cosmos, perfect convex mirrors reflecting, twinning, separating, *diverging* . . .

Each atom split itself into two, reflected its twin, drew apart from its twin, isolated itself in its own diverging universe and became unique.

Jonah Lightfoot looked inward and saw that he had been torn in two.

The divergence continued, radiating out from his core like an explosion, or super-heated ash pouring down a volcanic slope. Everything it struck became divided . . . no, not divided: *multiplied*! Two Jonahs, two rivers, two seas, everything doubled and pulling slowly apart. Two skies.

Two Stones.

Descent. Insensibility.

'. . . up.'

His eyelids fluttered as if being tugged by tiny strings. 'Wh . . . ?'

'Wake up. Jonah, wake up.'

Mouth dry, limbs aching, ten thousand needles pressing against his skin from the inside. Regaining control of the small things first: fingers and toes, tongue separating parched lips, eyes. Opening them he saw Annie's face, racked with concern.

'Jonah, thank God! Are you all right?'

'I . . .' He fell back, weaker than he had ever felt in his life. 'Wait.'

They both waited patiently, she for him to speak, he for the needles to retract. They did so, slowly. When his skin had stopped throbbing he raised his head, relieved that he could do so without fainting. A line of pain on his neck reminded him first of fire, then a knife. Lifting his hand he touched a trail of clotted blood standing proud of his skin like an ancient scar.

'Annie,' he mumbled. 'I . . . I brought her back.'

She nodded through her tears, reaching forward as if to stroke his face but withdrawing before making contact, as if she were afraid to touch him, afraid of what he had become. 'Oh, Jonah.'

'Tell me . . . what did you see?'

'I saw light all around you, Jonah, like an aura. You went . . . limp. Then there was a screaming sound, and at first it sounded like Archan and then it was Gerent and then it was you. And all the time it was Malya. It doesn't make any sense, I know, but that's how it seemed. She *appeared*, Jonah, she just appeared, and for a moment I thought there were two of you, only one was on fire, and then the one of you that was on fire looked like a reflection in a mirror and disappeared. You pushed Malya into Gerent's arms and fell, and Kythe caught you.'

They were resting on a small ledge that Kythe had managed to locate. Both dragon and Shifters were perched nearby, looking on anxiously. Gerent, with Malya wrapped in his arms, was flying in slow, lazy circles.

'I know what happened, Annie. Dear God, it was not what I had expected, not at all. And when I consider what I have caused to happen . . .'

'You're tired. You don't need to tell me now . . .'

'But I must tell you! I brought Malya back from my memory just as I once brought back Darwin's book. Do you see? I did not remove her from the past, I *copied* her. I created her anew, Annie. I *created* her. The Malya I brought with me is both resurrected and new-born. That was as I had expected it to be – wonder enough, I thought. I believed that was the limit of my powers. I was wrong.

'In stepping into the memory – a memory of Stone only a few weeks old – I did a simple thing: I stepped forward and took Malya's arms. But in doing so I caused Frey to attack me, where he had not attacked me before. He killed me, Annie. Yet I returned here with Malya; I am still alive. This can mean only one thing: *I have created Stone anew also.* I have made a change in history which even the river of time cannot absorb. Until now I have tampered with time only at the most superficial level, and even then in the distant past. History has been able to adapt to the minor alterations I have made, without significantly affecting the future. But now I have stretched it beyond breaking point. In causing Frey to kill me, I removed the possibility that I would ever return to *allow* him to kill me. Such a contradiction cannot be tolerated and so the river has diverged in order to accommodate both truths. Just as the copy of Darwin I carry is not an original but a duplicate, just as the woman Gerent is holding is a duplicate, so I have made a duplicate of Stone itself, along with all its past and future. There exists now a version of Stone in which I was killed by Frey, a world out of which I have since fallen but which I created. I have created a world, Annie; is it any wonder I am tired?'

As he talked about it, it seemed that twin world was very close, a ghostly presence drifting through the spaces between the atoms. Not outside at all, not *beyond* but *within*. But already it was moving away as its track forked from the reality into which he, Jonah, *this* Jonah, was embedded. Could he ever reach that other world again? He thought not; he certainly had no desire to. Were he to attempt a journey to that new world, to prevent his own death for example, he would only end up creating a third world; in the second he would still be dead. No, the new Stone, and all it contained, was as unreachable to him now as the moon had been to a Neolithic man.

Memories, once made, could never be forgotten. Histories could not be unwritten, only transcribed.

Still, the knowledge of what he had done made him shudder at his very core.

His body was free of pain now, except for his head, which ached abominably. He told Annie this and she forced him to lie down with his head nestled in her lap; as he rested she stroked the back of his neck with her hand. Her long hair rested on his, its weight like silk. He knew there were more and greater tasks to be done but for now he wanted only to close himself up like a flower and wait for the sun to rise again.

'Even God had the seventh day,' he murmured.

Annie was humming softly and for a time he dipped in and out of sleep. Eventually the headache subsided and he was able to keep his eyes open without the light hurting them.

'I miss the stars,' said Annie, gazing at the pin-points set into the curve of the pipe. 'Kansas stars are beautiful, Jonah.'

'You loved your home very much.'

She nodded. 'I didn't think I'd ever want to go back, not once I'd left. But now . . . I'd like to see the plains again, even if it's just for a moment. I'd even . . . I want to see Rance again.'

'Annie, if we manage to deal with Archan I will . . .'

She pressed a finger against his lips. 'Ssh. Don't promise me nothing, Jonah.'

They watched the starlight together.

'Remember the scoop, Jonah? How I used to love swimming in it? Way back before you measured Stone and went up into that damned forest? Well, when I was swimming I used to think about the charm, all that magic we were breathing in. I wondered if maybe it was like breathing in woodsmoke. The Indians do that, you know – they seal themselves into their tepees and set a fire and breathe the smoke, and they say it makes them fly and gives them far-away eyes. Visions, you know. I used to wonder if that's what the charm would do to us.' She touched his lips again, very gently. 'You told me it was the charm making me crazy, making me love you then not love you. And now there's Gerent . . .'

'You do not have to justify yourself to me, Annie.'

'I'm not, I'm just saying. I think . . . I used to wonder something else too. I got to thinking about how there used to be magic in our world back home, before what Esh called the *turning of the world*, and I got to wondering what happened to all that magic.'

'The basilisks had a saying: "Nothing goes."'

'I remember; you told me that once. So, what if the charm did linger on somehow? Or what if it went away, but left something behind? Like . . . like salt on your cheek when your tears have dried. I've always thought, since I was a little girl . . .' she regarded him shyly, her hair falling in front of her face, '. . . that being in love is like having a piece of magic inside your heart.'

Jonah smiled weakly and kissed her fingers. 'Perhaps that is exactly what it is.'

'How strong do you feel?'

He thought for a moment, then replied, 'Strong enough.'

He spent a while talking quietly to Kythe, trying to reassure the young dragon who, despite her size, was still little more than a child. Her simple loyalty was touching, and when she no longer seemed to be paying attention to his words he wrapped his arms around her neck and hugged her.

'Can you make Archan go away?' she asked meekly.

'Yes, Kythe, I believe I can. With your help and a little good fortune.'

At these words she brightened, and Jonah's feigned confidence even helped him rally himself. Looking to his right he saw Tam, sprawled on Meem's back; the selkie's face was sad and drawn.

'I am sorry about Ruane,' called Jonah, pressing down his own sadness for the time being.

'She was dying, I think,' replied Tam. 'Perhaps it was for the best.'

Jonah doubted that, and resolved to question Tam further about his sister – there was more to her death than met the eye, he was sure of it. But for now the group needed to be gathered and roused; enough time had been wasted.

'Meem, Teget!' he announced. 'I made you a promise, then told you I was unable to keep it until Archan was vanquished. But in bringing back Malya I have proved myself a liar: I *can* still navigate the memory rods, despite Archan's presence. If you wish I will fulfil that promise now, and seek out your true forms. However . . . I fear we have no time left to spare. I beg you to indulge me just a little longer, to accompany me to the Aqueduct and see Archan brought down. Then, I swear, I will do as you have asked.'

The two Shifters regarded each other briefly, then Meem looked back at Jonah and said, 'We believe you. Do what you must. If we can be of assistance we will. The task you have to perform outweighs all others.'

Jonah breathed a silent sigh of relief. 'Thank you.'

Gerent and Malya were entwined some distance above them, near the twinkling ceiling. He had somehow strapped her into the harness Annie had once worn, so that she was suspended with her back against his stomach and her head resting back on his chest; his legs were clasped lightly about her waist. They were talking in low, intense voices, hands restlessly locking and unlocking, hair entangled.

Jonah asked Kythe to carry him aloft so that he could speak with them.

'Gerent? Is she all right?'

'She is well,' murmured Gerent. 'All is well.'

Malya looked down at Jonah with a mixture of fear and awe, and he wondered how much she understood of what had happened to her.

'She is frightened,' Gerent went on, 'but she will come with us.' Then he bowed his head. 'I have done you both great wrong. I do not regret what I have done, but . . . I am shamed nevertheless. I held a blade to your throat. My love for Annie was real but . . .' Here he glanced at Malya, who regarded him quizzically. 'I will explain it all, my love. But Lightfoot, if you must think of it as a madness then do so, a madness that took me and which has now departed. I cannot . . . please do not . . .'

Jonah spoke up to end his misery.

'Gerent, I already owe you my life for rescuing me at the Threshold. I do not pretend to like what you have done, but I understand the depth of the love that made you act the way you have. You need not feel ashamed. Once you had to remind me that you were my friend; do I really need to remind you of that self-same thing now?'

'Then we will fly at your side, Lightfoot, if you will have us there. We will be there when you need us.' He turned his head down so that his long, golden hair fell in front of Malya's face and Kythe dropped away again.

'We go,' said Jonah, and so they set out to cross the last few miles to the end of the pipe.

'Malya must be terrified,' Jonah mused as Kythe carried both him and Annie towards the light. 'How can she possibly comprehend what I have done?'

'I've been thinking about that,' replied Annie, 'and I think she'll be okay. Think about it, Jonah – her father was a magician, her people believed in magic, they lived in a world where the air is filled with magic. What she'll remember now is: she was standing on the ledge, facing up to her father, then you took hold of her and suddenly she was here. She's just . . . *jumped over* the days between. That's frightening, but it's not hard to grasp the facts, however strange the causes, and she's not stupid. I'll bet she'll just put it down to some weird magic and get on with things. In fact, I bet she'll deal with it a hell of a lot better than we would. They're tough, these Stone Age types. She probably thinks you're just a better wizard than her father.'

Watching Malya looking hungrily ahead, Jonah began to come round to Annie's way of thinking. This woman was of pre-Viking warrior stock, and that meant if nothing else she was resilient. He was reminded of his first impressions of her; with her well-muscled limbs and blonde mane she might have been a prototype Valkyrie.

'When I first met her I found her intimidating,' he said.

'That's because you're not used to women who answer back.'

'It is because she was carrying a spear and treated me like an insect.'

'Well you obviously ain't used to that either.'

'Where I come from women know how to behave.'

'Sounds dull as hell.'

Jonah studied the reflections of the star-lights in the speeding river, the wash of daylight across the dark metal of the pipe, the unseen patterns in the air as wings traced out invisible lines.

'Gerent apologized,' he said.

'People change.'

They were within half a mile of the exit when the water grew agitated. There had been no stars for some time now, but the expanding semi-circle of daylight gave them all the illumination they needed.

In place of the stars there were deep grooves in the

344

sides of the pipe. They spiralled around its circumference like the rifling in a gun barrel. To their right, where the grooves were curving upwards, the water was forced to rise in fractured waves; to their left the water dropped away as the falling spiral channels sucked it downwards. The rifling was not uniform however, nor did any of the individual grooves appear to extend all the way round the pipe, so the river was not spun completely around; if so they would not have been able to proceed. Nevertheless, enough of the white water rose high enough to force them to pick their way through the worst of the spray. At times it was like flying through an inverted rainstorm.

The disturbance did not last for long. Between the end of the rifling and the exit itself the pipe walls were quite smooth, devoid even of the plates and rivets that had characterized its upStone sections. A few hundred yards short of the exit a trio of squat metal stanchions broke through the water, sharp-sided islands set square in the flow; their top surfaces were flat and level, dark iron. The centre island was marked with a symbol that was unnervingly familiar:

It was a Mah-Jongg symbol, and Jonah knew it at once: the North Wind, the tile that had always reminded him of a man and woman dancing arm in arm.

These Oriental marks had pursued him across worlds even to this point, their calligraphy seemingly built in to the very structure of Stone, as meaningful to the basilisks as to the Chinese man who had made the set of ivory tiles for Annie in the first place. Esh had borne on her carapace the mark of the Red Dragon, and Jonah himself had wielded a solidified replica of that sword-shape during one of his earlier encounters with Archan.

This is no game, he reminded himself as they flew over the strange archipelago and left the oversized tile behind.

The end of the pipe flared like a trumpet. The daylight beyond was blinding – they could see nothing within its whiteness, neither detail nor distance.

After a quick consultation with Kythe and Annie, Jonah announced that they would be first to fly out. No argument came back; indeed their companions remained altogether silent.

They passed through the exit.

Eyes adjusted swiftly to the desert-bright glare. In sober mood they looked down upon the Aqueduct.

From above there was nothing to see but the river, swift and calm once more. It flowed on just as it had done through the pipe, cleaving a dead straight line towards the brilliance of the downStone wall. To Jonah it looked like a contradictory Styx, an epic waterway bound not for the underworld but Paradise.

Curious to learn what manner of structure was supporting the bed of this mighty river he instructed Kythe to take them over the side and underneath. As she traversed the stream he watched Gerent swoop low, nearly trailing his and Malya's legs through the water.

'Have a care!' he shouted, then Annie was clutching his shoulder hard enough to hurt.

'My God, Jonah, will you look at that!'

In imagining what colossal structure might be used to support such a body of water, Jonah had returned to a familiar image from the journals he had left behind in nineteenth-century London. In 1878, just five years before he had found his way to Krakatoa, Thomas Bouch had built the longest bridge in the world, spanning a two-mile stretch of the Firth of Tay at Dundee. He fully expected to see something resembling that structure here: soaring columns tied with struts and spars of delicately wrought iron. Annie too had described such a construction from her dreams, except in her imagination it was transparent as glass.

In reality there was nothing. No canal bed, no deck, neither beam nor pier. In fact, no bridge of any kind at all. There was just the river and the memory rod, the former encasing the latter, and that was all the Aqueduct was. If the water was held by anything it was held by the air alone, a fact which, given what they knew of the air's remarkable properties, was entirely consistent with the constantly surprising laws of Stone.

Jonah recalled that less than two years after completion, the central spans of the Tay bridge had collapsed. *And if this were to collapse in similar fashion now, all our problems would be solved.*

He suspected the architecture of the basilisks was rather more reliable than that of man.

Rising again he examined the opposite wall.

Like the wall from which they had emerged, the downStone wall was sheer, strikingly so. He had not realized how used he had become to Stone's constant ten-degree pitch, and to see a true vertical on such a tremendous scale was shocking. The far wall was made of small silver bricks, poorly aligned so that its surface looked rough and unkempt, despite its shiny appearance. Tiny plants huddled on ledges and in cracks, their branches long and spindly, their coppery leaves dull and tattered. Sunlight glistened off textured steel and streaks of gold, a palette full of variety yet with a single theme.

Metal world, he thought. *The world as it was before there was charm.*

He struggled to orientate himself with the rest of Stone. The Aqueduct ran parallel to Stone's main wall; the fire-break, this piece of air separating stone wall from metal wall was cut directly into Stone like a pass dividing a mountain range. To his left he could clearly see blue sky, to his right there was the indeterminate darkness of the slot's interior.

Somewhere beyond the metal wall, Archan was coming. The slot was barely one hundred yards across; she could practically leap from one side to the other, without even having to open her wings.

'Is this the fire-break?' said Annie suspiciously. 'Is this all it is? It might stop a fire but is it really going to stop Archan?'

'There might be more to it than meets the eye.'

'There'd better be.'

'Kythe,' said Jonah, patting the dragon's head, 'would you take us further across the gap, please?'

She did so, flexing her wings cautiously while Gerent and the two Shifters held their positions just outside the pipe exit. Below the river hung the abyss, made doubly vertiginous by the enclosing walls. It was cold out here and Jonah could feel Kythe trembling beneath him. Then again she was probably terrified. As was he.

As they approached the middle point of the canyon the air grew noticeably thicker. Jonah could feel it clogging in his throat; when he swung his arm around, his hand felt as though it were sliding through molasses. Then the world seemed to flip over and suddenly they were heading back towards the pipe again, without even having turned around. Kythe breathed a sigh of relief.

'It's a funny feeling, isn't it,' she gabbled. 'Oh, Jonah, I thought something awful was going to happen, but I wanted to trust you. Did I do all right?'

'Perfectly fine, Kythe. I had already expected Stone to pull that trick on us, but I had to be sure. You see,' he went on, addressing Annie now, 'it *is* an effective barrier. This twisting of space is Stone's way of defining its boundaries, just as it defines the line in the sky it does not want you to cross. The canyon is impassable by anything except the waters of the Aqueduct and the beams of light by which we see.'

'I guess so. So, d'you think Archan's planning to swim?'

'I suspect she is relying on sheer momentum to carry her across, just as it carried her clean through the timeless world where the faery queen ran to ground. I think in this case that will not be enough so, yes, she will ultimately be forced to use the Aqueduct.'

'Hmm. Have you noticed something about the air?' Kythe breathed in theatrically. 'Apart from the fact it's sticky, I mean.'

'What are you talking about?' put in Annie.

'Isn't it obvious? There's no wind.'

She was right: the air of Stone was utterly still.

When they reached the others they found Gerent pointing downwards, but not, as Jonah first thought, at the Aqueduct; he was squinting at something much further down, a thin grey line practically invisible against a slightly paler grey mist. Malya was whispering something to him; she jumped, startled, as Kythe drew near, and stopped talking at once.

'What is it?' asked Annie, craning her neck over Kythe's neck.

Gerent and Jonah traded glances, then both started speaking together. Bowing his head, Gerent allowed Jonah to take the floor.

'I could be mistaken, but I do believe it is another Aqueduct, or at least its equivalent.'

'Another one?' blurted Kythe. 'But I thought . . .'

'Let him explain,' said Gerent.

Jonah continued. 'The fire-break – this slot we are in – must logically extend all the way from the very tip of Stone down to its base – if indeed it has a base. That is the only way it can be effective. For all we know it may be just one of many such slots all the way round Stone's circumference. Add to this fact our knowledge that extended travel on Stone is permitted only along its spiral thread – sideways in other words, not directly up and down – and it becomes clear that at regular intervals up the height of the slot there must be a bridge to carry the memory rods across to the next section of Stone. *Our* memory rod, having crossed the divide by means of *our* Aqueduct, continues beyond the metal wall on its descending spiral downStone, and when it has passed all the way round Stone's circumference again it returns to this same slot, but much lower down.

'And that is what we can see down there: the next point at which the unbroken line of the memory rods crosses the fire-break.'

'Like drawbridges across a castle moat,' murmured Annie. Then she frowned. 'The air's moving.'

Jonah could feel it too, not a wind but a slight vibration. He felt it against his skin, in his ears, across the surface of his tongue, a bass sound well below the threshold of hearing.

'It's getting stronger,' wailed Kythe. 'I can feel my wings shaking!'

'Can you still fly?' demanded Jonah, suddenly aware that there was nowhere at all for them to land in an emergency. He did not fancy ditching in the fast-moving river. Kythe gulped and nodded uncertainly; he was hardly reassured.

The vibration was growing more intense, rising through the scale until they could actually hear it, a low screaming that soon became a banshee wail. While Kythe and the Shifters shook their heads in obvious distress, their human and selkie passengers clapped their hands to their ears. Eventually the wailing became a whistling, finally passing out of the range of human hearing. Jonah noted abstractly that Kythe continued to shake her head for a few seconds after he had ceased to hear the sound, and the Shifters continued to be affected for as long as a minute afterwards.

Tiny waves were lifting from the surface of the river: the effect spread swiftly downStone from the pipe exit, meeting an identical set of waves emanating from the exit's silver-lined opposite number on the far side of the fire-break. Where they met they died away, leaving a narrow band across the centre of the Aqueduct where disturbance was minimal.

Now they could hear nothing, but the whole canyon was shaking.

Dust was showering from the walls. Puffs of mortar appeared like small explosions; pale clouds of steel dust sparkled; broken shards of Stone-stuff tumbled as it was unloaded into the atmosphere. Some of the debris fell into the river, where the wavelets were now each the height of a man. Then, abruptly, the waves fell away and the water was calm again.

'It is Archan,' said Jonah, looking at the others one by one.

'Are we too late?' asked Annie, her voice flat.

Jonah closed his eyes, tentatively opening his mind to the memory rod. She was there, to be sure, and too close for comfort but . . . was she really *that* close?

'I do not know,' he began. 'I do not . . .'

'By the sky!' exclaimed Kythe suddenly. 'Look at that!'

Miles below them, the second bridge was surrounded by minute streaks of light, like fire-flies swarming, exploding sideways from the downStone wall. The individual lights clung to the bridge, growing larger as they progressed, then popped and disappeared, making way for fresh ones behind.

Then the downStone wall disintegrated.

This was no gradual collapse: one moment the wall was intact, the next it had fragmented into a billion pieces. Something punched these splinters clean across the fire-break and then Archan was there.

She crossed the fire-break in an eye-blink, yet afterwards all swore they could remember every detail of her appearance. What they remembered most vividly was the span of her wings: they extended beyond the limits of vision, momentarily creating a red carpet to the entire canyon. Buoyed by those massive wings was a body of bones, each bone a perforated architectural lattice. Here at last was the suspension bridge Jonah had been expecting to see, only it was alive and in motion; Archan was a monstrous skeleton as fabricated by Eiffel. The fact they could see clear through her body to the abyss below in no way lessened her presence, in fact it served only to emphasize her dominance over everything they could see. Archan was the frame through which they viewed the abyss, the only aperture through which the world below could be reached.

Except below her there was now no world. Below her, behind her, Stone was gone.

The instant Jonah recognized this, Archan was gone too, leaving only emptiness in her wake.

Jonah stared unbelieving at the ragged line where the walls had once been: it was like looking down from a battlement only to see that the castle's lower storeys had simply been wiped away.

There was nothing down there but whiteness, except it was an unsettling whiteness: a nothingness that burned the eye – brilliant shadow, dark highlight, saturated grey. It was a region where neither light nor colour seemed to know what to do with themselves, settling instead for the neutrality of white without any of its serenity.

Equally disturbing was the plain fact that the walls around them were no longer supported by anything at all. Stone was, to all intents and purposes, hanging in the air.

'Never mind the drawbridge,' said Annie, her voice dull with shock, 'she took away the damn foundations.'

'That is exactly what she has been doing all this time,' responded Jonah. 'Ever since she caught the faery queen, Archan has been spiralling up the thread towards us, consuming everything as she goes – Stone's wall, the memory rods, even the sky . . . everything. Which means that everything around us is now entirely unsupported.'

'So how come we ain't falling, Jonah?'

He rubbed his forehead, his brow furrowed, but it was Gerent who answered, dipping in the air to bring himself close enough to speak. 'It can mean only one thing: Stone does not rest on foundations at all. It hangs.'

Annie's eyes grew wide as she tried to imagine this; Jonah was nodding his head. 'Yes, by God, Gerent! It *hangs*!' He beamed at Annie, who did not seem to share his exaltation. 'Annie, my dear, imagine it! A vast cone made of, well, of stone. To its ten-degree slope cling all manner of creatures culled from all the ages of history, while behind its face run all the memories of the world. And what does this cone rest on? *Nothing!* It rests on *nothing*, Annie! Since the past is infinite, it simply turns, spiralling away down and down and down, widening as it goes but never ending, never ending. It has no base, no foundation, there is no ground to hold it up: it simply *hangs*. Up there, at the very tip of the cone, is the point from which all Stone is suspended.'

'And above that?' asked Annie doubtfully.

'Who can say?'

'It'd better not be a thread. I can think of better things to have my life hanging by.'

Conversation faltered as they tried to comprehend this new theory. Jonah found his initial excitement quickly evaporating as he grasped the fact that Archan was *coming*!

'We have no way of estimating how soon she will be here,' he announced, 'but I think we can assume there is little enough time for debate. We must surely have no more than an hour, probably less.'

'What is your plan, Lightfoot?' asked Gerent. Malya, looking remarkably comfortable in the crude harness, regarded Jonah with undisguised awe.

He knew the Neolithic man shared his thoughts. 'The islands,' he sighed. 'To be specific, the one island that looked like a Mah-Jongg tile. I think that will be as good a place to start as any. Gerent, would you examine it first? Try to determine its function, as I have no doubt it has one.'

'What will you do?'

'I want to take a closer look at the Aqueduct. We will meet you shortly.'

That seemed to suffice for Gerent. After a brief discussion, Tam and the Shifters elected to go with him and Malya, if only to use the islands as a resting place; both Meem and Teget were tired again.

'If you find anything,' Jonah called after them, 'such as a mechanism, or some clue as to how we can break the Aqueduct, do not wait for me. Do what you must.'

'Trust me!' came Gerent's faint reply.

'How much time do you think we've got?' asked Annie quietly when the others had gone.

'Little enough.'

Annie's hand brushed Jonah's. 'Do you?'

'Do I what?'

'Trust him?'

'Yes,' he answered, without hesitation.

Instructing Kythe to fly out as far along the Aqueduct

as she could without invoking the turning charm that would flip them back in the opposite direction, Jonah tried to peer through the water at the memory rod.

'See?' he said after a moment's scrutiny. 'There is a mark all the way around the rod, there, at the very centre of the Aqueduct.' Sure enough there was a knobbly raised section, like a line of scar tissue, ringing the black rod. 'I believe that is the . . . I suppose we might call it the *junction*. It is the weak point in the memory rod, the place where it is designed, as a last resort, to break.'

'Last resorts are what we need right now,' drawled Annie. 'Shame you can't get to it – that water would just sweep you away.'

'It may not be necessary. I can still manipulate the rods from a distance – rescuing Malya proved that; perhaps I can break them from a distance too.'

'Is that what you're going to try now?'

'Yes, it is.'

'Then why d'you send Gerent and the others back inside? Don't those islands mean anything after all?'

'They almost certainly do mean something, but if I can do this without them I shall. As for the others – I simply wanted to get them to a place of safety.'

Annie arched her eyebrows. 'Just in case something goes wrong? Hmm. But you thought you'd keep me and Kythe out on a limb, right?'

Jonah had to smile. 'I did not think you would go, even if I insisted.'

'Damn right!' said woman and dragon together. Kythe even managed a passable impression of Annie's Kansas accent. Jonah could not help but laugh.

'Um,' put in Kythe. 'I've been thinking about what you said, Jonah, and if it's true then what about the future?'

'I beg your pardon?' Jonah was only half-listening: he

was eyeing the scar in the memory rod, trying to imagine how he might bring his strength to bear on it.

'Well, you said that Stone hangs from something, and the further down you go the more it unwinds, only it goes on forever because the past goes on forever.'

'That's right, dear,' said Annie when Jonah did not reply.

'But what about the future?' blurted Kythe, jerking her long dragon head upwards. 'What happens up there? Up there it all just comes to a dead stop, doesn't it?'

'She's right, Jonah,' said Annie gravely. 'If it all comes to a point, isn't that the point in the world's future where history just comes to an end?'

Jonah broke his attention away from the memory rod. Kythe was right, of course (and this held true whether Stone were suspended or supported on rocks or even afloat in the very bathtub of the gods): the uppermost tip of Stone was nothing less than the apex of time. He had discussed this with Gerent on that night on the Bark, when they had first deduced the screw-thread course of the rods; Kythe's reminder seemed ominous. This was the proof that the river of time was infinite in one direction only, that at some point in the future, history came to an abrupt end.

That the world, in short, was ultimately doomed.

'Jonah!'

The bellow came from the pipe exit and echoed around the narrow confines of the fire-break canyon. Kythe swung her head round, her eyebrows raised querulously.

'Damnation! It sounds urgent!' Jonah glared at the scar. 'Come on, Kythe. Let us see what he needs – but we must be quick now!'

Within the fire-break the air was still again. In the sky beyond however, thick clouds – thicker than any Jonah could remember seeing here – were dropping in front of the sun. The temperature was dropping too, and as the

356

light began to fail Jonah actually saw his breath misting in front of his face – another first on Stone.

'Gettin' cold,' commented Annie as Kythe swung them into the shadow of the pipe.

Gerent and the Shifters had landed on the central island; Tam had dismounted and was squatting beside Meem, the larger of the two Shifters. They were clustered round the large Mah-Jongg sign, but their attention was on one of the other islands.

'What is it, Jonah?' Annie murmured.

Something was breaching the water beside the island, a smooth, humped shape. From a distance it appeared both featureless and motionless, but as Kythe drew cautiously nearer Jonah began to see a pattern of lines and swirls across its surface. The object was deep red, the colour of terracotta, with the lustre and grain of highly polished cherry-wood. Simultaneously strange and familiar, it sat unmoving while the river crashed both past and over it, throwing up white spray: however it was anchored, it was anchored well.

The object revolved, revealing more of its skin. Knots and rings rolled past; ribs and vein-like swellings lifted clear of the water only to be submerged again; a single fin, sleek and tapering, rose dripping from the foam then plunged under.

Soon it had made a half-turn. Now, instead of smooth wood, the onlookers were confronted by a face.

Jonah stared in astonishment as deep green eyes blinked open and broad lips parted to reveal tangles of briar and bramble within. A wooden brow frowned briefly, then relaxed into contented crinkles; the eyes blinked, then the whole face smiled.

'About time, I might say! Waited a long time, I have. Oh ye, an age or more. Still, here you are now, and not soon enough. Work's to be done and time's rotted away. Ideas I've got – plenty of them. You want to hear?'

20

Aqueduct

'Such a tale I've to tell, but where to start? Best to keep the pith for another day – there's worlds to be saved, so I'll just sketch you the bark of it for now.

'Dark it was in the belly of the Goddess. Oh ye, dark indeed. I nearly got out – pierced her flesh from within – but beaten back I was. My control over the Bark, ah, poor it was. Back I fell into the acid, ready to die.

'It etched the Bark, that acid, etched him all over. Etched me too. I could feel it eating into Bark-wood and lesky-wood alike, a biting sea. Nothing to see, nothing to hear but the grinding of her belly. The Bark was tough, I knew, and would last many days, but would I? Likely not.

'Then, light came. Broken light, busy like a swarm of bees. The Goddess . . . opened up. She was *peeled*. The juruas came, glass bodies in a frenzy, tiny gluttons flaying the Goddess alive. They ripped open her belly, spilled the acid into the ocean, swarmed towards the Bark, enveloped him . . . and passed him over. On they scurried, consuming the Goddess from outside and in until all was gone.

'The Bark sank, and I sank with him. Riddled with holes he was, stricken and heavy. Down through Stone's sea he fell, until he struck a fist of coral. There he lay, drowned.

'Time passed. Air bubbled through the Bark, sucked from vents behind the coral fist. The air filled the holes and the Bark began to float. Smaller he was, just a sphere of wood, stripped of all but his innermost workings. But charm was still in his reservoir, and soon he was drinking new strength from the air.

'Then it was that the Deathless came.

'Six they were, as they've always been, the ghosts of the makers of Stone. They gathered round me, taking their old places in the lining of the Bark, the places they'd used in ancient times – the days when Stone was young and they were yet to lose interest in its wonders. The days when they'd voyaged. The basilisks said:

'. . . *You have been punished enough, Lesky. Amara has greater needs now than to see you subdued. Take the Bark and join the Faery in his quest. All you once were, you are again, with one exception: you still lack the power to change the memories. That power belongs to two alone now: the Faery and the Red Dragon. When they finally meet, you must be there.*

'There was more they told me, which I'll tell you shortly. When they left, I felt the Bark . . . *thicken* around me. Holes were plugged, tendons rethreaded through long-abandoned ways. Charm-skeins woven anew. A shining hull, sleek and fast. And at his centre – a place for me! A place for Grandfather Tree at last! A branchless tree whose root is all Stone, a ship both anchored and free, with a lesky at his helm. I filled Bark veins with lesky sap, looked out through Bark lids with lesky eyes, sent lesky thoughts plunging through Bark mind. We became one, Bark and lesky, and in becoming one each became more than he had ever been.

'The rest is mere navigation. The river – you'll have guessed this – drains from the ocean. I found the outlet, squeezed myself through and hurried here. Dozing I must have been when first you flew past, hidden under the waves. But now you're here, now I'm ready to help you.

And believe me, Jonah Lightfoot, when Grandfather Tree says: your humble servant I am.'

They had watched unbelieving as Grandfather Tree steered the Bark across the river's flow, resisting the devastating current with ease. He even found time to spin the spherical vessel once more about its axis; his craggy, brown face came up dripping wet and grinning broadly. Having fetched the Bark up against the North Wind island, he told his story while the river forged its way past. As he spoke, it struck Jonah that the old lesky had acquired something he had never exhibited before: a look of contentment.

Malya, extricated at last from the flying harness, was regarding the wooden face with undisguised suspicion. Gerent placed his arm around her and whispered reassurances, none of which changed the expression on her face, though some of the tension left her shoulders. His words, unheard by all except Malya, condensed in the cold air, making mist around his mouth. Out of the corner of his eye Jonah saw Annie watching the couple, her fingers fidgeting against the side of the painting box she still had slung around her neck.

'Grandfather Tree,' he said as soon as the lesky had finished, 'I am truly pleased to see you alive and well. I am sure you will regale us with a fuller version of your tale, but for now we must simply act. Tell us what you know of the Aqueduct. What is it that the basilisk ghosts told you?'

The first blow – not that Jonah was surprised to hear it – was that it was impossible to break the rod by anything other than physical contact.

'It was I who encouraged you to enter the rods from a distance,' said Grandfather Tree. 'But now I tell you here it will not work. Touch it you must, or the breach cannot be made.'

'Is the only way across through the water?'

'Oh ye, the water. Those who go by air are turned aside; only the river flows on downStone, and only a river vessel can make that journey. There's no other way.' He beamed. Were he a bird he would have been preening himself by now.

'Then it is a blessing you are here.'

'Nothing more than what the Deathless wanted. We're all pawns in their game.'

Jonah cocked his head on one side. 'Is that what you believe?'

Grandfather Tree held his gaze for a moment, then laughed uproariously. 'I believe they lost track of the rules a thousand aeons ago. Clutching at flimsy twigs they are!'

'With you and I the flimsiest of all.'

Green-tinged tears were squirting from the corners of the lesky's eyes. By degrees he managed to control himself, then, suddenly, his face straightened. 'It's not a safe thing to do.'

'Tell us.'

So Grandfather Tree explained. The mechanism was simple, as they had come to expect from the basilisks: on each side of the Aqueduct was a lock. By using the correct key, the two locks could be de-activated, allowing access to the part of the memory rod Jonah had already identified as the weak point: the scarred ring at the Aqueduct's central point. Comparatively easy though this might be to achieve, it was only the introduction of an adept such as Jonah into the scar region that would finally break the memory rod in two, thus making the fire-break a truly impenetrable barrier.

'You make it sound easy,' commented Annie. 'You got the keys?'

'No,' chuckled Grandfather Tree. 'No keys, not me!'

Annie threw her hands up in disgust and rounded on

Jonah. 'Can you make sense of this? Because I'm getting a mite edgy here!' She was close to tears, but drew back when Jonah stepped towards her. 'Don't, just . . . just get it done, both of you. Quit jawin' and just get it done!'

Under Grandfather Tree's direction they cleared the area around the Mah-Jongg symbol. This was the first time Jonah had examined it properly; he shivered, as much from apprehension as from the coldness of the air. He blew into his hands and rubbed them together, conscious of a growing stiffness in his fingers.

The island was a perfect square, about ten yards on each side. With the two big-winged Shifters and a handful of humans aboard it felt just short of crowded. At the centre was the sign of the North Wind, a collection of calligraphic strokes set deep into the polished black floor and covering an area around six feet square. Jonah knew instinctively that he was looking at the first of the locks.

'And the key?' he called to Grandfather Tree, whose face was just visible, peering over the edge of the island.

'Just press the shape of the symbol into the slots,' the lesky informed him. 'Doesn't turn, doesn't move. Just fill the holes.'

Jonah scratched his head, wondering why the lesky had assured him it was easy when it seemed he would need a ton or two of cement to fill in this particular excavation. Then a deep voice behind him said,

'Make way. I will do this.'

It was Teget. The Shifter lumbered towards the symbol, folding his wings away as he advanced. As Jonah stepped back to let him pass he saw he was doing more than this – he was actually absorbing his wings back into his body. At the same time his neck was shortening, as was his tail, both withdrawing until almost nothing remained. Legs contracted until they resembled the stumps his wings had become, and now Teget looked more like a turtle than a dragon, lurching into position on top of the carved symbol with a clumsy rolling motion. Once there, he flattened his newly sculpted body still further until all the cracks were covered. Then he *settled*.

Though he could not see it, Jonah knew what was happening: the Shifter was moulding his body into the shape of the Mah-Jongg symbol, using his malleable flesh to fulfil the requirements of the key. Presently he lifted his new face – half dragon, half turtle – and managed a fraction of a smile.

'It is not comfortable,' Teget announced. 'And the metal is cold inside. I am in some discomfort. But I will remain here as long as necessary.'

'Then we must waste no time!' cried Jonah, shaking off his astonishment at hearing the Shifter speak for the very first time. 'Meem! Will you come with me to the other side of the fire-break? There is but one way to make the journey: under the surface of this river. Will you accompany me into the Bark?'

Meem stopped to exchange a few words with his fellow Shifter, then joined Jonah at the island's edge. Grandfather Tree's mouth was wide open, the brambles pulled back as far as they would go; nevertheless it looked dark and uninviting in there, not to say prickly . . .

'What happened to the entrance hatch?' enquired Jonah.

Though he had no shoulders, Grandfather Tree managed somehow to shrug. 'Et in,' he gargled as a wave broke across his chin.

Stepping across on to the lesky's wide lower lip, Jonah gingerly descended into his mouth, wondering how it came to be that he was allowing himself to be swallowed for the second time by a monster from the deep. One of the brambles jabbed at his arm and he cursed under his breath, but once he was past the first clump the way opened up. Not that it was spacious: the inside of the resurrected Bark was smaller than the charm-reservoir had once been on its own. Indeed, Jonah realized, this *was* the charm-reservoir, the very place where Annie had pricked herself on the dryad's nail, after they had shared such a memorable few hours together . . .

The interior was smaller, he guessed, because the outer hull was thicker. After all, if Grandfather Tree was now a permanent resident he needed enough room to stretch.

He was about to push his head back outside when the yellow bulk of Meem squeezed in. Hastily moving aside he watched apprehensively as the giant creature folded himself unceremoniously into the cramped chamber. Then, before he could move again, Grandfather Tree's mouth closed and the light failed.

There was only a second or two of darkness before a phosphorescent glow spilled upwards from the floor of the chamber, but it was enough to scare Jonah half to death.

'Grandfather Tree! Let me speak with Annie. I would not leave her without saying "goodbye".'

There was a brief pause, then the lesky's face appeared in miniature, protruding from the curved ceiling directly above his head. 'A thousand apologies. We're off already – hold tight!'

'But . . .'

'No time! You said it yourself!'

Jonah felt something pushing against the backs of his knees, and found that Meem had extended one of his weird flipper-wings behind him. 'Sit down, faery,' the Shifter said. 'Since your kind lost their wings, it is all you can do.'

He did not imagine it would be a long voyage, but he settled back all the same; the Shifter's pliable flesh was as comfortable as a lounge chair and he could even feel his eyelids beginning to droop. It was hot inside the Bark, a marked contrast to the uncharacteristic coldness outside, and he felt the stresses of the past few days beginning to creep up on him. He felt tired and dirty; his stomach was emptier than he could ever remember it being, and though he knew Stone's nutritious atmosphere would sustain him indefinitely, still he felt the need for some ballast. In fact, he could not imagine feeling less prepared for the task ahead than he did just then.

'Meem?' he said. 'I must confess to feeling intimidated by you and your silent companion – your once-silent companion, I should say. Please trust me when I say I will keep my word.'

'We do not doubt your integrity. You are more important to us than you can know, Jonah. Do not think ill of us simply because we wish to stay near the one on whom we are relying for salvation.'

'Does Teget feel as you do?'

Meem laughed, a remarkably human sound from such an alien creature. 'Pay no attention to him. He is angry for his own reasons, not because of you. You see, ours is in many ways a simple life. Teget yearns for complexity.'

'Complexity? In what way?'

Jonah felt his living armchair wallow beneath him as Meem shifted to a more comfortable position.

'We Shifters are simple because when one changes we all change. Have you not noticed this? Individuality is not prized among us, because the primal shape is lost. Until we know that, one form is as good as another. Many of us are merely curious, but Teget is desperate for the knowledge. He wants desperately to be unique, whether his shape is true or not. But we Shifters have what you might call a . . . a *group-mind*. The will of the collective is difficult to resist. And so Teget is constantly trapped in forms he cannot control.'

'Yet both of you have been changing shape constantly on our journey,' Jonah pointed out. 'At one point you resembled caterpillars, then dragons. And Lawal chose to resemble me, on the night when we first met.'

'Lawal chose nothing, he merely responded to his instinct. All around him, unseen by you, the Shifters were changing in the same way. You were an intruder, and as such an irresistible stimulus. As for our present journey, the group has relinquished control to me and Teget. We are making the decisions, but you can be sure that behind us the rest of the Shifters are matching us shape for shape.'

Jonah tried to imagine the great band of Shifters they had left behind, spontaneously altering their forms in response to the unseen signals transmitted by their companions. By doing so they were all, in some small way, sharing in the adventure.

'So you see,' concluded Meem, 'why we have come. In our own ways, we all yearn to be free.'

'We've arrived!' proclaimed the lesky's disembodied voice, and daylight poured in once more.

Metal wall, metal world.

The island was square, just like the one he had left; around it poured the river, its velocity unabated; the air was cold, like winter. Apart from these things, he was in a world like none he had ever seen.

The tunnel was high and wide, much larger in section than the other. The island on which he stood was set very close to one of the walls. The wall – at least thirty storeys high – had been woven from strands of silvery metal, each strand as thick as Jonah's wrist, the construction as elegant as a spider's web, as mighty in scale as, well, as the rail bridge across the Firth of Tay. And everywhere there was movement: beads of mercury chasing each other up and down the web, exploding as they crossed the larger intersections and showering down into the water, where they sent out probing tendrils that latched on to the lowest reaches of the web and pulled them back up before they could sink.

Behind the web, pinioned between it and a secondary wall of worn and rusted iron, thousands of faces peered out.

The faces looked like masks cast from bronze, and they were anything but human. Many of them Jonah found himself unable to look on, so alien were their forms; a few bore some semblance of recognizable features – eyes like pools of gold, mouths filled with steel teeth – but what disturbed him most was their fluidity. Every few seconds they would melt and flow into their neighbours, their unreadable expressions merging and evolving into new and ever more elaborate forms, their complexity multiplying until he felt dizzy just looking at them. And all the while those mercury beads were flashing past, disintegrating and hauling themselves back into the fray.

He had to look away, look down at the river: on that at least he felt he could rely.

But even the river betrayed him: scant yards downStone the water took on the sheen of copper. The dense liquid metal surged and dipped, expanding into the distance so that it looked more like a sea, a brown ocean world from another age, another myth. He sucked at the cold air and found that even that tasted of iron; in fact, it tasted like blood.

This is the world as it was before even charm appeared, he reminded himself. *It is two ages removed from your own. Do not try to understand it; simply do what you are here to do – deliver the Shifter and be gone.*

Into the floor of the island had been engraved the North Wind symbol. Dropping to his knees, Jonah ran his fingers down one of its cracks, grateful for something familiar in this alien place. A shadow fell across him: it was Meem, emerged from the Bark at last. The Shifter, to Jonah's surprise, was gazing around in obvious delight.

'A vibrant place!' Meem intoned, scrutinizing the wall-web. 'A Shifter could feel at home here. I confess to feeling . . . intoxicated!'

Keeping his eyes fixed on the web, Meem flattened his body out just as Teget had done. The sight was both beautiful and disturbing – Jonah could not imagine what was going on *inside* the Shifter's body. He concluded they must be so saturated with charm that everything about them was flexible, even down to their bones – if indeed they had bones. *If they do, they must be made of India-rubber!*

'We will come back and get you,' he said when Meem had settled over the engraving.

'It will not be possible,' the Shifter replied. 'You know that. Keep your promise. I will stay.'

Jonah lowered his head, then said fiercely, 'No, Meem. It is enough that Lawal sacrificed himself – I will not have your blood on my hands. We will come back for you!'

'If you come,' answered Meem, closing its eyes, 'I will still be here. It is a good place; I shall not leave.'

Jonah was about to argue further when Grandfather Tree called to him.

'Hurry you must – there's trouble!'

Sparing a brief glance for the motionless form of the Shifter, Jonah ran back to the edge of the island. 'What is the matter?'

'The water!'

Jonah peered through the cloud of vapour that had condensed around Grandfather Tree's face as he had been talking and saw at once what he meant: ice was floating all around the island in small chunks. As he watched, the pieces grew larger, crashing together and riding up over each other to form icebergs and broad, flat plates. Looking beyond the pipe exit he could see it was the same out there. The entire river was freezing over.

'Archan!' he cursed. 'She has found a way to influence the river, even from this great distance.'

'Not so great. And getting shorter.'

'Well, Grandfather Tree,' Jonah growled as he jumped down into the Bark, hardly noticing when his blouse tore on the brambles. 'What are you waiting for? Let us go under the ice while we still can.'

The lesky was already spinning the Bark around even before Jonah had landed. Water slopped in behind him, along with several large lumps of ice; Grandfather Tree hastily closed his mouth.

'A window I've made for you,' he cried as Jonah fell against the wall. He was just a disembodied voice now, more concerned with steering his vessel than showing his face. 'Didn't need it before. Thought you might like to see where we're going. Apologies for the position – higher would make it hard to work the Bark. Charm flows, you know, like sap, and it likes to choose its own way.'

He had created a small aperture low down on one of the curves of the wall, so low that Jonah had to crouch to see through it. At first all he could see were deep blue shadows and streams of bubbles, but soon the whole upper half of the view had turned dull white. The Bark dipped lower, away from the ice, and Jonah saw the black curve of the submerged memory rod heave into view below like a dark and ominous sea bed. Then jagged white lines began to arc down from the ice ceiling like lightning from the sky, dividing and multiplying and not fading like lightning but growing instead, expanding and throwing out new crystals to the side, all the while thickening in spasmodic jerks until almost nothing was left of the blue but a few slivers; at last they too were gone. There was only the white and the black, and the Bark frozen between.

The floor shook, and Jonah was thrown forwards

against the window. It yielded a little, reminding him this was not glass but some trick of charm. He stayed there, his face pressed against it, staring out into the newly formed ice.

'We're stuck,' muttered the lesky. The Bark gave a lurch and something creaked outside, but it did not move again. 'And so close we were!'

'Frozen solid! Is there nothing you can do? Work some kind of charm, I mean?'

'Bark needs water. Without water, you walk.'

Jonah thumped his fist against the window. 'Damnation! There must be something we can do!'

Outside the window the ice had formed a barrier of crystal between them and the halfway mark. It was tantalizingly close, Jonah was sure of it, surely only a matter of yards . . . He held his breath.

'Grandfather Tree, how close are we to the memory rod?'

Still the lesky did not manifest himself internally, and Jonah wondered if he was casting his eyes around the outside of the vessel, seeking a weakness in the ice field. 'Close. Why?'

'Please – I need to know exactly *how* close we are!'

'An idea you have?'

'Just tell me!'

There was a pause, then: 'In your terms, three feet. Bark's belly is nearly touching.'

Slowly Jonah exhaled. 'Even though we cannot make any forward progress, is it possible for you to rotate about your axis, as you did when we first saw you?'

Instead of replying, Grandfather Tree tried. More creaking sounds found their way in, and outside the window a series of cracks and cavities appeared. For a moment nothing happened, then with a sudden crack and a jolt that threw Jonah on to his back, the Bark turned a few degrees.

'Ow!' exclaimed Grandfather Tree. 'If you don't mind – why are we doing this?'

'I want you to position yourself so that your mouth is directly above the memory rod. If there is only a yard of ice between me and the rod, I think I can cut my way through.'

'Cut? How?'

'I will tell you when you have managed to turn yourself round. *If* you can manage it, that is.'

With a series of explosive grunts, Grandfather Tree succeeded in bringing the Bark round nearly half a rotation before finally admitting he could turn no more. 'The fin,' he gasped. 'Holding us back it is. But more there is that I can do. Watch!'

The brambles, which formed a prickly curtain down one side of the Bark's interior, began to twitch and rustle as though they were home to an entire flock of birds. Jonah stood well back, reluctant to have his clothes ripped any more than they were, and watched in wonder as the brambles slithered down the curve of the wall to take up residence on the floor. The whole process was accompanied by a drawn-out scraping sound and occasional cries of pain from Grandfather Tree.

'There!' panted the lesky when the bramble carpet had settled into position. 'Not so easy to change myself . . . now Bark and I are so close. It's my will in his wood. Partners we are, but sacrifices we've both made. Mine's the ability to shift. Can still do enough though. Enough for you, Jonah Lightfoot, I hope.'

With a thick rustling sound the brambles parted as Grandfather Tree – who had just dragged his face around the circumference of the Bark to point it straight down at the memory rod – opened his mouth. Picking his way through the spiky foliage, Jonah lowered himself on to the ice. To each side were Grandfather Tree's great, brown lips, pressed flat against the ice like a boy's on a shop window at Christmas.

For a moment Jonah believed he was at the bottom of a deep well, with the twin walls of the lesky's lips leading up into a dark cavern above. Except this well was not prepared to give up its water as easily as some.

Beneath the ice, close enough to tease, was the black shadow of the memory rod.

Jonah reached into the waistband of his trousers and drew out the dryad's fingernail.

You are a fool, Jonah Lightfoot! Three feet of ice to carve your way through and only this flimsy spine to do it with. And all the time Archan is getting nearer! Do you really believe you will succeed?

The strange part was that he *did* believe he would succeed, at least at this part of the task. Whether he would be in time to repel Archan he would not have cared to wager, so critical had the time become, but he *did* believe the ice would yield to him.

Of course he did – he had no choice.

Grasping the curve of the fingernail with both hands, he began to hack at the ice. The nail went in much more smoothly than he had imagined, as though it were a hot needle, penetrating by melting the ice rather than piercing it. It felt quite cold to the touch, however, almost as cold as the ice itself.

Easy though it was to cut into the ice, Jonah did not make much real progress at first; all he managed to do was turn the slab of ice into a giant, frozen pin-cushion. Catching his breath, he adjusted his approach by slicing sideways with the nail. This proved much more efficient, and soon he was carving away large wedges of ice and throwing them up into the Bark, where they landed with a crash among the brambles.

By the time he was halfway down he was sweating hard, despite the cold. The black of the rod was clearly visible, though its smooth surface made it impossible to judge how close it really was – or how far. Jonah laboured on, hardly noticing as flying chips of ice drew blood on his hands and cheeks. He was no longer merely inside a well: he was digging one.

It was a moment or two before he registered that the dryad's nail was no longer cutting up ice but ringing against something much harder. He blinked, realizing belatedly that he had shut his eyes and been cutting in a partial daze. He was on his knees in a pile of ice shards, staring down at a circular hole barely as wide as his head. And there, framed by the ice, was the memory rod.

His own memory failed him – he could not remember the last time he had physically touched one of the rods. He had grown accustomed instead to handling them remotely, by the sheer force of his will. Now that he was confronted with the actuality of the rods again (and this was indeed *all* the rods combined into one) he felt weak and disorientated. He also felt as though he had come home.

'Jonah?' Grandfather Tree's voice drifted down from the interior of the Bark. 'You're through! Feel it I can – the memory rod! Ach, I would give anything . . . to travel just once more . . .'

'I plan to travel only a very short distance on this occasion.'

Reaching down, he pressed the palms of his hands on to the rod, revelling in the feel of it: a dry and slippery surface; beneath it a sense of restrained power, a monster in chains. Hidden electricity. Life-juices squirting through hidden vessels. And memories, of course memories.

Pushing down gently, feeling the rod bend beneath his hands, Jonah formed a depression in its surface. He could already feel pathways switching beneath his touch, patterns reconfiguring themselves as he distorted the outermost skin of the memory rod into a new shape. At the same time as his hands were moulding it, his mind was slipping into it, an intimate penetration, more gentle than any he had so far attempted: to make himself a crawl-space he had to change the rod's physical form, but he could not do so without changing its content.

Yet he would be as gentle as possible. In playing with the past he had already launched an entire world on the sea of eternity; he had no desire to perform such a feat again. Ever since he had rescued Malya, this was something he feared more than anything: if he could create a world so effortlessly, then surely to destroy one would be even easier.

Yet if I am forced to change history I can at least try to change it for the better. However, the procedure was not without risk: he could not know for certain the consequences of any change he might make.

As his physical self entered the channel he had made – the channel between rod and ice that would take him the last few yards upStone – his mind was . . .

. . . adrift in a metal sky. Rustling silver shapes surrounded him, a shimmering cloud of foil through which the ground was barely visible as a thin, gold sea.

Metal world? Have I come to the wrong place, the wrong time?

A break in the cloud. He saw the sea for what it was: a field of corn. He saw the cloud for what it was: a frantic swarm of large, ungainly insects, millions of them.

Jonah was inside the mind of a grasshopper, flying over the cornfields of Kansas.

A momentary flash of panic, as he doubted he could possibly isolate the one insect he wanted in such a colossal swarm. Then clarity, and reassurance that he was *right, that this* was *the one. He had brought this memory close, had made it his own to carve, to remould. It was in his possession, if only briefly. It was his to own.*

For a moment he was transported with the breathless beauty of the spectacle. Literally breathless, *he thought to himself, as he felt the air move not through windpipe and lungs but insect spiracles. He had too many limbs, his body felt hard yet incredibly flexible. The kin-cloud around him was buoyant as a salt ocean. Waves of energy poured through it as it flashed and darted like a shoal of fish, a composite creature with instincts of its own, the sum greater than the parts.*

Possessing, it came to him, some semblance of thought.

A dark, square shape passed below, a shape he had seen before: a human dwelling made of sod. Annie's house. Resisting the temptation to take control too soon, he let the grasshopper wheel him down towards the ground, part of a muscular spasm that emptied the entire lower half of the swarm on to the Rance fields.

The world down there was blurred and slow, the house huge. There was Annie, poised on one leg and swinging her other with sluggish grace as her head swivelled like that of a neglected automaton. Behind her loomed Rance, a lumbering hulk of a man, arms raised to thrash the air, eyes turned up to heaven yet only half-open, shoulders hunched, mouth just beginning to come open.

His mouth grew vast in Jonah's grasshopper vision, a black maw that was no longer Rance West's but Rata Kadul's, the lesky's, the fathomless abyss of Stone. The teeth with which it was lined looked like tombstones cut from ice.

He pulled back, actually started to pull his consciousness clear of the grasshopper. Rance's human throat expanded to fill his world, drawing him down, falling . . .

At the last moment he took control. Grasshopper wings tore as he wrenched the insect's immense back legs sideways. Something burst inside the little creature and he felt brief, insect agony as pieces of its body came apart. For a moment he thought he had failed, had left it too late, and that Rance had already inhaled him. Then brown flesh crashed into view and the grasshopper was glancing off the man's cheek and falling on to his shoulder.

Lying there inside the dying insect, Jonah watched as Rance started to raise his hand to the spot on his face where the insect had struck, then he drew himself out of the ruined chitin and . . .

. . . forced his way through the last few inches of the channel to flop gasping and sweating into clear air. He lay flat on his face for a moment while he caught his breath, relieved to find himself inhabiting comfortable human flesh once more. Then he got up and looked around.

It was like the parting of the Red Sea.

He was standing on the slightly curved surface of the memory rod between two towering walls of ice. This was the mid-point of the Aqueduct: there before him was the slightly raised scar, the place where the rod could be broken in two. Up to a few moments before, this whole region had been sheathed in water just like the rest of the rod; as soon as the locks had been activated, the water – now turned to ice by Archan – had simply peeled apart to create a void in which a man could stand.

The void was narrow: by standing in the middle and holding out his arms he could touch both the upStone and downStone ice walls. It was an unsettling place, and he resolved to work as fast as possible lest the walls start to close in on him . . .

Kneeling, he ran his fingers along the scar, shivering at the buzz of the memories beneath. Trying not to think about what he was doing, he took the dryad's fingernail from his belt once more and held its point against the scar's rough surface. It vibrated in his hand, almost singing in the still, cold air.

Abruptly he pulled it away, shocked that he could think to defile the glory of the rod with such an evil tool. It had cut the ice well enough, but he would not use it to cut the rod.

Drawing his arm back, he flung the nail as far as he could down the length of the walls. It rang like a bell as it bounced off one wall then on to the other, finally dropping out of sight over the curve of the rod. He heard it ringing still as it rolled down the incline, held his breath until the moment when at last the ringing stopped, indicating that the nail had plunged into the abyss, finally taking the same journey its owner had taken, far away on the other side of Stone's sea of charm.

Bending to his knees once more, he drove his hands deep into the flesh of the rod.

The rod yielded as though it were butter, melting away at his touch. Turning his hands so that they were back to back, Jonah forced them apart, literally prising open the memory rod. A crack opened up, shooting around the curve in both directions; at the same time a colossal groan rose up from the wound. Jonah pulled his hands free and stepped away, pressing his back against the downStone ice wall as the rod continued to separate. He remained there for several minutes as, with tremors and rumbles, the crack widened itself inch by painful inch. Presently he found the courage to kneel and peer into it.

He could see all the way through to the abyss below. The rod was broken; the task was done.

Can it be so simple?

An idea occurred to him. Taking a deep breath, he stepped across the crack. On the other side he paused, wiped his hand across his face, then stepped back again.

I can still cross over. And if I can cross over, Archan can cross over. It has not worked!

He realized his back was soaking wet.

The walls were melting away. Great plates of ice were detaching themselves and crashing to the ground, only to slither away around the curve of the rod; jets of water spurted from one side to the other, some so intense they carved notches in the facing wall; cataracts opened up from top to bottom, the water cascading down through the crack and into oblivion. Jonah was sure he would drown as the river fell back over his head, but some force kept the floods from completely overwhelming the exposed part of the rod; nevertheless he was at times knee-deep in freezing water, and only just managed to keep himself from being washed into the crack himself.

As he struggled to maintain his balance his mind was racing.

Archan has released her hold on the river! Why would she do such a thing?

If she was abandoning her attempts to foil his efforts it could only mean that she knew he had succeeded, and was pouring all her energy into maintaining her speed. Yet he had *not* succeeded!

'What do you know that I do not, Archan?' he bellowed, his voice practically inaudible amid the thundering of water. 'Why are you still in a hurry?'

A shadow loomed in the fractured ice of the downStone wall, and for a dreadful moment Jonah thought it was her. Then the enormous face of Grandfather Tree crashed through and the Bark's spherical form rolled to a halt across the still-widening crack in the rod. A pillar of ice broke over its back, hissing instantly to steam.

'Bark had a secret!' beamed Grandfather Tree. 'Got himself hot!'

'Then the thaw is not Archan's doing?' suggested Jonah, knowing it was a foolish hope.

The lesky looked around at the pandemonium. 'Bark didn't get *that* hot,' he replied dryly.

'But why is she doing this, or rather why has she abandoned her attempts to thwart our plans? The rod is broken yet the fire-break can still be crossed. The Bark demonstrates the fact clearly enough – though I would

378

suggest that is not a sensible place to rest, since the crack is growing steadily wider.'

'Your point is taken,' answered the lesky. 'We'll be gone again shortly. But Archan – she must believe what you've done is enough. Simple it must be. Perhaps . . . the crack, it just needs to get a little wider. Wait we must, just a little longer. Then – pouf! – the breach is made at last.'

'A little longer,' echoed Jonah. 'Long enough to rescue Meem?'

By the time they reached the island the river was entirely liquid again, but for a few shrinking icebergs still bobbing in its turbulent waters. The complex metal walls seemed even more alien than before; Jonah resolved to spend as little time here as possible.

With Archan's breath almost close enough to smell, it was not a difficult decision to reach.

They found Meem just as they had left him, sprawled across the symbol of the North Wind. His big yellow body was breathing slowly; Jonah almost fancied he could hear him snoring.

'Meem – we must go,' he announced perfunctorily. 'Your work here is done.'

When the Shifter did not reply Jonah poked him with his foot. He opened a sleepy eye and regarded Jonah balefully.

'It is a restful place. I would stay here.'

'No, Meem. I will not have it! If you stay here you will die.'

'This is a good place. Plenty of change. And . . . I am alone.'

'Damnation! Listen to me, Meem! There will be plenty of change on the other side of the Aqueduct too, I can assure you of that. Nothing will be as it was – nothing at all. Lawal sacrificed himself for a reason – I will not have you do the same thing for no reason at all. Have you forgotten the promise I made? Do you have no curiosity at all, or is your species' craving for self-destruction its most powerful driving force?'

Both Shifter eyes were staring at him now. When he spoke again, he did so hesitantly, like an uncertain child.

'To be a Shifter is not to crave self-destruction. Believe that much, I beg you. To be a Shifter is to crave many things, but foremost among those things is *change*. Death is simply a change that has not yet been experienced, and sometimes it seems to a Shifter that is all that remains. We are not . . . *imaginative*. We are not leaders. We re-create what we have followed, but we do not innovate. So when you see one of our number making the final change, do not think ill of it. He is merely doing what he has done all his life, and who is to say that even death is not the prelude to an even greater change, the like of which we cannot begin to conceive?'

'Forgive me – your ways of thinking are . . . strange to me. But I ask you this, Meem, and I ask you for the final time because there *is* no time: if you are not imaginative are you not at least *curious*? Do you not want to know what you really look like? Do you not want to see your own face for the very first time? Blind for so many years, do you not want, finally, to see?'

Jonah thumped the Shifter's flank in frustration. 'You do not need to be alone, Meem,' he added, exasperated. 'Can you not see that you do not all need to be the same? You told me of Teget's anger that he cannot change as he wants to change. Can you not imagine a day when your people might each one Shift in a different direction?'

Slowly, so slowly that Jonah was on the verge of turning and bolting for Grandfather Tree's open mouth, a broad smile spread across Meem's face. His yellow eyes were full of yearning.

'To my surprise, my answer to all your questions is, "Yes".'

Grandfather Tree halted the Bark at the lip of the exit to the metal-lined pipe. It pitched and rolled on the surface, the lesky having given up submarine travel because of the wild and unpredictable currents thrown up by the chaos outside. Peering through a newly fabricated transparent porthole, Jonah looked out across the disintegrating Aqueduct.

The river no longer flowed in a neat, invisibly supported cylinder around the rod. Now it sprayed violently outwards from both upStone and downStone walls, looking less like water and more like steam from a punctured boiler. Grandfather Tree took some pleasure in describing to Jonah and Meem the effort it was taking to keep the Bark from being swept over the edge.

As a result, the middle half of the Aqueduct now consisted of completely exposed memory rod, with fountains of water and clouds of spray pouring over both ends. At the very centre of the rod, the crack Jonah had made was just visible as a dark ring. It was, Jonah knew, still getting wider.

'I can fly you across,' suggested Meem, but Jonah shook his head.

'I suspect the air would flip us around just as it did before. No, the only way to cross the Aqueduct is by maintaining contact with the rod. Besides, you could not carry the Bark.'

'And I can't get far without water!' grumbled Grandfather Tree's voice.

'Then you and I can walk across, and only the lesky is trapped,' said Meem bluntly.

Jonah inhaled sharply, waiting for Grandfather Tree to lose his temper, but the explosion did not come. Instead, after a pause, the lesky said quietly,

'Right he is, Jonah Lightfoot. Go you must, and leave Lesky to his fate. This Bark aches all over.'

'I shall not!' snapped Jonah, surprised to find tears at the corners of his eyes. 'We came back for Meem; I will not abandon you again. There must be a way!'

'If you can find one,' Grandfather Tree sighed, 'nobody will be happier than me.'

Jonah was apprehensive as he approached the crack in the rod, now nearly four feet wide. He held his breath as he stepped across, fully expecting to be turned and hurled back downStone, convinced that he was as trapped as the lesky on this doomed part of Stone. But he took care to keep at least one foot in contact with the rod at all times, and so made the crossing without incident. Behind him came the thudding of Meem's footsteps, unnervingly human now that the Shifter had re-created the same giant human form Jonah had seen on his first encounter with Lawal.

'You are not built to fly,' Meem had commented just before they set off. 'But well made for running.'

The rod shook when Meem stepped across.

When they neared the pipe, Meem switched back to his dragon shape and flew Jonah over the waterfall, arrowing in towards the tunnel from which they had gained their first view of the fire-break. Jonah glanced back over his shoulder as they passed into the pipe, struck by how different that view was now.

The memory rod, black and trembling, looked naked in the thin afternoon light. On both sides of the canyon the waterfalls were growing steadily weaker. Jonah imagined some colossal system of valves shutting down the water supply, a tremendous basilisk fail-safe designed to prevent the entire ocean emptying itself into the abyss. The air flowing down through the fire-break looked flat and lifeless, as though it too had been drained.

Inside, the river level had dropped almost to nothing. The lower reaches of the cylindrical pipe were exposed, their black surfaces smooth and clean, having been scoured for countless years by the relentless flow of the river. Also visible were shallow slots and circular apertures; their function was not clear, but as they passed over Jonah fancied he could see pale eyes shining up at them from the blackness, and wondered what lonely creatures lived out their lives in such forsaken holes.

The three islands reared high, no longer islands but towering pinnacles standing a hundred yards clear of the drastically lowered water level. As they approached, Jonah counted heads: there was Gerent, unmistakable with his upraised wings, and Malya close by his side; there was the merman shape of Tam, sitting some distance away, while Teget's huge bulk was still sprawled across the island's centre. Kythe was just taking off from the island's edge, flying out to greet them. Annie! Where was Annie?

Kythe flew in front of the island, obscuring the view.

'Where is she?' yelled Jonah. 'What has happened here?'

'Oh, Jonah,' wailed Kythe. 'It happened so quickly!.'

Just as she said it her wing lifted, revealing Annie's body lying prone beside Teget. Gerent and Malya, as was now clear, were standing near her, looking anxiously out at Meem and Jonah as they approached.

'She is alive!' called Gerent as Meem swooped in to land. 'But what has happened to her . . . we cannot say.'

'She just collapsed!' Kythe wept. 'All of a sudden she threw her hands up to her head and just collapsed.'

'How long ago?' Jonah demanded as he leaped off Meem's back and rushed to her side. He felt her pulse: it was fast and shallow; her skin was cold as ice and slick with sweat.

'If you wish it in terms of your minutes,' replied

Gerent, crouching beside him and placing his hand lightly on Jonah's back, 'I would guess at fifteen, perhaps twenty. It is hard for me to judge, you understand.'

Now Jonah felt cold, and his stomach clenched. Annie had collapsed at about the time he had been forcing his way through his man-made channel between the ice and the memory rod. In fact, at about the time he had been journeying into the skies of Kansas and tinkering with the proper flow of history.

'I made a change,' he whispered. There were tears in his eyes again, but this time they flowed freely. 'I thought it would be for the best. Oh, dear God, what have I done?'

21

Annie's Journal – Six

Can't tell if I'm having a dream about writing, or writing about a dream.

Either way, I guess the words are real enough.

Can't remember where I am either. I can see the pages in front of my eyes, but I don't know if my eyes are open or closed. I guess if I can see they must be open, but they don't *feel* like they're open. I can feel the pen – that weird pen that flew out of the *Bonaventure* – I can feel it between my fingers, but it also feels like my fingers are numb. How can I see and not see, feel and not feel?

I remember – well, I remember the river, the way it hit the island. That Chinese mark on the ground, looking like two people dancing, and the river hitting the island and splitting into two streams to go around it, then meeting up again on the other side in a great crash of waves. I remember that, and then I don't remember much at all. Later on, the ground lifted up, or maybe I fell . . .

I've been home again. That's what I really wanted to write about. I've been back to Kansas. I guess that part had to be a dream, but it seemed so damned *real*.

Rance was there of course, and we were out back as the sun went down. His arm was round my shoulder as we sat with our backs against the sod and our legs sprawled on the soil. We were both a little drunk – must have been when old man Clayman was feeling a touch kindlier than usual and brought over a bottle from his still. We were hard pressed to afford liquor, and even though it was summer it felt a little like Thanksgiving.

There was a strong wind across the corn and the sky was filled with seeds. My belly was full and warm, and Rance was big and warm beside me, not saying a word but just filling the space as only he can. I was dozing, watching the seeds swirl above us like a cloud of spun gold. I knew I loved him, and all I could think of was the rest of our life together.

He said, 'Damned grasshoppers.'

I touched his leg. 'That was two years past, Rance. We're getting back on our feet.'

'Too slow, I reckon.'

'Times have been bad, I know. But this year there's a crop, and you're getting better . . .'

He turned and gave me the strangest look. 'What do you mean, "getting better"?'

I giggled. He looked so troubled, and the evening was so serene, I just couldn't help laughing. He just didn't seem to fit somehow, like a jigsaw piece in the right place but turned the wrong way round. 'Why, since the swarm. I thought you'd never stop . . .'

Then *I* stopped. I'd been about to say 'coughing', about to talk about the day when the grasshoppers fell like a blizzard and took all our crop and tainted the water, and Rance breathed one into his lungs and went stark crazy trying to retch it out, and how he'd never really got it straight in his head that it *had* come out – I'd seen it there on the ground between his feet – and how ever since then he'd been kind of sad and distant, less like a husband and more like a cousin you never see from one year to the next.

I'd been about to say all that, only suddenly it seemed

like it had never really happened, like that had all been a dream, one I'd just woken up from to find myself here behind the house on a glorious summer's eve. And the look on Rance's face told me it *had* been a dream, told me he didn't have an idea what I was talking about. The laughter caught in my throat as his face turned black.

'You laughin' at me, girl?' he growled, grabbing my wrist where my hand was on his leg and squeezing so hard I heard the bones crackle.

'No, Rance.' The liquor kept the smile on my face but inside I was scared, damned scared. 'I was just . . .'

'Just tellin' me I'm a crazy man, is that it?'

The sun had gone down now and everything had gone flat, like someone had pulled down a shade on all the happiness in the day. All of a sudden Rance looked too big, almost like he was two men in one set of clothes. He still had a hold of my wrist, and he stood up and dragged me across the dirt towards the field. I cried out with the pain, and this time I heard my wrist break, but he didn't let up. Even when we got to the corn he didn't stop. He hauled me in there like a sack and threw me down on the ground, then turned and strode away. The stalks moved to and fro, now hiding him, now letting me see, and each time I caught sight of him it was like he'd changed, like with each glimpse I was seeing a different man altogether, not my Rance but a different one, changing all the while, no longer the man I'd married, and who I still loved.

I lay there as the sun died and the stars came out, trying to work out what was a dream and what wasn't, and in the end it came to me that it had all been a dream. In the end I fell asleep, and when I woke up I was here, writing out the story and still wondering if it was all happening in my mind.

*   *   *

Someone's calling my name. I don't want to go but I guess I'd better. I think maybe I'll close the book now. I think I've written enough.

I feel – good. Content, I mean. I don't know why. I guess it's something to do with the dream, even though it wasn't far short of a nightmare. I still have memories of happier days, and they're mine to browse through whenever I choose. I don't need a dream to remind me of the good times.

And the bad times? Well, they happened too, and I'd no more meddle with that than change the cycle of the seasons or the track of the sun in the sky.

It's Jonah, I think. Yes, I'll wake up for Jonah – it'll be good to see his face again.

22

Impact

'Curse you, Annie West, wake up now!'

He shook her so violently that Gerent's hand flew in warning to his shoulder. He pushed the Neolithic man away, but lowered her back down to the cold metal all the same, clasping her hands between his own. His tears splashed on to his steepled fingers, running between them and around hers. 'Dear God in Heaven, Annie, please wake up.'

Her eyelids twitched, then parted momentarily before falling shut again. Jonah held his breath. The second time they moved more deliberately, fluttering only a little before finally opening all the way. Her eyes wandered before locking on to his own. When she saw him, she smiled.

'Jonah. Have you been meddling with my mind?'

'Annie! I am . . .'

'Running out of time, is my guess. Explanations can wait.' She started to sit up, winced then completed the movement, which brought her neatly into Jonah's arms. 'Right now, we've got a runaway train to derail.'

It did not take Jonah long to explain what he had done to the memory rod. The others regarded him with awe as he described the ease with which he had broken it apart.

'Is that all it took?' marvelled Kythe. 'Just one little tug?'

'Yes, Kythe. That is all that was required.'

'But it did not work!' cursed Gerent. 'You said so yourself. The fire-break can still be crossed. If anything, it is even easier to cross than it was before!'

'That is so,' agreed Jonah. 'But I believe that is only because the process of separation, though easy enough to initiate, takes rather longer to complete itself.'

'You mean you pulled the switch but the points ain't changed yet,' Annie drawled.

'Yes,' he smiled. 'If you insist on your railroad analogy.'

'Oh, I do, my dear man,' she replied, her English accent impeccable.

'And Grandfather Tree?' observed Kythe. 'What about him? He's stranded, isn't he? How can we possibly rescue him? Even with Meem's and Teget's help – and Gerent's too – I don't think we could carry the Bark.'

Glum-faced, the group returned to the mouth of the pipe, where they found a place to perch on a flat-topped iron tower that up to now had been hidden below the water. From here they watched the level of the river drop still further. By now the fountains at each end of the Aqueduct had died away, leaving only narrow trickles of water.

Gerent walked to the edge of the tower, his hand held over his eyes. 'I think we may no longer need to concern ourselves with the lesky.'

'Why?' demanded Jonah, running to his side.

'He is gone! And behold, Archan comes!'

The metal wall opposite was aglow with a shimmering internal light. Heat was pulsing off it in visible waves, great ripples distorting the view and discharging themselves in long strokes of lightning that earthed themselves on both walls of the canyon. Where the lightning crossed the invisible boundary between the upStone and downStone halves, it split and twisted, but passed over nevertheless. All the defences of the fire-break were down now; the border was open.

In the dark maw of the metal pipe opposite, there was no sign of the Bark at all.

Jonah felt a hand slip into his own. Looking round he saw it was Malya's: she had squeezed her way in between him and Gerent.

'Jonah Lightfoot,' she said, as if testing the syllables. 'I would say you saved my life, but . . . I think you *made* my life. Thank you.'

'You are most welcome,' he answered. 'I am only sorry I have brought you to this.'

With her jaw jutted forward she drew back her shoulders and puffed out her chest, looking every inch the warrior-woman he remembered. In her belt, he noticed, was a short sword, presumably given to her by Gerent. He smiled: the couple's penchant for keeping themselves armed was still alive and well. 'I will face it with you, if you will have my company.'

'I should like nothing more.'

'Nothing?' Annie slipped her arm into his.

Words eluded him. He started to mumble something, only to find her lips brushing his. They kissed, tentatively at first, then with passion. There was spray in the air, so it was hard to tell who was crying; Jonah thought that probably they all were.

Pin-points of light punctured the metal wall, each one expanding until they were no longer facing a wall but a lattice, a flimsy sheet that was nothing more than an array of cavities connected by diminishing strands of silver. Behind the lattice, growing brighter and brighter as more of the metal was etched away, was a red light the size of the sky. Within the light moved limbs big enough to hold up the world, giant wings and long woven bones. It was Archan, come at last, preparing to cross the Aqueduct.

She had slowed almost to a standstill. Had she been travelling as fast as when she had taken the lower bridge, they would surely have known nothing at all of her arrival. Their deaths would have been as clean as those of men in the path of a fire-storm – which was perhaps exactly what they were.

Apparently, Archan wanted their deaths to be anything but clean.

She was moving languorously now; the swaying motions and the red glare combining to make her true form hard to make out. As the last of the silver dissolved Jonah squinted into the light, trying to resolve her appearance, the scale of her.

Framed by the round aperture of the pipe, the view across the fire-break was now completely filled by Archan. She stretched far beyond the limits of vision, up and down, left and right. She was not merely a colossus – she was an entire world.

Naturally. She has consumed a world. She has eaten Stone, and in her belly is all the history of all the worlds that ever were. Is it any wonder she has had to grow to accommodate it all?

If she managed to traverse the fire-break, she would grow still further.

Now she had stopped altogether, and at last Jonah saw her clearly.

There was no flesh on her, only black scales perched randomly on an exposed dragon skeleton. They could see through her bones quite clearly, could see through to the appalling whiteness beyond, the void she had left behind her where nothing, not even memories, remained. Her bones were elaborately wrought, pierced through again and again with smooth-sided holes. Most of these were shapeless wounds, but some seemed carefully designed, with sweeping curves and artfully graded contours. A few resembled Mah-Jongg symbols, among them the Red Dragon and the North Wind.

Her head was a jagged skull. Set into it were two chrome eyes. White teeth jutted like steeples from her gaping jaw, their edges alive with crawling parasites. Though the direction of her gaze was impossible to follow, there was little doubt who she was looking at.

'Faery!'

Her voice: beyond all measure of sound, deep as the Styx and as black.

Lid-like dragon scales wiped her eyes, a monstrous blink. She was still a beast then, despite all else she had become, with the beast's simple needs.

Jonah tried to haul his voice into his throat, but could not raise even a whisper. He watched dumbly as Archan extended a claw out to grasp the Aqueduct. It was like watching a vulture taking hold of a human hair.

Maintaining contact with the memory rod (which, Jonah noticed, did not so much as bend), Archan's claw slid across the fire-break towards the mouth of the pipe, growing immense as it loomed before them. It halted just short of the tower on which they stood, a shining red mountain of horn. It rotated, rising up until its tip was six inches away from Jonah's face. It held there, utterly still.

Nobody breathed.

The claw withdrew with breathtaking speed, the sudden rush of air of air nearly spilling the four of them over the precipice.

Archan blinked again. Then she spoke again.

'Do you know hatred, faery? Do you know anger and envy? Do you know the fire they bring? If you did not before, then you know now, for you see it before you. You will continue to see it, even as you breathe your last. This is the fire of wrath. Though it cleanses, it is sick; though it scours, it is filthy; though it tears down all before it, still it builds resentment in its wake.'

Another massive blink.

'I once considered you a poor adversary, faery. When first we came to Stone, you and I, you were nothing to me. Yet by the time we came to the Threshold together you had grown. You . . . delayed me. No doubt you imagined you had defeated me. Now you are wiser, knowing as you do that I can never be defeated. Knowing that you have already lost.

'When you sent me chasing after that damnable ancestor of yours, it came to me that you had unwittingly been my aide. Of course unwittingly, since none of your species ever possessed anything more than the most rudimentary of wits. Yes, in sending me so far downStone, you in fact made it easier for me to do what I have since done. You sent me, as you might put it, to the very head of the table before inviting me to eat.

'And eat I have! Ah, the Deathless knew nothing compared to what I know already! Did they consider themselves immortal? They despised every drop of memory in the great river of time! Yet I have swallowed that river whole. In doing so I have become the past. Your precious histories are not lost – they are within me! I have not destroyed the lower reaches of Stone – I have assimilated them. And when I have swallowed the remainder, all eternity will be mine to digest. Immortal both without and within, I will be all there is to know, all there is to remember! All there is to be!'

Jonah swallowed hard and somehow found his voice. 'You will be the loneliest creature that ever lived!'

'The loneliness will be mine to command, faery, but you should know me well enough by now. I have rarely craved company.' Her enormous skull tipped to one side, and a shelf of bone folded into a frown that looked more like a landslide. 'And a million years' incarceration in a prison of ice gives a dragon a taste for solitude.'

As she moved her skull, Jonah felt Annie nudge him in the ribs.

'Look,' she whispered, scarcely moving her lips. 'End of the Aqueduct, under her jaw.'

He looked while trying not to make it obvious he was looking.

The Aqueduct – which was now nothing more than the naked memory rod, broken in the middle – appeared to be unsupported at its downStone end. With the metal wall dissolved away, now it simply vanished into the shadow beneath Archan's jaw. It looked a little like a harpoon sticking out from a shark's throat.

In that shadow, and apparently unseen by Archan, something was jutting up out of the rod, a slender, forked shape that looked as fragile as a tree made of porcelain.

'No doubt you would be content to have me talking for a little longer,' Archan was booming. 'No doubt you believe the process of separation of the memory rod is slow, and that if I delay for long enough then my way across will be barred. In fact, this is the truth: by your primitive measures there are only moments left before the last connections are torn and this gap in the fabric of Stone does indeed become impassable. If you had acted just a little earlier, faery, you might have managed to shut me out after all. However, a few moments do remain. Before I come for you – all of you – I wish you to know the fate that awaits you.

'You might imagine I will kill you. That is not the case. You will die some day – that is a certainty, since only I am immortal – but that day is a long way off. Almost an infinitely long way off, by some measures. Almost.

'No, you will not be killed. You will be consumed. I will swallow you, faery, along with your puny friends, just as I have swallowed everything else in my path. And in consuming you I will remember you, and in remembering you I will place you into the past of all the worlds, and because that past is mine to own and mine to control I will place you where there is only suffering. I will remember you as you were when your body was flayed over a pit of fire; I will remember you as you were when your offspring were gutted before your eyes and their entrails fed to the wolves; I will remember you as you were when all the ordure of the world was poured into your throat, and as you were when the one you loved most of all took her own life rather than look upon your face. I will remember you dragged through your pitiful, mythical Hell, then falling endlessly into a Hell your Devil could not even contemplate. I will remember your agonizing death and your resurrection into a new life of interminable sorrow. I will remember your tears, and the incurable wound of your broken heart. "These things never happened to me," you would say, but you would be wrong. Because when I own you I own your memories, and when I own your memories it is my place to say what happened to you, and it is my place to say how long you spend in recollection of those things. You may live thirty more faery years, but what you will remember during those years is a suffering that has lasted near eternity!

'You know I can do this, faery, because you possess that self-same power. Except you have not the courage to use it.'

Annie was shaking at his side, and even the indomitable Malya was clutching at Gerent for support. Then, to his astonishment, Kythe rose into the air, hovering shakily between them and Archan.

'You're a bully,' she shouted, her voice thin and wavering. 'And not worthy of the name "dragon"!'

Archan's mouth slammed shut, the sound like a meteorite strike. As her jaw moved, thin daylight glanced across the unidentifiable sapling-shape. Jonah held his breath; though he had no idea what the thing was, the fact that Archan did not appear to have noticed it made him unaccountably hopeful.

'Kythe,' he called softly. 'Come back, you can do no good.'

'But she isn't a dragon!' wept Kythe, slapping her wings against the air in frustration. 'Dragons are good creatures, full of charm, and . . . and . . .'

'It's all right, Kythe,' Annie soothed, reaching out her hands. 'Come here – don't make her more angry than she is.'

But Archan's frown had already gone. Now her bony skull had twisted into a vast smile.

'So let us come to it,' she said. She stretched her neck right across the fire-break, bringing her head up to the pipe where Jonah and his friends stood defiantly, hands and arms linked. Tipping her long, thin snout downwards, Archan peered in with one chrome orb like a cat inspecting a mousehole. They stared back at their swollen reflections. 'Do you see, faery?' she thundered, her voice still huge but muffled now, as her eye practically sealed off the pipe from the air outside. 'Do you see how I cross the moat? You have cut your way through the ropes, but the drawbridge has not yet fallen away.'

'All the time you talk, it falls a little further, dragon,' said Gerent. When Jonah glanced at his Neolithic companion he saw that both his and Malya's swords were upraised against their foe. He found the sight overwhelmingly touching, and had to look away.

'How true. In that case, it must be time to eat.'

Something lashed into the pipe, something long and thin, shining like silver. At the same time Archan's skull rose up, revealing the join between two of her teeth. It was from between the teeth that the rope-like thing had emerged, and Jonah realized belatedly it was a whip-thin tongue. It flashed past them, narrowly missing Annie's head as it coiled behind her then slipped back again. The last few yards of the tongue were wrapped around the waist of Tam, who was holding on to the coils more with bemusement than terror. Jonah wondered if he was glad to be tethered once more, glad to be sacrificed to a goddess.

And sacrificed he was. With blinding speed, before he could even utter a cry, his body was sucked between Archan's teeth. He became minute in Jonah's vision before finally vanishing, the comparison of scale shocking Jonah into appreciating just how big Archan really had become. He also realized that the entire fire-break must have expanded to accommodate her immense form. But then, if she had consumed Stone as she claimed, could she not make what was left of it any size she liked?

Even before Tam disappeared a second tongue had plunged forward and dragged Teget to the same fate. Meem took valiantly to the air, crying out after his companion, but it was too late. Teget writhed, his body flitting through a blur of changing shapes as he tried to squirm free of the tongue, but all to no avail. Yellow swords sheared towards his attacker but they were too late. Drawn like clay through a mere crack between Archan's clenched teeth, he was gone.

Foul-smelling air was whipping past them; Jonah realized it was Archan's breath. The draught was powerful enough to knock Kythe backwards through the air. As she struggled to stay aloft yet another of the chrome tongues darted out. This one seized Kythe's wing. The thin, transparent membrane collapsed and Kythe shrieked with pain, thumping the air with her free wing as the other was crushed like tissue.

'Kythe!' screamed Annie. If Jonah had not grabbed her round the waist he felt sure she would have leaped to her death from the tower in a vain attempt to jump to the dragon's aid. He looked on helplessly as Kythe was drawn like a crippled bird away from them and towards Archan's waiting jaws.

Then there was a new set of wings in the air, one

patterned with red and black scales. Gerent covered the distance to Kythe in less time than it took to blink, charm pouring from his heels in a dazzling stream, and Jonah knew then for certain that, though he still looked human, he was no longer exactly a man.

Balanced on his dragon-scale wings, Gerent skidded on the wind of Archan's evil breath and swung his sword-arm high. Then he bore it down with a single, devastating blow. The blade sliced through the tongue as though it were the softest butter. The severed end uncoiled from Kythe's wing; there were a few seconds as she fell when Jonah was sure she would not recover herself, but her crumpled wing filled and, though it was badly torn, sup-ported her weight. While Gerent hacked further lengths off the lashing tongue, she limped back to the tower, where she dropped heavily to the ground. Annie ran to her side.

Below them, the river bed was now completely dry.

The tongue retreated. No more came to take its place. Archan's teeth parted, drawing ominously close; her breath was visible now as a thin, sickly stream of reddish gas.

Then she halted. Something new slipped out of her mouth, and at first Jonah assumed it was another of the mobile tongues. Then he saw this was different: it was not chrome but dark brown, not smooth but textured with knobs and short spikes that looked almost like . . . thorns?

Another of the things emerged, elongating as it wrapped itself around and underneath Archan's jaw. They both split into two strands, forking and then forking again, their stems thickening and growing more robust as they began to entangle both each other and Archan's exposed teeth. With blinding speed, a forest of brambles was growing with impossible speed from the inside of the dragon-giant's mouth.

'Grandfather Tree?' he whispered as he looked on aghast.

Her entire lower jaw was now encased in a spreading network of thick, dark briar stalks. Where the thorns made contact with bone they latched on, digging in and holding fast. Leaves unfurled. Fat, black berries swelled along the longer branches, bursting as they were crushed in the mêlée; soon Archan's face was streaked with their juice.

She gnawed at the invading brambles, cutting through half the growth in a single bite. But the forest simply redoubled its onslaught, boiling out of her mouth with twice the ferocity and twice the speed. Her whole head jerked, retreating from the pipe so that she could shake it from side to side, like a dog trying to rid itself of a flea. As she drew back Jonah saw that her whole head was enveloped with the spiky growth; indeed, it was even thicker along the back of her head and neck. She tossed to and fro, biting through another swathe of the stuff only to have it surge back even more insistently. As she cut through the plump leaves they let out a sweet scent to drive away the stench of her breath.

Behind her, coming slowly into view as she retreated further and further into the clear air of the fire-break, was an entire wall of vegetation, a vertical tangle of brown and green leaf and massive black trunk, of twisted vine and tempered thorn. It was like seeing the whole great face of Stone laid out afresh, a vast backdrop, only it was not Stone but forest.

'Taiga!' shouted Jonah, raising his arms above his head. 'Taiga! Lesky!'

Malya looked at him with one eyebrow raised, apparently thinking he had gone insane.

There was a radial pattern to the forest, a centre about which the dark greenery was turning. That centre was, of course, the far end of the memory rod, now buried not in Archan's throat but in the heart of the wild-wood.

The brambles had coated the memory rod too, spanning the fire-break and embracing the tower with a thousand probing fingers. Through the middle of this flood thrust a single black trunk, laid on its side as it followed the path of the rod. Just before it reached the tower it bifurcated, flanking the tower on both sides then miraculously joining together again on the opposite side. The Aqueduct had effectively been re-created, using forest instead of water.

Out in the fire-break, Archan was fighting back.

Flames boiled from her skull – not just from her mouth but her eyes and bone-rimmed nostrils, from the cavities behind her cheeks, from between her horns. The brambles caught light instantly, exploding like firecrackers and falling away in a whirlwind of orange sparks. She howled and bellowed as charm-filled flames, blazing all colours of the rainbow from lightning-blue to the crimson of the furnace, poured from her. The taiga moved. Like great snakes its timbers wound around her neck, wooden sinews straining as they hauled her little by little back across the fire-break. These movements were accompanied by thick cracks and moans, the voice of the forest.

Jonah looked for her wings but found he could no longer see them: they had been utterly swamped by the taiga.

'Archan!' he shouted. He did not imagine she would hear but, incredibly, she stopped moving. The forest too fell still and silent. All that remained was the rustling of leaves and the faint creak of branches in the wind, an incongruous, unbearably Earthly sound.

Jonah paused, wondering what he might say. There seemed only one word left.

'Goodbye.'

Lightning poured across the scene once more, only

now it was coming from the air itself. It had no one source – it came in from everywhere, lancing from every direction but aimed at one place only: the centre of the Aqueduct.

At long last the drawbridge was breaking in two.

The cold blue fire instantly vaporized the bramble-and-branch coating, leaving only the smooth black cylinders of the memory rod, one on each side of the gap Jonah had made. The rod looked thin and fragile, and very old.

A million rapier blades of lightning skewered the gap, filling it and spilling out across the width of the fire-break. The light was blinding, and Jonah and all his companions had to shield their eyes from its glare. He looked back in time to see the lightning, dimming now, expand outwards again in a single vertical sheet. Like the spinning blade of a circular saw it sliced through everything in its path: the raining forest debris, the air itself . . . the very reality that held Stone together. The lightning blade was completing the task Jonah had begun, carving its way clean through the centre-line of the fire-break and creating an invisible, impenetrable barrier.

One hundred yards of memory rod, along with the miraculous forest in which its far end was buried, lay on the opposite side of that barrier.

And so, by the merest fraction of an inch, did Archan.

The disc of light continued to expand upwards and downwards, out towards the sky and into the hidden heart of Stone, extending the barrier to the limits of existence. A line had been drawn that could never be crossed. This was now the very end of Stone.

The edge of the world.

Beyond the barrier Archan was battling still, but the taiga seemed to have given up the fight. She spilled fresh fire on to its back and it caught readily. For uncounted hours a mighty pyre raged beyond the invisible barrier. From time to time, Archan's skeletal form could be glimpsed through the flames, prowling and lunging at what remained of the trees. As the taiga dwindled to nothing so she came to dominate the void that remained. Eventually everything was gone but the short length of memory rod, which she gulped down, hardly having to open her mouth to do so.

So now only Archan was left, flying free in a white and empty space. Sometimes she would swoop close to the barrier, calling out to the adversaries who remained forever out of reach on the upStone side. They could not hear her of course, since sound was no more capable of crossing the invisible divide than a dragon, even an immortal one. Occasionally she would move further away, returning like a battering ram at terrifying speed only to crash uselessly against the sheer wall of force preventing her escape. After a time she took to flying far away in the white, a distant speck of dragon dust, remote in the wilderness. They did not see her come close after that, though even as the daylight failed they saw that tiny mote again and again, cycling backwards and forwards like a caged animal.

Meem took Jonah out to the barrier.

Though he knew in his heart it was indeed impassable, still he felt the need to prove it to himself. The Shifter touched down just a few yards short of the tip of the memory rod, the place where all that remained of Stone came to an abrupt end. Clambering down from his mimic of a dragon steed, Jonah advanced to the very edge and stood with his hands on his hips.

The rod ended in a sharp, clean break. There was nothing beyond: a clean, white page. Here was the place where he had plunged his hands into Stone's fabric and torn it apart. Except it had not felt like tearing exactly – strange, for it had been such an invasive, catastrophic act. In fact it had felt a little like unbuttoning a woman's dress, an act both sensual and forbidden, an intensely private moment. He smiled at the thought; then his smile faded as he saw a speck of red dust drift across the white, far, far way.

Below the rod was spread the same unmarked page, a reminder of the eternal abyss over which the diminished Stone was now suspended. Jonah shivered, unable to contemplate the meaning of what he saw.

Instead he looked up, and was rewarded by a uniquely Stone-like view: blue sky, fading abruptly to white as it met the line of the barrier. From the high blue were cascading thin streamers of cloud; whatever Archan had done to Stone's lower reaches, there was still a whole world up there, sending down its falling wind, heady with the rich aroma of spice. Wind that nourished, the charm-soaked air of Stone.

Borne on the wind, dotting his upturned face with tiny pricks, were minute drops of water. He wondered from what ocean of the future they had been stolen.

'I have seen enough of this place, Meem,' he said, turning away from the precipice. 'You go on ahead – I will walk back.'

Annie and Gerent were waiting for him when he returned to the base of the tower. Behind them were tangled a few clumps of bramble and a twisted cylinder of tree trunk, all that was left of the forest.

'He saw two of his creations destroyed by fire,' announced Jonah, embracing them both. 'Though this second forest was built rather more quickly than the first.'

'I misjudged him,' Gerent replied. His face was solemn. 'You were right to trust the lesky, Jonah. He was our salvation.'

'Even I was never entirely sure where Grandfather Tree's loyalties lay, Gerent. Do not condemn yourself for your caution.'

'I regret that I will never be able to thank him for what he has done.'

'We none of us shall.'

Gerent looked up, clearly distracted. Jonah and Annie exchanged a smile.

'Go to her,' Annie said. 'She's waiting for you.'

Gerent's face broke into a sheepish grin, a youthful expression that transformed his features with a radiance Jonah had never thought to see on that tanned and care-worn face. 'Yes, go,' he laughed, clapping Gerent on the shoulder.

'I wish . . .' Gerent began haltingly.

'Fly,' Annie whispered, kissing him softly on the cheek.

As soon as he had gone she took Jonah's hand. They wandered together around the tower; on the other side they found a larger mass of forest debris barring their way. It was piled high like a funeral pyre, a jumble of dead branches and knotted briars.

'Can you forgive me for what I did?' Jonah blurted, unable to meet her gaze.

'Jonah – you're a damn fool, that's what you are!' There was anger on the surface, but something quite different beneath; Jonah did not dare believe it was what he hoped for. 'But I know why you did it,' she added.

'Do you? I am not even certain that I know that.'

'I know. You went back and stopped that damned grasshopper from flying into my Rance's throat, didn't you?' He nodded dumbly. 'You figured if you did that then he wouldn't turn into the man who started hitting me and hating me.'

'You told me once that was the day when everything changed for the worse. I just saw an opportunity to change it for the better.'

'I know. And I love you for that, Jonah. I knew something had happened to me. I felt . . . like I was in a dream, only I was the one doing the dreaming. It's weird – I can't describe the feeling, but I think what I experienced was my past . . . well, rearranging itself. Because of you. Knocked me backwards, I can tell you; knocked me out, to tell the truth. And you did change things, Jonah: you made it so that the day of the swarm was different, and the day after, and the day after that. But in the long run everything was the same. You changed the days but not the years. Rance still took to hitting me – he just found other reasons to do it, that's all. Do you see? You changed the past, but you didn't change Rance.

'Turns out I remember it all, both versions of my life. They're side by side in my head right now, and I know both of them are true. I know it, but I don't understand it. I guess that means you didn't just change things inside the memory rod: you created something new.'

'Yes,' mourned Jonah. 'That continues to happen, despite my best efforts to prevent it.'

He looked so forlorn that Annie could not help but throw her arms around his neck. Her eyes were shining. 'Oh, Jonah! What you did is more proof that you love me than anything else you've ever done or said before! Because if it had worked like you thought, I might not be here at all: I might still be in Kansas, living a happier life with my husband.' She paused, thinking. 'Though I guess what would really have happened is you'd have ended up making a new me, just as you made a new Malya. You wouldn't just have created Stone, Jonah – you'd have created the world.'

There was a moment of silence as they both considered this, then Jonah said, 'I do still love you, Annie. I have always loved you.'

She withdrew and went pale. 'I couldn't help what happened, Jonah. I'm not saying what I did – leaving you for Gerent – was wrong, but I know it wasn't right.'

'*Was* it the charm?'

'Oh, I don't know. We'll never know. What I need to

know now is . . . can you forgive me for what I did?'

Jonah grinned. 'Annie West – that is the very question with which we started this conversation, except I was asking you!'

'Then I'd better answer first.' She measured his gaze with her own, then said quietly, 'Yes.'

'Yes,' whispered Jonah.

They stood facing each other awkwardly, not knowing quite what to do next. Jonah had the briefest impression they were not on Stone at all but in an English glade, listening to the soft hiss of the wind in the treetops, the slow murmur of the branches as they creaked from side to side.

'Jonah?' murmured Annie. 'Something's moving.'

He came out of his reverie to find himself staring at the wooden pyre that had blocked their way. It was indeed moving, jerking and tumbling as the individual timbers from which it was made contracted in upon themselves. Like threads wound on to a bobbin the branches spun themselves inwards, solidifying into a spherical shape with a surface like driftwood. With a series of hard snapping sounds, this shape cut itself loose from the few straggles of vegetation still lying on the river bed, then rolled towards them.

It was the Bark.

Jonah took a step back, tugging at Annie, but she did not move, facing the wooden vessel as it came to a halt just yards away. It rotated once on its axis, sliding through the carpet of squashed leaves and twigs, and as it completed its turn a huge face appeared in its side.

It was the face of Grandfather Tree, and for a change he could think of nothing to say. Green tears, large as water melons, rolled from the corners of his eyes and puddled on the littered floor. As his lips parted, trembling into a nervous smile, fresh brambles quivered in the corners of his mouth.

Jonah felt Annie's arm linking through his, but for a moment all he could see was the face of the lesky, tall before him, crying the taiga's tears.

23

Beginnings

Kythe, as it turned out, was not badly hurt. In fact, once she had straightened out her crushed wing membrane and proved to the others there were no bones broken, she positively radiated excitement.

'Don't you see what this shows?' she cried, practically dancing on the spot.

'What, Kythe?' laughed Annie, unable to prevent herself from joining in the dragon's merriment.

'It shows what it means to be a charmed dragon, that's what!'

'I always thought that was what you were anyway, Kythe,' put in Jonah, a little puzzled. He too was in high spirits, but did not understand why Kythe was quite so exuberant.

'No, no, no! The dragons of Stone work charm a little bit, of course they do. But you know very well it's only since flying across the sea that I've got so good at wielding it. Look at me now!'

She rose into the air using only the lightest strokes of her transparent wings. Jonah grunted: he had noticed the changes to her body, of course, but only now did he become aware of the change to her *stature*. But then, perhaps it had only just occurred. She held herself in the air with a poise he could only think of as regal – indeed the new array of horns sprouting from the back of her head looked rather like a crown. She gazed down at him with a haughty air, an impression tempered only slightly by the breaking of a wide grin across her face.

'Why, Kythe,' smiled Jonah, 'you look splendid!'

'Thank you, Jonah. I feel splendid too. That's how I know I'm ready.'

'Ready?' He felt suddenly uneasy.

'Yes! Ready to go home!'

The flight back through the pipe was a chore, but time and distance passed quickly enough. Grandfather Tree amazed them all by displaying his new-found abilities. Eight legs, woven from green and limber branches, sprouted from the underside of the Bark, lifting the whole vessel up off the ground. Spider-like, it scuttled along the river bed, weaving in and out of the stumps and stanchions while all the time the lesky's happy face remained spread across the upturned curve of its hull, sending out prospecting tendrils of bramble from his mouth to test the ground ahead.

'Bark can do anything now!' he exalted. 'Even when he's dry. At last the Deathless have set him free!'

'You too!' called Jonah from Kythe's back. Annie hugged him from behind.

'Lesky too!' beamed Grandfather Tree.

Soon they reached the air lock. Here they discovered giant metal plugs sealing the ductwork from which the river had once flowed, proof that one of Stone's hidden mechanisms had shut off the supply of water automatically when the Aqueduct had been breached.

Just before operating the hatch that would lead them into the upStone section of the pipe, Jonah hesitated, fearing he would open it to a flood. But the basilisks had known their business, and whatever system of valves and locks they had built into the pipe-work had held the river in check. Nevertheless, they all agreed the water level was a little higher, and the air pressure a little greater, than when they had first passed through.

Grandfather Tree, who had climbed nimbly through the air lock like the giant spider he now resembled, bobbed gleefully on the smooth surface of the untroubled river. Though he no longer needed the water, clearly he was still very comfortable in it.

As they flew towards the second air lock, the one that would take them out on to the great wall of Stone again, Jonah thought about the selkies.

'I must confess,' he confided to Annie, 'that I suspected Tam had some part in his sister's death.'

'Do you really think so?' she asked, shocked. Kythe too looked round in surprise. 'I didn't reckon him to be a murderer. Seemed a bit of a lame horse, if you ask me.'

'He would not have killed Ruane,' asserted Kythe. 'He wasn't bad that way – if anything he was, well, sort of carefree.'

'He did not seem to care about anything very much,' agreed Jonah. 'Oh, I suppose you are both right. Nevertheless, Ruane's sickness began so suddenly, and Tam did not seem to know what to do with her.'

'So he wasn't a doctor,' Annie said, a little exasperated. 'Who knows – maybe the selkies don't *have* doctors. Maybe she did just fall off. Jonah, this is just one more puzzle we'll never know the answer to. For every mile we've trekked across Stone we've turned up a hundred such puzzles – that's the way it is here. You just have to accept it and get on with living.'

'Hmm. That is just what the selkies do. Perhaps I should take a leaf out of their book.'

'Maybe you should.'

'Still, I cannot help but wonder why there should be so much we do not understand. We have already divined

411

the true shape of Stone – why should we not learn everything else there is to learn about it?'

'Oh, *Jonah*!'

It was night when they finally reached the end of the
hexagonal tunnel leading from the second air lock out
to the surface of Stone. Jonah found it an emotional
moment as, hand in hand with Annie, he walked the
last fifty yards to the open air. They stood silently together
in the mouth of the tunnel, gazing at the unbroken black
of the night sky, and Jonah recalled his first view of
Stone. In his mind's eye he overlaid the blackness with
the vast confection of the Denneth castle, trying to
remember how it had felt to see Stone's abyss for the
very first time. Annie had been with him then too, and
Archan, the one riding inside the mind of the other.

It was a disorientating moment, one in which past and
present mixed with the heat of the falling wind.

'Is it really you?' he whispered, pressing his cheek
against her hair.

'Who were you expecting?'

'I just wanted to make sure there were no more sur-
prises waiting.'

Dawn found the whole group asleep outside the tunnel.
Jonah was first to wake, just before midday. The sun was
a hard disc punched into the cobalt sky, its light refracted
through the twisted fingers of glice flanking the ledge.

Meem's eyes opened as Jonah strolled past to look out
at the sky. The Shifter looked just as Lawal had done
when Jonah had first set eyes on him: a scissor-head
perched on top of a sinuous neck. His body was low
and wide, supported by stubby legs and hoofed feet. He
smiled, revealing sharks' teeth.

'Some forms are more memorable,' he explained. 'This
browsing shape has been ours for most of our time on

Stone. It is easy to return to, and easy to maintain.'

'I will walk back with you along the ledge, if you want me to,' said Jonah. 'I suppose the others will fly.'

Annie walked with them too, while Gerent and Malya and Kythe took a tour through the wild outcrops of glice. Their whoops of delight could be heard even when they were out of sight, diving through dense anemone clusters and swinging round tight corners, revelling in the freedom of the sky. Jonah wondered how Malya was feeling, strapped precariously to Gerent, but as they swooped past he saw she had her arms spread wide and her teeth bared in a ferocious grin.

Grandfather Tree was not with them. Having reached the second air lock he had announced his intention to return to the ocean by way of the river.

'Worked on the way down,' he said. 'See you there I shall.'

'What about the juruas?' Jonah had called when it had proved impossible to talk the lesky out of leaving them.

'Juruas don't bother Bark. Made of Stone-stuff he is. They know better! See you soon!'

The Shifters were waiting for them on a flat slab of glice projecting from Stone like a mantel shelf. Jonah held Annie's hand as they followed Meem into the semi-circular array of identical bodies; these Shifters too, like Meem, had reverted to the long-necked browser form. Yellow eyes watched as they came to a halt in the centre of the shelf. In the sky above, Kythe and Gerent hovered in the falling wind.

'Teget is gone,' announced Meem gravely. 'But the news is not all ill. The Red Dragon is vanquished. The adept is with me. What is more, he will keep his promise. Who here does not wish to hear him? Who here would live on without knowing his true shape? Who here would pass up the opportunity not just to store charm, but to wield it? That is what we are offered. Who would speak?'

There was neither movement nor sound from the ranked Shifters. It was as if they had turned to stone, yellow Shifter statues placed like identical chessmen in the hot afternoon sun. Meem turned a slow circle, dipping his pointed head with each quarter-turn.

Jonah gripped Annie's hand more tightly. He was nervous. For one thing, he was not sure what he would find when he tapped into the memory rod system again: would Archan still be in there, for instance, or some echo of her at least? In addition, he was beginning to regret the promise he had made so readily to Lawal. At the time, Lawal (and Ruane for that matter) had been so certain that an answer existed to the riddle of the Shifters' primal form that Jonah had simply gone along with them. But now, as he regarded this entire Shifter population – two hundred of them at least – he found himself distinctly unnerved.

How could he realistically bring back the information they desired? It had occurred to him that he might pluck a new-born Shifter from the past and drag it into Stone's present, but the image of all two hundred of these yellow giants gathered round a mewling infant creature that had been ripped from its proper time and place filled him with horror. Bringing back a book was one thing; bringing back Malya had at least been motivated by love (and from Jonah's point of view the blade of a knife). But this seemed cold-blooded and cynical.

The more he thought about it, the more likely it seemed that the Shifters would be disappointed. Assuming he did manage to witness the moment of their creation, and assuming he was able to describe it with sufficient accuracy that they were able to re-create that first Shifter shape . . . what would the Shifters then do with that knowledge? They would adopt that primal form, of course, but then what? They would become as bored by it as they had with the other forms they took

414

on. It would be like the latest Paris fashion, *en vogue* for a season then discarded, never to be worn again.

Heavy-hearted, he listened to the rest of Meem's speech, then he was invited to join the Shifter at the centre of the assembly. There was an awkward silence; soon he understood they were expecting him to say something.

'Um, I will try to do as I have promised,' he began uncertainly. Annie was smiling nervously at him, apparently sharing his apprehension. 'But I hope . . . I hope I do not let you down.'

Meem looked down at him, his head giraffe-high. 'Do not fear. Simply do what you can. We know the answer may not be what we desire.'

Some of Jonah's trepidation left him; nevertheless, he knew they had pinned their hopes on him. And he *did* want very badly to keep his promise.

An Englishman's word is his bond, he thought, amused by the thought that while he had shed both pounds and inhibitions during his time on Stone, his sense of duty was exactly as it had always been.

In an effort to relax himself, he lay on his back on the glice. Kythe was circling directly above him, her wings not so much blotting out the sky as painting it. Clouds streamed towards him like vast raindrops.

Concentrating on his fingertips, he plunged his consciousness down into the deep bed of Stone, seeking out the black roots that were always there, opening his mind into . . .

. . . a rising shower of water drops: rain falling up instead of down.

He gulped at the air between the droplets, found it bitter, and sank back down into embracing water. It was better: the water tasted sweet, filling his body with its nectar. He breathed the water in and out, drawing out of it the energies he needed.

415

It glowed yellow, a deep and miraculous hue.

Slowly he made sense of his surroundings. His vision was good, but he was seeing everything through a lens. Facets of crystal contained him within a narrow but deep pool of water; through them he could make out blurred movements, yellow-tinted by the water's dye.

There was a strong upwards current. Following it, he broke the surface with a gasp. Once more he drank in the air: it felt as though he were drowning so he closed his mouth and used his eyes instead. The rain was still rising, and as he looked around he chuckled to himself for being such a fool.

I am a fish in a fountain!

It was hard to see the body he had adopted in this memory. Eventually he found a crystal whose face was polished to a virtual mirror, and in it he admired his new reflection, that of a sleek, golden carp. Bobbing his head above water he could see the extent of the pond in which he swam, and the delicate spray of the fountain he had mistaken for rain. Willow trees hung weeping branches all around the pool, which appeared to be set within a forest glade. Crisp moonlight filtered through the branches, but the trees were aglow with the yellow light emanating from the pool. Cast across the trees were moving shadows – the same blurred shapes he could see through the crystal when he sank underwater; they were shadows of tiny figures dancing around the pool.

One of the shadows stopped, then grew larger. A face appeared over the lip of the pool, and as Jonah the carp breached the surface once more he found himself looking into the face of the faery queen.

She was much younger than he remembered; this was an earlier age than any he had visited with her before. It was a revelation to see her face so flawless, a reminder that the faeries were not immortal, that they too were born, though rather than dying they dwindled. To either side of her slender cheeks hung long silver plaits; on the crown of her head she wore a simple tiara of woven willow. She smiled a slightly puzzled smile at

Jonah the carp and said, 'Do I know you, Master Fish?'

'Not yet,' he replied. 'But you will.'

'On any other day I should be intrigued by that answer, Master Fish. But today is one I would rather see ended, and ended swift, so I shall not dally with inconsequential talk.'

She was more regal than the older faery queen he had known; her face, despite its silken complexion, was more troubled.

'May I at least ask why that is so?'

'You are polite for a fish, so I shall tell you. There has been war among the faeries – that is the awful truth of it. And my council has decreed that our race shall suffer for it, even more than it has suffered already.' She paused, catching her breath. 'Why do I tell you so much?'

Leaning forward, she brushed her hand across the surface of the pool. Though she did not touch it, the water leaped on to her fingers and gathered there in minute beads, so that when she withdrew them they looked as though they were covered in dew. 'Do I know you?' she whispered.

'You need tell me no more,' replied Jonah the carp. 'I know that the faery council will shortly remove the wings of the greater part of your population. I know that their legs will be fused and they will be cast out into the world to make their own way, no longer members of the clan of the Old Earth Dwellers. What I did not know until I came here is that they have decided this against your will, for I can see the sadness in your eyes. Is there nothing you can do to prevent this atrocity, my lady?'

'Nothing at all, Master Fish. But how do you know these things?'

'You will find out, in years to come. If there is nothing you can do then take heart, for I have seen the results of this day and I can tell you that much beauty will come of it, though it will also create much evil. Do not despair: from this act of war will come diversity. Your people, in different guise, will spread across the world. In time they will come to own it. They will evolve and grow, and for every new species you make here today a thousand more will be nurtured in the future.'

'You reassure me, Master Fish, though I do not fully understand your words.'

'In exchange for my reassurances, will you grant me a wish?'

'Name it.'

'Permit me to witness the moment when the council carries out its sentence. I wish to see the creation of the new species from the original faery form.'

'The wish is easy to grant, for it is not the council that will enact this deed. It is I.'

The faery queen turned sadly away. With a sudden gesture she halted the dancing of the unseen figures, who scuttled away through the trees in a flurry of muttered conversation. Wind fell into the clearing like a wind sent from Stone, pressing down on the surface of the yellow crystal pool. Jonah the carp retreated to the perimeter as the fountain sputtered and died.

'You have chosen the right place to bear witness to this act,' announced the faery queen, 'for it is in the water of the shaping charm itself that you swim.' He regarded the water with new respect, and not a little apprehension. 'Many years ago, a member of my council stole a charm from the giants of the Old Ice Peaks. It was a deed done in anger, for which the giants quickly forgave us. We did not deserve forgiveness, but the giants are kind and bury their memories quicker than most.

'This charm was a fundamental one, but only now have we found a use for it. It is a shaping charm, one quite different to the magic we use to move from the aethereal plane to the physical. It is a charm of physical stature only, and thus, in faery eyes at least, it is crude. So you will see that its use in these circumstances is doubly damning.

'As you know, the council has decreed that the race of faeries has grown stagnant and inward-looking. They have decided we must change. So now we have a use for the shaping charm at last. Beyond this ring of trees stand three out of every four *of the faery population. These faeries will be reshaped tonight, and this pool is the source of all the charm by which this appalling crime will be committed.'*

Crying openly, she knelt beside the pool and extended her hands over the water. More droplets flew up, except now they did not stop. The entire pond became a fountain, spraying water out over the tops of the willows in a damp mist. Jonah the carp watched it descend like a blanket behind the trees, and could only imagine the effect as it soaked into the bodies of the faeries awaiting the rainfall on the other side.

'Why do they not run?' he asked as the yellow-tinted water showered upwards all around him.

'They have been restrained,' she replied through her tears. 'I thought you wished to look upon them – I can arrange it.'

'Not yet.'

The water level dropped steadily as the fountain continued to unleash the charm upon the wretched faeries, and he began to worry that he would drown before he found the answer to the riddle. Whatever was going on beyond the willows, he was sure the answer to the Shifters' question was concerned with something rather different. Once the water was reduced to a mere puddle between the lowermost pair of crystals, the faery queen scooped most of what was left – and Jonah – into a large, silver bowl. Relieved, Jonah the carp circled his new home and watched the giant fountain run the pool dry.

In all that time there had been not a sound from the victims outside the glade.

'It is over,' sighed the faery queen. 'Yet you did not see what you wished to see.'

Ignoring her comment, Jonah the carp said, 'There is a little magic left, my lady. What will you do with it?'

Again there fell a look of puzzlement across the face of the faery queen. 'I do not know, Master Fish. Your question catches me unbalanced. What would you suggest?'

'Pour it on to the ground.'

'But it will soak away and you will die.'

'That does not matter. Please, just do as I say.'

So the faery queen took the bowl and upended it, allowing the yellow liquid to cascade in a single stream on to the ground.

Jonah the carp fell with it, wondering who had sent him the inspiration, sure that he had done the right thing.

The shaping charm worked only when it was set free. Thus, when the faery queen had transformed it into a shower of rain, each drop had worked its magic on the first thing it touched. Now she had set the remainder of the charm free, but in an unbroken stream.

As Jonah the carp tumbled through the air, he saw the charm come alive before him.

It held itself briefly in its stream-shape, then congealed into a perfect yellow sphere, denser than water, an opaque fluid pulsing with the joy of birth. So it fell, the origin of all the forms it would someday be, until it struck the ground.

Jonah the carp struck too, shedding scales and gulping at the lethal air.

The sphere of yellow liquid splashed into a crown but it did not separate. The spikes and pearls of the crown-shape reconverged on the whole and then it was falling still, dissolving into the bare earth on which it had landed, opening up a channel into the soil, digging itself a well that looked as though it would go on forever.

Wriggling so that one eye was positioned over the lip of the well, Jonah the carp stared down into the darkness, where a point of yellow light was growing steadily smaller as the encapsulated charm buried itself in the ground.

Then, without warning, dazzling blue light flared around the yellow sphere. As his gills closed shut for the last time, clogged with particles of mud, Jonah the carp felt his perception tilt over and found himself looking not down into the earth but along a vast tunnel, at the end of which was a cobalt blue sky streaked with falling clouds.

The sphere of pure shaping charm disappeared into the sky, then the well closed its one eye on the distant world of Stone.

Jonah the carp saw the faery queen bend down to pick him up, then convulsed as he drew in one final breath of . . .

. . . hot, spice-filled air.

He sat up with a start, clawing at his throat and coughing uncontrollably. Annie rushed to his side, but already the attack was over. He looked up, expecting to see the faery queen towering over him; instead he saw the face of Meem tilted down over him, his mobile mouth set with an expression of concern.

'I am all right,' he said to Annie. Then he addressed Meem. 'Give me a moment, and I shall give you your answer.'

'What are you doing, Jonah?' Annie demanded as he lay down again.

'I have one more journey to make. But do not worry – I shall not be going very far.'

When he returned she swore at him.

'I will not do that again, I promise you,' he reassured her. His kiss went some small way to appeasing her.

He called to the Shifters to gather round and, without preamble, described exactly what he had witnessed. The Shifters moved uneasily – this was not what they had expected. He took a deep breath.

'You have been asking the right question,' he cried, 'but in the wrong way! There was never any primary body form for your kind, at least, not the way you imagined it. There was no "first Shifter" with a long tail and a beautiful face, or bent arms and pointed ears, or bowed legs and claws for hands. You grew from what was left of the charm. After the rest of your kin had been created – the dryads and the selkies and Heaven alone knows how many other thousands of sprites and pixies and goblins and elves – there was still a little magic left over, the purest distillate of the shaping charm, if you will. And when the faery queen liberated that charm, not only did she create a being of perfect, shape-changing ability, but that being found its way here. If there was ever a "first Shifter" then that is what it was: a sphere of pure charm, breaking its way through to a new world.'

'If that is so,' rumbled Meem, 'then how do we come to be as we are?'

'That is why I made my second journey.'

'Where did you go, Jonah?' asked Annie.

'Over there,' he replied with a smile, nodding his head in the direction of the ocean. 'I returned to that very same moment, except this time I witnessed it from the other side – from Stone. In fact, I found myself inside another fish.

'What I saw was a fountain of water spray outwards from the surface of the sea. Within it was the yellow sphere of charm. The sphere fell, eventually striking the waves and spreading out into the waters. It turned the entire sea yellow – can you imagine it? It was but a single drop of dye cast into an entire ocean yet it was so concentrated its influence reached from one shore to the other! The waves rose, crashing against each other and throwing fresh spray into the air. On my world we call waves like that "white horses" . . . well, it was not horses that were formed from the waves on that day: it was Shifters – you, all of you! Each one of you was formed in a different shape – you were each one unique. That is how it was, on the day of your creation.'

They stared at him, dumbstruck. Annie pressed her lips against Jonah's ear and whispered,

'It's an amazing story. What d'you think they'll say?'

He shrugged, but Meem spoke before he could reply.

'Thank you, Jonah Lightfoot. You were right: the answer is not what we had expected. It will take us some time to . . . come to terms with this knowledge. But if I understand correctly what you have told us then . . . we *are* the ocean.'

'And the ocean is you.' Jonah beamed at him. 'Yours is a place of honour, Meem, for the same charm that built you built all the magic of the great sea of Stone. We have all seen the yellow lights that play behind the water's surface after the sun has set; now we know why you share their colour. You are them, Meem, and they are you. You can join them any time you like, but you are more than they are, for you can return to your lives in the morning. You are all shapes and you are no shape. You are exactly what you choose to be. I truly believe you have the very best of two worlds.'

They ended up spending the night with the Shifters. During the evening, a number of the yellow giants came up to Jonah, some singly, others in small groups, and asked him to tell them again what he had seen. By the time he settled down with Annie to sleep he had lost count of the number of times he had related the story.

As he lay with his head on Annie's stomach he could see the Shifters ranged in their broad semi-circle. The dusk light had turned them to featureless shapes cut from the darkening sky. Some of them still bore their long necks and pointed heads, but many more had transformed themselves. He saw humped backs and serpentine tails, he saw slender wings and tusks that reached all the way to the ground; he saw one individual who had created a body like a perforated balloon, spinning lazily in the falling wind.

And every one was different.

He watched them shift as he fell asleep, imagining he lay within a circle of ancient stones, a giant faery ring, and that what he was watching was the magic of the menhirs.

By daybreak they were flying again, having woken

early. Kythe was excited, keen to be on the move, and there seemed no reason to stay.

'We wish to see the sea again,' Jonah explained to Meem, who again looked like a dragon. 'And I would not leave Grandfather Tree waiting another day.'

'We understand. And we thank you again. I will accompany you, however, at least to the coast. Consider me your escort.'

The wind was kind to them as they negotiated the difficult towers of glice; gradually the Stonescape became less complicated, the terrain flattening out the further they travelled upStone. The sun had barely begun to warm the air before Malya spotted the brilliant blue line shimmering ahead.

'Is that it?' she exclaimed. 'By the Gods, it is a sight to behold!'

Jonah had forgotten this would be Malya's first sight of the sea. Gerent had described it to her, but as they all knew only too well, to appreciate Stone's wonders fully it was necessary to see them for oneself.

He confessed his own excitement to Annie, with whom he was sharing a perch on Meem's back. Kythe was flying ahead, alone; neither of them cared to dwell on her reasons.

'I feel like a child again!' he cried. 'I remember my first view of the sea back in our world, at a small cove on England's south coast. I watched the waves through an arch of rock; it was as if God had framed a picture for me.'

Annie nodded. 'All I knew was the Mississippi – when I was little of course, before we headed out west. That was big enough for an ocean, seemed to me back then. But the Pacific . . . that'll always stay in my head.'

'Yes, that and the southern seas of the Spice Islands . . .'

So it was that amid talk of their homeworld's wonders that Jonah and Annie crossed the coast and passed out over Stone's sea of charm. In the morning sun it was incandescent, alive with a light all its own and dappled with the drifting shadows of a thousand falling clouds. Neither of them could recall seeing a texture more rich than this liquid curtain, this many-layered series of veils into which one might plunge and journey forever. Even at the far-off vertex, where perspective drew the lines of light and shade together, there was endless variety.

Of them all, only Kythe seemed unmoved by the vision. No sooner had they reached over the water than she arrowed towards the whirlpool, clearly visible only a couple of miles off-shore. At Jonah's request, Meem sped after her, leaving Gerent and Malya in his wake.

They caught up with her in front of the spinning mouth of the maelstrom. Meem drew up alongside and Jonah saw the conflict on her face, her struggle to maintain the bravado with which she had started the day.

'You do not have to go through with this, Kythe,' he said gently. 'Nobody would think any less of you.'

She did not look at him, but her jaw clenched and she sniffed loudly.

'I'm going home,' she blurted. 'And that's that!'

I think I may have just made up her mind for her, thought Jonah wryly.

Kythe bent her long neck close enough so that Annie could reach up and stroke her long snout. Dragon tears ran down Annie's arm, soaking her blouse, but she did not seem to mind.

'Oh, Kythe,' Annie sobbed, unable to hold back her own tears. 'I wish you were staying.'

'Do you?' The young dragon sounded like a child still, one in desperate need of reassurance. 'Please say it's all right for me to go, please say it is.'

'Oh my dear, of course it is . . . it's just . . . oh, I'll miss you so much. I wish you weren't going, but if it's what you want . . .'

'It is. I know it is. I never felt so sure about anything in my whole life!'

'Then go. And remember that I love you.'

'We both do, Kythe,' put in Jonah. 'We will never forget you.'

'Who's going to catch you now?' Kythe sniffled, nuzzling his upraised hand.

'Well,' Jonah smiled, 'I will just have to make sure I do not fall.'

A gust of wind pushed them apart and the moment was over. Kythe looked anxiously at the whirlpool; a tremor passed down her whole body. 'The worst part,' she shuddered, 'is going in there on my own.'

'Then some help you will need!' came a familiar voice, almost lost against the rumble of the whirlpool. Jonah raised his arm to hail the Bark. It was holding station just to the downStone side of the whirlpool, denying the powerful currents like a stone set fast in the bed of the ocean.

'Grandfather Tree!' yelled Jonah with his hands cupped around his mouth. 'It is good to see you again!'

'You mean – I don't have to do this by myself?' quavered Kythe.

'You don't have to do anything alone,' said Annie. 'We're here.'

'But it's my trip. Only my wings can take me through. I wouldn't want any of you to risk your . . .'

'No risk!' bellowed the lesky heartily. 'Look! UpStone!'

They looked. At first there was nothing but a vague shadow behind the waves; at first Jonah passed it over, assuming it was cast by just another cloud. Then the darkness thickened, and it became obvious it was not a shadow at all but a massive shape moving towards the surface. Bubbles foamed at its perimeter, obscuring their view of it for a moment, then they subsided and something thrust its way slowly and gracefully clear of the waves.

It was an enormous fluked tail, like that of a whale, sleek and majestic in the low morning sunlight. Spray burst across its fine grey fur, drifting half a mile downwards before the slope of the ocean captured it again. Slowly, easily, the tail folded back into the sea and a huge back appeared, followed by a flank and a line of ribs and a human arm as long as London's Royal Mall. A head, covered in finely cropped grey hair. A familiar face.

'The Goddess!' exclaimed Annie.

'Ruane!' breathed Jonah.

There was movement all about the whale-woman now, a flurry of activity as hundreds of selkie bodies appeared from the surf at Her flanks and hips and hauled themselves on to Her living shore. With steady thrusts of Her mighty tail, She carved Her way through the water until She halted just short of the perimeter of the whirlpool.

'Good day, Jonah,' She boomed, Her voice as deep as the Pacific.

'Ruane!' he cried. 'I thought you were . . . what I mean to say is . . .'

'I too thought I was dead. Tam tried to catch me as I fell but he was too late. When I struck the river it carried me away, but my body became lodged against a metal island. The current held me there as the truth of my sickness manifested itself.'

'I can guess the rest! You were changing, were you not? Like a caterpillar becoming a butterfly, you were turning into Rata Kadul! If only we had known to look – we might have seen you as we flew over.'

'You would have seen nothing. I was beneath the water. During the transformation I had no need to breathe. Then, when it was over, all I wanted to do was swim upstream and return to my ocean. To find my people. I am still Ruane, Jonah, but now I am the Goddess too. I am Rata Kadul.'

'Ruane. There is something I must tell you. Your brother – Tam – he died. Archan took him. He died . . . bravely.'

Ruane's massive eyes blinked slowly. 'You are kind to say that of my brother. I knew him well enough. I suspect he was as unmoved by the coming of his death as he was by the flow of his life. But the news is sad to hear. Your presence here is proof that Archan was vanquished. Did she suffer for her crimes?'

Jonah watched a single tear, enough to fill an Earthly lake, well in the corner of the Goddess's eye.

'I believe she will suffer for a very long time,' he replied.

By now the selkies had spread themselves across Ruane's upturned belly, a large catch of shellfish laid out to dry in the sun. They looked busy: lines of females were working their way methodically through the catch and dividing it according to size, while some of the males were working with strips of driftwood and weaving weeds. It looked to Jonah like the kind of scene he might have seen had he flown over one of the islands of the South Seas: a native village united in the common cause of sustaining their lives.

And there was not a tether in sight.

'Quite a sight, isn't She?' called Grandfather Tree, who had made his way round to Her side. 'And She'll help you through, dragon, if it's what you want.'

'It is!' replied Kythe, her eyes wide.

With a wave of Her arm Ruane shooed the selkies back into the sea. Once they had all swum to what She considered to be a safe distance, She eased Herself towards the whirlpool. Jonah held his breath, but She stopped before She was near enough for the current to take Her. Then, revolving on to Her back, She lifted Her arm out of the water again. This time She extended Her hand outwards, reaching for Kythe.

The young dragon cycled her wings anxiously, back-tracking from the approaching hand, which was big enough to crush her as Jonah might have crushed a moth.

'Trust me, little dragon,' soothed Ruane. 'Alight on my hand and let me send you on your way.'

Jonah watched as Kythe closed her eyes. He saw her mouth working: she was talking to herself, no doubt words of encouragement. Then she folded her wings and settled like a snowflake into the huge cup of Ruane's outstretched palm.

Rolling over in the water, Ruane reached into the upturned bowl of the whirlpool. In this way, She was able to position Kythe beyond the violent air pockets at its mouth. Meem moved a little to the side, affording Jonah and Annie an uninhibited view clear down the whirlpool's throat. If there was a passage through to the old world it was obscured by the spray. The immense risk Kythe was taking had become a tangible thing; he could taste it on the wind.

Kythe opened her transparent wings . . . then froze.

'I can't do it!' she howled in agony. 'I can't go in there.'

Jonah tried desperately to compose words of reassurance but could think of none. Then Annie touched his arm.

'The faery queen,' she whispered. 'The names.'

Standing precariously on Meem's back she called out. 'The names, Kythe! Remember the message in the shell!'

'But what did it mean?' demanded Jonah.

'I don't know.' Annie's eyes shone. 'But she does!'

Kythe was chanting words – names – aloud. Instinctively Jonah knew they were dragon names; whether their recitation simply calmed her, or whether it had magic of its own, he did not know.

'Brace and Ledra,' she chanted. 'Cumber, Mantle, Halcyon, Ordinal . . .'

While she uttered the dragon names she began to beat her wings very fast, faster than Jonah had ever seen her move them before. Soon they had blurred to invisibility; she looked like a giant hummingbird.

'. . . Gossamer, Tallow, Destater . . .'

Rising slowly from Ruane's hand she darted forwards, then veered a little to the side.

Then she turned her head and smiled at Jonah and Annie.

'. . . Fortune,' she said.

With a sudden turn of speed, she plunged into the spray and disappeared.

Jonah thought he saw something beyond the spray. As Kythe passed out of sight, the turbulence she created whipped the spray into coils. These coils parted briefly, and for a moment he saw a line of pale orange light. A horizontal line.

Perhaps it was wishful thinking. Annie admitted to having seen nothing, and she had shared his viewpoint; perhaps she had blinked at the wrong moment.

Or perhaps he truly had seen the dawn on the world of his birth.

Though they lingered there for several moments they saw nothing more than the spinning vortex. The spray came and went, but there was only darkness in the depths. Having withdrawn Her hand, Ruane went back to the selkies, who climbed eagerly back on board and returned to their work.

At last Meem turned away, confessing that his wings were aching and he was more than ready to rest.

'Would you like me to take you back to the shore?' he asked.

Jonah and Annie exchanged a glance.

'There is a spot down there,' said Jonah, pointing at

the grey mountain of Ruane's hip. 'It looks like a good place to be. Perhaps we could stay there for a while.'

Two days later Annie came to Jonah. It was late evening, and the sun was just sliding behind the coast, illuminating the transparent fingers of glice from behind so that they seemed ablaze. She was holding something in her hands. Her eyes, like the sunset, were glowing.

'What do you have there?' Jonah asked.

Ruane's fur was soft and short here, a perfect bed. Behind them it rose high as the pelt-meadow curved down into the forest covering her tail. Several Shifters were moving unseen through the undergrowth, quietly browsing, a comforting presence at their backs. Still more were in the air in a multitude of different body forms, floating and flying and gliding, or swimming through the warm waters, no one the same as his neighbour.

Saying nothing, Annie brought forward her prize.

'One of the selkies found it and brought it me,' she said. 'She knew right away who it was meant for.'

It was a conch shell the size of Jonah's fist. He took it, turned it over, fascinated by the simple beauty of its spiral. He looked at Annie, raised his eyebrows.

Annie nodded. 'I've listened already,' she said. 'Now it's your turn.'

Tentatively, he lifted it to his ear.

I've been here for two days and I still get confused by the shapes. Everything's turned on its side. This really is a topsy-turvy world we all came from, isn't it? The sea looks so peculiar, lying flat the way it does, and the sky ... well, that's just incredible! It looks like it goes on forever.

Getting through the whirlpool was easy, thanks to Ruane of course. And the faery queen. I felt myself turn over, just like when Stone's sky flips you round, you know, then I was flying upwards, out through the whirlpool in this world. The

431

homeworld. The sun was setting (going down, not sideways!) and the sky was orange and, well, it was just gorgeous!

The whirlpool's right next to a shore, just like the faery queen said, so I was able to land straight away. Good thing too, since my wings were shaking fit to throw me right out of the sky. After a while I calmed down a bit and took a good look round.

There's a beach made of rock, just a flat shelf really, and high cliffs – very high – behind it. Lots of boulders have fallen down from the cliff; if I want to walk along the beach I have to pick my way through them, like a maze. I blundered around for a while on that first night, while it got dark, thinking I ought to find a spot to sleep. But then something amazing happened.

The stars appeared!

I know you'd told me about them, Jonah, but it's hard to understand something until you see it. I'd never seen anything so wonderful before in my life. In fact, I can't wait for tonight to come round so I can see them again. At first I tried to reach up to touch them, even though I knew they were a long way away. Then I just sat and watched them.

Then the moon came up. Oh, by the skies! Even the stars can't compete with the moon! It's, it's . . . oh, I can't tell you how I feel about seeing it! It's like a dream come true. It's as if this is the sky I was really meant to fly in, not just an empty sky with nothing but clouds and air and a few grumpy old dragons but a sky with lights of its own, a sky with stars and a moon and . . . and real magic! Even at night there's light all around – there isn't even a true black – just the deepest blue. Stone's sky is nothing compared to this, Jonah, nothing! As soon as I saw it I knew I'd done the right thing in coming here.

I really have come home.

Next morning I found some tiny bones. They were the faery queen's. Beside them was this shell. I'd like to think she knew I was coming, and left it for me. I couldn't think what to do

432

with her bones; in the end I gathered up a few of the smaller boulders and built a cairn over them.

Then I flew up to the cliff-top and looked over the land.

It's big and deserted. Over in the distance I can see some mountains with smoke coming off the top – I suppose they're the volcanoes you told me about. I don't like the look of them, so I think I'll stay well clear.

There are a few plants about, but they don't look right. Their leaves are heavy, like metal, and they're mostly dying. Nothing else living that I can see.

But it doesn't matter, because what there is here is charm. Loads of it! I really have come to the very earliest days of the charmed world. For all I know, this could be the day after one of the turnings of the world – the first day of all the days of magic.

If that's the case, then there are no dragons in the world but me.

And if that's true, then I'm the first dragon.

I'm not going to stay here. Soon the volcanoes will really start to make trouble, and I think that before long the first trolls will be lifting their heads out of the ground. I don't want to be around when that happens. Our dragon legends talk about the early days of the trolls as being pretty unpleasant. They were bigger than the biggest giants, with foul tempers too. I don't think I fancy getting mixed up in their wars.

So I'm going. The charm means I can fly as high as I like, so that's where I'm going to head. I'm going tonight.

I have this feeling, you see. If I'm now the first dragon in the world, then maybe it's up to me to see that the others come along when the time's right. So I need somewhere quiet to get things ready. Somewhere out of the way, but with a good view of the world, so I can pick my moment just right.

And I know the perfect spot.

When the moon rises again I'll be rising with it. I'm going to drop this shell into the whirlpool as I leave. I hope it gets to you. Somehow, I think it will.

Wish me luck, Jonah – there's a long flight ahead, and if there's one thing I'll need it's charm.

'Did you understand what she meant, Jonah?' Annie asked, taking the shell from him when he had finished and holding it against her breast.

'Yes, I did. She is the dragon queen, Annie, the mother of her race. At last she is where she belongs.'

'Shall I?'

He nodded, and she curled her arm far back. The shell skipped once over the waves before sinking. A single bubble emerged as it disappeared; as it popped a word floated back through the dusk:

'. . . charm . . .'

Annie nestled her head into Jonah's lap and together they watched the sun slip away.

'I've got a theory about love, Jonah. You want to hear it?'

'Do I have a choice?'

'Just listen, Englishman. When Kythe's world changed into our world, something must have happened to all the magic.'

'Perhaps it simply went away.'

'Ah, but the basilisks say that nothing goes, don't they? So maybe the magic just changed, the way things do.'

'Changed into what?'

Her face filled the night, a new moon rising before his intoxicated eyes.

'I love you, Jonah Lightfoot,' she whispered as she touched his lips with her own.

The sea was a dark curtain shot through with streaks of yellow light. They lay together, while beside them an ocean of charm fell silently into the night.

24

Annie's Journal – Final Entry

I've still got some questions.

Most of them are to do with Archan, I guess. And
Stone, of course. I figure writing them down might be
the best way to work them out. I'll talk to Jonah about
them sooner or later, but I want to get the thoughts
straight in my own head first.

My head – well, Archan lived there a while before she
finally found her way into a dragon body again. Sometimes I can still taste her there, like my mind's a cup
that's been badly washed, and there's a trace of milk left
in the bottom that's gone sour. She's trapped again now,
but I know what Jonah knows, what we all know, which
is that no prison's strong enough to hold her forever.
Especially when you remember she's going to live
forever.

The difference is that I don't just know it, I can
taste it.

So that's the first thing: the fear that she'll escape,
which I guess is really fear that she'll escape while I'm
still alive. When the day's bright and I can think straight
I don't reckon that's likely. I think that invisible barrier
will keep her out for even longer than the million years
she spent in the Arctic ice. In fact, I think the worlds will
have slowed to a standstill and the suns winked out like

candles by the time she finds a way through, and by that time she may very well be the last creature left alive in all creation, and as far as I'm concerned she's welcome to do anything she likes, because the only soul she'll damn will be her own. I think she's gone from our lives at last, gone for good. I think, between us, we did a good job.

But when the night comes I get a little more scared. I wonder what she's getting up to out there in that great white desert. I wonder what magic she managed to take with her. I wonder what she'll do with all those memories she swallowed. I figure it's only Stone that's holding her back, and she's got a lot of Stone inside her now. One thing's for certain, she won't waste time. It's one thing to have all the time in the world, but the strange thing is I think that just makes you more impatient.

Another thing – in the day I'm able to think of her like an animal in a cage. In the dark it's the other way round, and we're the ones behind bars.

All that I can mostly deal with. The thing I really can't get square in my head is Jonah making a new world.

He created a world!

When he brought Malya back, he dropped a great big rock in the river of time and made two streams where before there was just one. So now there's a new Stone hanging over a new abyss, somewhere we can't see, can't even imagine. And living on it is another Gerent and another Malya and another me, and Esh and Kythe and the dragons – not Jonah, because in making the world he sacrificed himself – and Archan.

There's another Archan out there.

And if that's a version of Stone where Jonah died, then its version of Archan was never defeated at the Threshold. Maybe, in that world, Archan won that first battle and went on to conquer all Stone, or even consume it as our Archan wanted to consume our Stone.

Two Archans, twin sisters of evil. Even if we destroy one we might still have the other to contend with.

Jonah did talk briefly about this, and he reckons the other Stone is beyond reach. That it's logically impossible for us ever to make contact with it, or it with us. Reckons it would create what he's taken to calling a 'temporal paradox' or some damn thing. He believes this, and I'm prepared to believe him.

Besides, what I said before holds pretty much true – I reckon we'll be long gone before our version of Stone has to worry about Archan again.

Which makes me think that maybe, just maybe, we might live happily ever after. I don't remember if Rapunzel ever managed that, but I think the Sleeping Beauty had a good shot at it. That must have been one hell of a kiss, to wake her up like that.

I think I know how she felt.

Words. All just words. Words are useful when it comes to stories, but I'm not so sure they do much for the heart. I've used quite a few in this book, but this miracle pen's getting scratchy and running out of ink. I guess I'm running out of things to say too.

The ocean's beautiful. The colours in it are – well, I don't have the words to describe them. All I can do is liken them to Kansas colours, the colours I know best. So when I see yellow in the water I have to write that it's the yellow of the corn, and the blue is the blue of the sky and the green is the green of the prairie. But what I'm really seeing is an endless chain of colours all linked together and spinning round and round each other, each one alive, and that's where the words fail me.

So I'm not going to use them any more. When I close this book, it'll be for the last time.

I brought a special gift with me when I came to Stone.

437

It kept Jonah and me afloat while Krakatoa erupted all around us, and it gave Jonah something to cling on to while Archan was in me, something to remind him of the real me. And that's what it represents – the real me – and I've all but ignored it since we've been near this ocean.

I opened it last night, the first time since I left Jonah. Now I'm back with him again it seems right.

As soon as I looked inside I caught that giddy smell of turpentine and linseed oil. Such a *real* smell, and so enticing. I picked up a brush and ran the bristles along the palm of my hand. It felt like the breath of a child. Sat there, with my painting box on my lap and the brush in my hand, I felt like I'd been reborn.

I picked up the tiles I'd painted one by one. Pictures of the Rockies, San Francisco, the Galapagos, Java, each one like an old friend. Looking into them I could remember the exact days I'd painted them, the weather, the temperature, the sound of the gulls or the wash of the sea. There's sea in most of the pictures, I realized then. Thirty-four little ivory memories. And one hundred and ten tiles I haven't even touched yet. One hundred and ten little blank canvases.

I'll start tomorrow. The view across Ruane's torso is inspiring, such a bizarre mixture of human form – on a giant scale of course – and strange village life, with the selkies busy fishing and hoarding. Gerent's started to spend time with them, showing them how to make nets. Malya's popular with the young females. They're fascinated by her skill with the sword, and I'll bet it's only a matter of time before we've got a selkie army on our hands. They're a popular couple, and they look well together.

I wish Gerent and Malya luck, I really do.

And as for Grandfather Tree, well you only have to glance at the sea and up pops the Bark out of the waves.

If he's told me the story of how he sent Archan packing once he's told me a thousand times! You can't help but listen, though – for a man of wood he's got a hell of a heart.

Before closing the box I unclipped the last tile I'd worked on – the view from the beach on Krakatoa where I first met Jonah. That day seems so far away, yet the painting makes it real again. It wasn't quite finished, but I put it away anyway. Then I picked a blank tile at random from the stack. I couldn't resist peeping at the Mah-Jongg sign on the back. I had to smile. I think it was Grandfather Tree who told us that Stone enjoys coincidences, or maybe it was Esh. Whoever it was, they would have appreciated the joke.

It was the sign of the North Wind, of course. Still looks like a man and woman dancing together to me. I clipped it into the brass holder, ready for me to start painting in the morning.

I can't wait.

I woke Jonah up afterwards. Boy did he grumble! Well, it was the middle of the night. Told him I loved him, which I do. Told him I wanted to stay with Ruane for a while, which I do. He told me he felt the same way. And he does. It's such a simple thing, to say things to each other and know they're the truth.

We danced then, arm in arm, just like the couple on the Mah-Jongg tile.

Just me and Jonah, and the charm.

Acknowledgements

As well as the usual suspects, I'd like to thank Andy Wicks for his pertinence (somebody publish this man). Phil too, and Joy, but most of all Helen for seeing me through a tough year.

Why not come and see me at
http://members.tripod.co.uk/amara?